D0733540

"STAY AWAY FROM ME," CATHERINE ORDERED.

"That's not what you want, and you know it."

As Rolfe spoke, she was again watching his mouth. Sensation spun through her as she remembered fully its mastery. "'Tis what I want," she insisted, stumbling away two more steps. She gasped when her back met solid wood. My God! She'd missed the door. "Stay away!" As she tried to break for the opening, his left hand hit the wall near her shoulder.

"Too late, Catherine. You're trapped."

Wide-eyed, she stared up at him. Why was he doing this? "Let me go . . . please?"

He pressed himself closer. "Not until I've answered your question."

"What question?"

"You've been staring at my lips again, which tells me you want to know if my kiss will feel the same now that your senses are no longer dulled by wine."

"You're mad!" she told him.

If he were mad, then she must be doubly so, for again she found herself staring at his lips. "Loose me," she demanded.

"If I do that, you'll always be left to wonder," he said, his warm breath fanning just above her lips. "But wonder no more, Catherine. 'Tis time you learn the truth. . . ."

Turn the page for more wonderful praise for Charlene Cross. . . .

BOOKSELLERS LOVE ROMANCE . . . ESPECIALLY CHARLENE CROSS'S

ALMOST A WHISPER

Books by Charlene Cross

Masque of Enchantment
A Heart So Innocent
Deeper Than Roses
Lord of Legend
Almost a Whisper
Splendor

Published by POCKET BOOKS

CHARLENE CROSS

SPLENDOR

POCKET BOOKS

New York   London   Toronto   Sydney   Tokyo   Singapore

This book is a work of fiction. Names, characters, places and incidents are products of the author's imagination or are used fictitiously. Any resemblance to actual events or locales or persons, living or dead, is entirely coincidental.

An *Original* Publication of POCKET BOOKS

POCKET BOOKS, a division of Simon & Schuster Inc.
1230 Avenue of the Americas, New York, NY 10020

Copyright © 1995 by Charlene Cross

All rights reserved, including the right to reproduce this book or portions thereof in any form whatsoever. For information address Pocket Books, 1230 Avenue of the Americas, New York, NY 10020

ISBN: 0-671-79432-9

First Pocket Books printing January 1995

10 9 8 7 6 5 4 3 2 1

POCKET and colophon are registered trademarks of Simon & Schuster Inc.

Cover art by Lee MacLeod

Printed in the U.S.A.

IN MEMORY OF:
Donald R. Cross
Edwin J. Baum
George and Doris Falconer
Maurice and Thelma Falconer

SPLENDOR

CHAPTER

1

WANDERLUST RAN IN THE VEINS OF ROLFE DE MONT ST. MICHEL
as though it were his life's blood. The thought of marriage
had never once entered his mind.

Not, that was, until four days ago.

The sinking winter sun at his back, Rolfe looked up at the
gray stone fortress and its imposing tower. What he sought
lay just beyond the castle walls. He had a quest, and by his
knight's oath, he'd not fail his mission, or the duke of
Normandy could fail his.

By Rolfe's calculations, the force of slightly over three
thousand should have made the crossing, perilous waters
notwithstanding. As the rightful heir to England's throne,
Henry would at last face Stephen, intent on claiming his
due. Should Eustace, Stephen's son, follow the invading
troops—and no one doubted that he would—it was Rolfe's
duty to keep the barons of Avranches and Mortain from
joining in the fray, Geoffrey d'Avranches especially. To that
end, a diversion was planned, one ensuring that both men
were kept busy for some time to come.

And if Rolfe somehow failed?

Henry would welcome the chance to again face Geoffrey,
to settle his grievance against the man once and for all.

1

Though Rolfe had vowed his allegiance to Henry, he knew he had not volunteered his services simply to ensure the duke's success. Something else had given Rolfe the impetus to seek this task.

As he continued to study the fortress, exhilaration surged through him; his confidence grew. Revenge. He could almost taste its sweet reward. Miles d'Avranches would suffer for his cowardice. This Rolfe promised himself.

A frigid wind swept the barren hillside, sending a chill down Rolfe's spine. He raked back the strands of hair that had whipped across his face to settle them at his shoulder. Devoid of the protection of his hauberk and the quilted aketon he wore beneath it, he shivered as the cold air penetrated his clothing.

Catching the edge of his hood, Rolfe covered his head. Five years had passed since he and Miles had last met, five years in which Rolfe had matured and hardened in both aspect and character. He was no longer the young knight-errant eagerly seeking wealth and adventure on his first crusade. Although Rolfe doubted that the weak-kneed Miles would recognize him, he nevertheless thought it might be wise to keep his face hidden.

His steed had strayed slightly from the path, and Rolfe reined the great destrier in line with the procession of men, women, and attendants as they made their way up the lane toward the gate.

"Smile, Garrick," he ordered his companion after spying the man's pensive visage. "You look as though you're about to attend a funeral."

The statement drew a sharp glance from the grizzle-haired knight. He pressed his mount close to Rolfe's.

"'Tis a possibility," Garrick replied in a low voice. "What worries me is that it may be our own."

Rolfe chuckled. "You're becoming an old woman. Stop wringing your hands. Naught will happen to us."

"Had you a solid plan in mind, I might agree with you. As it is, we go in blind. I don't like it, my young friend. 'Tis too dangerous."

"Have faith, Garrick. I know what it is I want to accomplish. 'Tis just a matter of discovering how to go about it."

2

"Risky, I say," the older man grumbled. "Especially when there is only we two."

"The smaller our number, the less suspicion we draw. Now lighten your mood and pretend you are enjoying the day. We promised Henry we'd keep the barons occupied, and that we shall."

Garrick snorted. "I hope by 'occupied' you have more in mind than our providing the entertainment at the wedding feast as we are baited by a pack of ravenous hounds. Should we get caught, that's precisely what we'll be doing."

Along with the others, the pair passed through the gates into the castle. "Have no fear of that, Garrick," Rolfe reassured the man as he carefully scanned the high stone walls of the inner courtyard. His gaze stopped on the comely young woman framed in an open window. "There'll be no celebration tomorrow. No wedding, either. *Not* without the bride."

Tomorrow was her wedding day.

Excitement bubbled inside Catherine de Mortain as she watched the activity in the courtyard below. Invited from far and wide, the guests were arriving with less continuity now, and she imagined that this particular group might be the last.

Miles.

The name of her betrothed whispered through her mind, and Catherine's heart raced with anticipation. To think, as had happened to all the young men who had previously sought her hand in marriage, their fathers eager to enter into negotiations with her own, that she'd nearly rejected Miles without so much as ever seeing him.

At seventeen, Catherine was well past the usual age to be wed; but, desiring a husband whom she could respect and love, one who respected and loved her in return, she'd resisted any proposed match, threatening to sequester herself in a convent if the man her father chose wasn't to her liking.

In the past, William de Mortain had always acceded to Catherine's wishes, she being his only heir. But when Geoffrey d'Avranches had sent word that he and his son were interested in arranging a contract for the joining of their two families, Catherine's luck had run out. This time her threats fell on deaf ears, her father stating it was time she wed. No amount of cajoling or badgering could change his edict. The marriage would go forth. Catherine was now glad her father had stood fast.

Their betrothal had taken place four months ago, and as was the custom, Catherine immediately withdrew to Avranches to learn her own responsibilities within the daily workings of the castle, to thereby become a dutiful wife. Now only the nuptials remained.

Miles, she thought again, giddiness overtaking her. Proud, handsome, and well-mannered, he was the epitome of what she desired in a husband. For unlike most men— her father being the exception, of course—he seemed genuinely interested in her opinions. Complete agreement with her views was something else entirely, but at least Miles didn't chastise her for speaking her mind, something that was highly uncharacteristic for his gender.

Yes, in an age when women suffered from the curse of Eve's deceit, when females were considered to be the lowest of all God's creatures, Miles exalted his betrothed, honoring and respecting her. *That* was why Catherine loved him so.

"A cold wind blows through that window. Come away from there, child, or else you'll catch your death."

A smile still playing on her lips, Catherine turned to see her nurse ambling toward her from the far side of the vast chamber. "But Eloise, much is happening below. Can I not watch?"

"No," the woman said firmly. "Now come away from there."

"I'll marry only once, you know. Don't be so eager to spoil my pleasure."

Eloise brushed past Catherine. "You'll not marry at all should you take a chill," she stated, shuttering the window and securing it with an iron bar.

"You worry far too much, Eloise. I have never been sick a day in my life."

4

"True, good fortune has shined on you. But remember, there is always a first time for everything. Come along now. You are expected below to greet your guests. Your father awaits you."

"And Miles?"

"He's there too."

Catherine studied her nurse. Eloise was akin to a mother to her, had acted in that very capacity since Catherine was twelve, when her mother had died of an illness. She valued Eloise's opinion and, in this situation, wanted desperately to win the woman's approval. "You don't agree with my marrying him, do you?"

"'Tis not for me to say whom you marry or don't marry."

"That's not what I'm asking. You don't like Miles. Why?"

"He is not what he seems," Eloise grumbled.

Catherine thought to defend her betrothed, but her words died on her lips as Clotilde scurried into the room.

"M-milady," she said on an awkward curtsy, then fell silent.

Eloise's niece was painfully shy and equally as plain. Catherine always felt the former in the girl was a direct result of the latter. Knowing Clotilde would say no more unless prompted to do so, Catherine smiled gently, then asked, "What is it?"

"I—I just came from the chaplain. H-he says the bishop has arrived along with several clerics. He will be meeting with them shortly, and he won't be able to hear your confession until tomorrow. He'll meet you at dawn in the chapel."

"Thank you, Clotilde. I know how difficult it was for you to speak to him on my behalf. Now fetch my comb, will you?"

After Clotilde did as she was bade, Eloise quickly groomed Catherine's hair, then the three exited the women's quarters and descended to the great hall.

Seeing the servants' strained expressions as they hurried about the huge room, Catherine instructed both Eloise and Clotilde to assist with the serving. The pair immediately took up flagons of wine and began filling the empty goblets at one of the many tables.

Searching out Miles's whereabouts, Catherine saw he was already seated in his place of honor at the head table. Miles's father sat to his right, while to his left, an empty chair between, was her father.

Her heart tripping lightly, Catherine promptly sought her betrothed's side. But her pace slowed when she heard the raised voices, particularly her father's, as they swelled in restrained anger.

"Don't attempt to convince me that Stephen is a strong and just king. If things stay as they are, England will not survive under his rule," said William de Mortain. "His barons do naught but pillage and rape the land. Because of their lawlessness, I must keep my own estate heavily guarded. You know as well as I, Geoffrey, that a knight's pay is not meager of coin. I cannot say about your circumstance, but my coffers are fast becoming empty. Stephen has lost control, I tell you."

Geoffrey d'Avranches issued a short laugh. "Since you have far more wealth than most, William, I think you exaggerate the magnitude of your financial woes. Likewise, you worry too much. Just because a few barons stand in disagreement with each other doesn't mean all of England is in the throes of civil unrest."

"'Civil unrest'?" William questioned. "With the empress and Henry's sympathizers gathered to the west and Stephen's gathered to the east and most of the south, England has been in the throes of civil unrest for the past fifteen years. You are doltish, sir, if you think otherwise."

"So a few skirmishes arise now and then," Geoffrey said with a shrug. "Tempers flare, then they are quickly soothed. 'Tis naught but posturing on both sides. In my opinion, Stephen's authority is no less secure than it ever was. Besides, as two of his barons, we stand to gain far more than we ever have. Stephen is not as strict as was his predecessor."

"That is my point," William snapped. "Where Henry Beauclerc was forceful and resolute in his actions, his nephew, Stephen, is weak and indecisive. As for the term *we,* you had best change that to the singular. I am content with

6

what I have. But I fear you are not. Greed, Geoffrey, is part of Satan's scheme. Beware your immortal soul, my friend, or you might find it lost."

Catherine noted how her future father-in-law's gaze had narrowed on her sire. "Milords," she said, her hands falling on her father's shoulders. "Such political talk is far too cumbersome, especially at a time like this. Our guests are enjoying themselves. And so should we."

"You're right, Daughter," William declared. His large, callused hand patted hers. "The night is indeed for merry-making. Come. Sit. There will be no more 'cumbersome' talk, as you call it."

While her father was speaking, Miles had risen from his chair. "And what, Catherine, do you know of politics?" he asked.

"I know that Stephen has a generous heart. Because he does, he tries to please everyone at once. For that reason, he is perceived as being weak. He might be wise to take a stand. His position as king could depend on it."

"A stand? Against whom?" Miles asked. "Those who support him?" He chuckled. "Catherine, you are such a delight, but I fear your woman's reasoning is not very sound. No man would be so foolish as to make enemies out of his friends, especially Stephen."

Catherine frowned. Her "woman's reasoning"? He made it sound as though she were a dunce simply by virtue of her gender. She felt Miles's touch. He lifted her hand from her father's shoulder, upward to his lips. His light kiss brushed over her fingers.

"Do not wrinkle your brow so, Catherine. It mars your exceptional beauty," he stated, his gaze penetrating hers.

Catherine was instantly captivated by the alluring look in Miles's dark blue eyes. Her stomach fluttered with excitement as her heartbeat quickened, and the disparaging remark was quickly forgotten as images of their forthcoming marriage bed flashed through her mind. Heat flamed from her neck upward to her cheeks, for Catherine knew her thoughts were anything but maidenly. She immediately feared the consequences of such a fantasy.

"Lustful" was what the chaplain would say when she made her confession tomorrow. Ten days' penance, starting with her wedding day, would undoubtedly be her reward.

Was feeling desire for one's future husband really a sin?

The question rolled around in her mind. Knowing that the castle priest was quite strict in his views, Catherine debated whether or not she should meet him at dawn. Though she desired to ease her conscience, thereby coming to Miles not only pure in flesh but pure in spirit, something told her she might be wise to forgo confession altogether.

From his position at a lesser table, Rolfe ignored the jovial throng of several hundred that feasted in the great hall and concentrated on the betrothed couple seated on the dais. A wooden partition stood at their backs, separating them from the hustle and bustle of the kitchens. The sable-haired bride-to-be, in particular, held his interest, had done so for the past hour.

A waste of woman's flesh, sweet and soft, he thought in disgust as he watched Catherine de Mortain from over the rim of his cup. Certain she was the one he'd seen at the window, he decided she was indeed fair, but Rolfe wondered if she possessed all her wits. To marry Miles would be a grievous mistake. A cowardly husband would afford her no joy, only a passel of spineless sons.

But the beautiful Catherine's future happiness was of no concern to him. What did concern Rolfe was the forestalling of tomorrow's nuptials. Opportunity was all he needed. He prayed the occasion presented itself, and quickly, else all would be lost.

Rolfe swilled his wine, then grimaced at its bitter taste. But the wine was no more bitter than the feelings he held for the comely Catherine's betrothed.

Memories of the road to Antalya filled the field of his mind. His heart began to hammer, and raw fear erupted inside him, just as it had on that day five years before, when he'd faced the prospect of his own death.

In the echoes from the past, he could still hear the eerie cries reverberating through the valley as droves of Turkish raiders swept down from the hills, catching the unsuspecting

Crusaders off guard. Incredibly, he could yet smell the sweat from the battle and the blood from the carnage that was left behind. Then Rolfe relived the greatest horror of all.

Away from the main troop of Norman warriors, the band of two hundred having allied themselves to the French king, was Robert de Bayeux, Rolfe's lord and mentor. His own sire unknown to Rolfe, Earl Robert had been akin to a father to him. Beside the earl was the man's son. To Rolfe, Francis de Bayeux was the older brother he had always longed to have, the friend and companion he had always desired. In their company was Miles d'Avranches, the one person whom Rolfe hated with a passion, and for good reason.

On seeing the heathen Turks streaming down on them, Miles had paled and fled, leaving both Robert and Francis to fight on their own. By the time Rolfe managed to traverse the expanse to their side, lifeless bodies lying in the wake of his sword and ax, he discovered he was too late. His only claim to a family lay dead, bludgeoned and maimed.

Rolfe's stomach lurched at the grisly picture that formed in his mind's eye. Swallowing hard, he quickly shut the door to the past. That the gutless Miles hadn't recognized him was no surprise. Though neither he nor Miles had continued on the sacred journey to Jerusalem, their return to Normandy had taken separate paths. Even so, Rolfe was determined to keep his distance, just to be safe.

A shadow fell over him, and Rolfe looked up to see that Garrick had returned. "Well?" he asked once his companion was seated.

The knight lifted his cup to shield his lips from prying eyes. "The talk is about the wedding and the bride ale," he whispered. "'Twould indicate they are still unaware Henry has invaded England."

"Even Stephen may not yet know he is about to be dethroned. But it shouldn't be long before he is faced with the truth."

"Aye," Garrick seconded. "Pray Henry is successful, for England's sake."

Both men lifted their cups in salute, then drank deeply. Grimacing anew, Rolfe wondered if everyone's wine was as foul as his. Then again, his mood might be the cause of the sour taste in his mouth. "What about the two women?" he asked. "Will we find any help there?"

"The plump one is the Lady Catherine's nurse—Eloise is her name. The younger one is Eloise's niece. The girl is pitifully plain and terribly shy. Of the two, I'd take my chances with her."

"If she is as shy as you say, I doubt I'll get within ten feet of her before she seeks to flee," he said, watching the girl in question.

"I've yet to know a woman who would willingly run from you. One glimpse of your wide white smile and her heart will melt. She'll be wanting to thread her fingers through your tawny locks and press her lips to yours. With luck, her tongue will loosen as well."

Garrick's words drew a sharp look from Rolfe; the older knight guffawed. "There have been times, my friend, when I've missed the mark," Rolfe said once Garrick had quieted. "I fear this might be one of them."

"If you wish to discover if that is so, I suggest you act now. She's headed behind the partition to the kitchens."

Knowing this might be his only chance to glean the information he sought, Rolfe came up from the bench and moved away from the table. His gaze on the girl's aunt, making certain she didn't spot him, he strode the hall's perimeter. When he reached the wooden screen he glanced at the betrothed couple, who were now only a few yards away from him. For some unexplained reason, the look of devotion that the sweet Catherine cast upon her future husband galled Rolfe. Dismissing the pair, he slipped behind the partition.

Rolfe kept to the shadows, watching and waiting for the girl to reappear. No more than a minute had passed when she came from the kitchens, two flagons of wine held in each hand. Her head down, she nearly collided with him as he stepped into her path. She stumbled back, wine sloshing onto her hands.

"Steady, sweet one," Rolfe said as he gently caught her arm.

At the endearment, surprise showed on her face; then, her

eyes downcast, she tried to twist from his grasp. Rolfe felt her tremors of fear, but he held her fast.

"I didn't intend to startle you," he told her. "Calm yourself. I mean you no harm. Never would I injure a woman who is as delicate and enticing as you." Under his hand, her quaking eased somewhat. Timidly, she peered up at him; Rolfe offered her a smile. "What is your name?"

"C-Clotilde," she squeaked, unable to look him full in the face.

"Clotilde," he repeated in a whisper. "A beautiful name it is." His smile broadened. "I've been watching you, Clotilde. And with great interest."

"M-me? Why would milord want to watch me?"

"There is a gentleness about you that intrigues me. The women I've known tend to be shrewish and bold. A man grows weary of such unfeminine behavior. When he comes upon a maid who is both quiet and shy, soft and tender, he is taken with her straight off. 'Tis the same with me, Clotilde. As I say, you intrigue me."

Rolfe watched as a blush crept across her otherwise wan cheeks. Her once lackluster gaze brightened.

"I—I don't know what to say, milord," she responded, now looking at him fully.

Though Rolfe felt guilty about using the girl this way, he nevertheless pressed on. "Say you will come with me so we can become better acquainted."

He stroked her arm lightly. A shiver ran through her, and her blush deepened. Several servants grumbled their annoyance as they attempted to slide by them, their arms laden with trenchers of food.

"Come, Clotilde." He urged her aside. "Let's find a secluded spot where we may talk."

Her look of expectation turned to one of regret. "I—I cannot. I have work to do."

"Later, when you are through with your work, say you will meet me then."

She shook her head. "I cannot."

"Why?"

"My aunt won't allow it."

11

"Your aunt need not know. Please, Clotilde," he implored, his fingers brushing the curve of her cheek. "Don't deny me this opportunity. I'll only be at Avranches a short while. Meet me tonight. Please?"

Leaning toward him, Clotilde moaned softly. Then, at the sharp call of her name from without, the spell that Rolfe had worked so hard to weave around her was suddenly broken; she blinked.

"My aunt!" she gasped. "She'll chasten me with a switch if she finds me here with you."

He caught her arm as she attempted to flee. "Later, then," he insisted, refusing to give up.

"No. I must attend to the Lady Catherine."

Again the girl tried to escape him, but Rolfe blocked her path. "When you are through attending your mistress, you could meet me then."

"I cannot," she replied in desperation. "I must be up well before sunrise."

"So early? Why?"

"Clotilde!" Eloise's voice sounded closer, sharper.

The girl looked to the wooden curtain, then to Rolfe. "The Lady Catherine is to rise early to make her confession in the chapel at dawn. I must help her dress. Please let me go. My aunt—"

"Clotilde!"

Rolfe ducked back into the shadows just as Eloise came around the barrier.

"What are you doing here?" the woman questioned sternly. "The guests are in need of more wine. Come!"

Rolfe watched as Clotilde scurried toward her aunt, then disappeared altogether. He waited, then rounded the divider.

As he headed back to his place at the table, he glanced toward the dais and noted that Miles and Catherine were missing from their seats. Suspecting the pair had slipped off for a private moment alone, he hoped they made good use of their time together; for after tomorrow, it would be a long while before they saw each other, if ever again.

* * *

12

Catherine experienced a familiar tingle in the pit of her stomach as she walked in silence beside Miles. They had escaped the hall to stroll the courtyard away from prying eyes. Though the cold night air nipped at her fingers and stung her cheeks, she hardly noticed its bite. The love she felt for Miles kept her warm, deliciously so.

Midway around the courtyard, Miles stopped. Leaning against the wall, he drew Catherine to him and linked his arms around her waist. "Tomorrow is the day for which we've waited, Catherine. Are you ready to accept me as your husband—in every sense of the word, that is?"

Catherine felt heat rise on her cheeks. "Aye, I am," she answered softly.

"Good. For I shall expect many sons from you in the years to come."

Catherine's blush deepened. "Only sons and no daughters?" she asked.

"Of course daughters. Once our eldest son weds, how else can other lucrative marriages be formed? The right alliance, whether it be political or monetary, is all important to me. Without daughters, it would be nearly impossible to achieve."

In the dim torchlight illuminating the courtyard, Catherine examined Miles closely. His statement surprised her. Never would she have thought that he would look upon his own flesh and blood as mere chattel—not when he'd made every effort to treat her as his equal. "You mean if each of our daughters approves of the match, don't you?"

"I, alone, shall decide such matters."

"Surely, Miles, you will consider each of their feelings in the matter. Besides, the Church says that no man or woman may be forced into a marriage he or she does not want. If you are not careful, you could find that, one by one, our daughters will reject the men you choose. I, as their mother, will have to stand behind their right to refuse."

"Despite what the Church says, those in charge have a tendency to look the other way in these matters, especially if, by doing so, they profit." Miles chuckled. "As I recall, your father was the one who made the decision about our betrothal. He insisted that we wed, did he not?"

"Yes. He insisted. But perhaps I should clarify something. You weren't the first who wanted to contract for my hand in marriage. My father considered me in all such proposals. If he'd been unfeeling, the way many fathers are, I would have been wed by age twelve. I can assure you, had I not found you to my liking, there would have been no betrothal, Miles. I'd have sequestered myself in a convent before marrying a man I could not abide."

"I fear, Catherine, that your education has made you too independent for your own good. Had your father sent you off to such a convent at an early age, as most fathers favor doing with their daughters, instead of keeping you at home as he did, you would probably be less outspoken and more demure. In case you aren't aware of it, the latter is considered a virtue among women."

Catherine bristled. "Is that what you hope I shall be once we marry? Demure?"

"It would be appealing at times."

"It is unlikely I shall change once we are wed. So do not fault me because I was educated the same way as a man. I cannot help that my father chose to keep me at home. In fact, I am glad he did."

"I don't fault you. I am simply saying, that because you were educated in such a way, you have a tendency to make all decisions on your own. As your husband, it is my right to make them for you."

"I will allow, Miles, that it will be your right once we are married. But I would hope you would consider my feelings before you make any decision that affects me or our children. Otherwise I fear we will have words over the matter, whatever it is."

"Catherine, since we met, have I not always considered your feelings?"

"Yes," she conceded. "At least most of the time."

"And when have I not?"

"Last week, when you wouldn't allow me to go on the hunt with you."

"Your safety was at issue. A boar hunt is dangerous. You know that as well as I." He shook his head, then sighed. "Let

14

us not quarrel on the eve of our wedding. If it will ease your mind any, when the time comes for our daughters' betrothals, I'll listen to their concerns before making any decision."

"Do you swear this to me?"

Miles looked down on her. He remained silent for a long while. When he spoke, he said only, "Come. The moon will soon be rising. Let's climb to the wallwalk and watch it from there."

Catherine allowed Miles to guide her to the stairs leading up to the battlements. As they ascended the steps, she contemplated his refusal to swear to his words. Twice tonight she'd seen a side to Miles that he'd kept hidden from her.

He is not what he seems.

Eloise's words tumbled through her mind, and for one brief moment, Catherine wondered if her nurse could be right. Just as quickly, she shoved the thought aside, attributing Miles's mood and her suspicions to naught but nervousness over their forthcoming wedding.

"Well?" Garrick questioned when Rolfe reached the table.

"Come. Let's make our way outside."

Once in the courtyard, Garrick asked, "Were you able to question the girl?"

"Clotilde? Aye," Rolfe said as he scanned the area. Movement along the wallwalk caught his attention.

"And?"

"In a few hours we'll gather our mounts and leave the castle."

" 'Leave'?" Garrick repeated, a frosty mist showing on his breath. "Have you given up?"

"No. We'll position the horses in the wood. You'll await me there."

"And where will you be?"

Rolfe's gaze remained fixed on the pair who were silhouetted in the moonlight high above him. "Here. I plan to return on foot."

"I think you'd draw suspicion—leaving, then returning."

"Dressed in a priest's robes, I doubt anyone will question me."

"A priest's robes?"

"Aye," Rolfe said, watching the couple as they embraced. "At dawn I'll be in the chapel, ready to receive the Lady Catherine's confession."

CHAPTER
2

"IT IS LATE, MY SON. IF YOU WISH FOR ME TO HEAR YOUR confession, come again on the morrow. Right now I intend to seek my cot."

Two fingers of Rolfe's left hand hooked the ties of the cloth bag that was slung over his shoulder. He remained silent as he continued his trek across the wooden floor toward the apse and the priest. From under the hood of his cloak, which was pulled low across his forehead, he eyed the scrawny man, gauging his height.

On his return from the courtyard, Rolfe had kept watch on the clergymen who were seated near the head table, trying to determine which one was the castle chaplain. True, Clotilde could have easily supplied the answer he sought, but he decided not to approach her, mainly because of her aunt.

Rolfe had no desire to tangle with the plump Eloise. It wasn't her girth that caused him anxiety but her tongue. Attracting attention to himself was the last thing he wanted. So he'd waited.

Several hours elapsed, the revelers slowly taking themselves to their pallets in the upper chambers. The betrothed

17

couple had retired long before, but not until they'd made their rounds, greeting many of their guests as they went.

On their approach, Rolfe and Garrick had escaped their places. Once the two had journeyed on past their table, the men regained their seats and continued their vigil. But as time crept by, Rolfe grew uneasy.

Then a thought occurred: Instead of returning to the town and its church, which lay only a short distance away, the group may intend to spend the night. Rolfe prayed that it wasn't so, or his plan would unravel like a tattered piece of cloth.

Finally, and to Rolfe's relief, the bishop and his clerics departed the hall. It was then that Rolfe received his answer.

Having bade his brethren farewell, the priest withdrew to the chapel, obviously unaware that Rolfe was fast on his heels. Presently Garrick stood just outside, ensuring that the pair were left undisturbed.

"Did you not hear me?" the priest asked.

"Aye. I heard you." Falling silent, Rolfe bore down on the man whom he'd concluded was only a few inches shorter than himself.

"Take your leave, sir. Return tomorrow and I'll hear your confession then."

"Since my conscience is clear, I have no need to confess anything," Rolfe said as he neared the altar.

"Then why do you invade these premises at such a late hour?"

"I have need of your robes."

Surprise showed on the man's face. "My robes?"

Rolfe stopped before him. "Aye. Your robes."

"Who are you?"

Alarm lit the priest's eyes. Unexpectedly he caught hold of Rolfe's hood and pulled it downward, a definite mistake. The man had no time to react, for the speed with which the fist met his jaw was blinding. He crumpled into Rolfe's arms.

"Sorry, my reverend friend, but I saw no other way," Rolfe whispered, easing the unconscious man to the floor. Quickly he relieved the priest of his vestments, including

18

the linen coif that covered the man's tonsure. Then Rolfe went to work.

Devoid of clothing, his hands and feet bound with strips of leather, his mouth gagged and his eyes blindfolded, the chaplain looked like a plucked fowl, trussed and ready for roasting. Rolfe dragged him behind the altar. "Sleep well and long, priest. Be aware, though: Should you awaken too soon, you'll be sporting another bruise."

Gathering the cleric's garments from the floor, Rolfe placed them into the cloth bag, positive they would fit him. Then he made his way from the chapel.

"'Tis done?" Garrick questioned, shoving his shoulder away from the wall.

"Aye."

"Now what?"

"To the stables," Rolfe answered as they began wending their way down the stairs.

"Are you certain it is wise to leave the castle? What if the guards refuse to again allow you entry? Worse yet, what if the priest awakens, or is found before you return? 'Twould be like walking into a nest of vipers."

Rolfe looked at Garrick as they stepped from the tower into the crisp, cold air. "Aye," he responded. A quick death would be merciful, but Rolfe knew there was always the threat of torture. "I appreciate your concern, my friend. But such are the chances I must take. Come. Let's make haste. Dawn is not that far off."

"Clotilde! Take your head from the clouds and pay attention," Eloise admonished. "Now fetch milady's comb."

Catherine poked her head through the top of the deep crimson bliaud. Made of soft wool, the overtunic was bordered in gold embroidery at hem and sleeves. Beneath the bliaud she wore a white linen ground-length chainse, which covered a chemise of fine samite, a gift from Miles. As Eloise draped a blue woolen mantle over her mistress's shoulders, fastening it at the neck with a jeweled brooch, Catherine kept her eyes on Clotilde.

The young woman, who was nearly Catherine's age, acted wistful. Catherine had never seen her behave thus. Though unsure of herself, Clotilde was always attentive, doing what she was told the instant the command was issued. However this morning was different, and Catherine wondered what had overcome Eloise's niece.

"Tend to the Lady Catherine's hair," Eloise stated on Clotilde's return, "while I see to emptying her bath."

Seated on a stool, Catherine waited to feel the pull of the comb through her waist-length hair. The stroke never came.

Turning around, she noted that Clotilde was staring into space, a dreamy look on her face. "You're lost in your thoughts today, Clotilde. What is it that has made your mind wander so?"

Before Catherine's eyes, Clotilde's cheeks flushed with color. The girl quickly looked away.

"'Tis a man, I'll wager!" Catherine exclaimed softly. Clotilde's blush deepened, and Catherine knew she'd hit upon the truth. "Tell me: Who is he?" she asked, her excitement for Clotilde growing.

"I don't know his name, but he is truly the most handsome man I've ever seen."

On hearing the reverence in Clotilde's voice, Catherine smiled. "When—how did you meet him?" she asked, genuinely happy for her maid.

"Last night, while I was serving, he approached me and asked that I meet him later on. He said he was intrigued by my gentleness. Most women are too bold. Oh, milady, can you believe it was my shyness that fascinated him so?"

"Yes, I can believe it. There is a sweetness about you, Clotilde, that is appealing to all who know you. Tell me: Later, did you meet him?"

"No. I had to be up early to help milady dress."

Catherine marked the disappointment in Clotilde's voice. "I'm truly sorry you couldn't meet with him as you'd wanted, all because of me. Does he live here in the castle?"

"Since he said he'd be here only a short while, I believe he is one of the guests."

"You mean a servant of one of the guests, don't you?"

"No, milady. His raiment was far too fine for that of a servant."

Catherine grew cautious. It was unlikely that a man of nobility would approach a young woman of Clotilde's class, not unless it was for a mere tryst. To be used then tossed away would devastate the guileless Clotilde. Though she wanted to advise Clotilde of such, Catherine didn't quite know how to go about it. She had to choose her words with care or she could very well hurt the young woman's feelings. Clotilde was all too aware of her own plainness. Because of it, she might misconstrue her mistress's words, thinking Catherine referred to her appearance and not her breeding.

Taking a moment to gather her thoughts, Catherine felt certain she had come upon a way to circumvent both issues. "I know you were disappointed about last night, Clotilde, but it may be for the best that you didn't meet this man straight off, as he wanted. From what I know of the male gender, they are most often enchanted by the chase, and not by the actual winning of a maid's hand. Should you respond to his overtures too easily, he may lose interest all too quickly. My advice is to keep him just at arm's length. That way he won't be too far, but he won't be too close either. 'Tis a game played between the sexes for centuries. What a man thinks he cannot have he'll desire even more. You have to make him want you beyond anything else."

"I understand, milady."

"Good. And, Clotilde, if he is at the bride ale tonight, point him out to me, will you? I'd like to see him firsthand. That way, if you wish my advice, I could better counsel you on what you should do next."

At a distance, Catherine hoped to measure this man's character for what it was. Not knowing he was being watched, he was more likely to show his true self. She intended to protect Clotilde, no matter what it took.

"I will, milady," Clotilde responded. "And I welcome your counsel. But please don't tell my aunt about any of this. She is too protective of me. Without even knowing him, she may forbid me to see him ever again."

"'Twill be our secret, Clotilde. I promise," she said,

smiling up at the young woman. "'Tis almost dawn. I don't wish to be late for my confession, or the chaplain will be greatly annoyed. Please see to my hair, and quickly."

Clotilde stroked the comb through her mistress's hair, allowing it to flow free to Catherine's waist.

"Thank you," Catherine said, rising from the stool. She looked for Eloise, but didn't see her. "Tell your aunt I will be in the chapel and that I'll be back shortly." With that, she scurried from the chamber.

As Catherine walked toward the chapel, she again prayed the chaplain would be lenient with her, her penance slight. But the nearer she came to her destination, the more anxious she felt. Something within her told her to turn back, but she ignored the warning. She must go to Miles pure of heart. She would offer him no less.

"Have you sought to tempt your betrothed by inviting him to your bed before the nuptials?"

Catherine stared at the priest, whose deep, clear voice resonated through her. Upon her arrival at the chapel a little before dawn, she'd found him instead of the chaplain.

"Your regular confessor has fallen ill," he'd told her. "Ingested something that didn't agree with him. He asked that I receive your confession. I hope, my child, that meets with your approval."

She'd been undeniably relieved by the announcement, for this man's manner was not as censorious as was the castle chaplain's. But his interrogation was coming ever closer to the one question she hoped not to answer. Catherine wondered if she would truly be so presumptuous as to lie, should he ask it.

"Should I repeat the question?" he asked.

Catherine scanned his face, its angles and planes drawing together into what could be termed perfection. A fringe of tawny hair brushed his wide forehead as it peeked from beneath the linen coif that hid his tonsure. Instead of the pallid complexion that most men of the cloth bore, his skin was a healthy bronze. His gray eyes, as soft in color as a dove's breast, gazed at her through lazy, long-lashed lids. He was indeed handsome—too handsome for a priest.

"My child, your concentration is straying. Shall I repeat the question?"

Catherine blinked. "N-no." What had she been thinking? "I—I've never sought to tempt my betrothed."

"You sound unsure."

Biting her lip, Catherine could no longer hold his gaze. "I've not sought to tempt him," she repeated.

"Not even in your thoughts?" he asked gently.

Again she stared at him. His eyes were clear, free from condemnation. She didn't know why, but on impulse she questioned, "Is it really a sin to desire one's betrothed?"

"Then you desire him?"

How could she lie and seek the Lord's forgiveness at the same time? "Aye, I do." Then she blurted, "Please be merciful. I'll exist on bread and water, for forty days if need be. But do not forbid the consummation of my marriage. I promise to be a good wife, obedient and submissive. I'll observe the days that we are forbidden to lie together, and when I am with child, I'll abstain altogether as the Church demands."

"You know the saints' teachings well," he replied.

Cynicism had tinged his voice. As Catherine looked at him questioningly, wondering at his tone, a muffled squeal, coupled by a slight scraping noise, sounded from behind the altar. Her eyes widened, and her heart beat faster.

"Rats," the priest explained. He caught her arm and urged her from her knees. "Come, my child. Let us leave here before the odious things overrun the place."

Catherine gladly allowed the priest to guide her from the chapel. She couldn't imagine what might happen if she actually saw one of the furry beasts. She soon found herself outside in the courtyard. "Why have we come out here?" she asked, shivering.

"By your confession, you must do penance. You know that, don't you?"

"Yes, but—"

"You have requested leniency, and I shall grant you such. By doing penance as I prescribe, you will be allowed to consummate your marriage. Otherwise you will wait ten days. The bishop will be notified of such before you state your vows at the church door."

Catherine searched his face. "What is it that I'm supposed to do?"

"We shall go to the wood below the castle. There you will kneel and recite your prayers for one hour."

"One hour?"

"Yes. And you shall be humble, my child."

Hesitant at first, Catherine felt she had no choice. Gooseflesh rose on her arms beneath the sleeves of her woolen tunic, and she was trembling uncontrollably from the cold. "I shall get my boots and a heavier cloak," she said, for she wore only her slippers and a lightweight mantle, both meant for indoors.

As she started to turn, he grabbed her arm. The action startled her. Twice he had touched her, the second far more forcefully than the first.

"No, milady." His grip eased, then his hand fell away from her arm altogether. "As part of your penance, you shall suffer from the elements. 'Tis this or a regular penance."

"As you wish."

Catherine followed the priest to the gatehouse. The watchman looked them over when she requested passage out. After listening to her explanation, then her assurance that they would return in about an hour, he ordered the gates opened.

While they traversed the hillside toward the wood, Catherine listened to the sound of the priest's dalmatic as it slapped sharply against his legs. His lengthy strides carried him onward, and she skipped quickly alongside him. Still, she was hard-pressed to keep up with his swift pace.

Once they'd reached the woods, she again felt his hand on her arm. Together they ducked the bare branches, traveling ever deeper into the forest. A sharp limb snagged her hair, and she cried out at the abrupt sting along her scalp. The priest's deft fingers hastily untangled her from the branch, and they continued on.

"Are we almost there?" she asked, fearing they might get lost. Were she to be late for her nuptials, Miles would not be at all pleased.

"Nearly," came his reply.

In less than a minute they were standing in a small glade. "Is this the place?" Catherine asked.

"Aye."

Expecting instructions from him, she received none. Then she heard the rustle of fallen leaves. Twigs snapped under a heavy foot. Horses, she thought, turning toward the sound.

A man entered the clearing dressed in a hauberk, two destriers trailing after him. Confused, Catherine turned back to her confessor. Her eyes widened as he pulled the linen coif from his head. A wealth of tawny hair tumbled to his shoulders.

"You're not a priest!" she cried the second she realized he bore no tonsure.

The priest's vestments were stripped from his body to reveal a knight's armor; Catherine felt her heart race with trepidation.

"Dear God! What is this all about?"

"You are coming with us, my fair Catherine," the stranger proclaimed.

"With you? Where?"

He caught her arm. "To England."

"But why?"

"A matter of politics."

The look in his eyes told her he was serious. Fear streaked through her body, and she tried to twist from his hold, but his grip tightened.

"Don't fight me, Catherine. 'Tis futile."

Futile? Never! she vowed in silence. She'd fight him unto her death, if need be. She'd not leave Miles. This was to be their wedding day.

Catherine's fear instantly turned to riotous anger. Unable to break her abductor's hold, she lunged at him, her fingers aimed at his left eye.

Adeptly he lurched back, but before he could catch her hand, her nails raked his cheek. The white streaks, marking their tracks, slowly oozed with blood.

Staring up at him, Catherine knew she'd done the wrong thing. His silver irises turned steely as his eyes narrowed.

"God's wounds, you are a vicious little thing," he said

through clenched teeth. Catching both her wrists in one hand, he wiped his cheek with the other. He stared at his fingers, and the red film covering them, then looked at her. "If you value your life, wench, you'll not attempt such a thing again."

A rustling in the woods caught Catherine's notice. The noise had also attracted her captor's attention, for he looked beyond her.

"Milady! Catherine? Where are you?"

Catherine recognized the voice as that of her nurse. "Eloi—"

The rest was a strangled garble as his large hand clamped over her mouth. Struggling against his hold, Catherine edged her mouth open and sank her teeth into his little finger. His breath hissed between his teeth as he yanked his hand away.

By now Eloise had appeared at the periphery of the glade. "Milady? What on earth are you—"

"Run, Eloise!" Catherine shouted, kicking out at her captor's shins. "Alert my father! Alert Miles!"

The breath whooshed from Catherine's lungs as she was pulled hard against a solid chest. Looking up at the tall warrior, she watched as he nodded toward Eloise. Catherine had forgotten all about his companion.

"Run, Eloise!" she cried again.

A thump and a thud met Catherine's ears, and she cringed. When she was spun around, she saw that her nurse lay unconscious on the frozen ground.

"What shall we do with her?" the older knight asked, inclining his head toward the woman he'd felled.

"She's seen our faces. We've no choice but to take her with us."

Catherine's wrist ached from the pressure of his fingers. Bending over, he scooped up the priest's vestments and wiped his cheek, then tossed all but the coif into the thickness of the brush. With the scrap of linen, he again blotted his wound. Catherine hoped the scratches became infected and festered. With luck he'd take the poisoning and die.

"What if she awakens and starts thrashing about?" his

companion queried while eyeing Eloise. "I imagine she'll be hard to control."

"Then show her no mercy."

Catherine fought back her tears as she was pulled toward one of the horses. "Barbarian," she denounced.

"If I were really a barbarian she would already be dead." They had reached the destrier's side. "Give me your other hand," he ordered after taking a strip of leather from across the saddle.

Catherine refused.

"Your nurse's life could depend on your present and future actions, so I suggest you do as you are told. Now give me your hand."

Catherine glared her discontent, but she obeyed. As he bound and tied her wrists, she looked to where Eloise lay. The older knight had just finished knotting the leather that secured Eloise's feet. Grabbing the front of her gown, he pulled the woman up from the ground and, with a grunt, lifted her fully across his shoulder.

"She's a heavy one," the man said as he moved toward his horse.

"If the added burden wearies your steed, rid yourself of her along the way."

His order given, her captor looked Catherine fully in the face. Immediately she berated him. "You odious bastard! When we are found, I pray you suffer mightily for this."

A hard glint showed in his eyes. "Since I am unsure of my parentage, your assumption may be correct. As for the other, I doubt we will be found. But if we don't leave here this moment, you may get your wish. Let's go."

Hysteria bubbled inside Catherine. If she didn't do something now, it would be too late. She opened her mouth, but before she could scream he had shoved the coif between her lips. A heavy cloak was draped across her shoulders, the ties secured; then she was cast upon the saddle, her abductor mounting behind her. With a nod at his companion, he looped his arm around Catherine's waist and reined his destrier toward the opposite side of the glade.

Miles!

His name tore through Catherine's mind as the foursome

entered the shelter of the forest. Looking over her shoulder, she could see the jutting tower at Avranches slip farther and farther away. A tear rolled down her cheek to fall upon her breast. Dismally, Catherine feared she'd never see her betrothed again.

An angry Miles swung Clotilde around by her hair to face the men who stood in the great hall, all of them blond in coloring. "Do you see the bastard?" he asked, the words gritting between his teeth.

"N-no, milord."

"Are you certain?"

"Y-yes, milord. He's not among them."

"Stupid wench," he said. "As unappealing as you are, it is beyond me how you could ever think a man would be interested in you solely for yourself." He shoved her away. "Get from my sight before I thrash you."

Tears streamed down Clotilde's pale cheeks. Her sobs followed her as she ran from the room.

When Catherine had not appeared in the hall to break the fast, William had gone to the women's quarters, looking for his daughter. At Clotilde's pronouncement that her mistress had not yet returned from the chapel, both father and maid sought her there. Behind the altar they found the priest, bound, gagged, blindfolded, and stripped nearly nude. William had rightly feared the worst and sounded the alarm.

Freed from his bonds and wrapped in William's mantle, the chaplain began recounting his ordeal. By then Miles and Geoffrey had arrived. It was when the priest described the man who had accosted him that a loud gasp escaped Clotilde. Naturally, all eyes turned her way.

Miles immediately began interrogating the girl, and without mercy. Although she'd been instrumental in leading Catherine's abductor straight to her, it was clear that Clotilde hadn't intended anything of the sort. Of all those present, only William took pity on her.

"You were far too hard on the girl," he now stated.

"Was I?" Miles shot back. "Since it is your daughter, William, I'd think you'd be more distressed than you are."

"No one is more distressed over this than I, sir. But maligning the girl won't give us the answers we seek. If we are to help Catherine, we need to keep a clear head and a keen mind. Instead you are behaving like a fool. Continue to comport yourself thus and I'll do worse to you than what you ever intended for Clotilde."

Miles and William stared at each other, long and hard. It was then that Geoffrey intervened. "William is right, Son. Keep your wits about you, or else we'll never find your bride."

"You called for me, milords?" the sentry asked as he tried to stifle a yawn, for he'd just been roused from his bed. All three men spun toward him.

"On your watch, did the Lady Catherine leave the castle?" Miles asked.

"Aye, she and a priest. Said she was going to the west wood to do penance."

"What hour was that?" William questioned.

"A little after dawn."

"What of her nurse? Did you see her?"

"No. The watch was changed right after the Lady Catherine left. Perhaps my replacement saw her."

Miles and Geoffrey, along with several guards, followed Catherine's father from the great hall. The sentry on duty confirmed he'd seen Eloise leave the castle shortly after he'd begun his watch. He hadn't seen her since.

"To the woods," William ordered.

A short time later, while skirting a small glade, a flash of white caught William's eye. Leaning from his horse, he snatched the wadded cloth from the brambles. "These are the priest's robes, and there's blood on them."

Miles and his father were across the way, searching through the undergrowth. On his hearing William's words, a hissing epitaph erupted from Miles's lips. "The bastard's tupped her."

Geoffrey captured his son's arm. "Remember to watch your tongue," he ordered in a low voice.

"Watch my tongue? 'Tis not to my liking to take a bride who is another man's leavings."

"Whether she's been defiled or not is not the issue. The bride's portion is what concerns us. We can ill afford to lose it. Now quit fretting about your own vanity and show some concern for your betrothed."

Wresting himself from Geoffrey's hold, Miles rode across the glade. Once beside William, he grabbed the robes and examined them. "If the bastard has harmed her, I'll kill him."

"I'll grant you that privilege after I'm through with him myself," William stated.

A shout sounded from deeper in the wood. "Milords," a guard called, "we've found some hoofprints."

William, Miles, and Geoffrey rode to where the others were. "From what I can tell, there are two horses. By the size of their hooves, I'll wager they are destriers," William said, then he turned to Geoffrey. "Instruct one of your men to return to the castle. We'll need arms, food, and more troops."

"Do you intend to follow?" Miles asked.

"Aye. Do you?" William countered.

"The tracks—the ground is frozen. These might be all there are."

"They are all I need, sir. They point west. With or without you, Miles, I am striking out for the coast." Turning his steed, William traveled deeper into the wood. He reined in. "Are you coming or not?"

For a long moment, Miles looked at his father. "Aye, I'm coming," he said, pointing his horse in the same direction as William's. "I'll not forsake that which I've so longed to have. Come. Let us find Catherine."

They were nearing their destination.

His back as rigid as a stake, Rolfe kept his arm tight around his captive's waist, pulling her snugly against his chest. Her hair, the color of rich sable, shone like shimmering liquid under the sun's rays, mesmerizing him. Her scent, like a field of wildflowers on a spring day, filled his head each time he breathed. The effect made him dizzy. As her body moved against his in time to the galloping motion of his steed, he gritted his teeth. Unequivocally, she was driving him mad.

It had been a long while since he'd held a woman this close. Never, though, was she as soft or alluring as the one now in his arms. Nor was she as treacherous.

Given the opportunity, Catherine de Mortain would kill him. Despite his growing fascination with her, Rolfe swore he'd not allow her the chance.

That he was exceptionally wary of her didn't surprise him. Since that fateful day on the road to Antalya, he'd trusted few. Garrick was an exception, of course; so was his squire, Aubrey, but in Rolfe's eyes he was yet a boy. Last there was Duke Henry, Rolfe's liege lord. Of the three, he thought Garrick and Aubrey to be the most faithful. They would lay down their lives for him, as he would for them.

As the great destrier carried his captive and himself easily across the low, rolling hills, Rolfe was thankful that the first leg of their journey was almost over. In less than a league, they would reach the coastline. Rolfe hoped that the sea was calm.

Without warning, his captive shifted in the saddle. Her small, round derriere rubbed against his groin, and Rolfe bit back a groan. She moved again, and he sucked in his breath.

God's wounds! Could she not be still?

As the question tore through his mind, he belatedly wondered why he had insisted on volunteering for this mission. True, he wanted to exact revenge on Miles, but from Rolfe's way of thinking, the tables were now turned. His mistake was in not anticipating how appealing his captive would be. Per Henry's own decree, Rolfe was to take great care not to despoil the fair Catherine. But as her appetizing young body continued its attack on his, Rolfe knew the command might prove impossible to obey.

His jaw set, he rode onward. Soon the group topped the last hill. He reined in and looked across the marshes toward the jutting rock and the building atop it.

"'Tis an abbey," Catherine said, the coif taken from her mouth long before.

"Aye, milady. Mont St. Michel, to be precise."

She looked at him questioningly, and he noticed how her hazel eyes had changed color. Where once they were a deep gray, now they were a muted green. He wondered absently their shade when she was in the throes of passion.

"The sacred mount of the Archangel?" she asked, disbelief ringing in her voice.

"Aye," he said. "'Tis my home."

CHAPTER

3

HIS NAME WAS ROLFE DE MONT ST. MICHEL, AND SHE HATED him.

In the dim candlelight, Catherine stared at her abductor, wishing beyond anything that he were dead.

He stood across the way, his squire helping him disrobe. His helm and mail coif, which he'd donned once they were away from Avranches, rested on a nearby bench. Beside them lay his broadsword, at most an arm's reach away. Steam rose from a wooden tub centered in the roomy cell inside the abbey. His bath awaited him.

As the layers of clothing were peeled away, first his hauberk, followed by his chainse, garters, and mail chausses, most maids would have looked away, but not Catherine. She hugged the wall, eyeing him the same as a cornered rabbit watched a hungry predator. Her hands were still bound, but she stood ready. Should he dare approach her, she'd lunge at him, inflicting as much damage as she could before he overpowered her.

He was now stripped to his braies. His long fingers caught the ties that held the garment snugly in place between his waist and hips. "Turn around, Catherine, and face the wall, or your maidenly eyes will see more than what is intended."

33

She defied him by ignoring his command. He shrugged, then jerked the ends of the string. The garment fell to his ankles.

He boldly met her stare for stare. Silence encompassed them, until he said, "Does milady approve of what she sees?"

Living in a castle where privacy between the sexes was as tenuous as a wooden screen or a cloth curtain, Catherine had some knowledge of the male anatomy. Grudgingly, she had to admit his was exceptional.

He possessed a warrior's body, well muscled, agile, and strong. Dark blond hair furred across his broad chest, then darted to his navel, and past, where it fanned and thickened.

Her eyes never wavered as she continued her examination of him, down to his feet. Save for three obvious scars—one on his left forearm, another at his waist, the last slashing across his right thigh—he was without flaw.

Unflinchingly, he withstood her scrutiny. Then she saw his lips twitch. A wide smile stretched across his handsome face, exposing straight white teeth.

"No answer, Catherine?" he asked, then shook his head. "I'm surprised at you. I thought by your confession this morning you were a virgin, but the mark of innocence evades your lovely face. I suppose that means your betrothed has already reaped his prize."

Catherine stiffened. Had it been Miles who was standing thus, her cheeks would be flaming like fire. She loved Miles. The mere thought of him set her emotions to spinning, pleasantly so. *This* man she despised. The only feeling she held for Rolfe de Mont St. Michel was contempt.

"Since I find you to be such an odious creature," she said, malice deliberately sounding in her voice, "there is no reason for me to blush."

She refused to respond to the last of his statement, but he wouldn't let it pass.

"Are you a virgin, Catherine?" he asked softly.

Should he decide to ravish her, she doubted it mattered whether she were intact or not. She was, but if he wanted the truth, he'd have to discover it for himself. "My physical condition is none of your affair. I am betrothed. That's all I will say."

Rolfe chuckled. "I admire your pretense at bravery. However, being a man who has had carnal knowledge of not just one woman but many, I can see you are as innocent as the day you were born. You may ease your worries. You are safe, and so is your virginity."

He stepped from the fallen braies and walked toward the tub. Unchivalrous lout, she thought. His touting the fact that he'd made numerous conquests of the fairer sex proved he didn't take his knight's oath seriously. No doubt he was a mercenary, his services rendered to the highest bidder. At first Catherine wondered exactly who stood to profit from her abduction and why. Then she decided it was Rolfe himself, and his motive was gold.

He stepped into the tub, then eased himself down into the hot liquid, whereupon he sighed contentedly. When he next looked her way, he asked, "Why are you smiling?"

Catherine hadn't realized she was. Naked and ensconced in a tub, he was at his most vulnerable. Fancifully, she'd been pondering his reaction should her father or Miles burst into the room, sword drawn.

Oh, what she'd give to see the expression on his face just before his bathwater ran red. Would it be one of surprise or embarrassment? Or perhaps a little of both? Whatever his response, Catherine wished she could witness the event forthwith.

"I asked you a question, milady. I would like an answer."

"I'm smiling because you are far too confident. By now there is undoubtedly a small army searching for me. Considering your present situation, perhaps you are not as intelligent as you would have everyone believe."

"If you refer to the fact that I've taken the time to bathe, let me assure you there's little chance I'll be caught unawares. The abbey is virtually impregnable."

"But not totally."

"Nothing is invincible. At least nothing of an earthly nature. However, this day I perceive no danger. After all, the Archangel is purported to guard not only this mount, but also the marshes and the sea surrounding it. I have every certainty he'll continue to do so. Hence, I am comfortable in my present situation."

"And I say the Archfiend holds dominion here. That is the real reason you are so at ease."

He chuckled. "That's sacrilege, Catherine. Had your chaplain heard those words you'd be doing penance for years to come. Be a good girl and sit and eat," he said as he leaned forward, allowing his squire access to his back.

The lad, whom Catherine surmised was only a year or two younger than herself, ran a soapy cloth over his lord's shoulders, then down his spine.

"You'll be needing your strength," her captor finished as the lather was rinsed away.

"Why?"

"Tonight, when the tide is right, we leave for England. Once we meet her shores, we'll be traveling overland. The journey ahead is long. As I say, you'll be needing your strength."

Catherine glanced at the half loaf of crusty bread and the thick chunk of cheese. The two rested on a linen square atop a small wooden table only a few feet from her. A chalice filled with wine sat in the table's center. It was now midday, and even though she hadn't eaten since the night before, she was far from hungry. She looked back at him.

"Why are you doing this?" she asked. She was desperate to know the true reason he'd carried her to Mont St. Michel, to learn the motive behind his taking her to England.

"It has been a while since I've had a bath. I thought for milady's sake I should take one."

"That's not what I meant," she snapped. "Whether you bathe or not is of no concern to me."

"Given the fact that we'll be in fairly close quarters from now on, I'd think it would hold *some* concern."

He bedeviled her, intentionally. In return, she glared her disdain. "I want to know why you abducted me. Was it for ransom? Do you hope to make your fortune through me?"

He lifted a long sinewy leg from the tub; his squire set to scrubbing it. "I am happy with what I have," he said, dunking the leg back into the water.

"Then what is your purpose?"

He lifted the other leg. "I told you it was a matter of politics."

"Whose politics, and what does it have to do with me?"

"The less you know the better off you'll be—at least for now. Once we are in England, and we are safe, I'll explain all. For the present, eat what has been served you. I repeat: You'll be needing your strength." Rebellion must have flashed in her eyes, for he added, "Food is far more enjoyable when it is not forced upon the partaker. I hope you understand my meaning."

Challenged by his words, she thought to knock the offering from the table with a sweep of her arms. However, she didn't relish having the fare picked from the floor and shoved down her throat, as he would undoubtedly do. He was right: She did need her strength, especially if she hoped to outmaneuver him.

Wisdom forbade her from reacting as she wanted. She moved to the stool and sat at the small table, where she lifted her bound hands and grasped the bread. With the first bite, she found it to be quite palatable, and not in the least stale. The cheese was equally good.

As she reached for the chalice to quench her thirst, she thought of her plight. There had to be a way to escape him, to escape from this fortress he called his home. That this spawn of the devil would be allowed anywhere near the sacred mount of the Archangel made Catherine wonder about the sanity of the Benedictines who resided here. Did they not know how truly wicked he was?

Wine flowed past her lips and over her tongue. Swallowing the sweet liquid, she remembered the greeting she'd received on entering the abbey. She was yet stunned by the event.

After their perilous trip across the marches, quicksand threatening to swallow both the destriers and their riders should they veer even a step off course, the group had wended their way up the steep granite rock path toward the monastery. Once inside, she'd spied a black-robed monk. Twisting against her captor's hand, she'd called out for assistance. Unbelievably, the monk had smiled and nodded, then continued on his way.

It had been the same with everyone she'd faced, her pleas for help falling on deaf ears. As a result, Catherine knew her bid for freedom lay solely with herself. There would be no aid from any of the brethren in this hallowed place. Like Rolfe de Mont St. Michel, Catherine imagined that they too were possessed.

Fury welled inside her, and the chalice hit the wood beside her food. By the saints, she'd find a way out. But she'd not leave without Eloise.

"Where is my nurse?" she asked, again looking his way.

Lost in her thoughts, she hadn't heard him step from the tub. Rivulets of water sluiced down his golden body, tracing his sleek contours, to puddle at his feet. Caught off guard, Catherine felt her cheeks blaze with embarrassment. As her gaze skittered back to the tabletop, she heard his laughter. Gritting her teeth, she seethed inwardly. This time her anger was aimed at herself, not him.

He accepted a large piece of cloth from his squire and began drying himself. "Don't tell me that milady's courage is wavering," he said, his tone lightly mocking. "Do you feel at a disadvantage without your nurse here to protect you?"

"I haven't needed her protection in a long while. I'm concerned about her well-being. Where is she?"

"Garrick is putting a poultice on her jaw. No doubt his ears are suffering for it too."

"I hope more is made to suffer than just his ears, the barbarian."

"Garrick acted on my command. If you need to vent your rage on someone, then vent it on me. Or your nurse."

"Eloise? Why?"

"Had she not come to the wood, searching for you, she'd now be at Avranches, none the worse for wear."

Catherine bristled at his logic. "And had you not come to Avranches, Eloise and I would both be there, none the worse for wear. But you did, and with malicious intent."

He tossed the towel aside and strode toward the chest where his clothes lay. Catherine watched him from the corner of her eye as he donned a clean pair of braies, handed to him by his squire. His lower half covered, he turned toward her, nimble fingers tying the lacing that kept the garment in place.

"You've suffered no abuse, Catherine. Nor will you, as long as you behave."

She stared at him as though he'd gone daft. "Suffered no abuse? You lied to me, tricked me, stole me away from my betrothed. What do you call that?"

"I didn't strike you."

"You bound me. See?" She held up her hands. "I am still tied. My wrists are nearly raw."

"When I am through dressing, I'll free you from your bindings. Will that appease you?"

"You could never appease me. Had it not been for you, I would already be wed, reveling in the knowledge that I was now Miles's wife. Because of you, what should have been the happiest day of my life has become the most vile. You've ruined everything for me. For fear that I've been defiled, Miles may no longer want me. I hate you for what you have done." Tears stung her eyes, yet Catherine fought to control them. She'd not cry in front of this beast. "Someday you will suffer for your treachery. On that day, I will shout with glee."

While she'd let loose her tirade, he appeared to ignore her and continued to dress. He'd drawn on a woolen chainse, its hem striking him at midcalf. Over that he placed his hauberk. Next came his mail chausses, both gartered at the knee. Afterward, while his squire girded a pair of prick spurs at his heels, their gilt finish proclaiming that he was a knight, he belted his broadsword at his waist. Catherine was wondering if he'd heard a word she'd said when he slowly turned her way.

"I understand your hatred, Catherine," he said softly, his silver gaze now trained on her. "You feel as you do because you are convinced that you are in love with your betrothed. You think you know him, but I say you don't. I agree. Someday you'll be shouting with glee, but it will be because you are truly thankful that I saved you from the misery you would have been made to endure had you married the bastard."

"How dare you speak about Miles in such a demeaning manner. He is not of ignoble birth as you are. Unlike you, he is kind, chivalrous—"

"You may see him as noble, but in truth, Miles d'Avranches is a coward, and his father is a traitor who is driven by greed. You are a very comely young woman, Catherine. Quick-witted and spirited. Any man would be proud to take you as his wife, including Miles. But I doubt his devotion to you comes solely from love."

"What exactly are you inferring?"

"I'm not inferring anything." He moved toward her. Once beside her, he unsheathed the knife that was tucked into his belt. "I'm telling you: You're not the true object of his desire. He wants your marriage portion. Your inheritance also."

"A lie!" she protested. "You know nothing about Miles. Nor about our relationship."

"'Tis well known that William de Mortain possesses vast holdings both in Normandy and in England. His wealth is said to be sizable. That you are his only heir is equally well known. What is not so well known, however, is that Miles d'Avranches and his father were in the process of arranging for a betrothal to another young heiress when suddenly all negotiations were broken off. Shortly thereafter came the announcement about your forthcoming nuptials. From all accounts the young woman whom he rebuffed is said to be blessed with considerable beauty. Her one flaw seems to have been that she wasn't as wealthy as you. It makes one wonder about your betrothed's loyalty, doesn't it?"

"I don't believe you."

"Nevertheless, it is true." He lifted her hands, slipped the knife between her forearms, and, with a quick slice, cut through the bindings. "Finish your meal, Catherine. Aubrey will stay with you and attend to your needs."

"What you really mean is that he is to keep watch over me," she said, rubbing her wrists.

"That too," he replied. He sheathed his knife, then headed away from her.

"Where are you going?" she asked.

"To speak with Garrick."

His back now presented to her, she turned her attention toward his squire. "What about Eloise?" she inquired while gauging the lad's height and weight. A swift blow to the head should fell him easily enough.

"If Garrick is done tending to her, she may join you."

He had stopped at the doorway. When she next looked at him, she saw he was assessing her.

"I should caution you, Catherine. Aubrey is not yet a man, but he is well trained. His reflexes are quick, his mind keen. Attempt to do him bodily harm and you will discover just how adept he is."

Catherine silently cursed him. Clearly he'd read her thoughts. "The notion of violence never crossed my mind," she said, feigning a look of innocence.

"I think it did. Likewise, don't seek to beguile the lad. He's far too smart to be led astray."

His edict given, he departed.

Catherine stared at the empty space where Rolfe de Mont St. Michel once stood. He was too astute by far. Because he was, any opportunity for escape would be slight. Even so, she had to try. That night, as they descended to the shore and the longship that was to carry them to England, she would make her break for freedom.

And if she failed?

She'd throw herself into the sea.

Rolfe strode the narrow corridor toward the almonry, where Garrick awaited him, wondering over his own boldness. There was something about Catherine de Mortain that provoked in him the need to taunt her, to challenge her, and yes, to hurt her.

He was surprised by her defiance, surprised by how she'd faced him squarely while he disrobed. Slowly, deliberately, she'd assessed him. He remembered how, on his part, it had taken tremendous control not to respond to the touch of her gaze as it raked him from head to foot.

As he relived the moment, his restraint was again tested. Gritting his teeth, he swallowed the groan of misery that threatened to break from his lips. God's wounds! Why couldn't she have been plain and unappealing, instead of the vibrant beauty that she was? And why couldn't he foster some contempt for her, instead of favoring her as he did?

Admittedly, from the first, she'd demonstrated courage and determination. Still, she was exceptionally naive, especially when it came to Miles d'Avranches. For the former, Rolfe admired her; for the latter, he wanted to take her by the shoulders and shake some sense into her.

He hadn't lied when he'd told her about Miles's attempt at an earlier betrothal. Through Henry and others he knew it to be so. An introduction to the young maid in question might prove the surest way to convince her. Even then, he doubted his captive would believe him.

The fact was that Catherine de Mortain had blinded herself to her betrothed's shortcomings, and no matter what Rolfe presented as testimony that Miles was a cowardly pawn enmeshed in the greater schemes of Geoffrey d'Avranches to attain power and wealth, she would disavow his words and call him a liar, just as she'd done a short while before.

Becoming angry with himself, Rolfe clenched his jaw. Why did he care what she thought? About Miles? About him? About anything at all?

In a short while he'd be rid of her. After she was securely installed behind the walls of one of Henry's strongholds, the place already selected by prearrangement, Rolfe planned to rejoin the duke. As far as he was concerned, someone else could act as her keeper. He had gotten what he'd wanted. He'd won his redress. And even though he could gain the ultimate revenge, the fair Catherine's virginity, he rejected the notion. He did so not because Henry had warned him off, but because the forcible misuse of a woman went against his convictions.

Regrettably, not all his brethren-at-arms agreed with his stance; to them rape was simply another privilege earned, one of the spoils of victory. From the first that he'd donned his golden spurs after taking his oath, Rolfe had shied away from such practices, gold, fine silks, jewels, and other comparable treasures being dividend enough for him. If he ever wanted a woman, he utilized his charm and enticed her into his bed, always allowing her to leave with her dignity intact. And despite his captive's declared hatred, an emotion that he often found to be erratic, Rolfe felt it could be the same with Catherine de Mortain.

Strangely, though, like a bird foraging along the bark of a tree, the voice of caution kept pecking away at him. Yes, he desired her, wanted from the moment he first saw her to feel her legs entwined around him, her sweet young body eagerly receiving him, their union culminating in explosive pleasure. But somewhere along the way, the question arose: Once he'd made love to her, would he be able to let her go?

Since his youth, Rolfe had purposely shunned the thought of committing himself to one woman. With adventures to be had, campaigns to be fought, and rewards aplenty, in his mind marriage was something to be scorned. Just the notion of his growing old and fat as he lazed beside a blazing hearth while a passel of children ran through some drafty keep overlooking a sleepy little village in a place yet unknown made him cringe. Catherine de Mortain was the type of woman who could cause a man to want to settle in, all else forgotten. For that very reason he was impatient to unburden himself of her. Before it was too late.

Over a prolonged period, Catherine sat at the small table. Tallow candles flickered in their holders, casting strange shadows on the stone walls. In the room's stillness, soft breaths the only sound to be heard, she continued to assess Rolfe's squire, forever wondering if he was as seasoned a lad as his lord and master believed.

He stood nearly a head taller than herself. He was muscular, but nowhere near as muscular as the cursed whoreson who'd brought her here. Nor anywhere as tall. Knowing she was no match for the lad, she decided if she couldn't lay him low, perhaps she could outwit him instead. At long last she intended to find out.

"May I have more wine?" she asked after draining her cup.

"As milady wishes." He laid aside the garment he'd been folding. Lifting a flagon from a side table, he came toward her.

"Are you also from Mont St. Michel?" she inquired as he refilled the chalice.

"No, milady. I am from Bayeux."

"Bayeux, is it?" She saw his nod. "Since you are now a squire, I suppose you are of noble birth."

"No, milady. My father was a blacksmith in the service of Robert de Bayeux."

"And who is he?"

"He was my master's mentor. Earl Robert, along with his son Francis, was killed in the last Crusade. Their bones lie here in the abbey, Sir Rolfe asking that they be consecrated and buried under the protection of the Archangel. The Abbot du Bec complied."

Catherine frowned. "This may be none of my affair, but I am curious as to how your master came to claim Mont St. Michel as his home. Was he born in the village below?"

The boy's reddish locks bobbed against his face as he shook his head. "No, milady. The Archangel saved him."

"Saved him?" she cried, stunned. From an early age, she had been taught that Michael and Lucifer were meant to face the other, good against evil, good winning out. So why on earth would he preserve the progeny of his most vile enemy? Deciding it was unlikely that he would, she laughed sharply. "Surely you jest!"

The lad's gaze narrowed on her. "I do not jest. His life was spared by the Archangel. The monks proclaimed it a miracle, one of many occurring on this mount. If you do not believe me, then ask the Benedictines. They will tell you it is true."

Catherine heard the indignation in his voice. It was coupled with pride. "I am sorry if I have offended you, Aubrey—may I call you 'Aubrey'?"

"That is my name."

His tone hadn't softened, and Catherine realized the insult had gone far deeper than she'd thought. "I didn't mean to suggest your words were false. As you know, I hold no fondness for your master. That the Archangel would

44

spare him, especially after what he has done to me, is very hard to accept."

"Particularly when you believe I'm the spawn of the devil, right?"

Catherine swung her head in the direction of the door. There, lounging against its frame, was her nemesis. "The thought has occurred," she said while lifting her chin.

"It has more than 'occurred,' Catherine. You've verbalized as much at least once so far. 'Archfiend,' remember?" Shoving from the stones, he stepped into the room. "Despite what you've conjured in your mind, I'm simply a man, albeit with a nebulous past. Instead of questioning Aubrey, why don't you ask me what it is you want to know?"

"I don't want to know anything about you, past, present, or future," she snapped. "'Tis unimportant—all of it."

"Then why were you talking about me?"

"We were simply making conversation."

He considered her at length. "As you say, my past is unimportant. However, what affects me presently, and in the future, *is* important."

"To you, maybe."

"And to you, milady. It affects you also. Like it or not, we are on a parallel course. We will be for some time to come. You might say our destinies are intertwined."

Until her father or Miles caught up to them, she deemed. At that moment she would be free, and he would be dead. "Since we are thus linked, then perhaps I should know about your past as well."

"Whatever for?"

"To complete the circle," she declared. "Without a past, you can have no present or future. Or so I would think."

The truth was that she'd become curious about the alleged miracle that generated such reverence from the Benedictines. She watched as he moved to a tall stool. The mail links of his hauberk scraped against wood as he edged his hip onto the seat. Again he regarded her.

"There is not much to tell," he said finally. "However, because you insist, I'll relate what I've been told, for I have no memory of it myself. At age one, I was left on the marshes—'deserted' would be a better term. How long I lay there no one knows, but my placement had to come after the tide had ebbed.

"Apparently, as the tide came in again, slowly surrounding the mount, one of the hounds let loose to patrol against robbers and thieves bounded from the pack and pulled me to safety before I drowned and was washed out to sea. Since the hounds seldom leave the mount, the brothers proclaimed it a miracle. They were convinced the Archangel had spared me. For what purpose, no one seems to know.

"Myself, I call it a stroke of luck." He chuckled. "The hound was probably hungry and saw me as a tasty morsel by which to supplement his diet. 'Twas simply my four-legged savior's misfortune that one of the brothers discovered me before he had the chance to follow through."

"And mine," Catherine grumbled, wishing the hound had made a fine meal of him.

He arched a brow at her. "That may be true. Then again, it may not. We will just have to wait and see, won't we?"

Catherine refrained from responding. He already knew how she felt about him. Instead she asked, "Is that why the Benedictines named you 'Rolfe'—because you were 'protected'?"

"The choice was apparently foreordained, since my name was given me beforehand. The brothers found it, along with my birthdate, embroidered on my swaddling. Other than those two facts, they know no more than I do about my past. 'Tis a mystery to us all." He came to his feet. "Now, milady, if you are finished with your meal, I suggest you get some rest. Our ship will be arriving soon to sit at anchor a short distance out. When the tide is high enough, we'll be meeting her. You have a long and unsettling journey ahead of you, one during which I doubt you'll find much comfort. If you are wise, you'll seek your pallet"—he motioned to the straw-filled bed that lay not far from where she sat—"and take your ease there, for it's unlikely you'll find it later."

"Where is Eloise?"

No sooner had the words left Catherine's mouth than a loud fuss arose in the corridor just outside the room, signaling the woman's approach. "If you've harmed one hair on milady's head, I'll disembowel the two of you and toss your entrails to the predators of the sea. More than likely the vicious things will rebuke the offering for fear they'll wither and die. The devil's own poison, evil and vile—that's what you are." At the last of her diatribe, Eloise showed in the doorway, the one called Sir Garrick holding her arm. "My dearest child!" she cried, her gaze snagging Catherine's. "He didn't hurt you, did he?"

"I am well," Catherine said, coming up off her stool. "And you?"

Eloise looked up at the man who held her. "I have experienced better treatment, milady," she announced with a sniff.

"Had you shown good sense and restrained your temper instead of behaving like the termagant you are, you wouldn't have suffered any further maltreatment," Garrick returned.

His tone was abrasive, and Catherine wondered what had passed between the pair since she last saw them. Searching for fresh bruises on Eloise's face, she found none. But the telltale marks could be hidden.

That Eloise had suffered such abuse further angered Catherine. Though she wanted to strike out at both men, she thought it best to stay calm. Then, on noticing the woman's hands were yet bound, she looked to Rolfe.

"My nurse is most protective of me," she said. "If she was remiss in her conduct, I'm certain it springs from worry. Free her, please, and I shall give you my pledge she will cause no more trouble to either of you."

To her own ears, her voice was excessively placid. Catherine pondered whether or not her abductor would believe her.

"And exactly how will you seal your pledge, Catherine?" Rolfe asked. "With a kiss, perhaps?"

At his words, Eloise shrieked disapprovingly. Catherine, however, simply returned him stare for stare. "My word is good enough, sir," she announced. "Accept it or reject it. The choice is yours."

Garrick scowled as he fought to keep a firm hold on Eloise. "'Twould be safer," he muttered, "if the shrew stayed thus, binding her feet for added assurance. She's untrustworthy, much like a raging wolverine."

Catherine's nemesis remained silent as he inspected her from head to foot, then back again. His silvery gaze halted briefly on her mouth, to caress it ever so lightly. Catherine's stomach trembled, for, unbelievably, she felt as though she'd actually been kissed.

Maddened that he had the power to affect her so, she squared her shoulders and lifted her chin. "Well? What do you say?"

"Free her," Rolfe ordered.

"'Tis a mistake," Garrick countered. Nonetheless he released his knife from his belt and cut through the bindings securing Eloise's wrists. The deed done, he hobbled back a few steps, as though he feared she might turn on him.

"You are wise to retreat, else you'd be suffering a wound on your other shin, far worse than the first one I struck." With those words Eloise rushed to Catherine's side, whereupon she took a protective stance. "Come near the Lady Catherine again and you will discover the consequences of your folly."

Garrick limped back beside Rolfe. "I told you she was not to be trusted."

"Her threats are simply the squawkings of an old hen guarding a lone chick," Rolfe said. "She poses no genuine menace. If she becomes too much of a nuisance, you have my permission to rid yourself of her. She is an encumbrance as it is."

He meant every word, Catherine realized. When Eloise's mouth flew open, the woman undoubtedly bent on delivering another verbal attack, Catherine quickly caught her nurse's hand and squeezed. Fortunately the action stilled Eloise before she erred, and Catherine said, "I gave you my promise that she would cause you no more trouble."

"Then see that it is so," Rolfe responded. He turned to his squire. "Are you finished here?"

During the interim Aubrey had moved from the table and set to packing his master's belongings. "Aye, sire. All is ready."

"Then bring the chest, so we may give our guests some privacy."

Catherine heard the key as it scraped in and out of the metal lock. Rising from his knees, Aubrey lifted the carved chest by its handles and carried it to the door, dodging the tub as he went. When the squire stepped over the threshold, her gaze jumped to his master. For a moment, he returned her stare; then with Garrick preceding him, he moved out into the hallway. Once the panel had closed, an iron bar fell into place on its outer side; Catherine shut her eyes and expelled her breath.

"What are we to do now, milady?"

Her eyelids fluttering open, Catherine looked to her nurse. "We need to plan our escape."

"The girl appeals to you, doesn't she?" Garrick asked.

Perched on a bench in the almonry, polishing the blade of his broadsword, Rolfe bided his time. Refusing to dwell on Catherine de Mortain, he focused his thoughts on other things. Their ship had not yet arrived. Still, until the tide was right, they were unable to leave. He fretted not, positive that all would come together, just as planned. But at the knight's words, he quickly glanced up. "What makes you think that?"

"By the way you gaze at her."

Rolfe shrugged, then set to polishing his sword again. "She's pleasing to the eye."

"'Tis more than her physical aspect that holds your interest. It goes far deeper. When the time comes to free her, I wonder if you'll be willing to let her go."

"Women and war do not mix, Garrick. I am a knight, and my allegiance belongs to Henry. When he says the time has come, she will be freed."

"What? So she can go back to Miles and wed him?"

"If that is what she desires, then so be it. There will be no one to stop her."

Garrick frowned. "I doubt he will want another man's leavings. No one would."

Rolfe jerked his head to attention. "If you think that I mean to bed her, you are wrong," he announced. "For one, Henry has forbidden such. For the other, she is merely a pawn who is being utilized for another's gain. Because of that, I'm unwilling to take advantage of her. She is, after all, quite innocent and will have suffered enough once this whole thing is finished."

"'Twill be interesting to see if you feel the same once we are in England. Besides scratching your face, she has stirred your passion, my young friend. That much I can see. I wonder just how long you'll be able to resist her, considering your continued immediacy."

"I have made other plans," Rolfe said, looking down at his sword. "Once we've reached our destination and the Lady Catherine is safely tucked away in another's care, I intend to join the duke. You are welcome to come with me, Garrick, if you so desire."

The older knight chuckled. "Your fear of what might happen between the girl and you is what drives you to Henry's side, isn't it?"

"My desire to see Henry succeed is what takes me to him. Naught else," Rolfe snapped. With a final rub at the center of the blade, he placed the broadsword beside him on the bench. "Your imagination has taken flight, Garrick. The girl means nothing to me. And so shall it stay."

"Aye. If you insist."

Rolfe's gaze narrowed on his companion. Just as he started to open his mouth to deliver a retort, a monk came scurrying down the stairs and into the almonry. Rolfe recognized him immediately.

"Brother Bernard!" he proclaimed with obvious delight. Bernard de Beauvais had been a young monk when Rolfe had been found on the marshes. The man had become one of Rolfe's teachers. Rolfe had not seen him when he was last here, having borne Robert's and Francis's remains to their final resting place. At the time, he'd been told that Bernard was now serving at a different abbey. "I'm happy to see you have returned."

The man, whose hair had since grayed, waved Rolfe off. "There is no time for amenities, my son. Your ship has arrived, albeit late. However, there is activity on the mainland shore. I think you'd best come see for yourself."

Grabbing his sword, Rolfe sheathed it at his belt. Then he, Garrick, and the monk ran the steps, up to the entrance at the abbey's north side. After skirting around to the south, they searched the shoreline.

"I count a dozen torches," Garrick said. "In the darkness, and at this distance, it is hard to tell what their bearers are about."

"There's no mystery to it," Rolfe stated. "I was hoping they wouldn't find us." He cursed soundly, then apologized to the monk. Afterward he silently cursed again.

Where the marshes now stood, there was once a great forest. But over time, the sea had claimed it. At high tide, the mount was severed from the mainland, at least to those who went by foot.

Likewise, on the north side of the mount, the brackish waters had slowly filled the bay with sand. No ship could come near, for fear of running aground. The only way out to sea was by a small boat, but the water's depth had to be suitable for such a journey, else the travelers would also be caught on the shoals.

Rolfe knew that, even then, it was a treacherous journey. For until the mount was cleared, there remained the possibility that a sudden wave could toss them back against the rock. Such a thing meant death to them all.

"The tide—at this hour, the water is too shallow. 'Twill be impossible to transport the horses. We'll have to leave them behind."

"Surely there's no need to panic—not unless they have the ability to walk on water," Garrick replied.

Along what was now the shoreline, the dozen glittering lights formed into two distinct ranks. One by one the torches were doused. When four remained, they were divided into two separate units, which began moving toward the mount. "'Tis more worrisome than that," Rolfe returned. "It looks like they have procured some boats." He pulled back from his position. "I do believe we'd better see to making our way out to the ship."

Striding around to the entrance, Rolfe loped down the steps, Garrick and Brother Bernard behind him. "Aubrey, gather my things, as well as Sir Garrick's," he called on spying his squire.

"So soon?" Aubrey asked.

"'Tis a matter of expediency." He turned to the monk. "Are the hounds on patrol for the night?"

"They were set loose an hour ago," the man replied.

"Good. Maybe they will allow us some additional time. Now, to collect the Lady Catherine."

"Her nurse too?" Garrick questioned as he followed Rolfe down the corridor to the room where the women waited.

"Aye."

"Why so? She is naught but a hindrance. We don't need her."

"For whatever reason, my instinct tells me to bring her along." He and Garrick were now at the entrance to the room. Lifting the iron bar, Rolfe tossed it aside and drew open the door, whereupon he strode across the threshold. "'Tis time to go," he announced.

Catherine and her nurse sat at the small table, their heads turned his way. Rolfe watched as they shared a quick look, then each rose to slowly cross the room.

When Catherine reached his side, he took her arm and guided her back to the almonry. Garrick and Eloise followed them. In the large room where the pilgrims were received, he thrust his captive in front of him. "Give me your hands," he ordered while pulling a strip of leather from his belt.

"Is this really necessary?" she asked. Nevertheless she obeyed his command.

"For the time being, it is."

Quickly he bound her wrists; then, seeing that her nurse's hands were also secured, he again gripped Catherine's arm and headed toward the stairs. Along the way, with his free hand, he grabbed the handle of the small chest containing his possessions.

At the top of the steps he came face-to-face with Aubrey. The lad's arms were filled with Rolfe's shield and ax, as well as Garrick's. "Where is Brother Bernard?" Rolfe asked.

"He waits at the entrance," the squire replied, then trailed the small group.

True to his word, the monk stood at the doorway, a torch in hand. "I'll guide you to the boat."

At Rolfe's nod, they made their way out to the steep path that snaked downward to the mount's northern base. Below him, he could hear the waves crashing against the rock. The sea was much higher than he'd anticipated, possibly caused by a distant storm. He prayed they were able to escape the current's force or they'd remain at the foot of Mont St. Michel forever.

As they began their descent, Brother Bernard at the fore, Aubrey behind him, Rolfe waved Garrick, who kept a firm grip on Eloise, ahead of him. The mists, carried by the steady wind, made the granite slick beneath his feet, and Rolfe tread lightly along the path.

Reaching the first turn, he glanced to his right. Surprisingly, the fair Catherine remained quite tame. Too tame, he thought. Then remembering the look that had passed between the plump Eloise and the young woman beside him, he pondered its meaning.

Halfway to the next turn, a screech exploded from Catherine's nurse. "You loathsome oaf!" she shouted, pulling against Garrick's hold. "I cannot fit side by side on this ledge with you. One of us is bound to go over. Loose me, I say, before I fall to my death."

Still holding on to the struggling woman, Garrick shot Rolfe a questioning glance. "Let her follow you," Rolfe said, keeping a firm grip on Catherine. "I'll watch her from above."

They made the second turn without further incident, as well as the third. But as they neared the fourth bend, Eloise appeared to slip. With a strangled cry, she snagged the rock facing and held on.

Having made the turn, Garrick looked up at her. "Keep your feet under you, woman."

By now Rolfe and Catherine were upon Eloise. "Can you go on?" he asked.

"Aye. Just let me catch my breath."

Eloise shortly eased away from the wall of rock; then, squaring her shoulders, she slowly headed down the path. At Rolfe's nod, Garrick continued onward.

The second incident over, Rolfe viewed Catherine from the corner of his eye. Twice her nurse had nearly fallen. Twice she'd not reacted. His suspicions rose.

His concerns came too late.

Meeting the bend, Eloise abruptly spun toward them. Like a charging sow, she rammed into Rolfe. At once a set of small teeth sank into his right hand. Reflexively he loosened his grip on Catherine's arm; she twisted free. He dropped the chest and snatched at her, but missed. Below him, Garrick uttered an oath, the heavy coffer having toppled over the ledge to nearly fell him.

Then, unbelievably, Eloise came at him again. Just as her girth hit him full force for a second time, she shouted, "Run, milady, run!"

In response, Rolfe heard footfalls running back up the rock.

He hissed a curse of his own as he thrust Eloise away from him. Spinning around, he was instantly after Catherine de Mortain.

CHAPTER

4

CATHERINE'S HEART HAMMERED WILDLY AS SHE SCRAMBLED UP the path under the light of a three-quarter moon. The group had descended midway down the mount before Eloise had sprung her attack.

Earlier, as the two had sat in the small storeroom, examining their options, all tenuous at best, the only solution seemed to be that of creating a diversion. Though Catherine had insisted she would not attempt an escape without her nurse, Eloise had insisted that she ought to.

You must save yourself, my child. You are the one they want, not me. Once you have made it to safety, I am certain they will set me free.

The remembered words streaked through her head, and Catherine prayed that her nurse would indeed be released unharmed. Instead, should her captors decide to seek retribution, she'd never forgive herself for leaving Eloise behind.

Her feet sliding on the wet rock, she made the first turn, but heavy footfalls tread close behind. Her captor was gaining on her. She crossed herself mentally, then beseeched the saints to plead with God to grant her special favors.

"Catherine, give over! You'll not make it."

The voice of Rolfe de Mont St. Michel lashed out at her. She ignored him and pressed her feet harder against the path. Rounding the next turn, she ran the narrow course, mindful that one slip could easily send her sailing over the edge. *Don't look down!* the voice within commanded. And Catherine kept her gaze fixed on the next turn.

Footsteps thundered in her ears, and she whimpered, believing she'd lost the race. Fingers raked at her shoulder. Crying out, she jerked free of the clawing hand. Behind her she heard a thud, followed by a biting oath. Glancing back, she saw he'd fallen to one knee. Hope sprang inside her, and she pushed herself into an even faster pace.

In a few strides she was around the next bend. Elation streamed through her, for she felt certain she was nearly free. Once at the top, she planned to circle the abbey, then angle down to the village, where she'd hide herself away. Surely by dawn her father and Miles would have found her. If not, she'd cross the marshes on her own.

Ten more steps, and Catherine slid to a halt. *No!* her mind screamed, for there in front of her and on the rocks above stood a pack of snarling dogs. Hounds from hell, she deemed them, for their eyes glistened like green fire in the dark.

"Don't move, Catherine," Rolfe said, his footfalls slow but sure. "If you do, they'll attack."

With those words, Catherine's hopes plummeted. She was trapped. Dare she attempt to pass the evil creatures? Tempting fate, she took a step.

Fangs bared, several hounds had sunk into a crouch. Snapping and growling, they were set to lunge at her throat. She glimpsed the pack above her, noting how the dogs now hovered closer to the edge, ready to spring. One small move and she'd be torn limb from limb.

"I told you not to move. This time obey me."

The voice behind her was steady, low. Then the scrape of steel against steel cut through the eerie stillness. The dogs had fallen strangely silent, but the danger, Catherine realized, was far from over.

She felt Rolfe's hard chest press against her back. His sword eased in front of her as he looped his left arm around her waist. His warm breath fanned the top of her head as he whispered, "Remain fixed and keep your eyes downcast. If you look at an animal, the action is perceived as a threat. Be patient, and they'll leave."

Willingly, Catherine did as he said. She waited.

High on the mount, the winter wind whipped around them. Catherine shivered. In response, he offered his body as a shield while pulling her closer. Without thought she huddled against him, seeking his warmth. As she did so, she looked at one of the hounds. It growled.

"If you'd like to remain thus all night, then continue to challenge them," he whispered harshly. "Otherwise keep your eyes down."

Catherine didn't miss the impatience in his voice. As the moments slowly passed, his body grew more taut, and she wondered why. Through her eyelashes she glimpsed the dogs, waiting, hoping they'd leave.

Abruptly their ears pricked. Nostrils quivered as they sniffed the air. Growling, the hounds on the rock above turned sharply. One broke from the pack and bounded across the rocks. The others circled and followed.

Sheathing his sword, Rolfe commanded, "Come on."

Catherine felt the bite of his hand as he grabbed her arm just above where her wrists were tied. He began pulling her down the path. By his haste, she expected they would tumble to their deaths.

Then as they turned the bend, she spied what she thought were torches at the western foot of the mount. Male voices lifted on the wind, and Catherine was sure that orders were being given. There was a shout, abrupt and forceful. Catherine felt her spirits soar. The call had come from William de Mortain.

Drawing a deep breath, she fairly screamed, "Father!"

"Catherine?"

Her name, bellowed with an edge of uncertainty, rose toward her, but before she could reply she was jerked in front of her abductor. Her back met his chest, this time with force; his hand clamped over her mouth. He hefted her at the waist; then, his arm holding her fast against him, he carried her down the path.

Her head turned in the direction of the torches, she watched as the dots of light waved over the rocks. Their bearers followed the rugged coastline, ranging toward the north. She heard a piteous yelp and imagined that one of the dogs had just been wounded or slain. She wanted desperately to cry out, hoping to guide her father and his men ever closer. Miles: Was he with them?

Rolfe's hand kept her calls to a strangled whimper. Catherine knew she had the power to remedy that. But when she tried to pry her lips apart, he grated, "Bite me again and I'll slit your lily-white throat."

By his tone, Catherine knew he meant what he'd said. This time she decided not to test him. As they rounded the last bend, they came face-to-face with Garrick and Eloise. The tip of the older knight's blade was pressed against the thick flesh at her nurse's neck. Seeing such, Catherine struggled furiously in Rolfe's arms.

"About time you got here," Garrick stated.

Her captor's grip tightened around her waist. Catherine could barely breathe. When she ceased fighting him, he eased his hold.

"We were detained," Rolfe countered.

At his nod, the foursome continued down the path. Shortly they caught up to Aubrey and the monk.

"Hurry," the Benedictine ordered. "They grow closer."

The last half of their descent was less worrisome, the mount sloping to the shore. When they reached the boat, Catherine watched as it bobbed precariously in the surf, straining against its lone mooring.

Without ceremony, she was tossed into the craft. Her knees struck the wooden bottom, near the bow. She flinched, then gasped. As she tried to straighten, a wave lifted the boat. She was tossed sideways. Somehow she ended up on her back. Before she could move, her nemesis leaped the short expanse that separated the rocks from the boat. His feet now planted firmly against the boards, he swayed above her, but the motion was one with the sea.

"You bastard," she berated him.

"Aye, 'tis very likely that I am."

His reply shot down at her, but his gaze remained fixed on

the shore. Then as Catherine struggled to pull herself up, his foot came down on her stomach, holding her fast in place. An angry growl trembled in her throat. He would pay for mistreating her so. This she swore.

Aubrey pitched the shields and axes into the boat, then jumped in after them. The monk, having discarded his torch midway along the mount, handed over the chests that he'd dragged down the hill. The things were quickly settled, then Eloise was thrust from the rocks.

When she landed, a wave of icy water rolled over the boat's side. Catherine sputtered as she was splashed in the face. Then she heard voices rise in the not-too-far distance.

"Hurry," the monk said. "They're drawing nigh."

"We'll not make it to the ship," Garrick announced once he'd joined the group. "Aubrey cannot possibly guard them both while we row."

"We have little choice but to try," Rolfe returned.

There was a shout, far closer than before, followed by her father's cry, "Where are you, Daughter?"

Abruptly another voice called, "Catherine. Answer us!" *Miles.* He had come for her!

"Here!" she yelled, but she feared the word had been lost in the sound of the surf.

"Get to the oars," Rolfe ordered.

As Garrick withdrew to the boat's center, Aubrey scrambled toward the bow. Rolfe's foot lifted from her stomach. At once, Catherine shot up to a sitting position. Simultaneously, Eloise rose from her crouch and lunged at Garrick. The air whooshed from his lungs as her shoulder struck his back.

The action set the boat to rocking, and water poured into the small vessel. Garrick spun on Catherine's nurse. "'Tis time we end this nonsense. Say your prayers, woman."

The knight caught Eloise's shoulders, and Catherine instantly realized he intended to toss her into the sea. Since her hands were bound Eloise couldn't possibly stay afloat. She'd drown. "No!" Catherine cried. "Leave her be. Please!"

It was then that the monk sprang from the rock into the boat. "You're needed at the oars, Sir Garrick," he said, his jeweled dagger aimed at Eloise's heart. "In the meantime, the woman and I shall take a seat. I foresee no more problems." He looked at Eloise. "Is that not so, my child?"

"Are you sure of your decision, Brother Bernard?" Rolfe asked as Garrick positioned himself at the unattended oar.

"I have never seen England," he replied, his hand pressing Eloise down into the boat; the dagger remained close to her breast. "I believe it is time that I did."

At that moment, Catherine's name thundered across the mount. Her rescuers were nearly upon her. "Fath—" The rest was cut off as Aubrey clamped his hand over her mouth.

"Take care. She bites," Rolfe said to his squire. He looked Catherine directly in the eye. "If you value your nurse's life, you will behave." His attention swung to Eloise. "And if you wish for your lady to remain unharmed, you will do the same."

Then on Rolfe's nod, Brother Bernard cut through the mooring rope. The severed end fell away, and the iron ring to which it was tethered clanged against the granite. Catherine shivered at the noise.

With a grunt Rolfe pulled against the oar. Beside him, Garrick did the same. The boat moved, over one wave and then another. The strain of their effort vibrated in both men's throats. Backs hunched, then straightened, hands and arms pulling mightily. At each dip of the oars, the mount grew farther and farther away.

Tears formed in Catherine's eyes as torchlight streamed over the area where she'd stood just moments ago. Though her vision was blurred, she recognized the three men at the group's fore. Her father, Miles, and Geoffrey—they had come for her, albeit too late.

England! He takes me to England!

Hoping that somehow her thoughts could be transferred through space and time, she screamed the words over and over again in her mind.

She gazed longingly at the mount and the men who lingered on its shore. Riding the waters that glistened like quicksilver in the moonlight, she wondered if they'd spied the vessel carrying her away from them. Thinking it was

60

possible, she offered up a multitude of prayers, asking that they had.

Shortly she noticed her abductors' breaths were not as pronounced. Similarly their motions appeared less strained. The oars dug deeper into the water, and the boat glided across the waves as though it were on ice. Then it occurred to Catherine that they had crossed the shoals, and the current was now taking them out to sea. Soon the lights along the shore were naught but four tiny dots.

A sob rose to her throat just as a faint call ferried across the water. The hand over her mouth fell away, and Catherine twisted around, whereupon she spied a longship sitting at anchor.

"The ship, sire," Aubrey announced, "'tis but a furlong away."

Rolfe and Garrick leaned into the oars, then stroked back as hard as they could. In no time, their small craft was within feet of its destination. Then the two men locked the oars, creating a drag, and they eased against the ship's side.

Rolfe and his squire quickly changed places, the former pulling Catherine to her feet. Hoisted by Garrick and aided by a seaman from above, Aubrey was the first to scramble from the boat.

Next the two chests, along with shields and axes, were handed up. Then Garrick turned to Eloise. "Your turn, woman."

Glaring at the knight, Eloise stood up, but offered no resistance. Her bindings were cut, then Garrick and Brother Bernard pushed from below while two men pulled from above. It was a struggle, but Eloise soon disappeared over the ship's side.

The monk went next, then Garrick. After Catherine's hands were freed, she was lifted at the waist and swung around. "Up with you," Rolfe said.

Reaching for Garrick's hand, she felt Rolfe's on her derriere. He pushed her over the side. In a moment, he was also aboard.

"I thought so: You're wet," he said, feeling the back of her heavy cloak. "Sodden, in fact."

"I wonder why," she snapped in return. She was turned toward him. His fingers worked at the ties just below her chin. She swatted at his hands. "Leave it."

"But you'll catch your death."

"'Tis better than having to suffer the likes of you."

Catherine immediately questioned the wisdom of her words, for his eyes had turned from a soft silver to a stormy gray. She was stunned when he ripped the cloak free and tossed it at his squire.

After ordering his coffer opened and a dry mantle brought to him, he turned back to her and fairly growled, "Whether you relish it or not, you'll be suffering the likes of me for some time to come."

The promise of such didn't sit well, and Catherine grew bolder. "Then I shall make your life miserable."

Aubrey returned with a dry cloak and handed it to his master. Rolfe swung the warm wool covering around her shoulders. Briefly he regarded her, then said, "I have no doubt, Catherine, that you will."

The gentleness in his voice surprised her, and she stared after him as he strode to the center of the deck. There he ordered the ship set underway.

At first Catherine questioned if she might be mistaken, then decided she wasn't: Somewhere in his soft utterance had been the sound of regret.

"'Twas as I thought," William de Mortain said. He released the iron ring anchored to the granite. The biting clink as it hit the rock sent a chill down his spine. He rose to his feet and turned to Miles and Geoffrey. "There was a boat moored here. The cut on the rope is recent. My eyes did not deceive me. My guess is that a ship sits out there, and Catherine is by now on it."

"For what purpose would he take her away on a ship?" Miles asked. "And to where?"

"That is something we'd best ask the monks," William returned. "Maybe they know the reason for all this."

"Since the good brothers here are allied with Duke Henry, and I, along with most of Avranches, favor Stephen, I doubt we'll get much help from any of them," Geoffrey declared, "especially if her abductor sought and was given shelter at the abbey."

William's eyes narrowed. "That remains to be seen. But I tell you this, Geoffrey: If your political convictions have had anything to do with Catherine's abduction, I shall not be in the least bit forgiving. Not to you, not to your son, and certainly not to this bastard who has taken her." He looked to the others. "Now, all of you, to the top of the mount and to the abbey. Perhaps with a bit of coercion on our part, the Benedictines will reveal the identity of this brigand, along with his purpose."

While the hounds circled ever so cautiously, William and the others set out on the path leading to the monastery at Mont St. Michel's crest.

Under the uniform strokes of the oarsmen, who heaved and pulled tirelessly, the longship skimmed across the deep waters that edged the Norman coast. Other than an occasional ripple and snap, the square sail billowed in the night wind, aiding their flight. Guided by the stars, the duke's supporters, along with their captives, sailed toward England.

From his position near the stern, Rolfe kept watch over Catherine de Mortain, who sat close to the bow. Her head resting at her nurse's breast, the pair huddled against the frigid winter winds. Twice on their journey, the ship's pitch had sent Catherine scrambling to its side. Each time, after her stomach had settled, she'd wiped her mouth and sent him a murderous look.

Her malice, Rolfe realized, was compounding. He couldn't really blame her for despising him as she did. Yet he could do little to change her conviction. Their course was set. In truth, to hope she might one day look upon him in a more favorable light was the least of his concerns. That he even worried about the prospect annoyed him greatly.

The ship rolled over another swell. This time the motion caused Rolfe's head to swim. His own stomach feeling as though it had climbed into his throat, he marked how

Catherine's wan face paled even more. She broke from her nurse's arms to again seek the ship's side, whereupon she retched into the sea.

Beside Rolfe, Garrick shook his head. "The girl is suffering mightily. If she keeps this up, she'll be far too weak to travel overland once we meet England."

"She'll have no choice in the matter," Rolfe returned. As Catherine pushed herself from the ship's rail, he expected to be speared by her gaze. He wasn't disappointed. "As soon as we reach Wareham, we will acquire some horses and head north."

"I take it you think her father will follow."

"Aye. He'll follow," Rolfe replied as Catherine again settled next to her nurse. "Miles too."

Garrick frowned. "Her father I can understand. She is of his own blood. But Miles? Coward that he is, 'tis more conceivable he'll remain in Normandy, where it is safe."

Turning his attention away from Catherine, Rolfe heeded his companion. "I have a feeling Miles has become his father's son. Unlike five years ago, his greed now outweighs his cowardice. He'll follow, all right. As will Geoffrey. Therefore, whether the Lady Catherine is physically sound or not, we won't linger when we reach shore."

"What if by some odd chance our pursuers find us?" the older knight questioned. "Do you intend to stand and fight? Or will we simply give the girl over?"

Rolfe looked back at the subject of their conversation. "We will stand and fight. Henry's cause is the reason we have entered into this. We'll not fail him, especially where Geoffrey and Miles are concerned. Unfortunately, there is also William de Mortain."

Rolfe sighed, knowing Henry's quarrel was not with William. Even so, they would be forced to face him just the same.

"I fear, Garrick, by what follows, the Lady Catherine will hate me all the more."

CHAPTER
5

~~~~

Wareham, England

CATHERINE'S LEGS WOBBLED AS THOUGH SHE'D IMBIBED TOO MUCH wine. The ground seemed to shift beneath her feet, and she had trouble gauging her steps. Silently, she cursed the sea and its unrelenting swells. Openly, she cursed Rolfe de Mont St. Michel.

Were it not for him, her head wouldn't be pounding, her limbs quaking, nor her stomach nearly turned inside out. Nor would she be in this forsaken land called England.

She eyed her nemesis's back as he walked several yards ahead of her along the path leading from ship to castle, his squire beside him. A short distance behind her, Garrick and the monk followed. Of the four, it was Rolfe de Mont St. Michel who elicited her wrath, for it was he who was the cause of her woes. "The whoreson," she grumbled, bitterness reflecting in her tone.

"Take care, milady, that he doesn't hear you," Eloise cautioned as she ambled alongside Catherine. "He looks to be in ill humor this morning. At the smallest provocation, he might turn on you."

"His mood cannot be any more foul than mine," Catherine returned as she gazed at her nurse. The day and a half that she'd spent on the ship did nothing to elevate her spirits. "However, you can put your mind at ease. I do not plan to provoke him. In fact, I intend to be most gracious to the beast." Surprise showed on Eloise's face, and Catherine explained, "'Tis the only way I know to get him to lower his guard so that we can make our escape."

"By your sudden complaisance, I'd think he'd grow suspicious. He may be a beast, but he's not a fool."

"Aye," Catherine replied, keeping her voice low. She again glanced at Rolfe. "He is no fool. That I know." She turned back to Eloise. "The change in my attitude will come by degrees. Slowly, surely, his vigilance is bound to weaken. Once I'm assured I've gained his trust, that's when we'll act."

"And I say he'll not be duped," her nurse insisted. "Instead of your freedom, the only thing you might gain from this is his wrath. Besides, if by some chance your plan does work, where are we to go? Alone, in a strange land with no one to assist us, we'll surely perish. 'Tis the dead of winter, milady. If the elements don't do us in, we'll undoubtedly starve. Worse yet, we could be set upon by a band of thieves or eaten by a pack of ravenous wolves. I say we should stay in his company and hope that your father finds us."

"And what are the odds of that?" Catherine snapped. "No, Eloise. I'll not wait for something as improbable as my father finding us to occur. I'd appreciate it if you'd stop being a gainsayer and offer your support."

Eloise harrumphed. "As you wish. One thing, though, is certain: We cannot go back to Normandy."

"No, we cannot. But there is another place."

"Not a monastery, I hope. Considering the way we were dealt with at Mont St. Michel, I'd think you'd want to shy away from such a place, especially if it is inhabited by the Benedictines."

"We were treated as we were only because the good brothers at Mont St. Michel are under the misguided impression that he is some sort of a saint. I doubt we'd be given the same reception elsewhere. But a monastery is not what I have in mind."

"Where then?"

"Have you forgotten my father has an estate here in England? If we could just reach it, we'd be safe."

"'Tis well and fine for you to be so optimistic, milady. However, since you've never been to England until this day, tell me: How do you propose we find the place?"

"What place?"

Catherine pulled herself up short. There in her path stood her abductor. By the arch of his brow, it was obvious he awaited a reply. Wondering just how much he'd heard, she searched his face, but received not the slightest clue. Somehow she had to come up with a response.

"A place where I might rest," she blurted. "I fear the voyage has depleted my strength." She pressed the back of her hand to her forehead. "Truly, I feel faint." With that she purposely went limp.

Well before she could hit the ground, long fingers caught her arm and she was scooped up by her captor.

"What's happened to the girl?" Garrick asked, having rushed up the hill.

"She's succumbed to her ordeal," Rolfe answered. "Get to the village and find a place where she can be given repose." Then, swinging around, he trailed Garrick, Eloise clucking like a mother hen beside him.

Forced to keep her eyes closed, Catherine was at once filled with sensations. She felt as though she were floating, her weight no more than a scant feather lifted on a light breeze. She marveled at his strength.

Likewise, when she inhaled, her nostrils tingled, for he smelled of the sea. Beneath her ear, his heart beat in a smooth, even rhythm. The sound, she credited, was strangely comforting.

In the cold, damp air, his breath fanned over the top of her head and warmed her face. Unbelievably, she was tempted to snuggle closer and draw from his own heat.

Catherine had never been held thus in a man's arms. She felt odd, all trembly inside. The feeling frightened her. Still, she had no choice but to bear the assault being levied on her senses. If he knew she was feigning, he'd no doubt drop her, dusting his hands of her as he strode over her, aiming himself up the path.

Before long, and to Catherine's relief, she was jostled through a doorway. Wood smoke filled her head while fire crackled in a hearth. Then she felt herself being lowered. She was eased onto a pallet filled with straw.

Catherine moaned, then twisted her head from side to side. She slowly opened her eyes to note how he knelt beside her on one knee.

One large hand stroked her brow, then his fingers lightly trailed across her cheek. "Feeling better?" he asked.

His silver eyes were filled with concern, while his voice was as gentle as the whisper of wind on a warm summer day. As she looked at him, strange stirrings arose inside her that she couldn't explain. Nor did she seek to do so. "Yes. Thank you," she replied, unable to hold his gaze. "I just need to rest a bit."

"Aye. Some food and water might help too." He turned to the peasant woman who stood by the hut's central hearth. "What have you in that kettle, good woman?"

"A fine barley pottage, sir."

"No bread or cheese, I suppose?"

The woman shook her head. "No, sir. We cannot afford anything of the like."

Catherine watched as Rolfe rose to his feet. He untied a pouch from his belt. Coins jingled inside.

"Is there a place where you can purchase the items I mentioned?" he inquired of the woman.

"Aye, sir. The market is only a short distance away."

"Go, then, and buy several days' supply for the women, myself, and my men. Your family as well," he added. "In the meantime, a bowl of that pottage will do nicely for these ladies. Some water, also."

After fishing in the pouch, he tossed a coin through the air. On the woman's catching it, her eyes widened when she realized it was pure gold.

"You may keep what is left once you've made your purchase," he announced. "Consider it payment for your gracious hospitality."

"Oh, thank you, sir," the woman said with a curtsy. Then she quickly dipped out two bowls of pottage from the kettle. Having served Catherine and Eloise their meals, along with some water, she hastened out the door, a tattered cloak thrown across her shoulders.

Rolfe again set his attention on Catherine. "Aubrey and Brother Bernard will stay with you while Garrick and I make our way to the castle. We won't be long. Rest and eat your fill while you can. We'll be leaving as soon as Garrick and I return." He eyed the monk. "Brother Bernard, do you plan to stay in Wareham?"

"I see no reason to remain here. If you have no objection, I'd rather travel with you."

"You are welcome to come along," Rolfe said. "But I must warn you: Danger undoubtedly awaits us."

The monk chuckled. "I found the last round rather exhilarating. Life at the abbey can become fairly dull, you know. Inasmuch as it does, I think I'll put my faith in the Lord and see what lies ahead."

Rolfe smiled amicably at the monk. "We'll be glad to have you in our company." That said, he again turned her way. "Do not cause these men any trouble, Catherine, or you'll regret you did."

From where she now sat on the pallet, Catherine stared up at him. The light of concern she'd once seen in the depths of his eyes had been replaced by the usual stoicism. Perhaps Eloise was right: He was not a man who could easily be duped. She refused to give in. "You may ease your mind, sir. I have accepted my fate. I shall remain here, peaceably so, until your return."

The way in which he regarded her told Catherine he didn't know whether to believe her or not. Then he announced, "A wise decision, milady. In the end, you'll suffer less for having made it." He motioned to his squire. "I'd like a word with you, Aubrey. You too, Brother Bernard. Let's step outside."

As soon as the men had exited the small hut, Eloise was at Catherine's side. "Are you now well, dearest child? I had no idea you were about to faint. Here." She took the scarred wooden bowl from Catherine's hands. "Let me feed you. If we are to travel soon, you must regain your strength."

"There is no need for you to feed me as though I were a wee babe. I'm as stout as I ever was. My fainting was merely a ruse."

"A ruse?" her nurse questioned.

Briefly Catherine again remembered the tenderness in Rolfe's eyes, as well as the gentleness in his voice, a result of his believing she'd actually fainted. "Aye. A ruse. 'Twas the first step toward his downfall. He may be a great warrior, but by the way he reacted, I'd say it is not in his nature to wish ill on the fairer sex. With continued agreeableness from me, he should soon relax his guard."

"Take care, for if you are too agreeable, you might find you've created another problem," Eloise declared.

Catherine frowned. "Another problem?"

"Aye. He may gain feeling for you."

"Are you suggesting that he might fall in love with me?"

"'Tis a possibility."

Catherine laughed lightly. "I doubt he knows the meaning of the word. But if he does 'gain feeling' for me, then so be it." She mused a bit. "Actually, such an occurrence might just work to my advantage."

Before Catherine's eyes, Eloise grew tight-lipped. She thrust the wooden bowl back into Catherine's hands. "I thought I raised you to show good sense, but apparently I've failed."

"What are you saying?" Catherine asked, confused.

"He is not a naive little boy but a man who is well versed—not just in the methods of war but also in the ways of love. Trifle with his emotions and you may find you've taken one step too far. I caution you, Catherine, to think twice about your words before you act. Once done, there will be no turning back."

"Do you think I cannot control the situation?"

"You lack the experience."

"There is Miles. He always accedes to my wishes."

"Pah! The man has no spine. In fact, he is no man at all. I imagine when he kisses you that his lips are as limp as a wilted leaf thirsting for water. 'Twould not be so with Rolfe de Mont St. Michel. Do not press the issue, Catherine. I am warning you."

That Eloise held no faith in her abilities angered Catherine. Didn't she realize how imperative it was for them to escape? Whether her nurse agreed or not, Catherine's mind was set. "Whatever it takes to ensure my freedom I'll do. Even if it means tempting the beast."

"Then be prepared to suffer the consequences, milady. For in the end, you may discover you've unleashed within him such a raging passion that it will be beyond anyone's control. Play with fire and you're bound to get burned. The decision is yours."

Catherine refused to believe what her nurse said was true. "Aye. As you say, the decision is mine."

Just over an hour later, Rolfe rode down the path toward the village on his newly acquired steed, Garrick beside him. Five horses trailed behind them, two of which were loaded with supplies.

While at the castle, the two men had learned that Henry had landed safely. The duke had not tarried, however, in setting out immediately for Devizes, where he would join forces with the earls of Chester, Cornwall, Hereford, and Salisbury. Regrettably, Rolfe had missed Henry by a day. But that wasn't what claimed Rolfe's attention at the moment.

His hand gripping the leads of three geldings, Rolfe rued the fact that they were a mount short. He wondered what Catherine's reaction would be once she learned she'd again share a saddle with him.

Not good, he decided, then questioned if that were so. She seemed less combative and far more passive. Yet he wasn't sure if he should give credence to her swift change in behavior and accept her statement about being resigned to her fate. Ruse or reality, Rolfe didn't know which, but he was certain that time would enlighten him to the truth.

A hard jerk on the reins broke Rolfe from his thoughts. Beneath him, the young stallion pranced sideways. Tossing his head, the horse attempted to slip the bit. Rolfe emitted a sharp command and guided his mount back to the center of the path.

"The beast is too skittish," Garrick said. "You should have left him behind."

"And have one of us walk?" Rolfe countered. "You know as well as I that we have no time to dally. Of course, if you'd prefer to again share your mount with Catherine's nurse, I could always return him to the castle."

"I'll drag her behind before she rides with me," the older knight pronounced with a scowl. "What about the Lady Catherine? I suppose she is to ride with you?"

"Aye. Like it or not, that she'll do."

"Then keep a firm hand on those reins. The beast has no fondness for one rider, much less two."

The stallion was untrained, yet Rolfe had little choice but to take the animal. True, he could have freed the other two horses of their burdens, but a cart and ox would have slowed their progress, something he could ill afford.

"I'll do as you've advised, Garrick," Rolfe returned. "Should he become too troublesome while carrying a double load, I'll hand the Lady Catherine off to you."

"Now *that* I can abide," Garrick said, smiling broadly. "As tempting as she is, I won't mind holding her in my arms."

Through narrowed eyes, Rolfe surveyed his companion; the older knight guffawed.

"So," he said, "the girl does interest you after all. Admit it, my young friend. You wouldn't object in the least to having her supple limbs wrapped around you while her soft lips eagerly received your kisses."

The picture that Garrick's words conjured in Rolfe's mind caused his loins to stir. The heat of desire swept through his veins like a torch set to a trail of oil. Rolfe gritted his teeth.

"Well?" Garrick prodded.

"No. I wouldn't object," Rolfe snapped, for the vision of Catherine lying nude on a downy-soft pallet beckoning him to come settle between her satin thighs had grown more vivid. "But such a thing won't happen, so stop badgering me about it."

"You grow testy," Garrick offered. "Perhaps that is precisely what you need."

"What? To deflower my captive?" Rolfe asked.

In his mind's eye, he saw himself doing just that. His hand glided beneath her enticing hips, and he lifted her to him, whereupon he eased inside, gently but surely. With a quick thrust, he claimed her.

The image became too much. Beads of sweat broke across his brow. Rolfe closed his eyes and swallowed the groan of longing that trembled in his throat. Madness, he thought, wishing beyond anything that he was now on his way to Devizes with Henry.

"Is that what you suggest I do?" he questioned, his gaze again on his companion.

"Not at all," Garrick returned. "Your own honor prevents you from taking her, not to mention your promise to Henry. I see that you suffer. If not the Lady Catherine, then another should do. Once we reach our destination, I suggest you seek out a fair young wench who will be happy to ease your pain."

Rolfe imagined that by the time they arrived at journey's end his "pain," as Garrick put it, would be unbearable. "I'll keep your suggestion in mind," he grumbled, then dismounted, for they had come upon the hut. Without preamble, he entered. Catherine was the first he saw. "'Tis time to go," he said.

Even to his own ears, his voice sounded unduly harsh, so he wasn't surprised by her stunned expression. What did amaze him was her acquiescence. He'd expected a challenge to spark in her eyes. Instead he saw the soft glimmer of acceptance. Had she truly resigned herself to her fate? Or was her present submissiveness merely the result of her arduous passage from Normandy to England? Whichever, the fire inside her had turned to ash.

Strangely, without that resilient flame, which burned into a man's soul and kindled his desires, this new Catherine wasn't as captivating. He was still bewitched by her beauty, but that was only the shell. Rolfe silently cursed himself, thinking he may have somehow destroyed the woman within.

And why not? He had stolen her from her father, from the arms of her betrothed, from the land of her birth, from all she held dear. His quarrel was with Miles, not Catherine. Likewise, Henry's feud lay with Geoffrey, not the man's future daughter-in-law. Nonetheless, Catherine had been drawn into it. She was a pawn in some political game she knew nothing about.

Drawing a breath, Rolfe released it slowly. If he could rectify the wrong done to her, he'd do so now. But he couldn't. He'd pledged his allegiance to Henry. As a knight, he wouldn't break his vow.

"'Tis time to go," he repeated, for Catherine had not moved.

Never taking her gaze from his, she slowly rose from the pallet where he'd last left her. "Where are you taking us?" she asked.

"North," he responded.

"How far?"

"Several days' ride. Now come. Gather your cloak about you and don your hood. The air is damp, and I cannot afford for you to take a chill."

Catherine exhibited no defiance as she did what she was told, and Rolfe again wondered at her mood. Then, as the others left the hut, expressing their gratitude to their hostess for her hospitality as they went, Catherine moved toward him on steady feet.

"You promised to tell me what this is all about once we reached England," she said, looking up at him. "I now hold you to that vow. In whose politics am I embroiled and why have I been brought here?"

"You'll have your answers as soon as we are on our way."

Taking Catherine's arm, he said farewell to the hut's owner, then, ducking under the door frame, guided his captive outside. Everyone was astride their horses. As he drew close to his own mount, Rolfe felt a tug against his hand. He looked down at Catherine.

"Is there no horse for me?" she asked.

"No. As it is, we were fortunate to get these."

Her expression said she was opposed to riding with him, but she offered no resistance when he lifted her onto the saddle. When her weight settled, the stallion snorted and bobbed his head. Rolfe yanked on the reins, whereupon the beast quieted. With ease, he hoisted himself onto the animal's back and settled behind Catherine.

The journey ahead promised to be a miserable one. At least Rolfe thought so. Besides the unknown dangers that awaited them on their travels north—something he'd discussed with Garrick, Aubrey, and the monk before making his way to the castle to procure the horses—there was his captive. How could he possibly keep alert with her cradled so close in his arms?

God's wounds!

The words exploded inside his head just as Catherine shifted in the saddle. She nestled closer to him, undoubtedly seeking protection from the frigid wind.

Gritting his teeth, Rolfe steadied himself, then turned his attention to Garrick and the others. "Remain watchful," he ordered. Then setting the stallion into a canter, he led the group up the path, past the castle and away from the village at Wareham.

With his captive huddled against him, they traveled in silence for miles on end. Soon they came to a great wood, which by right belonged to Stephen. Though the trees were barren, the forest offered some protection. However, Rolfe knew their pace would be slowed.

On entering the wood, he eased his stallion from its canter into a walk. The others followed suit. After a bit, Rolfe began to relax, but just when he thought he'd mastered the turmoil roiling deep within his gut, Catherine again moved. His loins quickened.

"'Tis time you fulfilled your promise," she said, having turned to look at him. "I want to know who is behind this so that I may thank him for my current misery."

Her wide hazel eyes were locked with his, and Rolfe felt as though he were sinking into their alluring depths. Misery?

he questioned in silence, positive she didn't know the word's meaning. For certain, she suffered no more than he.

"Well?" she prompted.

With her query, she squirmed against him, obviously impatient for an answer. Rolfe swallowed hard, then grated, "For our mutual agony, Catherine, we can thank Geoffrey d'Avranches."

CHAPTER
6

CATHERINE STARED UP AT ROLFE IN DISBELIEF. SURELY SHE'D heard wrong. It was inconceivable that Geoffrey d'Avranches could be the cause of her woes. And what did he mean by "our mutual agony"? If anyone was being made to suffer it was she, not he.

"You lie," she asserted, forgetting her resolution to remain agreeable. She noted how for a moment his eyes turned steely. Apparently he was offended by the accusation, yet she pressed on. "Geoffrey is not behind this. Now tell me who ordered my abduction."

"I do not lie, Catherine," he said firmly. "Were it not for your future father-in-law and his political ploys, you'd not be in England. Instead you'd be enjoying the so-called joys of wedded bliss—though I doubt such a thing is possible, considering the gutless weakling you've chosen to be your husband."

She was instantly incensed. "Miles is not a weakling," she protested. "You are the one who is gutless. Stealing me away while in the guise of a priest—if you were truly a valiant knight, you would have made known your convictions, then have stood and fought. As it is, you showed no honor to whomever it is you give your allegiance."

His lips curled into a lopsided smile. "At the time, the odds were against me," he replied. "In view of such, I doubt Henry will fault me for not announcing my intent. But have no fear, milady. The time comes when I shall have to stand and fight. The occurrence, I imagine, won't be all that far off."

Catherine's heart faltered when she heard the name. "H-Henry? Are you referring to the duke?"

"Aye. He's the one to whom I owe my allegiance. In fact, 'tis by his command that you are here now."

Unable to fully fathom his words, Catherine gaped at Rolfe. The duke of Normandy had ordered her abduction? What sort of madness was this? She didn't even know the man, just *of* him. "From what you say, Henry is the cause of my misery, not Geoffrey." The idea made her bristle. "I demand that you return me to Normandy so that I may *thank* him personally."

"Henry is not in Normandy. He is here in England, on his way to Devizes. We missed seeing him by a day. As for your misery, you can lay the blame on Geoffrey. As I said, if it were not for his political ploys, you'd not be here huddled in my arms."

With those words, Catherine wanted to bolt from the saddle. Using his body as a shield against the frigid air while simultaneously drawing from his warmth, she hadn't realized just how closely she'd pressed herself to him. He was her nemesis, her enemy. That she found comfort in his arms truly horrified her.

Nibbling at her lip, she wondered at Miles's reaction if he were to learn how she'd been so accepting of her abductor's nearness or that she'd been content nestled against him as she was.

Believing her betrothed wouldn't find favor with the knowledge, Catherine slowly pushed herself away from Rolfe.

Almost immediately gooseflesh rose along her arms, and she started to shiver. Apparently her captor noticed the slight tremors, for he tried to ease her against him, but she resisted.

"Is your betrothed the sort who would prefer that you took a chill and died rather than have you held in another man's arms, where it is safe and warm?" he asked.

On the query, his breath fanned across her head. But by the time it touched her face, it had lost its inviting heat. The plume of frost struck her cheek; Catherine shivered again.

"If he is," Rolfe continued, "he has little consideration for you. 'Tis shameful his pride means more to him than the woman he plans to marry."

"Miles is always considerate of me," she stated.

Even so, she couldn't help question which of the two— her death or her safety—Miles would choose if he were given the option.

"You know not what you say," she finished, then frowned as she puzzled over whether the words were meant to convince him or herself.

"Then it must be your own pride that causes you to pull away from me. You're being foolish, Catherine. You grow cold for no other reason than to soothe your own vanity. A pity, but it could mean your death."

In a situation such as this, Catherine understood that the honorable thing for a woman to do was to take her own life, especially if she were ravished. She hadn't been defiled— yet.

Even if that were to happen—and she prayed it didn't— she wasn't absolutely sure she could follow through. Her will to live outweighed any fanciful need to preserve her honor. But then she'd not experienced the horrors of being violated.

If that time ever came, she might change her mind. But until it did, she would accept anything handed to her, as long as it promised to keep her alive.

Slowly she leaned back against his chest, only to hear him chuckle. *Enjoy your mirth now, for in the end, I will be the one who is laughing.* Although Catherine wanted to shout those words aloud, she kept them from her tongue. Instead she asked, "Does something amuse you?"

"For a while, I was worried you had somehow lost your

desire to live. I am relieved to see the flame has been re-kindled."

"What flame?"

"The flame that gives expression to your temperament, to the woman you really are. 'Tis what sets you apart from all other women. 'Tis also the part of you that intrigues a man most.

"The fire within, Catherine, is what a man seeks. Without it, there can be no passion. And without passion, there can be no joy. If there is no joy, life is naught but an endless road of sorrow. Take care that you don't find yourself following that path. 'Twould be a pity, to say the least."

At first his words, along with the soft tone in which they were spoken, sparked an odd sort of warmth in the pit of Catherine's stomach, which she couldn't explain. But with the last of his statement, the tiny ember had cooled, for she understood all too well that he referred to Miles and the life he thought awaited her should she marry her betrothed.

"The only path that concerns me is the one we are presently on," she said. "Tell me exactly what occurred to set Henry against Geoffrey. What are these political ploys you spoke of? Why did the duke order me abducted? And why is he in England?"

"He is in England because he intends to claim what is rightfully his."

Catherine's eyes widened. "You mean he——"

"Aye. He plans to oust Stephen and take his legitimate place on the throne." He fell silent. "You act surprised," he said after studying her.

"Since his mother managed to insult all of England when she finally had the throne in her grasp, I'd think that Henry wouldn't make such an attempt on his own."

"You hold little esteem for the empress," he commented, his gaze now steady on the track ahead. "Do you know her, by chance?"

"No. 'Tis no secret, though, that her arrogance is what caused her downfall. She fought well, had captured Stephen, and had the opportunity to become queen——"

"A position her father had already settled on her by

naming her his heir," Rolfe interjected, "except her cousin
Stephen got to England before she did, whereupon he
usurped the crown."

"Obviously, Beauclerc's decision to name Matilda as his
successor was the wrong one. As I said, when she did have
the crown in her grasp, she chose instead to alienate her
barons, to spurn the peace terms, and to offend the London-
ers with her tactless behavior. That she was chased from
England shouldn't surprise anyone. As for Henry, when he
was here four years past, he had little success. Why should
he hope things will be any different now?"

Rolfe looked down at her. "Determination is the key to
his success. Besides, Henry is no longer a boy of sixteen. He
has become a man, one who is to be reckoned with. Mark
my words: This time he'll succeed."

Catherine cared little about politics. Who ruled England
mattered not at all to her. What did matter was that she'd
been forced into this situation. And she had the duke of
Normandy to thank for it.

"If he has become such a man, why didn't he show his
determination sooner? Why not some eight months ago, just
after he first married?" she asked peevishly. "Or is Eleanor
of Aquitaine the reason for his quest? I'm sure being
married to a duke is quite a descent in status for her,
especially when her first husband was king of France. I've
heard she is excessively ambitious. Tell me: Is she the reason
I missed my own wedding?"

"I know not what is in Eleanor's mind. I do know, over
these past eight months, Henry has been kept exceptionally
busy."

Catherine laughed sharply. "I imagine so. If Henry hadn't
the gall to marry Eleanor, thereby enraging Louis, the king
wouldn't have laid siege to Anjou and Aquitaine."

"Louis had no cause to be enraged. After fifteen years of
marriage, he chose to set Eleanor aside because the two had
suddenly discovered they were too closely related. The real
reason he requested the dissolution was that she hadn't
given him a son. Yet the Church, ever mindful of the laws of
consanguinity, had no choice but to issue a divorce."

Catherine noted the tinge of sarcasm in his voice when

he'd mentioned the Church. She wondered briefly if he lacked faith. Or did he abhor religion altogether?

She thought of the chapel at Avranches. *"Rats,"* he'd proclaimed when a noise erupted from behind the altar.

At the mere mention of the horrid creatures, she'd eagerly rushed from the chapel, straight into the trap that Rolfe de Mont St. Michel had set for her. Had he known about her fears? Purposely used them to entice her from the castle at Avranches? For a moment the questions plagued her. She quickly negated the possibility of his possessing such knowledge. Very few did. A coincidence, she decided.

As she looked back on the episode, she was now certain the sounds had come from the chaplain. Bound, gagged, and undoubtedly lying naked, he'd probably thrashed about, trying to warn her of her peril. If she'd only known that at the time, she'd not be here now. Oh, why was this happening to her?

"What?" Rolfe said after her prolonged silence. "Have you no retort? A pity, for our discussion promised to become quite lively. Or have you fallen asleep on me?"

Catherine snapped to as he leaned around to look at her. "I was thinking. As for what you said, Louis was not totally at fault. I had heard Eleanor was as eager as he to be on her way, for she'd grown tired of him."

"Gossip manages to travel far and wide, doesn't it? At least in this case. Nevertheless, whether it was by Louis's doing or by both of theirs together, Eleanor was free to marry whomever she pleased, which happened to be Henry."

"I hear tell she is eleven years his senior. Considering such, the marriage is not likely one of love but of convenience. After all, Henry stood to gain Aquitaine, didn't he?"

"Aye. The province is his by right of marriage. However, Eleanor shouldn't be cast off by you or anyone else simply because she is now over thirty. She is quite lively and a very attractive woman, Catherine. And once more, she can still bear children."

"You know her?" she asked.

"I've met her, but that was long ago."

A distinct melancholy sounded in his voice, and Catherine gazed up at him. His eyes held a faraway look, as if he'd slipped into a time gone past. The memories, she decided, were not pleasant. Shortly he blinked, and it was as if a door had slammed shut, barring all those unhappy thoughts.

Catherine contemplated what might have caused him such torment. Had it to do with Eleanor of Aquitaine? Or had the reminiscence of meeting her triggered another memory, one that he'd sooner forget?

Although he was her enemy, Catherine held empathy for him. No human should be made to suffer such heavy-heartedness, not even Rolfe de Mont St. Michel.

Catherine quashed the thought. Why should she feel pity for him, when he held none for her? Whatever misery he endured was his alone to bear.

And it would be the same with her, for in this vast land there was nary a soul to help her. Except her nurse. But Catherine wasn't fully certain she could count on Eloise.

The woman was fiercely opposed to Catherine's plan of escape. Catherine would normally regard Eloise's refusal as being something indicative of her character. She worried constantly, usually for no reason. But this was different. She'd advised Catherine not to go forth with what she deemed foolish, had even promised to abandon her if Catherine dared to disobey her warning.

Play with fire, and you're bound to get burned.

But what choice did she have? Besides, how could being agreeable to the man cause her any harm?

Sighing, Catherine knew she'd do anything to be free of Rolfe de Mont St. Michel. She'd become his laundress, his cook, his squire, if need be. She'd become anything he wanted, except his whore. With or without Eloise, some-how, someway, she'd again return to Normandy, and all this would be behind her.

The stallion's cadence changed, and Catherine felt Rolfe's arm tighten around her waist. He pulled her snugly against him. Ready to give protest, she realized he'd set the horse into a canter in order to gain speed so they could mount the steep incline ahead. Once they topped the hill, he eased his hold; Catherine breathed a bit easier. Again the stallion was slowed to a walk.

"You never told me how I fit into Henry's plan. Or why you blame Geoffrey for my abduction and not your duke," she said after a bit.

"He is your duke also, Catherine."

"Not after this," she said, only to draw another chuckle.

"Maybe you won't be so harsh with the man once you understand his reasoning."

"I doubt it. But in all fairness, I'll reserve judgment until you've explained exactly what his reasoning is."

"'Tis most kind of you, milady. I'm certain Henry will be pleased to hear of your impartial attitude when I see him next."

He mocked her, she knew. "And I suppose, once you've disclosed his reasoning to me, you will also tell him what my final word was?"

"*That,* I believe, he already knows."

They had come upon some heavy growth, and Catherine waited patiently until her captor had maneuvered them through the thicket. Twice the stallion attempted to stray from the narrow path; under his expert hand, Rolfe set him back on the trail.

The beast, Catherine noted, was skittish, untrustworthy, a far cry from the trained destrier that had carried them to Mont St. Michel. She decided not to make any sudden moves or else she might find herself lying on the ground, an arm or a leg twisted and broken. Possibly even her neck.

When they were free of the dense wood, she heard Rolfe breathe deeply. Then he said, "Before I begin disclosing Henry's reasoning, I want your promise that you'll sit quietly and listen to all I have to say before you speak. Once I've finished, you may question me on whatever it is you feel you need to know. Also I want you to understand the seriousness of the situation, for what I tell you is not to be taken lightly. This is not some simple little intrigue, such as who is sleeping with whom at court. In no way can it be laughed off. What is transpiring involves the control of a nation. Understand that men and women have died for much less. Now, do I have your promise that you'll keep silent?"

If she wanted to learn the truth—*his* truth, that was—Catherine had no choice but to agree. "Aye. I'll keep silent."

"'Tis best you do," he said. "The reason you should fault your future father-in-law for your predicament, Catherine —probably Miles, too—is that when Louis sought the force he needed to ride against Henry, it was the duke's rivals who responded. Geoffrey d'Avranches was among the first to join Louis's cause. Those who are close to Henry are well aware that Geoffrey's hatred for the duke even supplants that of Louis.

"Geoffrey is an avid supporter of Stephen. He stands to lose a great deal if Stephen falls. However, Geoffrey doesn't have the wherewithal to fund the small army needed to help Stephen defeat Henry. But if the house of William de Mortain were joined with the house of Geoffrey d'Avranches, money would become no object. Your dowry could easily buy the services of fifty knights. With some persuasion, your father might even contribute to the cause. Henry couldn't afford for such a thing to happen. The wedding had to be stopped.

"It was decided the best way to do that was to abduct the bride. You also became a diversion. Henry and his troops had already sailed for England, but if word had somehow reached Avranches that the duke planned to claim his throne, Eustace—who'd be expected to go to his father's defense—Geoffrey, your father, and who knows how many other men may have followed. As I said, Henry could not afford for that to occur.

"Presently, there is no reason to believe your father, your betrothed, his father, or those with them have any inkling as to what Henry is about. Just as planned, they are far too busy chasing after you. By the time they discover the truth, Henry's forces will be in place, the first battle probably already begun.

"Geoffrey will then have a choice: He can forgo his search for you and join Stephen's forces. Or, as Henry believes, he will see the folly of the situation and opt to find you, whereupon he'll quickly marry you to his son. As it is said: 'A bird in the hand is worth two in the bush.' Unfortunately, you are that bird.

"Although Geoffrey might desire all, he is wise enough to know that a portion is better than nothing. Being one of Stephen's supporters, his hopes of further gain in way of land and gold will be thwarted. But a lucrative marriage could give him added security. You, Catherine, are one of the wealthiest young maids available. Likewise, William de Mortain's name is irreproachable. Should Stephen fall, which he will, Geoffrey can always hope to hide behind your father, though it will do him little good."

The rest was left unsaid, but Catherine knew that if Henry were the victor, Geoffrey d'Avranches's life was in jeopardy. "What about Miles?" she asked, assuming Rolfe was finished. "Surely Henry holds no grudge against him, does he?"

"Your betrothed is not without fault. Since he has no spine, he coddles and bows to his father's wishes. I don't know what lies in store for Miles. As for Geoffrey, Henry won't be forgiving. The man's fate is sealed."

Catherine had trouble comprehending all that was said, possibly because she didn't want to believe any of it. Yet Rolfe de Mont St. Michel was obviously one of Henry's knights, probably part of the inner circle and privy to the duke's most intimate plans. And she was his prisoner.

Never did she think that her abduction would be connected with something as enormous as this. She could imagine herself being stolen away for reasons of greed or in reprisal for some petty grievance, but *not* for the want of an entire nation.

In truth, she was naught but a lowly pawn trapped in the grand scheme of things. The enormity of it all was hard for her to fathom. How could she conceivably fight something as big as this? Admittedly, Catherine knew she couldn't.

"Do you have any questions?" Rolfe asked.

"No," she replied, still feeling stunned.

Apparently he had said all he'd wanted, for he kept silent.

As they now rode at a canter through the wood, its density having thinned considerably, Catherine holed into herself and attempted to make sense of all she'd been told.

* * *

Occupied with various tasks, Rolfe and the other men were gathered around the campfire. While Brother Bernard and Aubrey engaged themselves in conversation, Rolfe and Garrick quietly polished their swords.

"The girl seems exceptionally withdrawn," Garrick said, breaking his silence. "She hardly spoke at all today while we traveled. Do you think she's ill?"

Rolfe looked up from his blade and glanced at Catherine. She sat huddled on a tree stump just outside their tent, staring off into the night wood.

It was three days since they'd left Wareham, three days since he'd told her why she'd been abducted. After that first day, the stallion had become increasingly unruly, so he'd handed Catherine off to Garrick. To Rolfe's relief—for he doubted he could have borne another moment with her pressed against him—she'd ridden with the older knight from that time onward. Hence Garrick's concern.

"I think she's yet suffering the effects of learning why she is in England," Rolfe stated, "and is probably trying to come to terms with it all."

"A pity that she was drawn into this," Garrick commented. "Of anyone at Avranches, she was the most innocent."

"Aye. But that is the way of things. We cannot change what has already been done. Had her father been more selective in choosing a mate for her, she wouldn't presently be caught in the middle."

"Perhaps. Yet I doubt you can fault William de Mortain for wanting to see his daughter happy. She claims she is in love with Miles. What father—especially if he is as doting as the Lady Catherine's—wouldn't welcome such a match?"

"Pah!" Rolfe exclaimed. "The man used bad judgment. If he were as devoted a father as you imply, he'd never have allowed the d'Avranches men near his daughter. He should have been more protective and less conciliatory. Besides, she has no knowledge of what the word *love* means. The choice she made proves what I say is true."

"But you *do* know the word's meaning," Garrick said, only to draw a sharp look from Rolfe. "My friend," the older man continued, "I believe you are in a quandary here. You are attracted to the girl, desire to have her, but are afraid of what might happen to your heart should you get too close to her. Certainly you could never offer her marriage—not the tried and true warrior that you are. Therefore you continue to suffer."

Suffer? He was in outright agony.

Though he had rid himself of his captive during the day, at night he lay beside her, for fear she might escape. That he slept at all was a veritable miracle.

In those hours before his eyes would ultimately close from utter fatigue, he would be tortured by her nearness. The sounds of her soft breath would fill his ears while her sweet scent invaded his nostrils. He'd been tempted more than once to pull her to him and curl around her. Always he'd fought against the urge, and in the end he'd always won. Yet at daybreak, when he awoke, he would find the fair Catherine snuggled against him, slumbering peacefully.

Rolfe preferred to think that she moved toward him on her own volition, possibly because the stones that were heated in the campfire, then wrapped in canvas and placed by her pallet, had cooled. But, he couldn't confirm if that were so. For it was possible that at some point when his eyelids finally closed, he may have lost his battle and had drawn her to him, to sleep nestled with her until dawn.

What Rolfe did know was that each time he'd roused to find her beside him he left his pallet and withdrew from the tent, allowing the cold morning air to leech the heat from his body—and, along with it, his desire.

"I assume by your lack of response you cannot deny my words."

Garrick's voice broke through his thoughts, and Rolfe focused in on him. "The last of what you said is true: I am a warrior, first and always. And because I am, there is no place in my life for a woman, much less a marriage. Let it be known, my friend, the only thing that suffers here are my ears. Once and for all, stop haranguing me about the Lady Catherine."

"If that is what you want, so be it," Garrick returned,

shrugging. "But first I think it's best I tell you that she is slipping off into the wood."

Rolfe cast his gaze in the direction of Garrick's nod. Cursing, he sheathed his sword, then loped across the clearing where they'd made camp and followed Catherine into the trees. Aided by the rising moon, which hung like an orange globe just above the horizon, he kept sight of her as she traversed the path leading down to a ravine. In short order, he caught up to her.

"A bit late for a stroll, isn't it?" he inquired, snagging her arm. By the way she jumped, he could tell he'd startled her.

"Not when nature calls," she snapped, trying to free herself of his grasp.

Chagrined, he released her arm. "Then lead the way and I'll follow."

"I can manage on my own, thank you."

"You shouldn't be walking in the wood alone, Catherine. All sorts of creatures could be lurking out here just ready to gobble you up." He tried to make light of the situation, but she wasn't amused.

"Since the most worrisome creature of all is standing here beside me, I doubt I have much reason to be afraid of anything that may lie in the shadows."

"There could be wolves running in the woods or a boar slumbering beside a tree. If you stumble onto either of those, you'll have good reason to fear." He took her hand and began pulling her down the path. "Come. We'll find a place where it's safe. While you attend to your needs, I'll stand guard." He heard her sputter, then added, "At a reasonable distance, that is."

Finding a location that looked suitable, Rolfe checked the bushes growing at the base of a tree. "I shall now give you some privacy," he said, then sauntered a short way up the path.

The moments passed endlessly, and he wondered what was keeping her. Just as he turned, intending to search her out, she stepped from the sheltering shrubbery and came toward him.

"I had thought perhaps you'd run off," he said when she reached his side. "I'm glad I didn't have to give chase."

She didn't respond. Instead she simply brushed past him and followed the narrow track leading to the top of the hill.

Rolfe frowned. He'd expected some sort of reply, even if it were hostile. She was unduly withdrawn. Her lack of energy concerned him, and he wondered, just as Garrick did, if she were becoming ill. He intended to find out.

When they reached the summit, Rolfe caught hold of her arm, then turned her toward him. "Catherine . . ." The question he thought to pose faded from his mind. By way of the moonbeams streaming through the barren branches, he saw tears shimmering in her eyes. "You've been crying," he said.

Foolishly, he'd sounded surprised. He should have expected the tears. She'd endured a lot this past week. Even so, he'd been taken unawares.

He moved closer to her and settled his hands on her shoulders. "Tell me what troubles you." Silence was his reward, and Rolfe decided she either wouldn't or couldn't reply. "Tell me what troubles you," he repeated with less intensity.

He knew the answer, yet he wanted her to voice it, but again she refused to speak. His gaze tracked each of her features, from her luminous eyes to the curve of her rounded chin. Then it moved upward and stopped.

Rolfe noted how her lips lay softly parted. They beckoned to him, and he was sorely tempted to kiss her, eager to taste the sweetness beyond. "Catherine," he whispered, all the fantasies he'd had about her from the first time he saw her again swirling to life. Fire kindled in his loins, and he edged himself closer to her. "I . . ."

"You want to know what troubles me," she said at last.

The spell was broken, but Rolfe's misery increased.

"By what you've told me," she continued, "I worry about my father, wondering if Henry's wrath will descend on him simply because he accepted Geoffrey's proposal that our two houses be joined. I worry over Miles, fearing he might receive the same punishment as his father should Henry succeed in his quest to oust Stephen. I am cold and tired. I long for a place where it's warm so that I may sleep in comfort. I want to go home to Normandy and to the life I had before you stole me away and destroyed my happiness."

The anguish in her voice nearly tore Rolfe asunder. She blamed him for all her sorrows. Whether she realized it or not, her world would still be in a shambles and she would yet be here in England, for if it were not him, then someone else would have done the deed. Though Rolfe knew that was true, he accepted her censure anyway.

"I cannot let you go home, but by tomorrow night you will have a warm place to stay and a soft bed to lie in," he said.

"And where is that?" she asked.

"Cartbridge Castle," he stated, now certain she would never accept his advances. "That's where you'll be kept until Henry's campaign is over."

And it was where Rolfe planned to find a comely wench who could ease his pain, even though it was Catherine he desired.

CHAPTER 7

Cartbridge Castle

LAUGHTER RANG THROUGH THE GREAT HALL INSIDE THE STONE keep. Trestle tables, once ladened with trenchers of roasted game and bowls of boiled turnips, along with assorted cheeses and loaves of brown bread, were now stripped clean.

In place of the viands sat pewter goblets containing wine or ale. The spills staining the tabletops attested to who drank what, and as Catherine watched the rowdy throng, she was well aware that the majority were deep into their cups. Even young Aubrey appeared to have imbibed too much. Brother Bernard was possibly the only one who was sober, except for Eloise and herself.

The current hour signaled the end of her first full day at Cartbridge Castle. Though she wanted to retire, she remained fixed to her seat and perused the revelers, seeking to learn something about each of their characters. If she could find just one among them who was similar in disposition to Clotilde, she planned to befriend the person, hoping he or she might take pity on her and help her escape. So far not one of them seemed worth approaching—the drunken lot.

Fighting back a yawn, Catherine grew weary. But she wasn't half as worn as she'd been the night before. When she'd arrived at the castle, far later than anyone had expected, she was exhausted from what had become a long and tedious ride. She readily blamed Rolfe for their lengthy journey, for he'd cut a wide path around Derby, one of Stephen's strongholds, because he feared they might be spotted.

When they'd at last reached their destination, she'd refused sustenance. Rolfe had taken pity on her, and while her nurse had remained below, eager to fill her stomach, Catherine had been shown to her quarters.

"Cartbridge has been without a lord since this past summer on the earl's death," Rolfe had told her. "Although the man is gone, his knights remained loyal and fought off several attempts by Stephen's supporters to claim it for themselves. The place sits here, waiting for Henry to name a new lord. You'll be sleeping in his bed. I hope it gives you comfort."

Catherine knew she'd been given the room because it could be secured. The bed, however, had looked positively inviting, and on hearing the door close and the lock trip behind her, she'd cared little that the room was now her prison.

Sleep—that's all she'd wanted. Strangely, though, when she'd snuggled deep into her bed, she'd felt as though something were missing. Unable to fathom what it could be, she'd closed her eyes and quickly drifted into her dreams, none of which she could now remember. She was certain that several of them, undoubtedly nightmares all, had had to do with Rolfe de Mont St. Michel.

Glancing across the way, she spied her nemesis lounging in a chair at the head table, which stood opposite where she sat. He had divested himself of his chain mail and now wore a dark blue woolen bliaud. In the torchlight, his freshly washed hair glowed golden, and even though she may have wanted to do so, Catherine couldn't deny that he was an exceptionally handsome man.

Besides his physical aspect, he exuded an aura that attested to his masculinity. Likewise his manner and smile were irresistible. That several young women had gathered around him didn't surprise Catherine. They were enamored of him, nearly as much as he was of himself.

"He certainly appears to be enjoying the moment," said Eloise, close to Catherine's ear. "I suppose since he is in one of Henry's lairs, he feels he can now relax his guard."

Earlier that day Catherine had related to her nurse all she'd learned from Rolfe. "That's what I'm hoping," Catherine said, turning her attention on Eloise. "The more he unbends, the better for us. 'Twould be doubly good if we could enlist someone from this den of iniquity who is not so partial to Rolfe de Mont St. Michel or his liege lord. Maybe then we could find our way to freedom."

"I fear you'll be searching beyond eternity," Eloise declared. "From what I've heard this day, all here think Henry is next to God."

Catherine noted how Eloise crossed herself, probably fearing that by her words she'd somehow committed blasphemy. "If Henry becomes king he *will* be next to God," she said. He'd already proclaimed himself judge and jury where her fate was concerned. "At least in his own eyes."

"Aye, that is probably so. Save Henry is not the one you should be worried about. He is not here, but your captor is. I doubt you'll be given the chance to find yourself an ally, for he'll be watching you like a hawk."

He had no such predilection at the moment, Catherine thought. By what she had seen, he was far too busy having his vanity stroked to pay much heed to her.

Catherine was about to express such when a burst of riotous laughter sounded across from her. Perched on Rolfe's lap was one of the young women who attended him—the comeliest, from Catherine's viewpoint. Her name, as Catherine recalled, for she'd had dealings with her during the day, was Ilona.

The wide grin Rolfe wore slowly faded as Ilona wriggled around to face him fully. Almost simultaneously, cups began to strike the tables. A shout went up, male voices urging Rolfe to kiss her.

Catherine noticed that his hands remained on the chair's arms, but as the cries got more tawdry, they moved to the woman's waist. Meanwhile Ilona linked her fingers behind his neck. The din grew louder.

Ilona was the first to advance. She brushed her lips temptingly across his cheek. Rolfe hesitated, then he turned his head. He parted his lips and kissed her soundly.

Shutting her eyes, Catherine blotted out the rest. The deafening cheers told her all she needed to know. Strangely, she felt a hollowness in the pit of her stomach; she grew oddly weak. "I believe I shall take my leave," she said to her nurse as she rose from the table.

On wobbly legs she started walking close to the wall, heading toward the stairs, her nurse fast behind her. As she went the boisterous voices, the smells of bitter ale and sour wine, pressed in on Catherine. Somewhere along the way she thought she heard her name shouted. She paid no attention to the call, uncertain that she heard it, and continued toward her appointed goal.

Three treads up the stairs, Eloise having preceded her, Catherine felt a hand snag her arm. Turning, she looked down on Rolfe and frowned.

"Where are you going?" he asked, his grip relaxing.

"To my quarters, where I may find some peace," she said, then noted the lovely Ilona was standing just behind him.

"Wait, and I shall send someone with you."

"If you mean so that he can lock me in, hand me the key and I shall do it myself."

"Do not be so disagreeable, Catherine," he said while his fingers feathered lightly down her arm. "The night is young." He caught hold of her hand and tugged gently. "Come and enjoy the festivities with me."

"I thought we were to slip away together somewhere," Ilona interjected. "Have you now changed your mind?"

Catherine forced her hand from Rolfe's. "I am still suffering the effects of our journey and would prefer to seek my bed."

He grinned up at her in a lopsided fashion, and Catherine realized he was nearly as drunk as the rest.

"As you wish, milady. Run to your bed and miss the fun. Go on." He turned her around and patted her bottom, drawing a gasp from Catherine. "I'll send someone up after you to secure your door. Good night and pleasant dreams." With a wave, he rotated on his heels, threw his arm across Ilona's shoulders, and swaggered off toward his chair.

Catherine stared after him for a moment. Then she cast her gaze over the room at large. Not an eye was turned her way. "'Tis time I depart this place," she muttered.

"What are you saying?" Eloise asked, catching hold of the same arm Rolfe had held. "Surely you don't mean to escape?"

"Aye. They are all into their cups. 'Twill be a long while before any of them miss us. 'Tis now or never, Eloise. Are you coming?"

"The dangers, milady—I don't think it is wise."

"Then you may stay, but I cannot."

Catherine scanned the room again, and again she saw that no one watched her. Her gaze leaped to the head table and to Rolfe. He was seated in his chair, Ilona ensconced on his lap. By what she had said, Catherine was certain he planned to bed the woman. Since they had not yet left the hall, she surmised he was probably waiting until he felt the mood was right. For her own sake, Catherine hoped his whore kept him entertained through the night.

It was time, she thought, after giving another cursory glance at the crowd. Shaking free of Eloise's hold, she hopped down the three steps and rounded the corner.

"Milady, don't!"

Catherine ignored her nurse's call and descended the dozen more steps that led to the keep's entry. On her way out the door, she caught hold of a cloak, lifting it from the peg where it hung. Quickly she was down the last flight of stairs.

Staying in the shadows, the wool mantle now around her shoulders, she made her way across the bailey to the curtain wall and the small gate she'd spied earlier that day as she looked through her window. That it was left unattended surprised Catherine. But then she doubted those at Cartbridge were expecting any trouble. Henry was far to the south of their location. If word of his arrival had by now spread, Stephen's supporters would have either ridden toward Devizes, where Rolfe said Henry had gone, or remained where they were, in order to fortify their own keeps.

Catherine nearly groaned aloud when she discovered the gate was secured. As her hands were fast becoming numb from the cold, she struggled with the heavy iron bar, raising it from its braces, then dropping it in the dirt at her feet. Exhilaration filled her when the gate easily swung open.

Free, she thought, racing down the steep incline, then across a deep ditch, which to her advantage held no water. Once she'd scrambled up its side, she stopped to get her bearings.

In front of her, she spied the full moon brimming on the horizon. Instantly she spun to her right and ran across the open field, heading south. A woodland stood not too far away. When she came to the forest, she'd shelter herself among the trees and slow her pace. Till then, she would run until she collapsed.

This was madness, she decided, just now realizing she didn't really know where she was going. Her father's estate was somewhere to the northeast of Oxford. But she had no idea how far the town was or, for that matter, in which direction it lay. It could be days before she came across anyone who might show her the way. By then she may have starved to death.

Catherine knew she should probably turn back, but she feared the repercussions if she did. Her abductor would be none too pleased, to say the least. Although she'd not yet seen him angry, she imagined he could be quite swift and forceful when roused. Then she questioned if he was the sort who would strike a woman, not just with his hand but with his fist. Woe unto her if he was, she thought, making her feet go faster.

Her side ached from her exertion, and her breath blew from her lips in a frosty stream, but she pressed onward, for she was nearly to the wood. Once she reached the haven, she planned to rest awhile. After she'd regained some of her stamina, she would continue on into the night, until she could go no farther.

Scanning the forest's edge, she thought she saw movement. Naught but the shadows playing, she concluded, after searching the area again. Shortly, she broke through the line of trees and pulled up.

Spent, she leaned against a tree, where she drew the crisp night air deep into her lungs. As the moments passed, she felt herself revive. Releasing one last long breath, she attended to the sounds in the wood, for a cloud had covered the moon, leaving her in virtual blackness.

Catherine heard leaves rustling in a wide arc around her, and at first she thought it might be from the wind. Then a low growl vibrated through the darkness; Catherine froze.

You'll have good reason to fear.

Rolfe's words tumbled through her mind just as moonlight streaked through the treetops and flooded the woods. Catherine stared wide-eyed at the large wolf, fangs bared, standing not more than five yards from her. The beast, she realized, was not alone.

Dear God! she thought as she eased away from the tree to slowly back toward the open field. What had she gotten herself into?

Eloise had warned her, so had her abductor, but she'd refused to listen to either of them. With each step she took, the pack kept pace with her, its leader the boldest of all. Snarling, he baited her, treading back and forth in front of her while always advancing.

The urge to run sparked to life inside Catherine, but she cautioned herself against it, positive they would attack. She envisioned herself being torn limb from limb, the carnivorous lot fighting with one another over the choicest piece. A ghastly sight it was.

She was now at the edge of the wood. If she could somehow make it back to the castle, she'd be safe. But its protective walls were an eternity away, and Catherine knew she'd never reach them.

They were coming closer. One more step backward and she would be clear of the trees. Taking that step, Catherine tripped, then found herself on the ground, upended by a fallen log. Her gaze shot to the pack's leader. He emitted a vicious growl, unlike any other.

"No!" she cried, knowing he was going to spring. She

shielded her face with her arms, praying it would all be over quickly.

Hearing Catherine's scream, Rolfe urged the stallion into a faster stride. They were only yards away, and he could see the wolf was about to attack. Rolfe drew his sword; then on his command, the horse vaulted over Catherine, placing them between her and the predator.

"Give me your hand," he ordered, leaning toward her while attempting to control the stallion. That the animal was performing as well as it was surprised Rolfe. "Hurry. The wolves are making him skittish."

She was up from the ground, reaching toward him, when the horse rolled its eyes and spun sideways, knocking Catherine away from Rolfe's outstretched hand. Trying to control the rogue with the reins, Rolfe discovered the bit had slipped.

At once the stallion reared. Its forelegs pummeled at the wind as a frightened whinney charged the air. When its hooves struck the ground, the horse twisted, then set to bucking. Rolfe was quickly unseated.

He hit the ground with force. Nausea instantly filled him from his gut to his head as pain shot through his right shoulder and down his arm.

As he attempted to pull himself from the ground, he saw the stallion running free across the field. Good riddance, he thought, cursing the animal. Then the hairs prickled along the nape of his neck, for he heard the snarls. The wolves, which had scattered with his appearance, were regrouping.

Rolfe gritted his teeth against the pain and forced himself to his feet. Looking for his sword, which had flown from his hand, he spied it lying several yards away. He took a step in its direction and immediately felt his head swim. A combination of the drink and the pain, he decided. "Catherine, my sword," he said, nodding toward it. "The wolves—we need protection."

She rushed to the weapon; then, grasping the hilt, she dragged it to him. His right hand dangling uselessly at his side, he took the blade in his left. "Get behind me," he ordered. "They come again."

"Can you stave them off?" she asked.

A good question, he thought. Though he could wield a sword with his left hand, he was far more proficient with his right. "I may not fell as many as I'd like should they attack, but they'll be fewer than they are." Because of his pain, however, he might not be able to slay a one. "They pace, waiting for their leader, but he acts as though he's having trouble gathering his courage. Crashing in on him the way I did, I think I made him take pause, but he'll not stay cautious for long. His hunger is too strong. Go, Catherine. Garrick and the others are somewhere out in the field looking for you. See to your safety while you have the chance."

"You're injured and cannot fight them alone," she told him. "I'll not leave you thus."

Rolfe was more than a bit surprised by her response. If anything, he would think she'd want him dead. "Your concern is well taken, milady, as is your bravery. However, I can fend for myself," he said while glancing over his shoulder. He wanted to look upon her face one last time, committing it to memory for all eternity. The dozen wolves were too many, he knew. Yet it was Catherine's safety that concerned him. "Now go," he ordered.

"'Tis too late," she said, her fear apparent. "He comes."

Rolfe jerked his head around to see the lead wolf stealthily moving toward them. The hairy beast now had a companion. Rolfe readied his sword.

"Get back," he commanded Catherine.

Just as the words left his lips, one of the beasts sprang through the air. The great broadsword was swung in an arc, slicing into its neck. Rolfe paid for the movement. Pain seared through his shoulder and into his gut. He had no time to pay heed to himself, for another creature was about to commit the same folly. Baring its fangs, the beast launched itself at Rolfe's throat. Again he swung the sword. The wolf fell dead beside its companion.

Beads of sweat had broken across his brow, and he wobbled on his legs. Rolfe fought against the agony encompassing him and stared at the lead wolf, noting the rest of the pack had gathered around him.

"Catherine," he said, "when the others attack, run from here. Once they take me down, they'll have no interest in you." He heard her strangled cry of protest and briefly shut his eyes. "Promise me you'll do that."

"Aye," she whispered, her voice choked.

Rolfe felt what he thought was the press of her cheek against his back. Though he wore no mail, it was hard for him to tell for the pain masked all else. "Be ready. They grow eager."

The snarls and yapping grew more vicious by the moment, then the leader drew back on his haunches, and Rolfe lifted his sword, certain this was the end. Pray God that Catherine made it to safety, he thought, wondering again how her lips might have tasted. Far sweeter than Ilona's, he decided, just as the huge wolf came at him.

All at once hoofbeats thundered in Rolfe's ears, accompanied by a fierce cry. Garrick, he realized, as the beast sailed at him. On contact, Rolfe was knocked to the ground. Sheer agony vibrated through him, and he groaned in misery. The wolf lay atop him, and Rolfe wondered why its fangs weren't tearing into his flesh; then he saw that the beast had been impaled on his sword. He relaxed his hold on the hilt and awkwardly shoved the lifeless wolf from him. Again he paid for the deed.

While Rolfe was trying to conquer his pain and make sense of what had just happened, Garrick rode straight into the pack, his sword swinging. When it was over, five more wolves lay dead. Those that were left quickly scattered off into the night wood, whimpering as they went.

His head clearing, Rolfe looked to his right. Catherine knelt beside him, concern etching her face. "I am not pleased with your actions," he said, glad that she was unharmed. He tried to ignore the searing heat in his shoulder by making light of the situation. "Running off as you did, you interrupted the festivities, thereby dampening everyone's spirits. Had your nurse not come to me, I'd still be enjoying my drink."

Her eyes widened in surprise. "Eloise came to you?"

"Aye. She feared for your safety. She had good reason, I'd say." He heard footsteps and saw Garrick approaching.

Once beside him, the man settled on one knee. "What took you so long?" Rolfe asked, then chuckled. Instantly, he wished he hadn't.

"'Twas a matter of discovering in which direction you went. If you had waited for the rest of us, you probably wouldn't be lying here now."

And Catherine would no doubt have been torn to pieces, Rolfe thought. "Time was of the essence," he replied, looking up at her. Guilt riddled her features; she couldn't hold his gaze.

"What happened to you?" Garrick asked.

"The rogue horse tossed me to the ground," he said. "I landed on my shoulder atop a log. My arm is useless."

The older knight grunted, then rose. Stepping over Rolfe, he urged Catherine aside and took her place, whereupon he probed the injury. Rolfe's breath hissed between his teeth.

"'Tis separated," Garrick announced. "If you hope to remain alert on the ride back, I suggest we take care of it here."

"Then be done with it," Rolfe stated.

Finding a stick, Garrick held it above Rolfe's face. "Open your mouth and bite down. And see if you can hold your temper while I'm about my task. 'Twill be better for us both."

Rolfe snorted. "I'm sure my agony will supplant my anger."

"At first, yes. 'Tis afterward which concerns me," Garrick stated, shoving the stick into Rolfe's mouth.

By now the men who'd ridden out with Garrick had found their location. Rising, the older knight ordered a litter be made. Then, lifting Rolfe's arm—which elicited an agonized groan from his companion—he set his foot to Rolfe's side.

"Ready?" he inquired, giving a firm jerk on the arm.

White-hot fire permeated Rolfe's body, from his head to his toes, just before his shoulder popped into place. The sound in itself was sickening. Through it all he heard Catherine's gasp as he was instantly relieved of his agony.

"We need to bind it," Garrick said. "If not 'twill surely slip out again. But we are lacking a bandage."

Rolfe saw a flash of skirt, then heard a tear. A wide strip of samite, interwoven with threads of gold and silver, was dangled just above his face.

"Will this do?" Catherine asked.

"Aye. This is just what we needed." Garrick took the length of silk from Catherine's hand. "Up with you, now," he said.

With Garrick's help, Rolfe came to a sitting position, whereupon the man bound the silk around Rolfe's arm and chest.

"Should do until we get back to the keep," the man offered.

Before long Rolfe was resting on a litter that had been hastily put together with tree branches and short strips of leather. As he was pulled along behind Garrick's horse, he gazed up at Catherine as she walked beside him.

"Why did you run?" he asked finally.

She didn't look at him, but kept her attention on the track ahead. "It should be obvious enough," she replied. "I wanted to be away from you."

Now that her fear had settled, she'd taken on a haughtiness about her, wearing it like a coat of mail, and Rolfe wondered if the change in attitude resulted from a feeling of uneasiness. She probably believed that she was the cause of his injury. In one way, she was; but in another, it was his fault. If he hadn't imbibed so much wine, he might have had a clearer head and been able to control the stallion, keeping it from heaving him from its back.

But he wasn't certain that was the whole of it. Her present show of disdain might have something to do with Ilona.

Just after the comely wench had planted herself on his lap, he'd noticed on a glimpse that Catherine was watching them. He'd kissed Ilona, not because of the boisterous cheers urging him to do so but because he wanted to see how Catherine would respond. When the kiss was over, he'd had his answer. She'd bolted from her seat and was headed for the stairs.

Whether the action came from disgust, from a slight twinge of jealousy—which he hoped was the case, for it would show that she was interested in him; or from the fact that she was truly tired—which he doubted, for she'd easily run the half mile across this field to the wood—he couldn't say. But he intended to discover which of the three it was.

"Why did you want to be away from me, Catherine?"

"Because you annoy me," she snapped.

"Why do I annoy you?"

That drew her attention. As she gaped down on him, he bit his cheek to keep from grinning.

"When you fell, you must have struck your head as well," she said.

"My head is fine. My shoulder is what gives me worry. Now answer me: What annoys you so much that you felt you had to be away from me?"

"Everything about you chafes me," she announced. "You are naught but a thorn in my side. Besides, I am obligated to attempt an escape. 'Twould be dishonorable of me if I didn't."

"In whose eyes? Your betrothed's?" he asked. "Knowing Miles, I'm certain he'd be exceptionally proud of you—doubly so if you hadn't called out and simply allowed the wolves to have their feast."

"Y-You know Miles?"

Since she didn't chastise him for the last of his statement, he assumed she'd only honed in on the first of it. "Aye, I know him." He didn't elaborate, but said, "The pity is, Catherine, if you had only waited until tomorrow, you would have been free of me. At daybreak I had planned to leave Cartbridge and ride south to join Henry. But now I doubt I'll be going anywhere. Not until my shoulder mends." She cast him a stunned look, and Rolfe chuckled. "I guess you're stuck with me."

They had reached the keep. Garrick dismounted and helped Rolfe from the litter. Once inside, the older knight shouted for Aubrey. The squire came running down the steps.

"Ready the lord's chambers," Garrick ordered. "'Tis the only bed, and he'll be needing its comfort." He turned to Catherine. "Up the stairs, woman. But stay within sight. We'll be having no more chicanery from you tonight."

Rolfe smiled when she took off up the stairs. By Garrick's

harsh tone, she was probably given to believe that her foolishness would not go unpunished. "You don't have to be so hard on her," he said as he slowly followed after Catherine.

"'Twould do her good to feel a piece of stout leather plying across her bottom. Maybe then she won't be so willing to cause us worry."

"I think she's learned her lesson. When I got to her, the pack's leader was about to pounce."

"Then she should be kissing your feet, instead of squabbling with you the way she was."

Garrick had obviously overheard their conversation. "She was unnerved by what happened and was trying to mask the fact. She stared death in the face, Garrick, probably for the first time. You remember the feeling, don't you?"

"Aye. When the fighting was done, I drank a whole keg of wine. My head pounded for two days after."

"And I found the loveliest young—never mind what I found," he said, nearing the lord's chambers. Actually it was now Catherine's room. She stood just outside the door, waiting. "Just let it be known I enjoyed myself immensely."

At Garrick's nod, Catherine opened the wooden panel. Rolfe noticed how she kept her eyes averted. With Garrick's help, he struggled through the doorway to spy Catherine's nurse on her knees, her hands folded. Her eyes were closed, her lips moving swiftly. "I appreciate your prayers, Eloise," Rolfe said, "but there is no need to continue them."

Her eyes flew open. First she looked to him, then to Catherine, who had followed through the door. "Oh, milady!" she cried, pulling herself to her feet. "I thought it was you who was injured." She speared Aubrey with her eyes. "His squire didn't tell me it was *him.*"

Easing himself onto the bed, Rolfe chuckled. "'Tis your fault I'm like this, Eloise. Hitherto your coming to me, I was taking great pleasure in the night."

The woman sniffed. "'Twas not the night that you were taking your pleasure in."

While Eloise spoke, Rolfe's gaze was on Catherine. At her nurse's reference to Ilona, she stiffened slightly. Disgust or jealousy? he wondered again. Unfolding her clasped hands, she moved toward the chest sitting against the opposite wall.

"I'll get my things, then depart," she said, reaching for the comb he'd given to her that morning.

"Leave it, Catherine," he said. She turned toward him and gazed at him questioningly as he added, "Henceforth you'll be sleeping with me."

CHAPTER
8

THE ROOM FELL INTO A HUSH.

"Sleeping with you?" Catherine asked.

"Aye," he said. "Obviously, you cannot be trusted. Therefore, you will make a pallet on the floor beside my bed so I may keep watch over you."

Catherine grew anxious. It was bad enough that she had to contend with him during the day, but to be locked in the same room with him at night was beyond comprehension. She positively abhorred the idea. The extent of her feelings must have showed on her face.

"I can see that milady has no fondness for the arrangements," he said.

An understatement if she ever heard one, Catherine thought. "You are correct. I have no fondness for the arrangements."

"You brought this upon yourself," he stated.

"But I have learned my lesson," she insisted, anxiety swirling inside her. Surely he could be made to listen.

"Though your desire to escape may be quelled for the moment, I doubt it will remain so for very long. Just as the wolf did, sooner or later you'll regain your courage. Next

107

you'll be knotting together strips of linen and dangling from yon window."

She would be the first to admit that he was probably right, but she had to convince him otherwise. She knew she couldn't withstand another night lying beside him as she had been made to do on their long journey here. Utter misery, she thought, certain it would be the same as before. "I'll give you my promise I won't do anything of the sort," she offered in haste.

"No, Catherine, I'll not chance your word. You stated yourself you were obligated to do the *honorable* thing. The next time you run, you may not be so lucky." He rubbed his shoulder. "Especially since I am now incapacitated."

"But—"

"I have spoken, and that is the end of it. Now ready your pallet. 'Tis time we sleep."

By his tone, Catherine knew better than to continue the argument. She turned to her nurse. "Eloise," she said, acknowledging the woman for the first time since entering the room. She didn't know whether to thank Eloise or to admonish her for having gone to Rolfe and telling him she'd escaped. "Find the necessary items so we can make two pallets and retire."

"That won't be necessary," Rolfe announced as Eloise started to move away from where she stood. "Aubrey will see to finding the items. Henceforth your nurse will be staying in the women's quarters." He looked at Eloise. "You may take your leave, woman. Your lady has no more need of your services tonight. Garrick, see that she finds her way."

"Wait!" Catherine cried as the man took hold of Eloise's arm. All eyes turned to her, but she saw only Rolfe. "Why are you sending her from this chamber?" she asked.

"I plan to have a restful slumber," he said. "I cannot achieve such if I am to constantly worry that I'll be pounced upon by the both of you while I sleep. Until I've recovered enough to join Henry, you and I will share this room alone. 'Tis the way of it, so do not question me about it again." He looked around the chamber. "Now everyone do as I've ordered and grant me some peace."

While Aubrey scampered to the far side of the room to

search through some chests for the necessary makings for Catherine's pallet, Garrick ushered the sputtering Eloise across the threshold and into the hallway, whereupon they quickly disappeared from sight.

Without her nurse there beside her, Catherine was devoid of protection. She gazed at the open doorway, longing to bolt from the room. The urge grew stronger, and her feet began to itch. She could almost feel her soles striking the floor.

Wisely, she resisted implementing the action, knowing she'd fail. Though he was injured, he was still far more capable than most. She pictured him bounding from the bed and heading her off, fury etched on his face. Then what? The thought weighed heavily that there was a good possibility he might strike her.

"Close the door, Catherine, and you'll not be tempted."

She looked at the bed. He lay there watching her intently.

"'Tis not hard to tell what you're thinking," he said. "Now shut the door and come undo this bandage so I can ready myself for bed."

Catherine traced the same path that only moments before had so urgently beckoned to her, but now it was done at a much slower pace. At the door, she pushed it to, then walked to his side. "You should leave the bandage in place," she stated. "Else, during the night, you may turn and cause yourself further injury."

With the aid of his left hand, he scooted up in the bed until he was at last in a sitting position. "You can replace it once I've disrobed," he said, leaning against the headboard.

"Disrobed?" she asked, gauging him carefully. Her expression must have betrayed the deliberate calmness in her voice, for she heard him chuckle.

"Aye. I'll not find any comfort otherwise. Come and do the task, so we can be on with it."

On with what? she questioned silently, an uneasiness settling in her stomach. Then she noticed how his eyes sparkled like sunlight on water. He baited her—purposely. Probably did so to punish her.

Pressing her lips together, she bit her tongue, afraid she might say something that would only add to her woes. With fast fingers, she attacked the bandage, only to hear his breath hiss between his teeth; he caught her wrist.

"Go easy," he said. "Whether you wish to believe it or not, I am human."

For the first time since they had returned from the wood, Catherine was aware of his discomfort. His face appeared drawn, while his color was a bit ashen. She remembered how his right arm had dangled at his side. The pain must have been unbearable. Nevertheless, he had stood in front of her, shielding her from the wolves.

When the others attack, run from here. Once they take me down, they'll have no interest in you.

His words replayed themselves in her mind, and Catherine grew quite still.

Promise me you'll do that.

It had been an impassioned plea, and as she gazed at him now, she understood fully that he'd been willing to give his life for hers.

Would she have left Rolfe to fend off the entire pack by himself? Or would she have stayed beside him, sharing in his death the same as he did hers? She'd never know the answer, for Garrick had saved them both.

Catherine blinked when the pressure on her wrist eased. His fingers traced lightly to her palm, then he squeezed her hand.

"What troubles you?" he asked as he searched her face.

She couldn't hold his gaze. "Nothing," she replied, feeling contrite. "I'm sorry I hurt you. I'll be more careful." Freeing her hand from his, she untied the knot.

"'Tis a pretty piece of silk," he commented, watching her. "Where did you get it?"

"From Miles. He gave it to me just after our betrothal and asked that I wear it on our wedding day."

"If it meant so much to you, why did you ruin it?"

"'Twas the first thing I put my hands on when Garrick asked for a bandage."

"In way of recompense for your loss, I'll buy you the finest length of silk I can find so that you may replace the garment."

"There is no need," she said as she stood back, the scrap

110

of samite now wadded in her hand. "What is ruined is ruined. It cannot be replaced. Besides, it is not the garment that matters but the spirit in which it was given. I'll always remember the moment Miles presented it to me, as well as the affection he displayed. No one can ever take that away from me."

At first, Catherine was surprised that he didn't scoff at her the way he usually did whenever she mentioned Miles. He lazed against the headboard, his silvery eyes regarding her. The silence stretched between them, then at last he sighed.

"That is a fine sentiment, milady, but are you certain he loves you?"

"Yes, he loves me. Why else would he marry me?"

"Money, power, greed—they are all good reasons for Miles to display affection, but it does not mean he loves you."

"And I suppose you know what is in his heart."

"I know him well enough to be assured it is not love. And you, Catherine, are foolish to believe it is."

She gave no credence to his words. All the same, she was curious. "You are forever maligning Miles, insisting you are familiar with him, that you know his character better than I. You expect me to believe what you say is true, yet you offer me no proof."

"I have proof."

Once again he did not elaborate, and Catherine grew weary of his nonsense. She gave him one more chance. "If you have such evidence, then bear witness to it and tell me how you know Miles."

"'Tis a long story, one I would rather not tell at the moment. But someday I'll explain what has transpired between Miles and myself. Afterward you may judge for yourself what sort of man your betrothed really is. Till then you may view him in whatever light you wish. Right now, you may ready yourself for bed. Aubrey will attend to my needs."

Catherine turned to see his squire standing behind her. He looked eager to fulfill his duties so that he too could seek his pallet. "I shall leave you to your master," she said, moving out of his way.

Aubrey nodded, then uttered, "Milady's pallet is ready. There is fresh water in the pitcher by the basin. I've laid your comb on the table beside them."

"Thank you." Not allowing her gaze to again fall on Rolfe, she moved to the opposite side of the room.

While Catherine cleaned her teeth with a piece of cloth and some salt, afterward combing her hair, Aubrey helped Rolfe from his bliaud. On occasion, a soft grunt or groan would whisper across the way. Catching the sounds, she was certain he suffered far more than he let on. Filled with remorse, Catherine blamed herself for his pain.

When she was finished with her task, she turned to see him lying in the bed's center, stripped to his braies. A length of linen covered his chest and wound around his right arm, securing it to his torso. The bandage replaced the scrap of silk, which now sat on the table beside the basin where Catherine had tossed it.

"Come here," he said.

She grew nervous, but did as told.

"Follow Aubrey to the door, then secure the lock. Afterward return the key to me."

Catherine accepted the key. At the door she waited for Aubrey to pass through.

"I'll see you on the morrow, milord," the squire announced.

"Do not be setting your fist to the wood too early or you may suffer for it," Rolfe told him. "Good night to you."

The door was closed, and Catherine locked it. Slowly she traversed the space between entry and bed, then handed him the key. He tucked it beneath his pillow.

"Get undressed and find your pallet."

"I'd prefer to sleep in my clothes."

"My temper is such that I'll abide no argument. You've worn those clothes for a week. Now remove them, or I'll do it for you."

By his expression, Catherine trusted that he'd do as threatened if she didn't comply. Boldly she stared at him while her fingers worked at the jeweled brooch securing her mantle. In return, his silver gaze bore into her. The garment fell at her feet in a puddle of blue wool.

Next, she reached for the hem of her short bliaud, snagging its embroidered trim. She yanked it over her head, exposing the linen chainse. Briefly she saw its bottom half was dingy and stained, and not the bright white that blanketed her torso.

The crimson bliaud landed atop the mantle, and she pulled the chainse from her, whereupon it joined the rest of her clothing on the floor.

Now in her silk chemise with its ragged hem, Catherine shivered, for the cold and dampness that had settled in the room passed right through her. "Are you satisfied?" she asked.

He inspected her from head to foot, his gaze lingering at her breasts, her hips, then dropping to her exposed thighs. He smiled. "More than satisfied," he announced. "Blow out the candles, will you? My body begs for sleep."

Catherine marched around the room, extinguishing each flame, then made her way to her pallet. After removing her slippers and stockings, she snuggled under the covers.

As she lay there in the darkness, the coals in the braziers glowing a reddish gold, she thought of the shame she'd just suffered.

He was far too impudent, she decided, and far too vain. In no way could he be equated with the chivalrous knights depicted in the minstrels' ballads. He'd treated her offensively, and she was determined to repay him in kind. Confident she could somehow double the embarrassment she'd sustained, she began to plan.

"By the way, Catherine . . ."

His voice flowed from the bed down to her; she glared at its source.

"I hadn't meant for you to undress in front of me," he said. "I intended for you to douse the candles first. However, with each article of clothing that fell away, the ache in my shoulder lessened. I thank you for the momentary distraction. 'Twas most enjoyable."

Her cheeks were instantly afire. Groaning, she pulled the covers over her head. He was truly the bane of her existence, the source of all her misery. How could she possibly be near him day and night and not go completely insane?

Catherine lamented her attempt to escape. If she only hadn't acted in such haste. He was right: She had brought this on herself. Therefore she would bear the consequences of her folly. By what had just transpired, Catherine was more than certain Rolfe de Mont St. Michel would see that she did.

"Your king is in jeopardy, my son," Brother Bernard said. "'Twould behoove you to pay attention to the game."

Without studying the board, Rolfe moved his pawn.

"I warned you," the monk declared, sliding his bishop into place. "That's check and mate, all in one move." He gathered the pieces, lining them up along the board. "Do you wish to play again?"

"No. The game holds no interest for me."

"There is always backgammon. Or how about a round of dice? I'll even dip into my purse and set a wager."

Rolfe sighed. "Sorry, Brother Bernard, but they hold no interest either."

"A gloom has settled over you, my son. Has it to do with your injury?"

"Aye. This inactivity is testing my sanity." That, and Catherine. "If it goes on much longer, someone will have to lash me to my bed."

"You must be patient. An injury such as yours doesn't heal in a day."

"God's wounds!" he erupted. "'Tis already been a week."

"I said you must be patient."

Rolfe's gaze narrowed on the monk. "How patient?"

The man shrugged. "A month, possibly six weeks. Even then your arm will be stiff. You'll have to work with it so that you can again wield a blade with proficiency. 'Twill be a slow process, I fear."

Just what he wanted to hear, Rolfe thought. His mood grew even more dour. His idleness was bad enough, but being kept in such proximity with Catherine was driving him mad.

The days could not be helped, but the nights were outright misery. He faulted himself for what he was made to endure. He now wished he had secured the window, preventing any attempt of escape, and locked her in the lord's chambers alone. At least then he'd have gotten some rest. Instead, just as when they'd journeyed to Cartbridge, he lay awake, listening to her soft sounds of slumber, imagining what it would be like to hold her, the way he had before.

What amazed him most was that he'd not rolled from his bed to seek her pallet, the urgency of his need demanding he seduce her. The knowledge that she'd attack him where he was presently most vulnerable—his shoulder—stopped him from following through. The added damage she would inflict would probably mean another lengthy spell of laying about. And that he could not abide. Nor could he abide being cooped up with Catherine. Something had to be done.

"I'll not be made to sit here for an eternity, nursing my shoulder," he said. "There must be something I can do to make it heal faster."

"While I was last in Rouen," the monk stated, "I had the opportunity to visit the natural springs which lay just north of the town. The waters there are said to have curative powers. I must say, I did feel a lot better after taking a good soak. I am tempted to try them again. Perhaps you could benefit from something similar."

"I know of no such springs this far north. The old Roman pools at Bath are the closest I'm aware of, and the town is too far south."

"We could always improvise," the monk announced.

"How so?"

"The water in the springs north of Rouen was exceptionally medicinal. However, I cannot decide if it was the water itself or the fact that it was extremely warm. If you were to soak in a hot bath, its temperature of the degree that I recall, the ache in your shoulder may ease. 'Tis worth a try."

"Agreed." The chess pieces scattered when Rolfe banged his knee on the table as he came up off the bench. He and the monk were in the great hall, and Rolfe's voice fairly rattled the beams when he yelled, "Ilona, come hither!"

She took her time getting to his side. "You called, milord?"

Rolfe realized she was yet perturbed with him. He supposed he should apologize to her for having dumped her from his lap on the night of Catherine's escape. Ilona had landed hard on her bottom, Rolfe stepping over her as he went. Just the same, he was in no mood to quibble with her.

"Obviously I did," he snapped, wondering why he'd ever considered bedding her. She was not as appealing as he'd first thought. The wine, he decided. It had the ability to make a woman seem far more enticing than she really was. Then there was Catherine. If he couldn't have her, he'd felt another could ease his pain. His mistake. "You are here, aren't you?"

"What do you want?" she inquired, her eyes narrowing on him.

"Start heating some water, then have the tub sent to my chambers. I am in need of a bath."

"The tub is already in use," she said.

"Oh? By whom?"

"By the woman you brought with you."

He'd brought two. "The fat one?" he asked, then watched as a slow smile spread over Ilona's face.

"Aye, the fat one," she returned. "She is in your room."

So, Eloise was enjoying herself in a warm tub, was she? The woman had been exceptionally bold of late. She opposed his locking Catherine in with him alone at night and was chastising him about it at every turn. It would serve the woman well were he to bound in on her unannounced. Rolfe's mood was such that he had no objection to doing so.

"Aubrey!"

His squire dashed from the opposite end of the hall where he and Garrick had been engaged in a game of dice.

"You called?" the lad asked, reaching his master's side.

Briefly, Rolfe bit his tongue, wondering if it were just he, or if everyone was dull of wit this day. The confinement, he decided, hoping it would be over soon.

"Aye, I called," he said at last. "After you finished straightening my chamber, did you lock the door on leaving?"

"Aye," his squire replied. "Just as you instructed."

"The key—give it to me." The article was quickly given over. "Now, go with Brother Bernard and see to the heating of the water for my bath. I do not trust that wench," Rolfe said of Ilona. "Considering her temper of late, she'll probably try to scald me."

"Where do you go?" Aubrey asked.

"To oust Catherine's nurse from the tub."

"But—"

"Just do as I say," Rolfe commanded from over his shoulder, for he was already on his way to the stairs.

Eager to try the monk's remedy, he took the steps two at a time. Once at the door, he didn't knock, just slipped the lock and entered. The screech that met his ears nearly deafened him.

Expecting to see Eloise in the tub, he instead saw Catherine, who quickly ducked beneath the water while her nurse came at him.

"You scurrilous oaf," the woman shouted. "Have you no manners?"

Rolfe eyed the empty bucket in Eloise's hands. She held the thing by its rope handle, swinging it around much the same as he would whirl a mace. He didn't wait to see if she would actually use it on him. In a trice, he was back out the door, the panel slamming closed behind him.

Leaning back against the wall, he released his breath. Then he dropped his hand from his shoulder, just now realizing he'd been protecting it. He should have known by Ilona's complacent smile that things were not as she'd said. The wench had been aware that Catherine's nurse would attack.

Women! Could he trust even one?

The sound of footsteps coming along the hall caught his attention. Garrick was striding his way.

"A messenger has arrived with word from the duke," he said when he reached Rolfe's side.

"And?"

"Catherine's father, accompanied by Geoffrey and Miles, has arrived in England. Apparently, they are in the company of a small army. From what Henry's spies could tell, they're just now beginning their search."

"'Twill be a long time before they find us," Rolfe said.

"Possibly," Garrick commented. "But it could also be a matter of a few days."

"What is it that Henry wants us to do?"

"We are to stay here."

"Here?"

"Aye. 'Tis unclear who hired the mercenaries. If it was Geoffrey, the detachment of warriors will undoubtedly be sent to join Stephen should the girl be found and taken too soon. At present Henry is on his way to Malmesbury, hoping to divert Stephen from Wallingford. Until the fight begins, he wants no surprises. We are to lay in supplies and make ready to stave off her rescuers. 'Tis the duke's wish."

"Then I suppose we'd better see that it is done," Rolfe said, pushing himself from the wall. "Let's go below and form a plan."

As the two men traversed the corridor, Rolfe questioned his own fate. Everything conspired against him. He had hoped to leave Cartbridge and join Henry well before the length of time the monk said it would take for his shoulder to heal—hence his need for a bath.

Now, by the duke's own word, it appeared that he and Catherine would be in one another's company for some time to come. Given that, he wondered how long he could continue to resist her.

CHAPTER
9

"I STILL SAY, BY ALL THIS PREPARATION, YOUR FATHER IS HERE IN England," Eloise said. "Why else would they be laying in stores and fortifying the keep?"

Catherine stood at the window in the lord's chamber, viewing the to-and-fro movements of those below. "You may be right, Eloise. I certainly hope so. But if anyone knows what this is about, I've yet to hear it for myself. No one is willing to talk."

"That's because they know your father is coming."

"We are not assured of that. Their sudden industriousness could also mean that Henry has finally engaged Stephen. Derby is not all that far away and is one of Stephen's strongholds. They could be making ready for a siege."

Over the past three days, the castle hummed with activity. Where its inhabitants were once content to spend their time in idleness, a minimum of work performed, they were now rushing from task to task, never taking a rest.

Out in the yard with the others was Rolfe de Mont St. Michel. Though he couldn't labor alongside them, he was certainly accomplished at directing the proceedings. Presently he was overseeing the positioning of a catapult that had been set under construction two days before.

As Catherine watched, the lever was released. A huge rock flew over the curtain wall, landing somewhere beyond the moat, which was now filling with water. He had supervised that also, ordering a sluiceway be dug from the empty ditch to a small stream that cut through the field, not far from the castle.

Apparently the catapult hadn't functioned to his liking, for he ordered it turned another degree. It was obvious to Catherine that he was seeking the optimum effect. She just prayed her father wasn't the recipient of the huge weapon's power. The lever was again released, the arm swung, and another rock sailed over the wall. With a smile and a wave, Rolfe signaled his satisfaction. The catapult was now in place.

Frowning, Catherine wondered at her own reflections. Why hadn't she also thought of Miles when she'd worried over her father's safety?

These last several days, her betrothed drifted in and out of her mind less frequently, and Catherine was troubled by the fact. Perhaps the lapse had to do with the strange happenings going on around her. Her head was already filled with questions and concerns, even to the point that there was little room for anything more. Until she had some answers, she doubted she would think of much else, Miles included.

Catherine again refocused on the yard. She saw Rolfe coming down the steps from the wall. Once his feet hit level ground, he strode toward the forge, where he talked to the smithy.

More weapons, she thought, then noticed how his fingers moved to his neck. His daily baths were helping, for his right arm was no longer bound to him but now rested in a sling. He adjusted the knot as though it were chafing him, then his hand fell away. Catherine viewed him for a long moment, then she turned to her nurse.

"Tonight, when he again bathes, I want you to keep Aubrey below."

"Why?"

"If we are to get any answers, I must gain his trust."

Eloise's eyes widened. "What are you thinking, child?"

"What I've thought all along, but nearly forgot. I intend to be excessively pleasant."

"'Tis not a good idea, with the two of you sleeping in this room alone," her nurse said.

"I know what I'm doing, Eloise. Just see that you keep Aubrey downstairs when his master calls for him."

"And how do you expect me to do that?"

"Sit on him if you must, but keep him from this room."

Exasperation rippled through Rolfe. Where was the lad? he wondered. His bath was quickly cooling. Three times he'd called for Aubrey, and three times there had been no response. By the time he undressed himself the tub would be a chunk of ice. He was tired, his shoulder ached, and he was in no mood to wait until his bath was filled again. Determined to find out what was keeping his squire, he started toward the door.

"May I assist you in undressing?"

Turning, Rolfe looked to where Catherine sat. Each night while he bathed, she claimed the same stool in the same corner and faced the wall, busying herself with needle and thread. That night she'd offered to mend one of his garments, which surprised him. But her current overture astonished him even more, especially when these past ten days she'd virtually ignored him.

"Aye," he said, moving back toward the tub. "I would welcome your help, for I cannot remove my tunic by myself."

Standing up, she grabbed the stool and crossed the short distance separating them. "Sit," she ordered, placing the stool beside him, "and I'll see what I can do."

Rolfe obeyed her command. As her nimble fingers worked with the sling's knot, he surveyed her from the corner of his eye. "Just now you sounded like a concerned mother tending her child."

"I'll be that someday," she replied.

Would that they were his children, they'd be a happy lot, he decided, then quickly quashed the idea. He had no room in his life for a wife and a family. Frowning, he took pause, questioning why the thought had even arisen.

The knot loosened, and she gently removed the sling from his arm. Next she stepped to his left side. Urging him from the stool, she drew his tunic up over his hips to his waist, then to his chest, before she prompted him to resettle.

"Pull your arm through," she said, having gathered the material up to his armpit.

He slid his left arm from the sleeve, then the tunic was pulled over his head, away from his injured shoulder, and down his right arm, where she slipped it off his hand. He was gladdened by the fact that he felt no pain. Had Aubrey undressed him, he would have been gritting his teeth. A woman's hands were far more proficient, he mused. Far less clumsy. Especially Catherine's.

She was now kneeling before him, removing the soft leather boots from his feet. Next she unwrapped the lacings that secured his chausses. Soon all that remained were his braies.

"I can do the rest," he said, coming up from the stool to stand above her.

Crouched at his feet, she looked a long way up at him. "Are you certain?"

"Aye," he said, his left hand moving to the drawstring. "'Tis a simple matter of undoing the bow."

Whether it was because Catherine was watching him or that he was simply inept, Rolfe couldn't say, but he quickly managed to tangle the string into a sizable knot.

Her soft laughter rang in his ears as she came to her feet. "You should have let me do the deed before you made such a mess of it." She eased his hand aside. "In a case such as this, two hands are better than one."

As her fingers worked against him midway between waist and groin, Rolfe stood as still as a mouse. Twice he had to remind himself to breathe. God's wounds! he thought. Would she ever finish with the task?

Sweat broke across his brow as the spark in his loins promised to become a raging inferno. If she didn't hurry, her hands would be occupied with more than a mere string.

"There," she said. "'Tis free."

Her hands moved away, and Rolfe felt the brewing fire that was storming inside him subside. Holding the garment in place, so it didn't slip from his hips to the floor, he drew a cleansing breath. On its release, he said, "You have my gratitude." The words were naught but a squeak; he quickly cleared his throat. "You may return to your sewing, milady. I can handle the rest on my own."

She hesitated and looked at her feet. "If you have need, I will assist in washing your back."

His brow furrowing, Rolfe stared at her. Something was obviously amiss here. She was too eager to help him, and he wondered what she was about. There was only one way to find out.

"Turn 'round then, and I'll get into the tub." When she did as told, he let the braies drop to the floor. Kicking them aside, he held his right arm to him, stepped over the rim, and settled into his bath. "You may aid me now."

Slowly she moved behind him, then took hold of a scrap of cloth and a crude bar of soap sitting on the table beside the tub. Rolfe soon felt the lathered cloth gliding over his left shoulder, then down his back. Her motions were gentle, but when she touched his right shoulder, he grimaced.

"I've hurt you," she said.

"'Tis more from reflex than from pain. I tend to favor the area, not really knowing I do."

Her slick hands began to lightly knead the spot. "You were too long on your feet today," she stated. "You are not ready to be moving about as you were."

Rolfe smiled. "I had no idea I held such interest for you."

"Interest?"

"By your statement, I assume you were watching me."

"I was watching all of you," she said. "Being locked in this room, day and night, there is little to hold my attention. The recent activity has become a diversion for my boredom. I've grown quite interested in the proceedings."

With her statement, Rolfe was more than certain he knew the reason for her sudden desire to serve him. Her curiosity was piqued and she wanted some answers. Not finding them elsewhere, she'd decided to come to him.

Over the last several days, he'd watched her during those times she'd been allowed from her room in order to partake of her meals. She'd become inordinately friendly with those who worked in the yard. No doubt she'd been subtly questioning each one as to the motive behind the fortification of the keep. Since he and Garrick were the only two at Cartbridge who were aware that William de Mortain and the d'Avrancheses were now in England or that they were the cause for the preparations, he knew she'd been thwarted at every turn. Even so, she may suspect the truth. Desperately wanting confirmation, she was probably willing to go to any lengths.

The knowledge tempted him, and he questioned just *how* far she would go. He was determined to find out.

"And I suppose you want to know what these *proceedings,* as you call them, are all about."

"I assume Henry has engaged Stephen and that you fear a possible siege from those at Derby," she said, her hands working at his shoulder.

"Ahh," he sighed. "Your fingers are like magic." He leaned back against the water-soaked wood. "Do the front, will you?"

She sidled around the tub on her knees and was now facing him. "That is the reason you are strengthening the castle, isn't it?" she asked, again massaging his shoulder.

"A little lower," he said, and her hands drifted down to attend to the right side of his chest. "In answer to your question, we could be attacked at any time. Over to the left a bit, please." Her hands moved and he sighed again. "Now, what was I saying?"

"You mentioned we could be attacked at any time."

"Yes, that's true. But I have no confirmation that Henry has engaged Stephen—not yet, anyway. When such a thing does occur, I doubt those at Derby will go too far afield. At least no farther than to see to the safety of their own boundaries, that is."

"If you aren't concerned about those at Derby, then why the added weaponry?"

"Back to the right a bit. *Ahh.* That's good. Now back the

other way." As Catherine's hands moved, Rolfe fought back a grin. "Now lower, please." She complied, her fingers tracing to the underside of his ribs. "Lower again." Her hands feathered almost to his waist, then abruptly stilled. "What's wrong?"

"You're using me," she accused, glaring at him.

"No more than you intended to use me," he replied.

With a strangled growl, her hands came up from the tub. Thinking she might strike him, Rolfe reacted. Lightning-fast, he banded both her wrists in his left hand.

"Loose me," she demanded, struggling to be free.

The action jarred his shoulder, but he held on. "Not until I learn the truth of it, Catherine."

"What truth?"

"This."

Releasing her hands, he caught the back of her head and pulled her to him. He kissed her hard, his tongue tracing her lips. Just as quickly, he freed her.

She fell away from the tub and rubbed her mouth with the back of her hand. "How dare you!"

"I dared because you offered."

"I did no such thing."

"Didn't you?" he asked. "You were eager enough to assist me with my bath. Even used your hands in an attempt to soothe me and loosen my tongue. 'Tis not in your character to touch a naked man. Not unless you want something. I'm curious. Had I played the game differently, just how far would you have gone to learn whatever it is you're seeking?"

"I'm not a whore," she defended.

"No, you're not," he returned. "If you were, you'd presently be in that bed with your legs wrapped around my waist." She gasped at his brashness, and he smiled. "Seek to tempt me again, and you'll know the consequences of doing so."

She couldn't hold his gaze. "I simply wanted an answer," she said.

"Then why didn't you ask the question straight off?"

"Because I didn't think you'd tell me the truth."

Rolfe sighed. "Get up, Catherine, and take yourself to

your corner. Before we go any further with our discussion, I think I had better get dressed."

She nodded, then rose and went to the far side of the room, where she waited, her back turned to him.

Rolfe attended himself as best he could, first drying himself with the linen bathsheet, then donning his braies, knotting the drawstring at his waist. Next he fixed his sling, pulled it over his head, then positioned his arm inside. Last, he threw a woolen mantle around his shoulders to ward off the room's chill.

"Come hither," he said when he was finished.

Slowly she came forward, then stopped several feet away. "If I ask, will you tell me the truth?"

"There's no reason for me to lie. Likewise, you don't need to ask the question, for I already know what it is. A messenger arrived three days ago with word from Henry that your father is in England."

"Miles too?"

He noted how her face had brightened. "Aye, the bastard made the journey." She began to sputter, but he waved her off. "Hear me out first, then you can defend him." After the tussle by the tub, his shoulder was now causing him pain. His mood was darkening as well. "Henry ordered that we fortify Cartbridge just in case your father should find you. We are to delay him until Henry is assured victory."

"Then they are on their way here."

Rolfe noticed how her smile lit not only her face but her eyes. She obviously expected to be free any day. "They are on their way somewhere. There's no guarantee that it is here. In fact, they may never find you. We are simply securing the castle as a precaution."

Her smile faded. "You intend to fight them, don't you?"

"If it becomes necessary, aye."

"My God. My father, Miles, Geoffrey—you could kill them all."

"If you're worried about Miles, you shouldn't be."

She frowned. "Are you saying you have no intention of harming him?"

"I'm saying he has no intention of putting himself in

harm's way. By chance, should your rescuers find you, I doubt you'll see Miles anywhere near the castle wall. More than likely, he'll be out in yon wood, hiding behind a tree." He could see his words didn't set well. "Apparently you disagree."

"You have continually maligned Miles, but you give no reason as to why you do so. You say you know him better than I, but you offer no proof. Is it because he favors Stephen and you approve of Henry? Is that why you attack him as you do? Simply because you are on opposite sides?"

Rolfe realized the time had come for her to learn the truth about her betrothed. He reached out and took her hand, then pulled her along to where the stool sat. "Seat yourself, milady," he said, "while I do the same."

As she perched on the stool, he shoved a chair close to her, then ensconced himself in it.

"This is my proof, Catherine." He lifted his arm and showed her the scar. "As is this." He pointed to the one at his waist. "There is another on my right thigh."

"I remember," she said, looking at her hands.

From when he'd boldly undressed in front of her at the abbey, he surmised, then continued on. "These wounds resulted from a raid by the Turks as I and a group of about two hundred Norman knights were traveling the road to Antalya five years ago during the Crusade. We had allied with Louis, but were well behind his army and were trying to catch up.

"Two men who were very close to me were also on the road that day. Robert de Bayeux was my mentor; I loved him as I would a father. Francis, his son, was like a brother to me. Also on that road was your betrothed."

"Miles?" she asked, frowning.

"Aye. He was there. I can tell by your expression you didn't know he was once a knight."

"N-no. He never told me that."

"I'm not sure I would tell anyone either if my sword and spurs were stripped from me, then broken as a mark of disgrace for my cowardice."

"Are you accusing Miles of being a coward?"

"I'm not accusing him of anything. 'Tis a fact," Rolfe said. "He was proved guilty of losing his courage and fleeing a battle. Two men died because of it."

For a moment she was very quiet, then she asked, "Your mentor and his son?"

"Aye."

"But many men lose their lives while in battle," she proclaimed. "I don't understand why Miles was singled out as the cause of their deaths."

"That day we were taken unawares. One moment all was peaceful; the next, the air was filled with terrifying cries as the Turks streamed down the hillsides upon us. Robert and Francis were to one side, Miles with them. At the first wave, Miles fled, leaving father and son to fight alone. By the time I was able to battle my way to them, it was too late. They had been hacked to death, their remains mutilated."

"How do you know it was Miles? It could have been another knight."

She was unwilling to believe her betrothed could do such a thing. Rolfe intended to put her straight.

"It was Miles, all right. I recognized him. I also saw him run, as did a dozen other men. We later found him among a pile of rocks, hiding from us all. Then and there, in front of his peers, he met his disgrace as each of us who witnessed his cowardice testified against him. The implements of knighthood were stripped from him and broken. He was exiled from our company."

Besides he and Garrick, Rolfe didn't know if any of the men who'd observed the event were yet alive. While Garrick had returned to Normandy with him, the others had traveled on to Jerusalem. Short of food and riddled by disease, only a small portion of the French army that had journeyed along the road to Antalya survived to join their king. Rolfe imagined that many of the Norman force were among the casualties, for he'd not seen or heard of any of them since.

"So you see, Catherine, I have good reason to call him a coward, a weakling, a bastard, because he is all of these. Robert and Francis were not the only ones to die that day. There were many. In fact very few of us survived. But of those who lived and of those who died, all stood their ground, except one."

"Miles," she whispered.

Rolfe watched her closely. She seemed to have drifted into another realm, possibly trying to comprehend what he'd told her. "I do not lie, Catherine. If you doubt my word, you may ask Garrick. He was there. That is how we became friends."

She looked up at him. "Your mentor—you said he was like a father to you, and his son, a brother. How is it you met?"

"I was seven when Robert de Bayeux came to Mont St. Michel on a pilgrimage. He spotted me, befriended me, and asked the monks if he could give me a home. The brothers agreed, for it was a time of unrest. Henry Beauclerc had just died, and Stephen had usurped the throne. The inhabitants of Avranches supported Stephen, while the Benedictines favored the rightful heir, Matilda. At the time, I think the good brothers wanted to get me as far from the mount as possible. As it later proved out, those at Avranches, Geoffrey among them, eventually attacked the abbey and burned the town."

"How do you know Miles's father was among them?"

"Ask Brother Bernard. He'll confirm that it was so."

"I will," she said.

By her tone, he knew she refused to believe what he said was true. He wondered what it might take to convince her. More so, he questioned why he felt it was even necessary. Once he released her, he doubted he'd ever see her again. Why then was he so intent on persuading her?

"Just think, Catherine: Had Robert de Bayeux not plucked me from the mount, I might presently be a monk instead of a knight." Her expression clearly told him what she thought of that idea. "I agree. I would have fallen far short of the piety expected of those who are affiliated with the order. As it was, Robert became my mentor and lord. He trained me to be a knight. Francis and I grew up together. Though he was two years older than I, we were the best of friends, brothers at heart. They were my family. And because of Miles's cowardice, they are now gone. My question is this: Knowing the sort of man Miles really is, do you still hope to marry him? Think about it. Think long and hard."

She acted as though she were about to say something, but a knock sounded on the door.

"Sire, 'tis me, Aubrey."

The announcement came through the wood, and Rolfe shook his head. "I suppose he thinks I wouldn't know him simply by his voice." He rose, found the key, and unlocked the door. "About time you presented yourself," he said upon opening the door. "Where have you been?"

"In the cellars, sire. But 'tis not my fault."

"The cellars?"

"Aye. Her nurse summoned me down there, saying she needed some cloth, so she could make her lady a tunic. She claimed she feared there were rats. Once in the storeroom, she shoved me down, slammed the door, and locked me inside," Aubrey announced. "I beat on the door from the time it happened. 'Twas a long while before someone heard me."

Rolfe's brow arched questioningly as he turned to look at Catherine; she had paled slightly.

"I—I asked Eloise to keep him below while I got some answers," she said.

"Your plan was well conceived, milady. But as you are now aware, not in the least necessary."

"I suppose I should have known better," Aubrey stated, his dejection apparent.

"Aye, you should have," Rolfe returned. "As I told you before, Aubrey: No matter who she is, never put your trust in a woman."

"'Tis your move, milady," Brother Bernard said.

Catherine stared absently at the chessboard. Her head was yet reeling from what Rolfe had told her about Miles. Though it had been a good week since their conversation, she still didn't know what to believe. The Miles she knew was not at all like the man Rolfe had described. She supposed there was one way to settle the matter. But she'd been reluctant to ask Garrick about that day at Antalya. In truth, she feared he'd confirm Rolfe's story, and she wasn't certain she could face the knowledge that Miles was indeed a coward.

"Milady?" the monk prompted. "Have you grown tired of the game?"

"No," she fibbed. "I'm just thinking about which man I should move."

She and Brother Bernard sat in the great hall. Since the fortifications had been completed and the stores laid in, she was no longer locked in her room during the day. However, her newfound freedom did have its drawbacks. She was constantly supervised.

Today it was Brother Bernard's turn to keep watch over her. Still examining what she'd been told about Miles, she decided to take advantage of her time alone with the monk. After all, she believed that one's perception of the truth could vary widely from another's. She wanted to know how Brother Bernard viewed the matter.

"How long have you known Rolfe de Mont St Michel?" she asked, moving her knight.

"Since the day the hounds found him on the marshes. 'Twas considered a miracle—one of many for the mount that bears the Archangel's name."

"He told me the story, but I was skeptical about its merit."

The monk moved his rook. "You should not have been, my child. He was abandoned on the marshes. Just as the tides came in, he was found by one of the hounds and dragged by his swaddling to the safety of the mount. There are at least two dozen of my brethren at Mont St. Michel who will confirm that it is true. As far as your skepticism, I've never known Rolfe to lie about anything."

Catherine moved her bishop and heard the instant clicking of the monk's tongue. "What's wrong?"

"Are you sure you want to do that?"

She studied the board. "Aye."

"'Twas a mistake, I fear," he returned, taking her bishop with his own.

As Catherine concentrated on her next move, she asked, "What do you know of Geoffrey d'Avranches?"

"He is a neighbor to Mont St. Michel—an untrustworthy one at that."

"Why?" she inquired. "Because he supports Stephen?"

"That is part of it, but mainly because he was considered instrumental in inciting the townspeople of Avranches into assailing the abbey and burning the village at its base. His politics are motivated by greed. When Henry became duke of Normandy, Geoffrey wisely became less vocal, and certainly far less bold. However, he yet practices his chicanery, albeit in the cleverest of ways. 'Tis your move, milady."

"Aye. I'm thinking," she said. She didn't know if she should accept the monk's opinion as true. His own views might be biased because of his affiliation with Henry and his closeness to Rolfe. "Tell me: Who is Robert de Bayeux?"

"Try your rook," he suggested.

"Thank you. I will."

After her move, it was the monk's turn to study the board. "I take it Rolfe has told you something of his past," he said, touching his knight. Shaking his head, he withdrew his hand. "And I assume you are uncertain whether or not to believe what he's said is true."

"Some of it is difficult for me to accept," she admitted.

"Such as?"

"He claims my betrothed is a coward—that Miles was the cause of Robert de Bayeux's death."

"And young Francis's," the monk inserted.

She released a long breath. "Aye. His too. Do you know that this is so?"

"I was not on the road to Antalya. Nor was I at the abbey when Rolfe brought Robert's and Francis's bones to the mount for burial. I can tell you only what the other brothers have said. Rolfe was devastated by their deaths. Because of it, his faith in God was shaken. He has not recovered his faith, nor has he forgiven the man whom he names as the cause of his great sorrow. I do know that if Rolfe says it was your betrothed, then it is so. As I said before, I have never known him to lie.

"As for Robert de Bayeux," the monk continued, "he was a good and generous man. He took Rolfe into his care, raising him alongside his own son, treating both equally. I would say Robert did exceptionally well, for Rolfe is a man who is readily trusted. He is loyal and forthright. In fact, even among my own brethren, he would rank far higher than most. I say this because I know him. So, milady, if you doubt him, perhaps you need to become further acquainted with him. 'Tis the only way to ease your mind."

Become further acquainted with him? she thought. What else was there to know? He was arrogant to a fault. And despite what Brother Bernard had said, he did lie. He'd posed as a priest, hadn't he? He'd tricked her, leading her into the wood. As far as she was concerned, she was as familiar with him as she wanted to be.

But then she'd thought she was familiar with Miles, knew his traits quite well. Geoffrey's too. Yet from Rolfe's and Brother Bernard's depiction of them, she was beginning to wonder if she really knew them at all.

Was it possible that both Miles and Geoffrey had duped her?

Perhaps it was her pride speaking, but Catherine remained undecided as to what the truth was. There was something she had yet to do. Scanning the vast room, she found what she sought.

"Excuse me, Brother Bernard," she said, rising from the bench, "but it is important that I speak to Garrick."

Rolfe viewed Catherine for the longest while. She had retired early to their chambers, Aubrey locking her inside. When he'd entered some time later, he'd found her sitting in one of the chairs, staring at nothing in particular. On greeting her, he'd received no reply.

At first he thought nothing of it and moved about the room, seeing to some minor tasks. But her continued silence and statuelike state soon began to concern him. It was unlike her to be so withdrawn. Though he felt he knew what was troubling her, he wanted her to voice it for herself.

"What's wrong, Catherine?" he asked finally. She didn't answer, and he moved closer. "I know you've been questioning Brother Bernard and Garrick. Have their responses caused your despondency?"

Her gaze hit him like a spear. "I am not despondent. I'm simply thinking."

"I take it you're still not willing to accept the truth."

"The truth?" she asked. "What is the truth? Yours? Garrick's? Brother Bernard's?"

"Are they not the same?" he countered.

Her gaze hardened. "The stories appear to match, but I have yet to hear Miles's side of it."

At once Rolfe was filled with the sudden desire to go to her, take hold of her shoulders, and shake some sense into her. "'Tis obvious, milady, that you wouldn't recognize the truth even if it were to somehow fall from the sky and smite you. You are too stubborn by far, but that is your failing, not mine. Two others have confirmed my words. Despite that, you refuse to believe.

"So hear me now, for I speak true. I have nothing to gain by anything I've said. The only reason you were told about my distaste for your betrothed is because you asked. I had thought that by telling you I could save you from what promises to be a miserable marriage. You will be the one who suffers, Catherine, not Miles. Think about it. If he has hidden his cowardice from you, what else has he concealed from you as well?"

His words said, she remained quiet, and Rolfe wondered if he'd reached her at all.

"I'll not judge him until I have his side," she said at last.

Exasperation swirled up inside Rolfe until it nearly choked him. He felt as though he could throttle her. As he stared at her creamy neck, the temptation grew. Knowing he had to get from the room before he followed through, he headed for the door. Once there, he pulled it open. Just as he was about to exit, he checked himself. Slowly he turned her way.

"'Tis only right that you should be prudent in your judgment by weighing all sides. However, I tell you this: In the end, should you decide to wed Miles, my words will one day return to haunt you. In your misery, you'll hear them again and again. Too late, you'll have learned the truth."

CHAPTER
10

CATHERINE SAT ALONE IN THE LORD'S CHAMBER, PONDERING HER dilemma. She now knew the angst she was meant to suffer on her refusal to accept Rolfe's words as being true. At the moment the door had slammed behind him, their relationship changed.

The days passed in endless succession, and the weather worsened. It was cold, gloomy, and as the pelting snows and frozen rains swirled outside Cartbridge Castle, a chilling dampness permeated its walls. There was no warmth to be found anywhere, not even by the hearth in the great hall. Why anyone would war over such a forsaken land was a complete mystery to her.

But the icy fury raging beyond the protection of the keep was nothing compared to the frigidness that had settled inside.

Rolfe de Mont St. Michel had become indifferent. *Cold* didn't describe him. *Glacial* suited him far better. And Catherine was well aware that she, along with her stubbornness, was the reason behind his wintry facade.

Since that day when he'd stormed from the room, they had spoken little, if at all. It was as though his warning hung between them. She could do with it as she pleased.

Not only had his mood changed, but their entire existence had taken a turn. She was now barred from the room whenever he bathed—which, in actuality, was a relief. Likewise, she never knew if he would be sleeping in his bed at night or if he would simply order her locked inside the room till dawn.

On most occasions, he chose to take his rest elsewhere. At those times she gazed longingly at the empty bed, desiring its comfort. But she dared not leave her pallet, for fear that sometime during the night he would enter the chamber and toss her to the floor.

Strangely, when Rolfe had rejected her, something happened. She couldn't explain why, but she likened her feelings to those of a small child who desperately vied for a parent's notice, only to be continually ignored.

Where once she was impatient to be away from him, she was now eager to see him. And when he turned away, as he always seemed wont to do, a sinking hollowness would settle inside her.

Her emotions were in a turmoil, and Catherine thought she was losing her mind. Not long before, she could barely abide his being near; now she hungered for his attention. Presently, even the smallest scrap would appease her need. But considering the recent turn of events, she doubted he'd offer even that.

Madness, she thought, launching herself from her chair. She strode to the window and threw open the shutters. The cold wind whipped over her. She readily withstood its bone-chilling bite. Breathing deeply, she hoped the frigid air would somehow clear her head, allowing her to regain her senses. Unfortunately, the act had little effect.

She thought about her father.

Gazing across the castle wall to the field beyond, she wondered how he fared. Was he out in the elements, suffering from the cold? Or was he safe and warm at his estate? She prayed that it was the latter, for she couldn't bear the idea of his searching for her in such horrid conditions.

In her mind's eye, she saw him fighting against the wind

and the snow, ice crusting his graying locks, his face chafed from the cold. What she feared more was that he'd become ill. If that were to happen, she might never see him again.

Adamantly, Catherine wished she'd never set eyes on Rolfe de Mont St. Michel. Life would be so much easier as a result. She wouldn't be worrying about her father. She wouldn't be suffering doubts about Miles or about her love for him. Nor would she be feeling dejected because her abductor no longer acknowledged her.

She lifted her face to the heavy gray heavens. "Oh, the misery of it all," she lamented aloud.

"Milady, don't!"

Startled, Catherine blinked. Turning, she saw Rolfe's squire standing just inside the doorway. His face was as white as the snow on the window sill. "What is it, Aubrey?"

"I, uh—well, I thought you were going to jump."

"Jump?"

"Aye, milady, jump."

"What gave you such a notion?"

"The open window and what you said."

Catherine's laughter bubbled into the air. "The thought of exiting by this window has crossed my mind several times, but I fear the fall will kill me. Hence, I have resisted the idea from the start."

The color slowly returned to his face; he smiled. "I'm glad it was only a whim, for Sir Rolfe would be very upset had you seen fit to follow through."

Upset? she questioned silently. Unlikely. He'd probably be relieved. "Where is the most noble knight?" she asked, while closing the shutters.

"He is down in the hall. That is why I have come. He says you are to join the others for your meal."

The window now secured, she turned to face Aubrey. "I'd prefer to take my meal up here alone."

"He won't allow any excuses, milady. He said you are to come to the hall at once."

"In other words, he has *commanded* my presence."

Aubrey looked at his feet. "Aye, milady. His words are a behest."

Catherine had been in this room for so long that she was

about to go completely mindless. She could tell anyone who cared to ask that there were two hundred and twenty stones on the chamber's front wall and one hundred and seventy-five stones on each side wall.

She could also inform them that it had taken the spider that resided in the high corner nearest the door approximately four turns of the hourglass to weave its web. There was also a huge cobweb in the opposite corner, but she didn't know if it had once belonged to the current spider or to a past resident, long since dead.

Alongside that, she—

"Milady," Aubrey said. "Shall I escort you to the hall?"

It was time she left this place, she decided. "Aye. I will welcome the change."

"You shouldn't drink so much," Eloise said sternly. "The wine will soon muddle your head, if it hasn't already. You might feel cheery now, but on the morrow, you're certain to be in the depths of your own gloom."

Catherine glanced at her nurse. The two women sat side by side at one of the tables in the great hall, their guards for this night posted not far away. Since the evening Eloise had locked Aubrey in the cellars, both had been kept under watch. Neither was to be trusted, at least according to Rolfe. He was right, but the thought nettled Catherine just the same.

She took another swallow from her cup. "This is the only way I am able to forget my problems," she announced. "Considering everything I've been through, I should be allowed some succor. If the wine promises such, I shall gladly take it."

"'Tis well and good, milady, that your worries are given some ease. Just see that you don't regret it tomorrow by making a fool of yourself tonight."

How could she possibly make a fool of herself? Except for her guard, no one watched her—especially not Rolfe. For all the attention he gave her, she could soon slide under the table into the rushes from the drink and he'd not miss her one whit. Frowning, she wondered why he'd insisted she come to the hall at all.

Some time before, when she'd come down the steps, she'd been surprised to see the sumptuous feast spread along the tables. If Rolfe had thought to be prudent with their stores because he feared a possible siege from her father, he showed no sign of any such concerns tonight.

Maybe he wanted to lift the castle's inhabitants from their winter mopes or perhaps he'd learned that Henry had garnered a victory over Stephen, hence the need for a celebration. Whatever the reason, the mood inside the hall was exceptionally festive. Weary of her own depressed state, Catherine had decided to join in the fun, thereby elevating her spirits.

"As usual, you worry too much, Eloise. I doubt I'll make a fool of myself. Especially when I intend to do naught but sit here."

"We shall see, milady."

Catherine chose to ignore the warning and summoned the server to again fill her cup. Twice more she did the same.

Somewhere along the way she heard the thrumming tones of a lute coupled with the melodic whistle of a flute. Several in the crowd rose from their places and came together in the center of the hall. There they twirled merrily in a carol.

As Catherine watched the dance of the common folk, its participants circling around and around, she was tempted to join in. She resisted the urge, aware that Eloise would not approve. Instead she tapped her feet against the floor, imitating the steps beneath the table. Likewise, she clapped her hands in time to the beat. Though she was not among the dancers, she enjoyed herself just the same.

Well into her fourth cup of wine, she found herself staring at her abductor. He sat across the way, his head close to Garrick's.

At first she wondered at their discussion; then, with no evidence whatsoever, she quickly concluded he conspired against her father. No doubt he planned his assault for when her sire rode upon Cartbridge.

The scurrilous rogue, she berated silently, her gaze narrowing on Rolfe. Had she a knife, she'd slit his throat and be done with him, once and for all.

He'd obviously anticipated such a move, for she had no

such instrument. Even at mealtime, she was forced to eat solely with her fingers, as was Eloise. He was too shrewd by far. But one day he'd have his comeuppance. She'd see that he did.

Catherine took another swallow from her cup, and her gaze resettled on Rolfe's lips. Supple yet masterful, she mused, becoming mesmerized by their movement. Heat streaked through her body as she remembered his kiss. She was on fire, she thought, her face feeling as though it were ablaze.

Certain it was the wine and not the man that had caused the sudden rush, Catherine felt more at ease. Yet as she continued to stare at him, she couldn't explain the tiny flame flickering low in her stomach. Nor could she fathom its source.

Her head began to spin in the oddest fashion, and Catherine giggled. The wine, she concluded again, noting that the music had stopped. Wanting to hear more, she peered over her shoulder, whereupon she spied her guard.

He leaned against the wall, his expression one of boredom. His duty apparently kept him from participating in the revelry. It was all Rolfe's fault, she decided, and was immediately impelled to remedy the situation.

Turning around on the bench, she crooked her finger at the young knight, beckoning him to come forward. "You look to be most unhappy, Sir Knight," she said once he'd approached her. "Mayhap some wine will cheer you up. Shall I summon the server and have her pour you a cup?"

"My name is Paxton, milady," he stated. "I thank you for your kind offer, but my obligations prevent me from partaking of any wine—at least for the moment."

Catherine frowned. "All because of me you are made to miss the fun. How very unfair." An idea struck, and she smiled. "Would your duty also prevent you from joining with me in conversation?" Uncertainty flashed in his eyes. "Your orders were to watch me, correct?"

"Aye."

"What better way to do so than as we talk?"

"What you say sounds logical, milady."

At the knight's words, Eloise reacted. "You are far too brazen," she hissed in Catherine's ear.

"Hush. All we will do is talk." She looked back at her guard. "'Tis very logical," she said. A slow smile crossed his face, exposing strong white teeth and deep dimples on each of his cheeks. Coupling that with his black hair and deep blue eyes, Catherine realized he was far more handsome than she'd originally thought. "Come, sit beside me, and we shall become better acquainted."

Without hesitation, Sir Paxton did as requested.

"Young Paxton appears to be taking his duty more seriously than intended," Garrick stated.

"Aye," Rolfe agreed.

He stared at the fledgling knight who was part of the castle's detachment, had been doing so for quite some time. Catherine also. She was far too happy. Unbelievably, with all the voices humming around him, Rolfe could hear her laughter rising merrily from across the way. Paxton's deep chuckle would follow. Admittedly, Rolfe was a bit more than just annoyed. In fact, he was becoming downright angry.

"'Tis not hard to tell that our young associate has received his spurs in the past year or that he has taken to heart the minstrels' songs lauding the merits of chivalry," Rolfe said. "Experience will soon teach him that all is not what it seems, especially when it has to do with a woman." He paused, and his eyes narrowed as he considered the young man more fully. "He resembles a lovesick hound, don't you think?"

Garrick chuckled. "'Tis certain she holds him spellbound. He is as equally entranced with her words as he is with her smiles."

"She trifles with him for a reason. Probably hopes to besot him, then use him as a means for another escape."

"I will find someone who is less impressionable to relieve young Paxton from his post."

Rolfe caught Garrick's arm just as the man started to leave his chair. "No. That won't be necessary," he announced, rising himself. "Paxton's one failing is that he is naive. For that, I do not want to embarrass him. After this night, assign him to a different post and make certain he stays as far from Catherine as possible. Besides, 'tis time she retired. She has been too long sipping from her cup."

"Since you intend to put an end to her pleasure, she'll not be of a mind to treat you with favor. The sling is off. Your shoulder is almost healed, so take care and protect it."

Rolfe smiled. "Your concern is appreciated, Garrick. However, I believe I will be able to control her."

Moving away from the table, Rolfe made his way to where Catherine sat. Once again her laughter overrode the room's din. Inexplicably, his mood darkened. When he reached her, he took hold of her arm. She gasped as he plucked her from the bench.

Paxton was instantly on his feet. "Your action, sir, is most offensive. Unhand the Lady Catherine at once."

Rolfe eyed the man, who was about his own height. "'Twould do you well, Sir Paxton, to take yourself to your quarters. The Lady Catherine is about to find her own."

The young knight remained firm in his stance, and Rolfe hoped he'd not be called upon to use his sword. Then Catherine giggled; her hand met his chest.

"Will I be sleeping alone tonight?" she asked. "Or will you be joining me?"

With those words, young Paxton's hardened expression quickly fell. Though Rolfe knew exactly what Catherine had meant, it was obvious Paxton had taken her words the wrong way.

"Sir Rolfe. Lady Catherine," he said with a bow. "I bid you good night." He then strode to the far side of the room.

"Did I say something to upset him?" Catherine asked, swaying slightly.

Rolfe heeded her fully. She was much farther into her cups than he'd thought. "Sir Paxton was given an order, and as an exemplary knight, he obeyed." He looked at Eloise. "She's going to her chamber," he informed her.

The woman squared her shoulders, then said stiffly, "'Twould have done her better had you taken her there some time ago."

"I fear I wasn't as attentive as I should have been," he replied.

"Agreed," Catherine announced.

At her tone, Rolfe stared down at her. She accused him with her eyes. Slowly, he began to understand. She was angry because he'd been ignoring her—not just tonight, but for the past three weeks. "Say good night to your nurse, Catherine."

"Good night, Eloise."

He then guided her to the stairs. Along the way, the lute was again strummed melodiously. He felt Catherine slow her pace.

"Might we dance?" she asked, pulling at his hand.

"Not tonight," he said, positive that with one spin she'd quickly meet the floor.

As he led her up the steps, he heard her humming. The soft sounds continued down the corridor. Once at the door of their chamber, he steered her inside. Humming louder, she immediately whirled from his grasp, throwing her arms wide. He winced as her hand struck his shoulder.

"Oh my!" she cried, obviously mindful of what she'd done. She was promptly standing before him. "I didn't mean to hurt you."

As her light kisses fell upon his shoulder, Rolfe was instantly bemused. He caught her chin and tilted her face upward. "Catherine." She stared at his lips. "Are you aware of what you're doing?"

"I'm making it better for you," she said, then smiled.

"It would be more advantageous for the both of us if you simply don't go spinning about."

"Why?" she asked, still staring at his mouth.

He smiled down at her. "For one, you won't be hitting my shoulder again. For another, you'll probably remain on your feet."

"You have the nicest lips," she said, her finger having risen to trace their contours.

Her words and actions had more than surprised him; he stood rigidly still.

"Eloise says your kisses would be those of a man," she whispered, her finger playing more boldly. "She says Miles doesn't know how to kiss a woman. That his lips are as limp as a wilted leaf thirsting for water."

Rolfe fought to keep a straight face, but he could not stop the laughter from sounding in his voice when he said, "That's what Eloise said, hmm?"

Her finger stopped its trifling. "Aye—but don't tell her I told you."

She touched his bottom lip, and Rolfe drew breath deeply. "And does he?" he asked, the air slowly passing from his lungs.

"Does he what?"

"Have lips as limp as a wilted leaf?"

"They look fine to me," she said. "But they *are* rather thin, not full like yours."

He understood he should set her away from him. He would do so, save he was far too tempted to learn something. Wine, he knew, not only had the ability to loosen the tongue, such as it had with Catherine, but it also possessed a magical elixir. Inhibitions fled, and one became exceptionally honest. What would she say if he asked? he wondered, then launched ahead.

"Whether his lips are thin or full, the question remains: Does he know how to kiss you?"

She frowned. "I suppose. But then he is the only man I've ever kissed—except for my father. And that was always on the cheek."

"Have you forgotten, Catherine? I kissed you once."

"You were angry," she said. "'Twas not at all the way Eloise said it would be."

Her finger yet rested at his bottom lip. Daringly, he drew its tip into his mouth and sucked gently, then allowed his tongue to swirl around it. She trembled with the action. Smiling to himself, he slowly released her finger.

"Would you have interest in knowing how I kiss when I'm not angry?"

Dazed, she stared up at him. "I, uh—I think so."

She sounded very uncertain. Rolfe knew he was being less than chivalrous, but he couldn't resist. "Close your eyes," he said, his left arm circling her waist. He pulled her closer. "When it is over, you can decide who is better with his lips."

As he spoke, he lowered his head; her hand had drifted to his chest. "Close your eyes, Catherine, and savor the experience."

Her eyelids fluttered shut over irises that were now a luminous green. Her lips parted, and he realized she was eagerly willing. He hesitated, knowing he'd goaded her. At first it had all been a game. But no longer. She was far too enticing to let the moment pass, especially when it might never come again. He shouldn't. On the other hand . . .

Moist and inviting, her lips beckoned to him. Damn her sensibilities! She was the one who'd been baiting him. His misgivings scattered, and his mouth covered hers.

Rolfe tempered his urgency for fear he might frighten her. He moved his lips in a slow, easy fashion and waited for the right moment to intensify the kiss. Soon she responded to his urgings, and her lips stirred impatiently against his. It was time, he decided, and his tongue broke the barrier of her lips.

At the intrusion, she withdrew slightly, and he knew Miles had never kissed her thus. If the bastard ever hoped to take her, he had better well know how to prepare her, he thought. But he imagined Miles cared only about his own pleasure. Catherine would forever be left wanting.

Determined to let her know what she'd be missing were she to wed Miles, Rolfe teased her with his tongue until she relaxed against him. She opened to him. Deeper and deeper he probed. She trembled, moaning softly. He relished the sound, a dividend for his efforts.

Thrusting and withdrawing, he savored the sweetness of her mouth. His loins burned with desire. He felt himself harden as never before. He restrained his lust, reminding himself this was simply a kiss; the act would go no further. Then her tongue sliced between his lips, to play with his own, and he nearly came undone.

He shook from the force of her invasion. She tempted and tantalized him, not realizing what could happen. He wanted desperately to lift her in his arms, carry her to the bed, lay her in its center, throw her skirts up, and bury himself inside her until they were fully joined.

The illusion quickened, and he saw himself thrusting into

145

her, felt the dewy caresses that enticed him deeper, watched as ecstasy streamed across her face, then was rewarded with the same sort of rapture as he quickly sought his own release. The vision was so strong that his body nearly fulfilled the last of his fantasy.

Fighting for control, Rolfe abruptly set Catherine from him. He breathed deeply, seeking to clear his head and to tame his lust. After a moment, he realized she was smiling up at him.

"'Twas far better than the first kiss," she said.

By her giddy expression, Rolfe wondered if she'd been affected at all. The wine. No doubt her senses were dulled. "'Tis time you take yourself to bed, Catherine."

"Don't you want the answer?"

He was yet dazed. "Answer?"

"Who is better with his lips, remember?"

Why had he been so bold, so presumptuous? What had made him think he could kiss her, then simply walk away? She was the sort of woman who could work her way into a man's heart, thereby trapping him. Marriage was not in his plans. He was a warrior, a wanderer, always eager for the next battle. Although Catherine was very tempting, he refused to be swayed from his purpose.

"I'm certain it is Miles," he responded, turning her toward the bed. "Now it is time you take your rest."

"How do you know I chose Miles?" she asked, wheeling from his grasp. "I've not given my answer yet."

When she'd twirled around, he'd noticed her eyes had trouble adjusting. He didn't know how much longer she could stay on her feet. "'Tis likely you'd choose your betrothed," he said, trying to herd her to the bed. He relaxed some when she flopped onto the mattress, only to hear her giggle.

"I guess I'm expected to remain loyal to Miles, so I'll simply say this: Eloise was right."

Rolfe watched her weave on the bed, then chuckled. "And Eloise was right when she said I should have brought you up here some time ago," he said.

She stared up at him. "Will you be spending the night with me?"

The question, though innocent, again incited his fantasies. Were he of a mind, he could easily take advantage of her. But the kiss was enough. "No, I'll not be staying here."

"Then may I sleep in your bed? The floor gets so cold sometimes."

He hadn't realized all those nights he'd been away that she was taking to her pallet. "Henceforth, the bed is yours, Catherine."

Her face beamed with pleasure. "Thank you," she said. Then, kicking her slippers from her feet, she snuggled under the covers, fully clothed. Within a few moments, she was asleep.

Rolfe looked down at her for the longest while. He noted how her long lashes feathered lightly against the soft tissue beneath her eyes, how her cheeks were flush from the drink. As he listened to the soft breaths whispering between her parted lips, he thought she resembled a small child. But he knew she wasn't. And therein lay the problem.

Lifting his hand, he lightly brushed his knuckles against her cheek. "Good night, Catherine. Sleep well." Then he strode from the room.

Out in the corridor, the door locked behind him, he stared at the panel, wondering at his own temerity. Soon he turned on his heel and headed for the stairs. Tonight, she was in a blissful state created by the wine. Tomorrow, she'd be sober. Considering what had transpired between them, he contemplated her reaction.

The Lady Catherine, he decided, would be none too pleased.

CHAPTER

11

SHE HAD BEEN WARNED. NEVERTHELESS, SHE'D CHOSEN NOT TO listen. Now Catherine suffered with the knowledge that she'd made a complete fool of herself. What was worse, Rolfe knew it too.

From the open window in her chamber, she watched as he stood in the yard, his boots caked with mud and snow. He was working with the same stallion that had tossed him to the wolves. After running afield for several weeks, the beast had returned to Cartbridge. Rolfe apparently believed the horse showed promise. Or maybe it had simply become a matter of pride. Either way, he attempted to befriend the animal.

Holding the tether, he talked to the stallion, soothing it with his soft utterances. As Catherine stared at his mouth, mindful of its fluid movement, she thought of that night a week past, remembering how he'd used the same maneuver with her. The wine had made her susceptible, his words enticing her with ease. And his lips . . .

The tantalizing memory of his kiss swept through her. She was instantly aflame. Dear Lord! she thought on a groan. Would she ever stop reliving that moment? With the slightest recollection, the same delicious shivers quaked around inside her, leaving her breathless and shaken.

This had to stop. Instead of hiding in her room, as she'd done all week from embarrassment, she needed to face him. If she explained that she'd not been herself, that she hadn't meant to trifle with him, that she certainly didn't mean to elicit his advances, maybe then she could put the situation to rest, his kiss forgotten.

Certain she had the answer, she turned from the window and marched to a low chest. Opening it, she pulled one of Rolfe's woolen mantles from within. Donning the thing, she continued on to the door and set to pounding on the wood.

After a short while, she heard the key turning in the lock. When the panel swung inward, she saw Garrick. "I want to see him," she told the frowning man.

"'Tis not a good idea," he said, obviously understanding whom she meant. "His mood is not the best today."

"Nonetheless, I must speak to him."

Garrick shrugged, then motioned her from the room.

As Catherine followed him along the corridor, she wondered if she should heed Garrick's warning. Had she attended Eloise's cautioning words about the wine, she'd not presently be going to Rolfe.

When they exited the keep, she saw that Rolfe was no longer in the yard. The stallion was missing too. Thinking he may have taken the beast into the stables, she mentioned such to Garrick.

"Is it so important that it cannot wait?" he asked.

"I must see him—now."

After descending the steps, they started across the bailey. With his hand on her arm, Garrick assisted her as she hopped the puddles and skimmed through the slush. Finally they entered the stables.

Once her eyes had adjusted, Catherine saw Rolfe at the far end. He held the tether in his right hand while his left was at the stallion's muzzle. She assumed he was feeding the animal some grain.

"The girl says she needs to talk to you."

Garrick's voice boomed through the quiet environment;

startled, the stallion jerked its head, pulling on the rope tether. Simultaneously a curse erupted from Rolfe. Catherine questioned whether she should stay.

Rolfe lashed the rope to a post. Rubbing his right shoulder, he turned and moved toward her. "You should not have come out here," he said. "But since you did, what do you want?"

"I'd like to speak to you if I may—alone."

His silvery gaze raked over her, then he looked at Garrick. "Leave us." The man nodded, then strode from the stables. "What is it you have to say?"

On examination, Catherine decided that Garrick was right: He wasn't in a very agreeable mood. Even so, if she wanted any peace, she knew what she had to do. Taking a deep breath, she plunged ahead. "I wish to apologize to you for what happened last week. As you know, I'd had too much wine. I hadn't meant for—well, uh . . ." This was harder than she'd thought.

"To provoke me into kissing you?"

Provoke? As she recalled, he was the one who'd made the suggestion. But then the night in question was a bit hazy. Perhaps she had proposed they kiss. Uncertain who'd said what, she decided to take the blame. "Yes, that's what I'm trying to say. I hadn't meant to provoke you into kissing me. I was confused. Certainly I was not myself. Had I been, the event would never have occurred. I feel you should know I do not seek your advances, and I hope, in the future, you will remember such."

He looked her up and down as though she were a loathsome thing. "You came all the way out here just to tell me that?"

Catherine blinked. His mood was darkening. "I thought it necessary to let you know where we stand."

"And where do we stand, Catherine?"

She frowned. "What do you mean?"

"'Twould seem to me that if you really didn't want for me to approach you, you'd stay as far from me as possible. Instead you make a point of leaving the warmth of the keep to tromp across the yard through the mud and snow, asking to speak to me alone—*alone,* Catherine—all to simply tell me that you don't want me anywhere near you. Curious, I'd say. For some reason, I have a feeling my kiss affected you in such a way that you can't get it from your mind, and your actions make me wonder if you aren't actually hoping it will happen again. Am I correct? Is that why you came out here?"

Catherine could only stare at him. Was he right? Did she want it to happen again? *No!* That's not why she'd come here at all. "If you believe what you say is true, then you deceive yourself, for 'tis naught but a fanciful notion."

"And I suppose next you'll be telling me Eloise was wrong."

"Eloise? What has she to do with this?"

His lips broke into a dark grin. "Wilted lips, remember? Or how about Rolfe de Mont St. Michel kissing like a man?"

Catherine felt her cheeks flame with embarrassment. Had she really told him all that? The wine had affected her more than she'd thought. What else had she said—done!—that she didn't remember? She was instantly rewarded with an answer.

"I suppose, too, that you don't remember asking if I would stay the night with you?"

She gaped at him. Surely not! Not wanting to believe she'd do such a thing, she went on the defensive. "I may have been drunk, sir, but I was not *that* drunk. Never would I have invited you into my bed. The truth be known, you repulse me."

"Do I?"

He took a step toward her; Catherine backed up one.

"From the way you responded to my kiss, I doubt that's true."

She remembered the moment, and those delicious shivers quaked through her anew. "Believe it," she fibbed, and she moved another step back.

He advanced one pace. "You lie, Catherine. I can see it on your face and in your eyes. You remember how my lips felt on yours, and you're eager to experience the same again."

Why had she come out here? Her gaze remained on his

mouth as she stumbled back two steps; he progressed the same. "Stay away from me," she ordered.

"That's not what you want, and you know it."

As he'd spoken, she was again watching his mouth. Sensation spun through her as she remembered fully its mastery. "'Tis what I want," she insisted, stumbling away two more steps. She gasped when her back met solid wood. My God! She'd missed the door. "Stay away!" she fairly cried. As she tried to break for the opening, his left hand hit the wall near her shoulder.

"Too late, Catherine. You're trapped."

Wide-eyed, she stared up at him. Why was he doing this? "Let me go . . . please."

He pressed himself closer. "Not until I've answered your question."

"What question?"

"You've been staring at my lips again, which tells me you want to know if my kiss will feel the same now that your senses are no longer dulled by wine."

"You're mad!" she told him.

"Am I? Or do you say that simply because you're afraid to admit I'm right?"

With each word, he'd edged closer until their bodies touched; Catherine thought she might swoon. "Why do you do this?" she asked on a whimper, at last expressing her thought.

"Because, as you say, I'm mad."

If he were mad, then she must be doubly so, for again she found herself staring at his lips. She squeezed her eyes shut. "Loose me," she demanded. She rolled her head against the wall and tried to break free.

The effort was for naught, for he was far too strong. Her eyes came wide when he checked the toss of her head. He held her still, his right hand framing her face.

"If I do that, you'll always be left to wonder," he said, his warm breath fanning just above her lips. "But wonder no more, Catherine. 'Tis time you learn the truth."

She closed her eyes and opened her mouth, thinking to scream. A decided mistake. In a trice, his lips were on hers.

Hot and wet, they foraged with determination, sending fiery prickles down her spine. His tongue sliced past her teeth, probing deeply, and flames burst to life in the depths of her stomach. She throbbed between her thighs. Unbelievably, she was warm and moist. Mother of God! What was happening to her?

His kiss became more ardent, his tongue thrusting and withdrawing, and Catherine heard herself moan. She was on fire from the top of her head to the tips of her toes. Insanity, she thought, as she began to respond. In that instant, his lips left hers.

Cold air rushed over her. Her eyes sprang wide. She saw him standing several feet away.

"Are you yet wondering, Catherine?"

His tone was mocking, his smile complacent. Like lightning slicing into a giant oak, the realization struck: He'd baited her, then used her. For what purpose, she didn't know.

Seek to tempt me again, and you'll know the consequences of doing so.

His words, uttered while in the tub, streaked through her mind.

"No answer?" he questioned.

Feeling utterly mortified, she ran from the stables, across the yard, and up the steps to the keep. On entering the great hall, she came face-to-face with Eloise.

"Why is your mouth all red?" the woman asked, frowning at her.

Catherine's fingers quickly covered her lips. Unbidden, the memory of what had just transpired streaked through her with a force that left her gasping for air. "'Tis cold out," she muttered, then she rushed toward the other set of stairs.

Climbing them, she wondered at her own purpose in seeking him out. Was her intention what he'd said? Did she desire his kiss anew? Whatever the reason, she felt certain she was now worse off than she had ever been before.

It had to be done, Rolfe thought.

Absently playing with a piece of straw, he crouched down,

his back pressed to the same wall where he'd pinned Catherine. The shattered look on her face just before she'd run from the stables was forever etched in his mind.

Blessed Virgin, why had she come out here? If she'd just stayed in her room, he wouldn't have had to embarrass her as he did.

From the moment he'd approached her from the back of the stables, he'd sensed something was amiss. When he'd clearly seen her face, he knew what it was.

True, she'd offered some speech about wanting to apologize, about not desiring his advances. But beneath that confident facade, she was filled with uncertainty. The first time she looked at his lips, he knew exactly what she wanted. Though she might not have been fully aware of it, he had no doubts. The trouble was that he wanted the same himself. Maybe more than she. That's why he'd mistreated her as he had.

This past week had been a living hell for him. By day, she was constantly in his thoughts. By night, she invaded his dreams. What transpired in his vapory visions was magical. More than once, he'd awakened in a sweat, his body aching for release. Yet he knew that to go beyond his fantasies would be nothing less than madness. And that's why he'd used her as he had. She'd thought of him as a spurious spawn of Satan once, and he wanted her to continue doing so. It was the only way he knew to assure they remained apart.

Springing from his haunches, Rolfe rubbed his shoulder. Though not fully healed, it was far better than it had been. Yet it would be a while before he could use his sword, and that to him was another worry.

Then there were the nightmares.

He'd thought they'd been put to rest over a year before. Apparently all this talk about Miles had again stirred them to life. God's wounds! He wished he'd killed the bastard years ago. The deed done, none of this would be happening now.

Between his lustful dreams about Catherine and his nightly terrors of Antalya, his mood was suffering. This eve, after his promised game of chess with Brother Bernard, he intended to retire early.

As Rolfe left the stables, heading toward the keep, he prayed that *this* night he'd get a decent round of sleep.

She saw it lurking in the shadows.

And it wasn't alone.

In the dim candlelight, Catherine watched the shaded area along the floor near the wall.

There.

She wasn't imagining things.

There.

She saw its companion.

Her heart leaped to her throat when she heard the squeal; one of the pair suddenly charged toward her.

Bounding onto the chair, Catherine screamed with all her might.

Rolfe bolted straight up from his pallet.

Was he dreaming?

Beside him, Garrick jumped to his feet.

The two men looked at one another as the shrill cry sounded louder.

"'Tis Catherine!" Rolfe said. Grabbing up his sword, he raced from the common quarters and down the torchlit corridor to her chamber, Garrick beside him all the way. Once there, he viewed the lock and hissed a curse. "The key."

"We have our shoulders," Garrick said.

"'Tis easy for you to say."

"Here!" Aubrey cried as he waved the key in the air while he ran toward them. Brother Bernard ran beside him.

"What is the trouble?" the monk called.

Above all the commotion outside, Rolfe could hear her screams on the inside. "Catherine," he yelled through the door. "What's wrong?" She responded with another scream.

His squire was now at his side. The key was inserted into the hole, the lock tripped, and Rolfe opened the door, whereupon he bounded into the room, his sword ready.

There on the chair, her skirts raised, stood Catherine, yelling at the top of her lungs.

"Christ, woman!" he fairly exploded. "'Tis only a rat."

With one swing of his blade, he felled the furry creature.

"Come down, Catherine," he said, offering her his hand. "The thing is dead."

"There's another one. I saw it. Oh please, kill it too!"

Her words were a piteous plea, and on closer inspection, Rolfe saw the sheer terror in her eyes. She was deathly afraid of the creatures, he decided. Somehow he had to convince her the things wouldn't hurt her.

"Catherine—"

"Oh, milady! Do not move."

Rolfe turned to see Eloise standing in the doorway. Her gaze was centered on the dead rat.

"There is another one, Eloise. Please make him kill it."

"I will, milady. I will."

Rolfe noted the soothing tone of Eloise's voice. Catherine's fears, he surmised, were more grievous than he'd thought.

"Find the thing and slay it," her nurse whispered as she drew alongside him. "Or she'll be struck by a madness from which she'll never recover."

"Stay there, Catherine," he said, motioning for Garrick, the monk, and Aubrey to join him, "and we'll look for the thing."

"Kill it too?" she asked.

"Aye, and kill it too."

Each man took a different corner, whereupon they began a thorough search around the furnishings. The shadows obscured Rolfe's vision. Twice he poked his blade at something he thought could be the rat. Twice he went unrewarded.

Behind him, Garrick was apparently doing the same, for Rolfe heard the ping or the thud of the man's sword against stone or wood. Then Aubrey cried, "'Tis here!"

Rolfe rushed to the spot. With a stabbing thrust aimed behind the low chest, he skewered the thing. Bringing up his blade, he stared at one of his boots.

Aubrey turned red. "I guess I forgot to put it with the other one."

"Aye," Rolfe said, pulling the ruined boot from his sword. They began their search anew.

A moment later, Rolfe turned when he heard Garrick growl, "Come here, you little bastard, so I can lop off your head."

"Is it the rat?" he asked.

Garrick stood by another chest, his sword poised. Brother Bernard was at his shoulder. "Aye. For certain," the monk whispered, hopping back several steps. Just as Garrick was about to strike, the rat scurried from its hiding place. The knight's blade hit the wall as he tried to fell it.

"It goes for the door!" Eloise cried.

At once, Rolfe, Garrick, the monk, and Aubrey were after the small gray creature. The rat scuttled into the hall just as all four men hit the door. Squeezing through the opening practically shoulder to shoulder, they stumbled out into the corridor. The rat was nowhere to be seen.

Rolfe shook his head. "Imagine, will you? This valiant effort came from two of Henry's best knights."

Garrick arched a grizzled eyebrow. "Had he knowledge of this right now, I'm of a mind he'd be glad we are here and not with him."

"Aye. 'Twould be comical, save for Catherine's fear. Her reaction was more than simply a woman's squeamishness. Let's see to her," Rolfe said.

"Should we say we killed it?"

"No. She may want proof, and we cannot provide it. I think the truth is better."

Rolfe was the first to enter.

"Is it dead?" she asked from her position above him.

"I'm sorry, but it got away."

"Dear God. 'Twill be back. I know it."

"I doubt it will, Catherine," he said. "By all our fumbling around, I think we scared it nearly to death." He offered her his hand. "Come down now. 'Tis gone. I promise."

He watched as Catherine looked away from him to her nurse. She appeared to question Eloise with her eyes.

"He's right, child," the woman said. "The thing is gone and cannot hurt you."

She hesitantly slipped her hand into his, and he helped her from the chair.

"I'll not stay in here alone," she said. "It might come back."

She truly *was* frightened by the creatures, Rolfe decided. He wondered what had precipitated her fear. "Then go with Eloise to the women's quarters. You may sleep there."

Her eyes widened. "On the floor?" She shook her head. "No, I cannot."

"I will stay here with you," Eloise offered.

Rolfe carefully studied Catherine. She looked somewhat relieved, but not fully convinced that Eloise would protect her. "Even better," he announced, "I will stay with you. Should the thing reappear—which I doubt—my sword will be ready." She still seemed unconvinced. "I slew the first one, didn't I?"

She looked at the rat on the floor several yards from her, then nodded.

"I am certain," he said, "I can slay the second as well —that's if it returns. I promise, Catherine. I'll not let it harm you."

"You'll not leave me?"

"No. I'll stay beside you the night through." Her fears subsided some. Then he noticed she was not yet ready for bed. "You are up quite late."

"I was thinking," she said.

Their meeting in the stables, he surmised. "I'll be just outside while Eloise helps you undress."

Her gaze whipped toward the bed. "Did you check under there?"

"Aubrey, look under the bed."

His squire quickly complied. "Naught but dust, sire," he said, his head popping up over the bed's side.

"Good. Now get rid of this thing," Rolfe ordered, pointing at the dead rat.

He watched as Aubrey lifted the creature by its long tail to carry it out the door. Brother Bernard followed the young man down the corridor.

Rolfe strode to one of the chests and set his sword aside. Opening the lid, he pulled from within the same mantle that Catherine had worn that afternoon. He swung it around his bare shoulders. Her scent instantly drifted into his nostrils. Another long night, he thought, as he retrieved his weapon.

He moved to the door. "I'll be just outside," he said, then he walked into the hall.

"What do you think caused such fear in her?" Garrick asked in a low voice.

"I don't know, but I intend to find out," he answered. "Eloise will stay until after Catherine is asleep. I'll ask the woman about it then."

"If you don't need me, I shall find my pallet. 'Tis cold in these halls," he said, a great shiver running through him.

Like Rolfe, Garrick was barechested, barefoot, and in his braics, except Rolfe now had the benefit of a heavy cloak. "Retire, sir, before you catch your death. When you see Aubrey, tell him to bring my pallet down here. The Lady Catherine has removed the other from sight."

"You hope to sleep, then?" Garrick questioned.

"I shall try."

"The nightmares—any tonight?"

"Not so far. But I had not been asleep too long before this."

"Rest well," Garrick said, lightly patting Rolfe's left shoulder. "And keep your sword close to you. 'Tis possible this was all a ruse."

"Another attempt at an escape?" Rolfe asked. He saw his friend nod. "I'll keep your words in mind, but I doubt this was a ruse. The fear in her eyes was genuine. I've seen such a look only in battle, and that's just before I laid low my opponent."

"If you say it is real, I'm certain it is. Good night to you. I'll see you on the morrow."

Rolfe watched as Garrick trekked along the corridor back the way they'd come. Before long, Aubrey came hurrying toward Rolfe, dragging the pallet and covers behind him. With a wave, Rolfe cautioned him to be quiet; then, peeking into the room, he saw that Catherine was already abed.

As they entered on silent feet, Rolfe noticed how she lay

curled under the covers. Eloise was singing to her. While Aubrey spread his master's pallet, Rolfe watched Catherine and her nurse from the shadows. Soon Aubrey left; then a bit later, Eloise stilled her lullaby. The woman rose from the chair and came toward him.

"I suppose you would like to know why she reacted the way she did?" Eloise whispered.

"Aye. She was overwrought and exceptionally fearful."

"And for good reason," Eloise stated. "When she was a small child—five, I believe—she had gone deep into the cellars, down to the dungeon, thinking it was a fine new place to play. No one knew she'd gone there. Actually it was forbidden for her to do so. However, always having been a bit independent, she slipped off on us.

"'Twas dark, very dark, and she did not see the creatures lurking alongside the walls. Apparently she stumbled into a nest of them. Her screams could be heard through the entire castle. When we all realized where they were coming from, her father rushed the stairs and saved her. She was bitten many times.

"Thank God she didn't take the sickness from the bites. But from that day onward, just the sight of one sends her into a near state of madness. Never will you see her go into the cellars or the dungeons. *Never,*" Eloise pronounced.

As Catherine's nurse related the story, a chill ran the length of Rolfe's spine. Such a small child suffering from so terrible a horror, he thought, understanding fully why she was mortally afraid.

True, he suffered from his own horrors, but he was a man, capable of facing his fears. However, her fears stemmed from childhood, and when they came upon her now as a woman, she reverted to that time long ago when she was small and helpless.

Rolfe promised himself that tonight, and every night thereafter, he would protect her from whatever troubled her. This he would do until the time came for them to part.

Rolfe twisted on his pallet, locked in a macabre dream.

His sword, painted with blood, swung with an inordinate slowness. Then he heard the deliberate clang of the blade as it met another. The sound reverberated forever. Red droplets dispelled, flying endlessly through space. He felt the splatter of one, then another, and another, as they struck his face.

Why couldn't he wield the thing faster? Why were his movements so laggardly?

Robert!

Francis!

He saw them across the way, at least thirty men surrounding them. But he could not bridge the distance between them. Then the span stretched farther and farther away.

He plied his sword again, and the same pattern repeated itself.

He groaned, for he felt the pain.

An iron blade sliced into his forearm. Another lacerated his thigh. The last cut into his waist. How many men had he felled between each wound? A dozen? Fifty? Had he slain any at all? He fought onward, Robert and Francis held in his sight.

They were going down. He watched as merciless swords rose and fell, hacking and gashing. Blood saturated the ground, the air.

Noooo!

The word echoed and re-echoed in grisly horror. Desperately he tried to advance, but something held him back.

Hands were on his shoulders. Where had they come from? Then through narrowed eyes, he saw the dark-skinned, dark-eyed Turk. Sunlight flickered off the blade as a knife drove toward his chest.

Instantly, he caught his adversary's wrists. He flipped the savage on his back. Grabbing his sword, he set its point. One thrust and his blade would penetrate the heathen's heart.

It was then he heard the scream.

Blinking, he swirled out of the past and into the present to find himself astride a pair of slim hips; the tip of his sword was centered between two ripe breasts hidden beneath a film of silk. His gaze shot upward to stare into a set of wide hazel eyes. The terror within their depths reflected back at him.

"Catherine?"

A great shudder ran through his body as he tossed his

sword away. It clattered against the floor, then stilled. Twisting, he lifted himself off her, then settled on his backside, facing away from her. Drawing a cleansing breath, he raked his fingers through his hair. They came away wet, and he realized he was drenched in sweat.

He felt her soft hand on his shoulder. He squeezed his eyes closed and shook his head. "How can you touch me when I nearly killed you?"

She didn't withdraw, but placed her other hand on his adjacent shoulder as she knelt behind him.

"'Tis not your fault. You were dreaming."

A strange laugh sounded in his throat. "Dreams are sweet little fantasies of slumber. This was a nightmare, Catherine."

"About Robert and Francis?" she asked.

"Aye. 'Tis always the same." He looked at the ceiling, the pain inside him mounting. "No matter how hard I try, I can never get to them. I fight and fight my way toward where they are, but they grow farther and farther away. 'Tis never-ending. And then I see them fall. I'm too late, just the same as before."

"Do you blame yourself for their deaths?" she asked as though maybe she shouldn't.

"No. Miles is to blame."

She was silent for a moment, then said, "If you really believe that is so, why do you keep reliving this scene you've described night after night? Could it be from guilt?"

He whipped his head around and looked at her. "I suppose that's possible. I should have been with them. Perhaps then things would have ended differently."

"And perhaps you also would have died."

"'Twould have been easier if I had, for I'd not presently have to carry the memory of their deaths with me, both day and night."

"But you lived, Rolfe. You tried with all your might to help them. You were even wounded—several times—while attempting to save them. You did all you could. Maybe if you accepted such, your nightmares will stop."

"I don't know. It may sound strange, but I ask myself:

What if I had stayed with them, instead of riding ahead? What if I had been more vigilant? What if we'd taken a different route? Would they still be alive? Over the years, I've *what-iffed* myself nearly into a state of madness."

She shifted from behind him. Sitting hip to hip, they now faced each other. He watched as she smiled gently.

"That affliction isn't meant solely for you," she announced. "I do the same myself."

Her smile was contagious, and he offered one in return. "When?"

"Most recently I've asked myself: What if I hadn't gone to the chapel for confession, would I now be married?"

That particular *what-if* didn't set well with Rolfe. Before he thought it through, he said, "'Tis trivial. How about: What if you hadn't gone to the cellars when told not to . . ." The rest died on his lips as he watched her expression change. "I'm sorry, Catherine. I didn't mean to remind you of your fears."

"No. You're right. That is the one question which continually plagues me. I suppose it is much like your questions about Robert and Francis. The thing is, neither of us can change the past. Our only hope is that someday we can face those things which terrify us and put them behind us."

Aided by the candle, its flame left burning in case Catherine had awakened in a fright, Rolfe gazed into her eyes. He was intrigued by the fact that they were now a soft gray. "You're right. We cannot change the past. Maybe, as you say, someday we will both overcome our fears. For now, though, I want you to promise me something. Should I have another nightmare, don't approach me while I'm in the throes of it. I'd never forgive myself if I harmed you. It grieves me now that I nearly did."

"'Twas not your fault."

"Promise me," he insisted.

"I promise, but only if you'll promise me that you'll not leave me alone at night. Someday I will face my own fears, but I haven't the strength to do it now. Not alone, anyway."

"You already have the strength," he said.

"Why do you say that?"

"When I was suffering with the horrors of my past, you left the safety of your bed and came to me. Likewise, you are now sitting on the floor. 'Twas just a short while ago that you said you couldn't do such a thing."

She looked to her hands. "The only reason I am here now is because you're beside me."

She seemed hesitant to admit those words. He caught her chin and forced her to meet his eyes. "For as long as we are together, I'll protect you. You'll never be alone. This I promise."

"'Tis good," she said, and smiled.

In that moment, Rolfe felt as though everything around them had suddenly moved away. The walls swept beyond infinity, the furnishings disappeared. All that remained was himself and Catherine. "You're beautiful," he whispered, his gaze roving across her upturned face. "More beautiful than any woman I've ever known."

Whether it was from nervousness or just an unconscious act, he didn't know, but her tongue quickly flicked across her lips. The deed had instantly caught his attention. He was spellbound as she did it again. Somewhere between the stables and now, he forgot his vow that they should stay apart. One small kiss, he thought, positive he could end it there. Afterward he'd send her to her bed—alone.

"'Tis time we got some sleep." Bidding her good night, he brushed his lips across hers. His plan nearly worked, until he felt the feathery touch of her tongue. Drawing back, he looked at her questioningly. Then he felt her cool hand in the center of his chest. It moved over his flesh, upward to his neck, then around to his nape, where it burrowed beneath his hair. "Catherine, 'tis risky for—"

"Kiss me again," she whispered, her hand urging him closer.

The soft plea felled Rolfe emotionally, for it was obvious she needed his reassurances as much as he needed hers. He smoothed an errant tress from her cheek, then threaded his fingers through her rich sable hair, its texture like satin to the touch. Cupping the back of her head, he breathed the words, "Most gladly."

He drew her face within a whisper from his own; his lips separated, then covered hers in a devouring kiss. He was delighted by the way she responded to his every urging. Her lips parted farther; his tongue slipped inside, and he was instantly aware that she tasted far sweeter than any confection he'd ever consumed. Better than honey, he thought.

Her free hand skimmed his shoulder, circling around to seek its mate. Her fingers linked at the back of his head, and she prompted him even closer.

Rolfe needed no such inducement. He eagerly deepened the kiss. His tongue plunged and withdrew, imitating the motions he wished he could enact elsewhere. She moaned, the sound trembling in her throat.

Blessed madness, he thought, wondering why he was doing this. Hadn't he pledged to stay far away from her, fearing something like this might happen? Her tongue darted into his mouth, teasing playfully. In this case, he decided on a groan, promises were meant to be broken.

Their positions were awkward to him, probably because he couldn't be as near to her as he'd like. He pulled his mouth from hers and allowed his lips to track across her cheek to her ear. "I want to lie beside you," he said. Wrapping his arm around her waist, he lifted her and rolled her over onto his pallet. Stretched on his side, he hovered above her, one leg trapping her thighs.

As he looked down on her, he marveled how her eyes were now a smoky green and, more important, glazed with desire. Her mouth was moist, swollen from his kiss. The way it lay invitingly parted, waiting again for their lips to meet, he was tempted to see if it was as sleek to the touch as it appeared.

His hand came away from her waist, and his thumb traced along her bottom lip. His breath hissed between his teeth when she drew it into her mouth. She sucked lightly, her tongue teasing its tip.

After a moment of enjoying her game, he eased his thumb from between her lips. "What made you do that?" he asked, his thumb playing beside her mouth.

"'Twas what you did to my finger the night we kissed," she replied.

"Aye. I remember," he said, his gaze now on her throat and its tiny pulse.

Eager to feel it, he pulled his thumb to her jaw, then down her throat to the fascinating vibration. It leaped to life when he touched it, and he smiled. "'Tis active," he said.

She frowned at him. "What are you doing?"

"I'm exploring."

His gaze tracked lower, stopping at her breasts. Beneath the thin silk, their rhythmic rise and fall entranced him. He wanted the pleasure of holding one in his hand. Boldly he sought the intriguing mound.

At first his fingers glided easily across the slick material, then oddly they began to drag. It was the silk, he thought, as remembered segments of the road to Antalya flashed in his mind, particularly those containing Miles d'Avranches.

Capturing her breast, he caressed it skillfully. The nipple, to his delight, budded against his palm nearly on contact. Yet all he could feel was the silk.

What fair justice it would be if he took her, he thought, his jaw tightening. He could see the act now. Rending the chemise from her, he'd place it fully under her hips. In one thrust, her virgin blood would stain Miles's gift. In a half dozen more, he'd leave his own mark mixed with hers.

Unknowingly he curled his fingers, his hand compressed, the silk tore, and Catherine gasped.

At the sound, Rolfe snapped from his trance. He beheld her startled expression, then looked to his hand. Through the jagged splits in the silk, four red welts showed on her flesh. He'd bruised her.

Cursing, he rolled to his feet, then strode to the window. Jesus, Mary, and Joseph! Why the hell had he done that?

He heard light footfalls coming up behind him, then felt Catherine's small hand on his back.

"Are you all right?" she asked.

The words shot to his gut. "'Tis the question I should be asking you." He stiffened when he felt her cheek press against his spine. "You're tempting fate, Catherine. Take yourself to bed."

"But—"

"Do as I say!" he fairly exploded. With that, she ran from

him. Then he heard the rustle of covers. "And drop the curtains too."

They wooshed from their anchors. The instant they'd settled, Rolfe tore open the shutters and let the cold night air rush over him.

Mother of God! What was happening to him?

CHAPTER

12

THE INCIDENT HUNG OVER THEM LIKE THE SWORD OF DAMOCLES.

As Catherine sat cross-legged in the middle of her bed, covers tucked around her, she carefully watched Rolfe, vitally aware of the danger. Something was happening to them, something neither of them wanted to admit. That certain something was . . .

Desire.

Three weeks had elapsed since their separate fears had erupted into a mutually gratifying kiss, three weeks since he'd ultimately yet unintentionally bruised her. Nothing was ever said after that night. It was as though the event had never occurred. Even so, the air around them remained charged. He felt the force the same as she. One word, one gesture, and the fine hair that held their passions in check would snap.

What then?

A stupid question. She knew exactly how it would end. The concept alone stirred her blood. Because it did, she knew she dared not disturb the fragile tenor of their relationship. Presently they were guardedly polite, a distinct wall existing between them. But if that barrier ever came crashing down, the consequences would be irreversible. Especially for her.

Blessed misery! Why did he always have to be so near? Maybe if he were elsewhere, she'd not constantly find herself in such a dither.

Catherine knew the reason he kept close. By her own request, he'd vowed his protection. Perhaps if she released him from his promise, he'd again seek the common quarters, and they could both find some peace.

"Why are you still awake?"

His question snapped Catherine from her thoughts.

He sat at the table, dressed in naught but his braies. A candle burned near his hand, its flickering flame illuminating him. With his tawny hair brushing his broad shoulders, his head slanted regally, he resembled a lion, golden and powerful.

Until a moment before, he'd been poring over a hastily drawn map of England, attempting to trace Henry's movements. A messenger had arrived that day. Malmesbury, it was learned, had fallen, giving the duke his first victory. Henry was currently in Bristol, but he soon planned to move to Gloucester, where he would hold his Easter court—or so Rolfe had told her.

By his prior study of the map, Catherine wondered if he wished he were presently with the duke. If he had no such impulse, she certainly had it for him. The farther he was from her, the better it would be for them both.

How to broach the subject was rather tricky. She didn't wish to offend him. She certainly didn't want to anger him. Yelling *"Get out!"* seemed a bit too harsh. If she were too subtle, though, he might miss her meaning altogether. What to do? she questioned silently.

"Catherine. Perchance are you sitting there asleep?"

"No. Just thinking."

"A risky procedure," he declared.

She frowned. "Why do you say that?"

"Because, milady, when you set yourself to contemplating too deeply, you usually manage to elicit nothing but trouble."

"And how are you able to draw such a conclusion?

"Experience. With you, it has taught me well."

His mood was not the best tonight. He looked tired, tense. Maybe she should forget about asking him to move to the common quarters—for now anyway.

"No comment?" he asked as he folded the scrap of linen on which he'd drawn the map.

She recognized the material as being a remnant from when she'd sewn her new chemise. First by her own hand, then by Rolfe's, the samite silk was now ruined. Since that night, she'd been left to wonder if his actions had stemmed from his knowing the garment was a gift from Miles. Finding no other explanation, it became the only plausible answer.

"No," she said. "I have no comment. But I do have a question."

Half the room away, he kept to his chair as though it were the safest place to be. He lounged back, his gaze fixed on hers. "If you have a query, then pose it."

"When the messenger arrived today, did you learn anything about my father?"

"There was no mention of him." He shrugged. "However, I'm sure he's safe and hale."

His flippant manner nettled her. Forgetting herself, she bit back, "How could you possibly know that? The weather has not been the best. If he has been out in these horrid conditions, looking for me all this time, he may have fallen ill."

Across the distance, he viewed her intently. "Your concern for your father is well taken. Yet I'm puzzled."

The statement dangled between them. "About what?" she asked when he didn't expound.

"I've yet to hear a word of concern about your betrothed. Is it possible the bastard has fallen from your favor?"

The question was antagonistic, his tone rancorous. What should she say? That Miles hadn't really crossed her mind?

Over the weeks, she had begun to think less and less of her betrothed, while Rolfe filled her thoughts more and more. Likewise, her attraction for this blond warrior was growing, while her affection for Miles was diminishing.

170

Confusion and guilt dominated her emotions, for she couldn't explain the reversal. She didn't know why or how the turnabout had occurred. She cared about Miles, but she was beginning to care even more for Rolfe.

Wisely, Catherine remained cautious. She'd be foolish to allow him the advantage of knowing what was happening in her heart. He would undoubtedly gloat with the knowledge, rejoicing that he'd at long last triumphed over his opponent. To him, she'd be the spoils of Miles's defeat, naught more than a trophy to remind him of his victory. This she could not abide.

"If you must think on the question," Rolfe announced, "I am of the mind that your concern for your betrothed is not as strong as it once was."

"You are wrong," she snapped. "I'm concerned about all of them."

He chuckled. "But it was only your father whom you asked about."

"He is older than Miles. This horrid clime could affect him more."

"From what I saw of him, he looked quite fit for a man his age. I doubt he'd succumb to a little snow and ice."

"When did you ever see my father?" she asked.

"At the banquet, I was seated among the guests."

Catherine realized he'd been watching, waiting for the right moment to strike. Then she posed the question that had troubled her all along: "How did you know I was to make my confession in the chapel at dawn?"

"By a stroke of luck, the information was given to me."

As Catherine recalled, there were only three people, besides herself, who were privy to such knowledge: Eloise, the chaplain, and . . . "Clotilde," she whispered.

He is truly the most handsome man I've ever seen.

The young woman's words spun through Catherine's mind. She could yet see the blush of excitement on Clotilde's otherwise pale cheeks. Anger burned inside Catherine.

"You purposely used her," she accused. "How could you be so cruel?"

"'Twas a matter of necessity," he returned with a shrug. "The girl suffered no harm."

At his show of indifference, which also sounded in his voice, Catherine fairly boiled. Forgetting herself, she shot straight out of the bed and marched to the table.

"Suffered no harm?" she questioned, her hands planted at her waist. "You arrogant beast! How do you know what she suffered?

"With your silken words, you charmed her, gave her hope that a man had at last found something appealing about her. You lied to her for your own designs, used her just to get at me. I'm sure she is overcome by your deceit. Even worse, the small amount of confidence she did possess is probably now lost to her, all because of you.

"You are cruel, sir. Cruel beyond anyone's reasoning. 'Tis unforgivable what you did to her."

His jaw tightened. "I did not lie to her," he replied. "Not fully. She did intrigue me. Clotilde is shy and gentle. She is also forthright. Unlike you, there is no pretense about her."

Catherine gaped at him. "What do you mean by that?"

"I mean she doesn't disguise her feelings. She speaks what is actually in her heart. She hides nothing. Are you able to say the same for yourself?"

The question surprised her. "I've always spoken what's in my heart," she stated, wondering at his true purpose. "Besides, what is there to hide?"

"You tell me," he countered, his tone challenging.

He was searching, she thought. "You digress, sir. We were discussing how you managed to injure Clotilde's feelings."

"And I am more interested in *your* feelings," he declared. "Why the pretense, Catherine? What are you trying to hide?"

Never would she give him the satisfaction of learning the truth. In her mind's eye, she could see that fine hair stretching. Disaster was imminent. Somehow she had to persuade him to leave before it was too late. "I excuse you from your vow."

The statement came from nowhere; befittingly, he sent her a confused look. "What vow?"

"Your promise to protect me. The rats—they are nearly all gone, correct?"

"A dozen have been poisoned. Another half that amount have been caught in the traps and slain. I cannot say, however, they are *nearly* all gone. I don't know their exact number."

"'Tis good enough," she said, not knowing which she feared most. She abhorred the ugly creatures. She could still feel the things herding around her feet, clawing their way up her legs, biting her thighs and hands. But if he stayed . . . "I no longer need your protection. 'Twould be best if you returned to the common quarters."

He grew very quiet. "Best?" he asked after a moment.

His eyes were a placid gray. The calm before the storm, she thought. No longer able to hold his gaze, she stared at the wall behind him. "Aye. I appreciate the security of your being near. However, I feel the threat has passed. Since it has, I'd very much enjoy having my privacy."

He rose slowly from the chair. "Privacy, is it?"

He started around the table toward her, and Catherine tripped back a step. Not again, she bemoaned silently, remembering how he'd stalked her in the stables. Determined not to allow him the upper hand—not this time!— she rooted her feet to the floor and squared her shoulders.

Relief washed through her when he stopped after rounding the table. Crossing his arms over his bare chest, he leaned his backside against the wooden top, his long legs linking at the ankles. He appeared as relaxed as a cat lazing in the shade on a hot summer day. But Catherine knew not to trust him, especially when nothing separated them but air.

"Why do you suddenly feel it's necessary to be alone?" he asked.

"A woman is entitled to some solitude. 'Tis simply the way of it."

"I suppose you want me to believe the thought of another rat invading these chambers no longer bothers you . . . that by some miracle you've mastered your fear." He cocked his head to one side and regarded her carefully. "I think not, Catherine. Something else has unsettled you. What?"

Annoyed because he wouldn't just let the subject lie, Catherine clenched her jaw. He knew the answer. From the first, when he'd compared her to Clotilde, he'd been angling for a confirmation. Obviously, by his constant prodding, he was determined she should say the words openly. But Catherine was equally committed to keeping silent.

She'd not give him that sort of power over her. Nor would she award him the opportunity to boast about his conquest. But most of all, she'd not jeopardize her chance at securing a loving and lasting marriage—if not to Miles, then to someone else. Not simply for a moment's passion. No matter how marvelous it was.

"Nothing has me unsettled," she declared. "I simply want some privacy. So please leave!"

A dark smile crossed his face. "Milady's composure is slipping," he said, pulling himself to his feet to tower above her. "Could it be because she is lying?"

He stood a few feet from her, his broad shoulders and solid chest filling the field of her vision. With the candle's flame dancing behind him, shadows played along his flesh, rising and dipping over corded muscle. Catherine was at first spellbound. Her fingers tingled, for she was tempted to explore the intricate pattern. Then he moved.

Forgetting her resolve to stand firm, she paced backward, her gaze locked with his. He followed her. "You talk gibberish," she proclaimed, remembering he had just accused her of lying. "If I act perturbed, 'tis because I want some privacy and cannot get it. Your pallet is there." Not fully comprehending how she'd gotten beside it, she pointed at his bed as she trod past it. "Now gather the thing up and—"

Stone met her back, and she gasped. She tried to turn away, but his hands hit the wall. Woefully, she knew she'd lived this scene before.

Smoke-gray eyes stared down at her. "It seems we are where we once were. The question is: What will the outcome be this time?"

As he spoke, he pressed fully against her. Only the thin chemise separated his chest from her breasts. In the chilly room, his body felt like a brazier brimming with hot coals.

She resisted its appealing warmth. "Get away from me," she demanded.

"Why?" he asked, just before his lips met the base of her throat to tease the fluttering pulse.

Longings that she could not have imagined swirled to life inside her. She trembled from their compelling force. Every nerve she possessed felt as though it were on fire; Catherine thought she might swoon.

Fighting the urgency rising inside her, she pushed against his chest. "Don't," she pleaded.

He nibbled his way to her jaw, then upward. His mouth played at her ear. "What are you afraid of?" he whispered.

You.

Me.

THIS.

The words screamed through her mind just as his tongue began tracing across her cheek, working slowly toward her mouth. The action robbed her resolve not to let him win, and Catherine realized she was fast losing the battle against him.

Oh, how he would laud his victory, standing forever triumphant. The thought cut deep into her mind and sliced straight to her heart. Merciful Lord! This had to stop.

But as his tongue flicked lightly at the corner of her mouth, the want inside her grew. She squeezed her eyes closed, and on a pitiful moan, she asked, "Why can't you leave me alone?"

Oddly, Rolfe was wondering the very same thing. He'd promised himself he would keep away from her, swore he'd not touch her again. These past weeks, since they'd last kissed and he'd subsequently hurt her, he'd managed to keep a feeble hold on his vow. He fought constantly against his yearnings. To master them took every ounce of mental strength he possessed.

Tonight was no exception.

But tonight he lost the war.

He remembered how she sat innocently yet provocatively in the center of her bed, covers tucked protectively around her. More than once, he'd been tempted to rise from his chair, kick the thing back, cross the distance between them, and join her there. Somehow he'd kept the urge in check. Yet the tension inside him abounded.

He'd purposely provoked her when she'd questioned him about Clotilde. Even so, he hadn't expected to incite such righteous anger from within her.

What a glorious sight she'd presented as she'd leaped from the bed. Her long hair swirled around her in a curtain of rich brown satin before it settled, cloaking her shoulders and cascading down her back. Once at the table, she'd set her fists at her slender waist, and her ripe young breasts rose and fell as she railed at him.

Enchanted, he eagerly viewed the pinkish crowns showing through the thin chemise, scrutinized the budding nipples at the center of each perfect sphere, and his loins stirred more powerfully than he could ever recall.

Through their conversation, he glimpsed the enticing globes that beckoned to him. Always he baited her, wanting to have the truth. Then, when she claimed she needed *privacy,* something inside him snapped. He'd come from his chair, determined to prove it wasn't seclusion she craved. In fact, her sudden longing took another party to appease it, preferably one of the opposite sex.

Just in time, he remembered his vow and stopped himself. But the lust within him wouldn't subside. Once more, he knew she felt the same raw passion as he. Although she refused to admit it, *that* was the reason she'd asked him to leave. And *that* was the reason she was now against this wall, his body pressed tightly to hers.

By the saints, if it was the last thing he ever did, he'd hear the words from her own lips. He stilled the teasing play of his tongue near the corner of her mouth. Pulling his head back, he waited. Her eyelids fluttered, then opened, and he looked deeply into her eyes.

"Why can't I leave you alone?" he questioned, repeating her query. He fitted his hips more snugly to hers, then moved against her, his hard member caressing her belly. "Because, Catherine, I desire you too much."

She groaned miserably. "This is madness."

"Madness?" he repeated. "Not so. 'Tis the natural response of a man who yearns for a woman. 'Tis my response for you." He swayed his hips in an erotic manner. "This should tell you how much I want you. I *do* want you . . . want you more than any woman I've ever known. And you feel the same toward me. Don't you?" Her answer was a strangled whimper, and he bore against her harder, determined to make her admit the truth. "Don't you?" he demanded.

YES.

Catherine shouted the affirmation in her mind, but she resisted having it pass from her tongue. If she admitted she wanted him, said she desired him with every inch of her being, she'd be lost forever, and so would her virginity.

That one word had the power to change her life. Speak it, and the smoldering passions inside them would quickly find their release. But to what end? she wondered as she searched his face. Having reaped his prize, would he offer her marriage? Or would he see himself as the conqueror, she as the vanquished, and look upon her simply as his whore?

Lost in her thoughts, she hadn't seen him move. She gasped as he worked his hand between the wall and her hips. Long fingers kneaded her bottom, then he lifted her. Her back slid along the cold stones until her face was level with his. Pulling her legs around his hips, he again clenched her derriere, supporting her. Then he pressed into her.

"Don't you, Catherine?" he asked, moving himself against her most intimate place.

Her reaction was spontaneous. Moisture seeped from inside her; she throbbed where they touched. Nearly overwhelmed by this new assault on her senses, she rolled her head against the wall. "'Tis madness," she repeated.

"Aye," he whispered in return, his lips feathering along her throat, ascending to her chin. "But a wondrous madness. You want me, don't you?"

While he spoke, his hands expertly caressed her bottom. His hips swayed in a provocative manner, eliciting the most delicious sensations, and Catherine thought she might burst from the untamed yearnings burgeoning inside her. Then they were again face-to-face.

"Don't you?" he repeated one more time, his warm breath fanning her mouth.

Unexpectedly his tongue traced her lower lip in a tantalizing fashion; Catherine moaned.

Play with fire and you're bound to get burned.

Somewhere in her mind, she heard Eloise's words. But they made no sense. She was already ablaze with desire. If he didn't stop bedeviling her this way she'd soon erupt into flames.

"Catherine—"

"Aye! I want you." The words tore through her lips as they were wrested from the depths of her soul. "Are you now satisfied?"

He rewarded her with a vainglorious smile. "Satisfied? Not yet. Not until I have you."

Her breath was instantly trapped in her lungs as his hands moved along her bottom. Fingers stretched forward. His eyes darkened with desire when he found her secret place. With the skill of an experienced lover, he stroked her through her chemise. She trembled anew.

"You're ready for me," he said, the play of his hands growing more erotic. "You're wet and as eager as I. Say you're mine, and I'll show you what ecstasy means."

In a daze, she stared at him. What wizardry was he working on her? she wondered.

"Say it, Catherine. Say you are mine."

His words acted like an aphrodisiac, and she could no longer resist him. "I'm yours," she breathed, not realizing she had.

With a low growl, he swung her away from the wall; she clung to him, for she was at once dizzy from the motion. Then she felt herself being lowered to his pallet. When her back met the soft bedding, he pulled her legs from around him. As he knelt between her outstretched thighs, she realized her chemise had been gathered well above her hips. As she reached for its hem, wanting to cover herself, he caught her wrist.

"No. Don't hide yourself from me."

His harsh tone at first startled her, and she searched his eyes.

"Your beauty is for me to gaze upon . . . all of it." He relaxed his grip, and her hand fell to the pallet. "All of it," he repeated as his knuckles brushed lightly through her curls.

At his enticing play, a delectable shiver ran the length of her; then she watched as his hand moved to a point between his waist and hips. He jerked the string securing his braies; the garment slid down his thighs to his knees. He worked it from his feet, tossing it aside. If she thought he was magnificent before, she believed him to be doubly so now. Proud, noble, his desire for her evident, he clearly welcomed the caress of her eyes.

Then his hands were at her hips. Catching the chemise, he pushed it up her body and quickly stripped it from her. The wadded scrap of linen joined his own clothing beside them on the floor. His heated gaze swept over her, stopping at her breasts. His palm grazed the peak of one. The nipple jutted. He smiled, obviously pleased by its instant response.

"You're beautiful," he whispered. "More beautiful than I had imagined."

He moved, and her golden warrior was leaning over her, muscles rippling in his arms as he supported his weight.

"I may regret this tomorrow," he said, his fingers gently priming her. "But tonight I shall glory in knowing you gave yourself willingly. Sweet Jesus, how I want you."

All her senses were attuned to his hand as it worked its magic in the delicate area between her legs. Except for the last of his words, which were an agonized moan, the others were lost to her. The ache inside her became unbearable. She wanted him as much as he wanted her.

"Love me, then," she beseeched, her hands meeting his solid shoulders. As her fingers glided over his sinewy flesh, circling around to the nape of his neck, she marveled at the smoothness of his skin, at the power beneath it. "And kiss me."

"Aye, I will do both."

Hot and moist, his mouth covered hers in a searing kiss. While his tongue delved between her parted lips, thrusting and withdrawing, the sleek crown of his manhood probed at the juncture of her thighs. Mindless with longing, Catherine relished his amorous play. Then he was slowly easing into her. The sensation was both exhilarating and frightening.

Reaching her maidenhead, he stopped his progression. He dragged his mouth from hers and looked down at her.

"There will be pain," he warned. "Then there will be pleasure . . . pleasure far greater than you've ever known."

She saw the promise of the latter written in his smoldering eyes, and she nodded her acceptance.

His large hand moved under her hips, lifting her to him. "Then kiss me, Catherine. Kiss me with all the passion you feel."

Their lips were again coupled in a heated foray, their tongues playing wildly. With all the sensations whirling inside her, she barely felt the sharp twinge as he thrust forward, breaking through the thin membrane to claim her virginity. Within moments, she was filled with him, welcoming him eagerly.

His mouth left hers. Again he gazed down at her. "'Tis done, Catherine. Now for the pleasure."

As he spoke, he waited, allowing her to adjust. Then his hips began to move in the most tantalizing manner. Though unsure of herself, she was at once anxious to please him. She joined him, matching the rhythm he'd orchestrated. With each sure stroke, a river of fire rushed through her veins. Her skin burned from some unfulfilled need. His hard body mastered hers, delighting her in ways she could not have imagined.

Yet something was lacking, something even more powerful than what they presently shared. Somewhere in the back of her mind, she wondered if he felt the same. What was this exotic thing that teased her, then eluded her? Did he know?

Rolfe knew exactly what evaded them. Each time her lithe hips rose to meet his quickening thrusts, he thought the heavenly plunge might be his last. She was like liquid silk, wrapping around him, enticing him ever deeper. His body was ablaze with his need for her; the fire inside him was intolerable, and he craved his release. But he'd not seek his own fulfillment, not until he could feel those tiny spasms caressing him, coaxing him to share in her own rapture.

He'd promised her pleasure, pleasure beyond anything she'd ever known, and she would have it. Tonight, and for every night she was willing to come to him, he would quench

her desires, along with his own. Would do so until the day
they parted. Enjoying her as he was, he prayed that day was
a long way off. Yet regrettably, he knew the time would come
and it would be all too soon.

Surprisingly yet gratefully, he felt her legs circle his hips.
Her passion, he understood, was as great as his. As he lifted
her to him and rotated against her, the question arose: How
could he bear to let her go?

Then another query shot through his mind, waylaying
him: After this night of their shared bliss, was she still
intending to marry Miles?

The notion angered Rolfe, for he knew the bastard didn't
deserve her. He was instantly determined to make her forget
her betrothed.

She was his. He was the one initiating her in the ways of
love. Once he'd satiated her desires, granting her the ecstasy
he'd promised her, she'd want no man but him. To that end,
he mastered her with his body.

Passion blurring his vision, he watched her as he worked
his own brand of magic on her, the act exciting him all the
more. Soon he was rewarded with the first indications of her
climax. Her small teeth dented her lower lip. Her eyes closed
as she arched against the pallet. A soft cry trembled in her
throat just as he felt the seductive little tremors that coerced
him to seek his own release. He didn't hesitate. Two more
thrusts and his whole body shuddered, then shuddered
again as he recklessly spilled his seed deep inside her.

When his heart was no longer racing, his breath coming
more steadily, his senses less dazed, he remembered his
thoughts about her betrothed, about making her forget
Miles. The idea she might yet lie with the bastard fostered
his scorn. The old hatreds surged within him.

Pulling back, he looked deeply into her eyes. "By what
we've just shared, you are now and forever mine," he said
with force. "Do you understand me?"

Her brow wrinkling, Catherine stared up at him. Joined
as they still were, she understood him all too well. Despite
her vow to the contrary, she'd given him her virginity. Done
so readily, eagerly. Any thought of marriage to Miles was
now lost to her. Strangely, on that point, she held no regrets.

What troubled her was the way Rolfe gazed at her. Contempt and loathing showed in his eyes.

"Do you understand?" he repeated.

The lump that had formed in her throat swelled as tears stung her eyes. "Aye," she whispered, fighting against her sorrow. "I understand."

Her heart lurched as satisfaction replaced his look of disdain; he smiled.

"'Tis good, Catherine," he said, his face coming ever closer to hers. "For I want to make love to you again, and again, until dawn breaks the horizon."

When his lips met hers, she didn't refuse their domination. What choice did she have? Especially now? Especially when she'd willingly allowed him to conquer her?

Not realizing she'd misread his look entirely, Catherine felt certain she was not only his captive but also, and to her greatest heartbreak . . .

His whore.

CHAPTER

13

HENRY WAS GOING TO KILL HIM.

The thought repeated itself in Rolfe's mind as his sword met Garrick's, then sliced away. Since shortly after dawn, when he'd risen from his pallet, his beautiful Catherine slumbering like a contented child, he'd been weighing the concept perpetually.

He could picture the scene now, the duke winking at him as if to say he hoped Rolfe found his little liaison with Catherine de Mortain to be exceptionally enjoyable and well worth the resulting punishment for his disobedience. Afterward, at Henry's command, Rolfe's head would be swiftly severed from his body.

A high price to pay for one night of passion, he decided ruefully. But, oh, what a wondrous night it had been. Be that as it may, Rolfe worried about the duke's reaction. His only hope was that once Henry personally looked upon Catherine's fairness he would understand, from a man's perspective, how Rolfe had failed to contain his desire and forgive the indiscretion. The final outcome, Rolfe knew, remained to be seen.

And what of Catherine?

He glanced at the shuttered window to their chamber. As he did so, the question needled. Now that daylight was upon them, did she regret their night of love, lament giving him her virginity?

If he had stayed beside her, he might now have the answer. But he'd left her before she'd awakened. Admittedly, he knew why.

On many a battlefield, he had confronted some of the most savage and fiercest opponents possible. Unflinchingly he'd stood against each and every one, winning time after time. Never had he thought of himself as a coward, never had he run. Not until this morning.

On rousing from his short sleep, he'd gazed upon Catherine's sweet countenance for the longest while. But as the moments passed, the warm feeling inside him slowly subsided. He was soon overcome by doubt and uncertainty, emotions that were both foreign to him where women were concerned. Leaving his pallet, he'd quietly gathered his things and crept from the room, afraid to face her, afraid of what he might see in her ever-changing eyes.

God's wounds! If he had only kept his vow, he'd not presently be worrying over Henry or Catherine. How easy it was to make that call now, he thought, knowing that hindsight was always clearer.

The two swords came together again with a loud clang. Rolfe skillfully deflected the blow with his own blade. But at the next onslaught, he swung and missed. His momentum caused him to stumble; Garrick caught him before he fell face-first into the mud.

"You are not as agile this morn as you have been," his companion stated, releasing Rolfe's arm. "You're having difficulty concentrating as well. From the looks of you, I'm of the impression you didn't get much sleep. Is something troubling you? Your shoulder, perhaps? Or is it the Lady Catherine who occupies your mind?"

For the past two weeks, Rolfe and Garrick had taken to the yard early each morning, practicing with their swords so that Rolfe could regain his accustomed strength and efficiency with the weapon. Other than a mild ache, which lessened day by day, the injury no longer plagued him as it once had.

184

He wasn't of a mind to divulge the truth about last night to Garrick. *That* was between he and Catherine.

"'Tis my shoulder," Rolfe snapped, rubbing it.

Garrick arched a graying eyebrow. "I would tend to believe you, except for two things."

"What two things?"

"For one, the blows you just struck against my blade were every bit as powerful as they were prior to your injury."

"And?" Rolfe asked after Garrick's prolonged silence.

"You keep glancing at yon window with a troubled look in your eyes. Your shoulder isn't what worries you but the Lady Catherine. She is the reason your concentration is off. Likewise, my friend, I imagine she is also the reason you were robbed of your sleep."

"You are wrong on all counts," Rolfe stated. He pulled a scrap of cloth from his belt and wiped the tip of his sword where it had dug into the mud when he'd stumbled. "'Tis my shoulder that troubles me and naught else." He plunged the blade into its scabbard. "Come. I'm hungry. Let's go inside and break the fast."

Not waiting for Garrick, Rolfe strode across the yard to the stairs. Once inside the keep, he ascended to the great hall. Aubrey was quickly at his side.

"Did your practice go well, milord?" his squire asked.

"As well as can be expected," Rolfe replied, his gaze sweeping the room. He was disappointed not to see Catherine among those seated at the tables. "Has the Lady Catherine requested to come down to break the fast?"

Aubrey shook his head. "A short while ago, I inquired through the door if she wanted to come to the hall. She said she wasn't hungry and told me to go away. From the tone of her voice, she sounds to be in ill humor, milord. I didn't insist that she come down."

His squire's words weren't at all encouraging. However, Rolfe decided it was time he stopped acting the coward and faced her. "The key, Aubrey."

Retrieving the item from his belt, the lad placed it in Rolfe's hand. "Mayhap, milord, you should not disturb her."

"The longer I wait, the worse it will be," he said, dismissing his squire.

Circling the hall's perimeter, Rolfe headed for the stairs, loped up them, then strode the corridor toward their chamber. After what Aubrey had said, he doubted he'd be received very warmly. In fact, he imagined she might be inclined to pitch the first thing that came to hand straight at his head. Now standing at the door, he decided there was only one way to find out.

Oddly, his hand shook as he slipped the key into the lock. Added to that, he felt his heart trip a little faster; his palms had grown sweaty. One would think he were some untried youth suffering the effects of an unrequited love. As experienced with women as he was, he would normally have laughed at the prospect. But the physical changes couldn't be denied. He had contracted a bad case of the jitters, and Catherine was the cause.

With a twist of his wrist, the lock clicked; then, on releasing the latch, he pushed the door wide and stepped into the room. His gaze immediately met the young woman who was wreaking havoc with his emotions.

Hugging her knees to her chest, she sat in the middle of the bed, wearing naught but her chemise. Closing the panel, Rolfe felt certain she'd heard him enter, yet she refused to look at him. Unable to gauge her temper, he moved across the room, heading toward the area where his possessions were stored. "Why aren't you dressed?" he asked, his manner purposely nonchalant. "'Tis time we break the fast."

"I didn't know if my dressing would be acceptable to you."

Her tone was undeniably hostile. Frowning, Rolfe stopped in his tracks. He turned toward her slowly and saw that she looked past him. Her mood, he decided, was far worse than he'd imagined. "Why wouldn't it be acceptable, Catherine?"

"This is all new to me. I'm not sure how I should behave."

"Behave?"

"Aye. Now that I'm your whore, I need to know if I'm to

be at your beck and call whenever you choose. If that is the case, there's little reason for me to don my clothes."

Through narrowed eyes, Rolfe stared at her. "My whore?"

She raised her chin a notch. "'Tis what I am."

Beneath her show of aloofness, he saw what he thought was pain. How in God's name had she arrived at such a notion? As far as he knew, he'd done nothing to make her see herself thus. "Have I ever used that term with you?"

"No. But words are not always necessary. 'Tis apparent that is what I am to you."

"My whore," he repeated, suddenly seething from the accusation.

"Aye. Your whore."

"Tell me, Catherine: If the word never crossed my lips, how are you so certain I think of you in that vein?"

"By the way you looked at me."

"*Looked* at you? And how, pray tell, was that?"

With the explosiveness of his question, she hugged her knees closer. "With contempt."

"Contempt?" He saw her nod. "When?"

"Last night, after we first copulated—"

"I prefer to think we made love," he interjected, not liking the word she'd chosen.

"Think what you will. 'Tis not what we did."

"As I remember, there was more to the act than just your panting and my thrusting. There was emotion—*deep* emotion, Catherine. That's what made our first joining so special."

"The only emotion I remember is one of loathing and disdain. 'Twas there in your eyes. I knew then how you felt about me, that you saw me as your whore."

More confused than ever, Rolfe shook his head, negating her words. "You must have been imagining things, for I don't recall looking at you in any other way except with tenderness and desire."

"I didn't imagine it," she defended. "I *saw* contempt."

Tears shimmered in her eyes, and Rolfe inwardly questioned if they were from hurt, from anger, or from both. He was tempted to go to her, but he knew she'd reject him, so he stayed near the foot of the bed. "Exactly when did you see this expression?"

"'Twas when you told me that I was now and forever yours. You asked me if I understood. By the way you gazed at me, I understood all too well what those words meant. I was now and forever your whore, to be used as you wished."

Rolfe remembered the moment, remembered what had been going through his head at the time. No wonder she'd presumed what she had. "Whatever you saw in my eyes—contempt, disdain, loathing—the emotion was not meant for you but for Miles."

Surprise showed on her face. "Miles?"

"Aye. I was wondering whether you still hoped to marry him, to lie with him the same as you did with me. After what we had just shared, the idea didn't sit well. It bedevils me. He doesn't deserve you, Catherine. He never has."

Her gaze dropped from his. "I shall never marry Miles—not now. Not after last night."

For his own satisfaction, Rolfe had to ask, "If last night never happened, would you yet be wanting to wed him?"

"I don't know."

"Do you love him?"

"I don't know that either."

Had she said yes, he would have called her a liar. No woman who was truly in love with one man would give herself to another. Not the way Catherine had given herself to him.

He thought to press the issue, to make her admit that Miles no longer held a place in her heart. But at the moment her emotions were far too fragile. To force her into confronting her feelings could do more harm than good. The truth, he decided, could wait. Yet there was one thing that could not.

"Catherine, I want you to understand something, and understand it well. Never would I defile the memory of what we shared by thinking of you as my whore. Nor should you be inclined to look upon yourself in such a demeaning manner. In my eyes, you are no less virtuous than you ever were."

"If that were only true," she said, her eyes downcast.

Her regrets were far greater than he'd thought. The knowledge tore at his heart. He wanted to go to her, take her in his arms and give her comfort. He resisted, knowing he was the cause of her pain.

Blessed Heaven! Why couldn't he have left well enough alone? But no. He'd had to prove she desired him as much as he desired her. Now she despised him. Worst of all, she despised herself. All this simply because he'd needed to stroke his own vanity.

He stepped closer. High on the bedpost, he braced his forearm and rested his brow against it. "Believe it," he said, looking down at her. "For it's true."

Her gaze met his, and she laughed sharply. "The man I marry might not agree with you, especially when he learns I'm not a virgin."

"That he was not the first shouldn't matter, not if he really loves you." Her response was to look away; Rolfe sighed. "By the uncertainty you're suffering, I know fully that what occurred between us should never have happened. It did, though. 'Tis done, and nothing can change that.

"You're very precious to me, Catherine. No woman has ever stirred such longing in me as you have. So I shall tell you this, hoping it will help ease your mind: I'll not approach you again in that manner, not unless it's by your own invitation." He pushed himself from the post. "Now dress yourself and come down to the hall."

"I'd prefer not to."

"Behave normally, and no one will ever suspect we were intimate. Act as you are now, and speculation will fly. No one knows except us. Unless you tell someone, your secret is forever safe."

"Someone will know someday."

If last night's joining produced a child, all at Cartbridge would know far sooner than she thought. He'd been reckless. But in the throes of his own passion, he hadn't cared. Catherine was the first to ever receive his seed. For her sake, he prayed it didn't take.

"When that time comes," he said, "then you have my permission to say you were forced by Rolfe de Mont St. Michel to submit to his lustful desires. Until then, 'twould be best if you say nothing at all." With that, he aimed himself at the door. Opening the panel, he turned. "Your meal awaits you. I'll expect you shortly."

Not locking the door behind him, he strode down the corridor, wondering what Catherine would do. He'd given her the instrument whereby she could protect her name, casting the guilt fully on him. The question was: Would she indeed use the device for her own purposes, one day pointing her finger to falsely accuse him of rape?

He believed her to be more honest than that. But as with all women, the answer, he knew, remained to be seen.

You're very precious to me, Catherine.

Rolfe's words echoed in her mind several times over just as the door closed behind him. Resting her cheek against her knees, she hugged her legs closer and stared at the entry. She'd misread him and, in doing so, had accused him wrongly. Even after he'd explained how thoughts of Miles had evoked his contemptuous look, she'd whined and complained, much like a petulant child, openly lamenting the loss of her virginity, claiming no man would ever want her.

With a sigh, Catherine wondered at her reasoning for doing so. Had she hoped to absolve herself of her own guilt by placing the blame totally on Rolfe? If that was her expectation, she'd been well rewarded, for he'd granted her a charitable way out.

But she questioned if she'd be so bold as to take that path. Charging a man with rape when no such defilement had occurred was to her way of thinking odious indeed. On having second thoughts about what they'd done, other women might be predisposed to indict a man falsely, but not her. Not when she'd given herself willingly.

Besides, her own nature prevented such chicanery. She could thank William de Mortain for that. All through her formative years, he'd preached against deception, had always rewarded honesty. Because of it, she was now her father's daughter.

Deep down she thanked Rolfe for offering her a way to protect her virtue. But if there was any guilt to bear, she would share it with him equally. His honor would go untarnished.

So why was she still in the grips of a melancholy? Did she really fear no man would want her now that she wasn't a virgin? Or did this weightiness inside her stem from some nebulous hope that after what they had shared Rolfe would ask for her hand, disappointment filling her when he made no such offer?

Certain her unhappiness originated from the latter, she chastised herself for being a fool. That he had not yet married should have given her fair warning. His life was that of a warrior, forever moving from battle to battle. It was unlikely he'd change his chosen course. Not because of a night's worth of pleasure. Not unless the woman with whom he'd shared it somehow stole his heart.

Oh, he wanted her, took pleasure in her lips and body, satisfied her as well as himself. Yet Catherine knew desire was not love. To that end, she was thankful he'd given her a reprieve by promising not to approach her again, saying he would do so only if she issued him an invitation.

As she remembered his ardent lovemaking, her whole being was aflame with longing. Though she felt certain there was no future for them, no hope of his ever falling in love with her, she couldn't help wondering if she'd be able to resist him. More so, did she even want to?

Catherine grew weary of all the questions teeming inside her head, especially when she could find no answers. And this glumness that was encasing her, a product of her own making, it too began to annoy her.

The truth was that she'd made her choice last night. Now it was time she accept the fact and endure the consequences, whatever they might be.

With that knowledge held firmly, she scooted from the bed. Once dressed, she left the room, ready to again face Rolfe de Mont St. Michel, but this time with far more pride.

Rolfe rose from his seat when Catherine appeared at the foot of the stairs. Under her blue mantle, she wore a new bliaud fashioned from the fine wool that he'd taken from the castle stores and given to Eloise, with instructions to sew the garment for her mistress. The soft yellow suited her, he decided, thinking she looked like a ray of sunshine wrapped in a clear azure sky. As he approached her, he wondered if her mood had lightened any.

"I'm happy you decided to emerge from hiding," he said, once he reached her side.

Elevating her chin, she looked directly into his eyes. "I didn't realize I had a choice in the matter."

Since last he'd seen her, she'd grown quite proud. Yet beneath her show of haughtiness, there lurked uncertainty. "The option of whether or not you left your room was yours, Catherine. I wouldn't have forced you to come down to the hall. Not if you'd strongly insisted against doing so."

She tilted her head. "Oh? And I suppose, if I'd rebelled more vigorously from the start, you would not have abducted me, nor have carried me all this way to Cartbridge, correct?"

"In that matter, you had no choice. However, since then, and albeit not very wisely in one such case, you've elected to make several decisions on your own." Her eyes told him she knew he referred to her attempted escape, to her coming to the stables, and, of course, to what had occurred last night. "Nobody coerced you into taking those steps. But you already know that, don't you?"

Her gaze fell from his. "Aye. I know that."

"Are you hungry?"

"No."

Her mood, he noticed, had become morose. Catching her chin, he inched her head upward. "What's wrong?" he asked, again looking into her eyes.

"Nothing's wrong."

"Then why the long face?"

"If you must know, 'tis this place. The walls are closing in on me. I sit locked in my room the day through with naught to do. Other than at meals, rarely am I allowed to come to the hall. And that is only when someone is available to keep watch over me, which lately no one has the time to do. This inactivity I'm made to suffer is driving me mad."

"Then I suppose we shall just have to remedy the situation, won't we." He turned toward the table. "Aubrey, come hither." When his squire was beside him, he ordered, "Get a cloak for the Lady Catherine. And one for myself too."

With a quick nod, Aubrey was instantly up the steps.

"What are you intending?" Catherine asked, staring up at him.

A smile touched Rolfe's lips. "I plan to cure you of your gloom."

CHAPTER
14

THE COOL WIND BRUSHED CATHERINE'S CHEEKS, WHILE THE SUN'S rays warmed her head and shoulders. Inhaling the fresh, sweet air wafting across the open field, she marveled how the castle's staleness quickly ebbed from her pores. She felt alive, invigorated, and very much aware of the man behind her.

With Rolfe's arm circling her waist, his hard thighs cradling her hips, they rode across the snow-patched earth, heading away from Cartbridge. Beneath them, the stallion, its skittish behavior having long since ended, stretched its legs into an easy canter.

As sure hooves struck the ground, the ensuing vibration quivered through the saddle and into her bottom. The movement accentuated the feeling of fullness between her legs, a ghostly remembrance of Rolfe's masterful invasion and the night of lovemaking that followed.

Though glad that she'd been freed from the keep, Catherine didn't know which was worse: being cooped up in her room, its walls closing in around her; or having Rolfe situated so near, his body heat charging through her. Both were inevitably a source of madness to her, for one was her prison, the other her release.

Last night, all her inhibitions had fled under his expert touch. In her innocence, nothing she imagined could have prepared her for the delirious joy she'd found in his arms. Even now, as images of what they'd shared flashed unbidden through her mind, her body trembled with want, and she wondered just how long she could resist him.

Her tremors didn't go unnoticed.

"Cold?" Rolfe asked, his warm breath touching her ear. Not waiting for her response, he pulled her more snugly to him.

With the action, his groin seductively caressed her derriere; flames of longing licked low in her stomach. Catherine closed her eyes and bit back a moan.

Blessed misery, she lamented in silence, wishing now she'd not complained and kept to her room. For once its dreaded confines promised a welcome relief. At least then he'd not be this close. Nor would her emotions be so unsettled.

Yet Catherine could be thankful for one thing. As they journeyed afield, they didn't go unescorted. To each side, three well-armed knights rode parallel to their position. Ever watchful, the six men kept their distance. They were not so far away that they couldn't quickly group around her and Rolfe should the need arise.

The added protection, she knew, resulted from Rolfe's being shrewdly cautious. If by some miracle her rescuers were to happen upon them, he didn't want to be caught alone in the open, his captive fighting him as he tried desperately to make it back to the safety of the castle.

Frowning, Catherine questioned whether she would indeed assail him should that very circumstance come about. In one way, she wanted to be free of him; in another, she hoped they would never part.

One need opposed the other, and Catherine wondered which of the two was the stronger. The latter, she decided. But why?

Like a hard slap, the realization struck. *No,* she told herself. She couldn't possibly be falling in love with him. Or could she?

"What deep thoughts are roaming through your head?"

His voice snapped her from her musings. Blinking, she noted the stallion had been slowed to a walk. Rolfe had leaned around and was now gazing squarely into her face. His expression said he expected an answer. Lord help her! She certainly couldn't tell him the truth.

"M-my head?" she stammered, while searching for a plausible lie.

"Aye. That pretty thing that sits atop your shoulders. What's going on inside it to make you frown so?"

"I was wondering about my father," she said, by way of a half-truth.

"You're still concerned about his welfare?"

He apparently accepted her answer. Inwardly she breathed a sigh of relief. "Aye. I worry about him. If you had a father, wouldn't you do the same?"

An odd look crossed Rolfe's face just before he straightened in the saddle; Catherine wished she'd bitten her tongue.

She turned to look up at him. "I'm sorry. I didn't mean to say that."

He shrugged. "You don't need to apologize. I did or do have a sire. I wouldn't be here otherwise. To answer your question: Had I been afforded the luxury of knowing who he was, aye, I would no doubt worry about him also."

He hid his feelings well, but behind his mask of indifference, Catherine felt certain there was pain. "Do you ever wonder about them?"

"My parents?"

Hoping he'd be honest with her, she nodded.

"When I was a youth living on the mount I did."

"Very often?"

"Often enough. In fact, my daydreams were filled with them."

"And how did you picture them?" she asked, glad he wasn't averse to talking about his past.

"I pictured them of noble blood. In one such imagining, I saw them grieving over my loss."

"How so?"

"The fantasy went as follows: Because my vengeful nurse was sternly reprimanded, then dismissed for being lax in her duties, she stole me from my cradle and carried me to the marshes, expecting the sea would take me. Of course, as she made her retreat, the quicksand swallowed her as payment for her wickedness. Thinking that was how I came to be on the marshes, I waited, praying my parents would one day find me. They never came."

Catherine's heart ached for the small boy he once was. Always longing to be returned to his loving family, he was never rewarded. "They could be of noble blood."

He smiled. "Aye. But more likely I'm of common birth—a bastard whose mother didn't know what to do with him. It doesn't matter, Catherine. Once Robert de Bayeux claimed me from Mont St. Michel, I wondered less and less about my parentage. He became the father I never had."

His bearing exuded a regal quality, and she very much doubted he was of common birth. Even so, for his mother to have left him just beyond the mount, where the sea could claim him, was heartless indeed. That, or she was exceedingly desperate. Catherine wondered which it might be.

"One day you may learn the truth," she said. "For now, whether you are of ignoble birth or not, it matters little to me."

He chuckled. "I wonder if your father will feel the same."

"My father?"

"Aye. Especially when he discovers we've been intimate."

Catherine indeed feared William de Mortain's reaction if he ever learned the truth. He'd call Rolfe a bastard, all right. Afterward he'd kill him. "What makes you think he'll ever find out we have?"

"As you've said: Someday, someone will know."

"Certainly I'll not offer such information. At least not any time soon."

"By chance, Catherine, what if during last night's union, you managed to conceive? If that is so, the truth will be out far sooner than you think."

She felt the blood drain from her face. As stupid as it

might seem, she hadn't even considered that. The notion that their lovemaking might have produced a child frightened her. By the same token, it also warmed her heart. Dear God! If she believed her emotions were a jumble before, they were doubly so now.

"Have you nothing to say?" Rolfe asked.

She had comments aplenty. None were very kind. And all were directed at herself. From him, however, there was only one thing she wanted to know. "If I did conceive, I presume you will do what is considered proper."

"Proper?" he questioned. "If you mean, will I claim the child as my own, the answer is yes."

She waited, hoping to hear the words that would put her mind at ease. They never came. "But you don't intend to legitimize our daughter or son, correct?"

"I have a feeling, Catherine, that I come from a long line of bastards. That being so, I see no reason to break tradition," he said heedlessly.

The statement jarred her. A hollow feeling settled in the pit of her stomach while incredulity filled her. Never would she have expected him to behave so callously. Though no proof existed he was actually a bastard, she imagined he bore the stigma just the same. How, then, could he have said what he did?

He'd apparently read her disbelief, for he announced, "Before we speak of legitimizing our child, let's first see if there is one." With that he reined the stallion around. "'Tis time we go back."

Catherine offered no objection when he called out to his men. Once he had their attention, he motioned toward the castle. Signaling they understood, the entire troop headed in. She again sank into her own musings.

Any joy she may have found in their offhand outing had quickly ebbed, for the idea that a night's worth of pleasure could so readily bring a lifetime of sorrow pained her deeply. She wasn't thinking of herself, but of the child she might be carrying.

Being branded a bastard was a fate that would be hard to endure. The lack of a legitimate heritage, she realized, brought with it a constant barrage of slurs, insinuation, and ostracism from family and strangers alike. How could any child sustain such cruelty and survive unscathed?

The silent query made her think of Rolfe. Proud and self-assured, he had come through the ordeal without too much ill effect. Yet his situation was unique.

In his extreme youth, he'd been protected by the Benedictines, for they saw him as their miracle child. Later, his mentor undoubtedly foiled any scurrilous attacks. In any event, he had to have suffered some indignities over the years. Because he had, one would think he'd be averse to having his own flesh and blood treated in a like manner. But then what did she really know about him?

For one, he was no fledgling when it came to the art of seduction and lovemaking. Such skill suggested he'd probably bedded more than his share of women. Who was to say he didn't already have a passel of offspring, scattered far and wide, wherever his travels had taken him?

For another, he was yet unattached. So if he knew about any such progeny, that in itself would signify his lack of concern for either his child or its mother, however many they were. Why, then, did she think he'd behave any differently with her?

Amidst all her questions, Catherine was certain of only one thing: If she had indeed conceived, she'd not desert her child the way Rolfe's mother had abandoned him. Under no circumstances could she act so unconscionably.

But what of her father? How might he react?

William de Mortain was a caring and just man. Even so he harbored a great amount of pride. She doubted he would fully reject his own grandchild, but he could very well distance himself, embarrassed his lineage was no longer pure.

Right now, however, her father's acceptance of her bastard child was the least of her worries. Her concern centered more on what might occur several months from now when her condition became quite obvious. If, by some miracle, William de Mortain found her then, and if by some equally wondrous phenomenon he breached the walls at Cartbridge, the events that followed would be terrifying.

In her mind's eye, she pictured the scene. Furious that his

daughter had been violated and his own honor besmeared, William would undoubtedly face her defiler, his sword drawn and ready. Though her father was more skilled with the weapon than most, Rolfe had the advantage of being younger, more agile, possibly even stronger. In the end, one would live and one would die. But which would it be? She knew she couldn't bear to see either of them fall.

Erasing the horrid visions from her head, she sighed heavily, for all that had crossed through her mind was nothing more than conjecture. She didn't even know yet if she'd conceived. Whether she was with child or not, she couldn't imagine her father letting her abduction go unpunished. Again she feared the outcome.

But if he didn't find her . . .

The stallion slowed from its canter. Her gaze focusing, Catherine saw the castle gates yawning before them. Hooves sounded hollowly as they struck the deck of the drawbridge.

As they passed into the yard, she again thought of her father, of Rolfe, and what could possibly pass between them. Once Henry's campaign was completed, she'd be freed, so she saw no reason for her father to continue his search. Closing her eyes, she silently beseeched:

Please, Father, don't come nigh. For all our sakes, just stay away.

William de Mortain had no such inclination.

He was closeted in the lord's chamber at Geoffrey's estate, west of Farnham. As was his practice when he was worried, he paced, his thoughts on his beloved Catherine.

She was here in England, and he'd not rest until he found her. On that day, he hoped the bastard who'd abducted her was in her company. She could then have the satisfaction of seeing just how swiftly justice was served on her behalf.

As for himself, William would take great pleasure in splitting the whoreson from groin to gullet. That was his right, and he'd settle for no less.

"You are torturing my floor, sir."

At those words, William turned on Geoffrey to spear him with his gaze. "Your floor be damned. 'Tis Catherine you should be worried about and naught else."

"I am, William," Geoffrey returned. "But your pounding the wood is not going to solve anything. Come. Let's again study these charts and see if we can come up with another plan."

The two men were engaged in a strategy session with Miles. Having scoured the southern part of England, while taking care to avoid the troops of both Stephen and Henry along the way, they'd had no success. Yet William was fairly well assured as to why his daughter had been taken.

That the quest for England's crown and Catherine's abduction happened nearly on the same day seemed quite peculiar. Certainly it was more than coincidence, especially when both the duke and Catherine had managed to land at Wareham, again nearly on the same day.

If naught else over these two and a half months, that much he had been able to ascertain. As before, William suspected Geoffrey's politics were the cause of their chase. But until Catherine was again safe, he'd not press the issue, for he needed both the father and the son to assist in finding her. After that, he and Geoffrey would have much to discuss.

"You are right, Geoffrey," he said, moving to the table. "My pacing is getting us nowhere. However, I doubt a new plan is fully in order. Not yet. We have searched much of the south. The midlands are next. If we don't find her there, we'll move north. Instead of us riding around willy-nilly, as we have been, I believe we should concentrate on Henry's strongholds."

"Whatever for?" Miles asked from his position by the table.

William surveyed the man who was to be his daughter's husband. Over the interim, he'd come to know Miles better. If he had it to do over again, he would have refused the proposed match. In fact, he was tempted to rescind the betrothal here and now. But Catherine had fallen in love with the young fool. When she was found, if she still wished to marry Miles, he'd not disappoint her.

As to his future son-in-law's question, William countered with one of his own. "Does the prospect of meeting Henry face-to-face unnerve you, Miles?"

"Considering the political climate, I would think it rather risky to attempt what you propose."

William's ire rose. Hadn't the dolt yet unraveled the reason behind Catherine's abduction? William doubted the man was that thickheaded. Indeed, perhaps Miles knew exactly why his betrothed had been carried off. Hence his opposition to William's plan.

Releasing a long breath, William glanced at Geoffrey. Where once there were none, lines of tension now etched the man's face. The possibility of confronting Henry did not appeal to either of his companions. Undeterred, he said, "Nevertheless, that is what we'll do. Tonight we should feed ourselves and the men well. Afterward, everyone is to retire early, for tomorrow we'll ride north and west."

Miles grunted his displeasure. "'Tis risky, I say."

William frowned at him. "Is your betrothed not worth the risk?" William noted how Miles glanced at his father. "If you harbor uncertainties, perhaps you are not the man for my daughter."

"Stop badgering him, William," Geoffrey cut in. "He's concerned about what might happen if we find ourselves caught in a fray between Henry's and Stephen's troops. Caution is not a deficiency. He's simply being practical."

"I asked your son a question, so stay out of this, Geoffrey." William's gaze shifted to Miles. "Is she worth the risk?"

Miles squared his shoulders. "Aye. She's worth it."

"Well, since that's settled," Geoffrey stated, "I suppose we should alert the men as to our plans." He rose from his chair. "Is there anything else, William, that we should know?"

"Only that when we find her, you are to leave the bastard who took her to me."

"Easy, big fellow," Rolfe said as the stallion nudged his chest, eager to have more grain. He held his empty hands in the air, wiggling his fingers. "All gone. See?"

The stallion snorted and shook its head. Chuckling, Rolfe patted the animal's neck. He was amazed by its progress over these past weeks since its return to the castle, and he thought the beast would make a worthy destrier in the not-too-distant future.

The animal pranced and tossed its head. "You're restless, aren't you?" Rolfe asked, understanding the stallion was impatient to stretch its legs.

More than a week had passed since the animal was last exercised. Rolfe remembered the day, as well as its previous night. Catherine had barely spoken to him subsequent to their outing. He believed he understood why.

Telling her that he saw no reason to break tradition was not the wisest thing he'd ever done. In fact, he'd been exceptionally callous. But when she'd made reference to his doing what was proper, meaning did he intend to wed her if she'd conceived, he didn't entirely know how to react.

From the first time he ever lay with a woman, he'd shunned the thought of marriage. Pleasure was all he wanted. But with Catherine? The notion didn't leave that familiar feeling of distaste whenever the word rolled through his mind. Nor did the idea that she might be carrying his child threaten him.

He'd always imagined that if he were presented with such a claim, he'd beat a hasty retreat, just as his own sire undoubtedly had. Notably, though, there was no riotous urge to break through the castle gates and ride to the farthest corner of the land in a pressing need to escape. Rolfe was rather bemused by the lack of turmoil inside him. Strangely, the only emotion he felt was one of calm acceptance. Even that of pride.

Had he gone soft? he wondered. Or was there something else going on inside him that he wasn't fully aware of yet? Surely he wasn't falling in love with Catherine. Or was he?

From the corner of his eye, he caught a flash of blue. It was Catherine. He watched as she descended the steps from the keep, her mantle pulled around her against the light chill in the air. Since she'd barely spoken to him the week through, he puzzled over why she'd come searching for him here in the yard. Yet the tilt of her head and the squaring of her shoulders told him she definitely had something to say.

"Hold on, big fellow," he mumbled to the horse. "I believe we're about to get an earful." When she was beside him, he greeted, "Good afternoon, milady."

"'Tis that," she said, looking up at him.

"I presume you wish to speak to me?"

"Aye. I thought you should know that any fears you may have had about my conceiving can now be put to rest. The tradition, therefore, will not be carried on. A pleasant good day to you."

The last of her words had been tossed over her shoulder at him, for she had turned and started back across the yard. Rolfe watched as she ascended the steps and disappeared into the keep. He stared at the closed door for an endlessly long time.

She hadn't conceived.

He should feel relieved.

He didn't.

Blessed creation! What, then, did he feel?

Bereft.

As though, twice over, he'd just lost something exceedingly precious.

CHAPTER
15

SHE'D LIED.

Catherine bemoaned the fact, but she wasn't about to beg a man to marry her simply because she carried his child. Unless Rolfe wanted her solely for herself, could offer her the love and devotion she would always require from the man who'd be her husband, she saw no reason to burden either of them with an unwelcome union. She'd thought that when she told him she hadn't conceived, and she believed that today.

Even so, she was beginning to worry.

And for good cause.

Two months had elapsed since she'd gone down into the yard to inform him he could put his fears to rest; nearly three months since she'd been visited by her last monthly flow. Though her breasts were a bit fuller, and certainly more tender, her stomach was as flat as ever. But she couldn't keep the truth from him forever. Not at this rate.

Oh, misery of miseries, she thought. What was Henry doing? By now, she'd have expected him to defeat Stephen, or vice versa, and she'd presently be away from Cartbridge, away from Rolfe, and home again in Normandy. But instead, here she sat in the great hall, staring at the unappetizing fare that had been set before her, her stomach churning as it was wont to do of late.

"What's wrong, child?" Eloise asked. "You're not eating as you once did."

Catherine wondered if the woman had somehow read her thoughts. "I'm just not hungry."

"Are you becoming ill? You do look a mite feverish," her nurse said. She placed her hand on Catherine's brow. "As I thought: You're overly warm."

Catherine understood Eloise's concern. But she wished the woman wouldn't make such a fuss, especially in the open as they were. The less attention drawn to her, the better. No one knew about her pregnancy, and that's the way she wanted to keep it.

"'Tis the heat," she announced, her stomach starting to flip-flop. Odors that had once been satisfying now nauseated her. The roasted venison was the culprit this time. "Excuse me. I need some fresh air." Shoving from the table, she quickly headed for the door.

Once outside, she gulped the night air into her lungs, hoping it would settle her nausea. Unfortunately, it had the reverse effect.

She dashed down the steps and ran to a corner of the yard, where, behind some stacked kegs, she relieved her stomach of its contents. Straightening, she wiped her mouth with the back of her hand, praying no one had seen her.

Catherine felt far better than she had. Wanting to rid herself of the sour taste on her tongue, and to also allay any further nausea, she slowly made her way to the small herb garden, in search of a sprig of peppermint.

She plucked a few leaves from the tender young plant, which was used not only for medicinal purposes but to sweeten the air inside the castle as well. In the dim moonlight, she inspected the leaves carefully, making certain the edges were jagged and not smooth. If this were pennyroyal and not peppermint, she could abort.

On first discovering her condition, she'd considered taking that route. Her deliberation, however, had been a short one. The babe was not at fault. So why cause it harm for something she should have governed from the start?

Damn him for making her want him. And damn herself for still wanting him!

Popping the leaves into her mouth, she chewed and strolled at the same time, her thoughts on Rolfe.

The man was infuriating. As promised, he hadn't approached her since that night. Even so, he slept in the same chamber with her. Sometimes she believed his decision to stay was precipitated by some perverse need to see who held out the longest.

It was as though he'd laid siege to her willpower. Strutting about the room at night in naught but his braies, his upper torso glowing golden in the candlelight, he purposely tempted her, hoping she'd come to him. So far she'd managed to keep her wits about her and her desire in check, but she didn't know how much longer she could stave off these yearnings swirling inside her.

The rogue! she berated silently. Simultaneously she turned her head, spitting the chewed leaves from her mouth.

"Is that really what you think of me?"

Catherine jumped. As her heart hammered in her ears, she stared at a pair of feet. A greenish muck smeared the toe of one boot. Slowly her gaze rose, until she was looking Rolfe full in the face. "I—I didn't know you were there."

"Obviously." He kicked the loathsome-looking clump from his foot. "What was that stuff?"

"Peppermint."

He nodded knowingly. "Eloise said you weren't feeling well."

Catherine tightened her lips. She'd cut the woman's tongue from her mouth yet. "Eloise is wrong."

"Why, then, did you rush from the hall?"

Had he been watching her? "'Twas the heat," she said. "I simply wanted some fresh air."

He cocked his head and studied her more closely. "Are you sure that's all?"

"Aye. That, and I also felt restless."

"Not thinking of trying to escape again, are you?"

"No. I learned my lesson the first time around. However, I'd be exceptionally pleased if Henry would stop dawdling about England and finish what he came here to do."

Rolfe chuckled. "I doubt he's dawdling, Catherine. Since Easter, when he was at Gloucester, he's been to Evesham and taken Tutsbury. Next, if he's not already there, he'll be in Leicester, then on to Coventry. Or so the last messenger he sent had told me. War is much like a game of chess. Who wins and who loses is based on who has the best strategy."

"Do you think Henry will win?"

"Outright, you mean?"

She nodded.

"Either that, or he'll come to a suitable compromise. Whatever the outcome, it will take time."

"How much time?" she asked anxiously.

He shrugged. "'Tis only a guess, but I'd say another six months, more or less."

Catherine thought she might faint. "S-six months?" she questioned, trying to remain calm.

"Aye. But for both our sakes, I hope it is done sooner."

To Catherine, he'd sounded as though he were as eager to be away from her as she was from him. "I take it, then, you are as restless as I," she said, wanting confirmation.

"I'm a warrior. Naturally, I'd prefer to be in the thick of battle. That is what I've been trained for. My skills are useless to Henry with me sitting here idle."

His ability, she knew, was as keen as ever, his shoulder now fully healed. Each day he and Garrick would practice with various weapons, ensuring their adeptness. She imagined this situation was indeed tedious for him, especially when he'd much rather be in the fray. Perhaps she could persuade him to join his duke.

"Then why aren't you with him, if that is what you want? There are others here who could guard me equally as well as you."

"Duty, Catherine. My liege lord has instructed me to remain at Cartbridge. A good knight never disobeys his orders."

"Not even when he knows he can be of more help somewhere else?"

"Not even then," he replied, stepping closer. He lightly caught her arm. "You sound as though you are impatient for me to be gone. Is that what you really want? Do you wish I would leave here this moment, never to see me again?"

Yes.

No.

Oh, blast the man! she thought, his warm touch having sent her emotions reeling. She didn't know what she wanted.

Her heart ached at the prospect of never again setting eyes on him. Yet if he stayed, he would soon learn the truth. He might grudgingly offer to wed her. Henry could force him to do so. But what she feared more was that he'd just walk away, without even so much as a backward glance.

His rejection would surely destroy her. Already she understood why. Unbelievably, she, Catherine de Mortain, the betrothed of Miles d'Avranches, had fallen in love with Rolfe de Mont St. Michel. Instead of bringing her joy, the knowledge saddened her, for she doubted he felt the same.

His hand was on her chin. He tilted her face to his. "Is that what you want?" he repeated on a whisper. "Do you wish me gone?"

"No, but she couldn't tell him such. "'Twould seem I have no say in the matter," she answered, hedging his question. "Henry is the one who controls your movements. You've told me that when this is all finished, we'll part. I trust that is still the plan."

"Aye. That is the plan."

"At that time, I further trust you'll be off to some other battle or perhaps a tournament, whichever catches your fancy."

"'Tis my way of life, Catherine. I'm a knight, first and always. Nothing will change that."

Though the light was murky, she could see his eyes. They were clear, forthright, free of any regret. The life he'd chosen was what he wanted above all else. Catherine knew what she must say.

"Then for your sake, I hope you'll be gone tomorrow, so you may join Henry and do whatever it is you feel most comfortable doing. As for myself, I care little if you stay or go."

His hand fell from her face. "'Tis late," he said dully. "You should be getting back inside."

She began to turn, then quickly looked his way. "Are you coming?"

"Not yet. I have a few things I must do."

"Then good night to you, for I think I shall retire."

"Pleasant dreams, Catherine."

She heard the words just as she started away from him. She didn't acknowledge them. Instead, she kept on course toward the steps. Had she turned for a second time, he would have seen the tears shimmering in her eyes. And that she couldn't allow.

Knowing nothing would ever change his desire to be in the fore of every battle, Catherine was now certain she'd done the right thing by lying to him about not conceiving.

As she climbed the stairs, she hoped something would occur to put an end to this madness once and for all.

She prayed it happened soon.

Well before he learned the truth.

Rolfe watched Catherine as she ascended to the keep's entry. When the door finally closed behind her, he took to walking the yard.

Over two months had passed since he'd made love to her, over two months in which he'd suffered in utter agony. Tonight was no exception.

He desired her, longed to enjoy her, was eager to take pleasure in her, wanted to give her the same. Yet he'd given his word not to approach her, to come to her only by her own bidding. So far he'd kept his promise, but his discipline was cracking. Soon it would crumble altogether.

True, he could seek his relief with Ilona, the woman having warmed to him again. Or, if she refused, another willing young wench would do. But the thought didn't appeal, not when it was Catherine he wanted.

He found himself at the stables. Nodding to a guard, he strode inside to check on the stallion. Next he examined his equipment. As expected, all was in order. The only reason he'd come in here was that he dreaded going to their room.

Leaving the stables, he bade the guard good night, then

walked the yard some more. A game of chess with Brother
Bernard didn't interest him. A round of dice with Garrick
and Aubrey didn't excite him either. The only thing that
held any attraction was Catherine.

He stared at the heavens. *Blessed St. Michael, I beseech
you to cease this agony within me.*

Realizing he was actually praying, something he hadn't
done in a long, long while, Rolfe strode toward the keep. His
protector had better end his misery for him, or he'd damn
well do it himself.

"Tomorrow we'll begin our search north," William said,
his tone indicating his frustration. His mood was not the
best, for he'd become weary of scouring the countryside,
never to be rewarded. His daughter was out there. This time
he was certain she'd be found. "'Tis the only place we
haven't looked."

"Are you certain we won't again be chasing naught but
air?" Geoffrey asked.

The men were again situated in the lord's chambers at
Geoffrey's estate. "Aye. This time we'll find her."

"How can you be so certain of that?" Miles asked. He
tossed the chart he'd been examining onto the table. "We've
been unsuccessful thus far. Why should *this time* be any
different?"

"Because, Miles, 'twould stand to reason that Henry
would hide her at the farthest point possible. No doubt he
understood her rescuers would start their search in the
south, constantly inching northward. If it was time he
wanted, we gave it to him. I am now of a mind that we
should have headed straight to the upper regions when we
first landed. Had we done so, our search would be long
over."

"You are undoubtedly right, William," Geoffrey stated,
"especially since we have, as Miles said, been unsuccessful
thus far. But why do you think Henry is behind this?"

"'Tis certain, Geoffrey, your favor lies with Stephen.
Likewise there has been bad blood between you and Henry
for a long time. Because of that, I have a strong feeling the
duke was averse to our families being joined. He wanted the

marriage stopped. What better way than to abduct the bride?"

Geoffrey sat forward in his chair. "Do you oppose my having supported Stephen?"

"Whom you support matters not," William snapped. "My daughter's welfare is what concerns me. Now, this is what I propose." He leaned over the table to view the chart. "Miles, you are to take thirty men and ride toward Derby. Just to the northwest lies Cartbridge." He pointed to the location. "Before his death, the earl was one of Henry's most avid supporters. I imagine the castle is yet held for the duke."

"And what do we do once we get there?" the younger man asked. "I doubt they will just open the gates and welcome us in."

William stared briefly at Miles, wondering if the man had any sense of strategy. "No, they'll not let you in, not if you approach in the company of an armed force. But a weary traveler, with a few unarmed attendants, might be asked inside. When you come upon Cartbridge, leave your men behind. They can set camp several miles away, but make certain their fires cannot be seen. Any smoke by day will surely alert those at Cartbridge that you are not alone."

"What about at night?" Miles asked.

"Logic dictates that if the men camp in a valley, the firelight will be masked by the surrounding hills," William returned, questioning whether he shouldn't go to Cartbridge himself. Watching Miles nod, he continued. "I suggest you post several lookouts to watch the castle. Also devise a signal of some sort. Should you get inside, you may want to advise your men as to what is going on. Also, if Catherine is indeed there, you'll need to get word to us so we can join forces."

"How do you expect me to signal anyone? If I do get inside, I'm sure I'll be watched."

William tempered his rising ire. Could the man not think for himself? "Can you write?"

"Certainly I can write," Miles stated, obviously affronted by the question.

"Then, I'll make certain there's someone in the troop who can read. Before you make your approach, do some reconnaissance. Find a spot where you think it's safest and leave your message there. Whether you drop the thing from a window or tie it to a stone and toss it over the wall, I care not. Someone is to go each night and search the area."

"And what if there's a moat?"

"Then I hope you have a sure aim. For if you find yourself in trouble and need assistance, you'll not get it otherwise." William proceeded to tell Miles that he and Geoffrey would search to the north and east, naming each place they would go. "If you find Catherine, I want a messenger sent to us. We'll be back at my estate by the end of next month. If you don't find her, be there yourself. If you do find her, make certain someone is there to alert us."

"The place is northeast of Oxford, correct?" Miles asked.

"Aye. If you doubt you can find it on your own, ride straight to Oxford. You can receive directions there. Since the town and castle are in Stephen's hands, I don't think you'll have any worry."

"If she is there and I'm allowed inside, how do you propose I get her out? Certainly they won't just let us leave with a wave and a fond farewell."

"That, Miles, you'll have to determine for yourself. Use your head for once. Whatever you decide, make sure it is done with caution and stealth, for I don't want Catherine harmed. Understand?"

"Aye," Miles said. "I will be cautious."

"Good," William returned. He looked at Geoffrey. "I presume you are agreed to this?"

"I have no objections," the man stated.

William stood up. "Then tomorrow we ride. For all our sakes, Catherine's especially, pray God our search will soon be at an end."

In their chamber, Catherine stared across the way. Surrounded in darkness, Rolfe stood by the window, its shutters thrown wide. She heard his deep, cleansing breaths as he gulped the night air into his lungs. He'd suffered another nightmare, this one far worse than before.

At his first agonized stirrings, she'd instantly come awake. She didn't go to him, but instead, as he'd instructed, kept to her bed. Feeling powerless, she'd watched him thrash about, mumbled cries vibrating in his throat. The ordeal, though lasting only a short while, had seemed to go on endlessly.

Pity had swelled inside her, and she could take no more. But just when she started from her bed, he suddenly roused. Like a great bear rising on all fours, he bounded up from his pallet. There was a wildness about him that frightened her. She was now thankful she'd stayed from his reach. Half awake, but still caught in his horror, he might have killed her.

From where she lay, she could tell he yet bore the memories of this latest terror. Again she wanted to go to him, to offer him comfort, but she held back.

His fist struck the stones beside the window. "Why?" he groaned.

All the misery inside him emerged with that one question. Catherine didn't think. She was away from her bed and across the room. As her hand settled on his sweat-dampened back, she felt him stiffen. "Rolfe?"

He reared his head back and stared at the ceiling. From his reaction, she thought he was no longer fighting his nightmare but something else entirely.

"Go back to bed, Catherine," he said, looking back out the window.

"Why?"

"You shouldn't have come to me."

"I know you said not to when you were yet asleep, but now you're awake."

He sighed heavily. "Your closeness only adds to my misery."

She didn't understand him. He suffered emotionally; yet, tormented as he was, he wanted her away. "I came to give you comfort. How can my offering to assist you possibly make you feel worse?"

A sharp laugh erupted from his throat. "You have no idea what I'm saying, do you?"

Catherine frowned. She was a bit dazed from her sleep, but she thought she'd heard him clearly enough. "I'm not sure. If I've missed something, please tell me."

For a moment, there was silence between them, then he

said, "I want your comfort, need it desperately. But I need something else from you equally as much. I'm afraid if I accept the first, the other urge will become uncontrollable. Even if you refuse, I may not stop." Slowly he turned toward her. "In other words, I want to make love to you. I told you I would approach you only by your own bidding. If you don't want to again lie in my arms, go from me—now."

Catherine didn't move. How could she run from him when she felt his anguish? She loved him and, though he might not return the sentiment, she'd do anything to help ease his pain. Gazing at the familiar angles and planes of his face, which lay in shadow, she knew the choice was hers.

"Catherine, please," he implored, turning again to the window. "Go, before it's too late."

"'Tis already too late," she whispered, pressing her cheek to his back. "The urge is in me as well. I want you to hold me as you once did, make love to me as I remember. Nothing could make me happier. Therefore, I bid that you come to me."

He inhaled deeply, jaggedly. His breath flowed slowly from him. "Are you certain?"

The question rumbled through his body into her ear. "Aye. I'm certain."

He spun around. "Later, you'll hold no regrets?"

"None."

"Then so be it."

Catherine gasped as he swung her up into his arms, the abrupt movement making her head spin. On his way to the bed, he sidestepped his pallet. At his destination, he easily lowered her to the center of the mattress. Her chemise came over her head. His braies fell to the floor. Naked, he joined her.

Kneeling, they faced each other. Then Rolfe's arm was around her waist, pulling her to him. "You don't know how much I've longed for this," he breathed just above her mouth.

Somehow her hands were at the nape of his neck, her linked fingers urging him closer. "Say no more and kiss me."

He complied eagerly. As their parted lips joined, their tongues hungrily entwining, he pressed her to the bed. Preliminaries were unnecessary, as their banked passions were already ablaze. Delirious with desire, Catherine needed no prompting. Her thighs opening, she welcomed him.

He was inside her, filling her. His hand lifted her hips, and he moved in the most enticing manner. Their joining was wild and wonderful. As she met him stroke for stroke, Catherine knew no man could elicit such joy in her as did Rolfe.

In their frenzied search for the ultimate gratification, she thought she heard him utter praise to St. Michael for having answered his prayers. She couldn't be certain, for at that moment all her senses began to spin. She tossed her head and moaned.

"Experience the ecstasy, Catherine," he whispered in her ear. "Let it take you where it may."

She obeyed readily. But as he joined her in that rapturous place that only he could take her, he promptly withdrew. Holding himself, he groaned and shuddered as he won his satisfaction. Even in the furor of the moment, Catherine understood the reason he'd pulled from her. He wanted to ensure there would be no bastard child from their union. Again she believed her decision not to tell him was the right one.

Once his breathing had settled, he kissed her soundly, then rose from the bed. She watched as he went to the basin, whereupon he washed his hands. Soon he rejoined her.

His long, hard body stretched out beside her, his head propped on one hand, he looked into her eyes. "No regrets?" he asked.

Only that he didn't love her, she thought. Even if he did, she doubted things would be very much different. His chosen profession meant all to him. Nothing would ever change that.

"You don't answer," he said. "I presume that means you're having second thoughts."

"Not so," she replied, knowing that no matter what the future brought, right now there was no place she'd rather be except here beside him. "I have no regrets."

He smiled. "I'm glad to hear that."

As he spoke, his fingers lightly ran from her curls to her breasts, then down again. Catherine's stomach quivered at his touch.

"If milady agrees, we could spend our nights together as we just have," he said, his fingers sliding deeper into her curls.

Catherine's breath caught at this new assault. Other than his saying the words she most wanted to hear, she desired nothing more than to be with him. "I have no objection."

His fingers eased between her folds to play and probe. "Then 'tis decided. For whatever time remains for us, we'll enjoy each other fully."

Her throat choked as tears stung her eyes. "Aye," she whispered, urging his mouth to hers. "For whatever time remains."

CHAPTER
16

Catherine awakened to feel the touch of Rolfe's tongue at the corner of her mouth. It sliced deliciously through her lips, then withdrew to lick her chin, down her neck, and on toward one breast. There the wet sliver laved the crown, bringing her nipple to erection. The act was performed on her other breast, then his tongue tickled to her navel, where it probed lightly.

His face moved lower. "Open to me," he said, his warm breath fanning her curls.

Stretching, Catherine arched her back, her thighs spreading wide. Her breath caught as his tongue worked its magic, delving and flicking. Her senses reeling, she moaned, thinking what an exceptional lover he was. These past two weeks had been pure heaven. Nothing, she was certain, would ever compare.

Just as her hips began to writhe, he abandoned her. The mattress sank as he bounded from the bed. Deprived of fulfillment, she sat up with a jerk. "Why did you leave me?"

Standing naked at the foot of the bed, he grinned wickedly. "I felt like tempting you."

"Tempting me?"

"Aye. To make you eager."

"You've already done that. Now come finish what you've started."

His golden locks brushed his solid shoulders as he shook his head. "That's only a sampling of what is to come."

Frustrated, she glared at him. "And why can I not have the sum total, here and now?"

"Because 'tis time we dressed." He shot the words over his shoulder as he made his way to the basin. "Rise, Catherine. We've slept too long. Everyone will be wondering where we are."

The rogue. Had he not kept her up most of the night, they would have risen far earlier. As she gazed at his body, which to her bespoke perfection, she remembered those wondrous hours they'd shared. Considering what had passed between them, she decided to forgive him for leaving her just now. Tonight they would again come together in a promise of ecstasy. She wished giddily that the sun would set within the next hour.

Breathing deeply, she noted that Rolfe's scent clung to her. She wasn't opposed to its presence on her skin. Indeed, she enjoyed the aroma. Still, someone else—such as Eloise —might notice the telltale fragrance. Questions were one thing she wanted to avoid.

By now Rolfe was through at the basin. Catherine rose and attended to her needs. Washed, her teeth cleaned, her hair combed, she set herself to dressing. Poking her head through a clean chemise, she saw Rolfe, his clothes donned, leaning lazily against the bedpost. He watched her.

"Enjoying the view?" she asked, feeling strangely embarrassed.

"Aye," he returned. "'Tis breathtaking."

Noting the way he gazed at her, Catherine felt her heart trip a little faster. Oh, why did this have to end? "And once your eyes can no longer behold me, how will you feel then?"

"Saddened, milady. Very saddened."

"Why?" she asked, then held her breath.

"Once we part, I cannot imagine any woman I look upon thereafter possessing such beauty as yours."

His answer cut deep into her breast. There would be

others. Dozens, no doubt. The thought of him eagerly plea-
suring another woman, the same as he'd done with her,
filled her with such misery that tears gathered. Afraid he
might notice them, she quickly turned from him.

Throwing on her clothes, she questioned why she was
forever weeping at the least little thing. Her pregnancy, she
decided, the last of her garments now donned.

Her emotions again under control, she circled toward
him. "I thank you for your compliment, sir, but I'm certain
that, in time, you'll forget what I look like. Perhaps one day
you'll even find you can no longer recall my name."

"I doubt that, Catherine," he said, studying her intently.
"I doubt that very much." He shoved from the post and
came toward her. "Are you ready to make your appearance
in the hall?"

At his approach, Catherine held her head high. "Aye," she
responded, praying he didn't touch her. Were he to do so,
she would undoubtedly fall at his feet, wailing like an
injured child.

He stopped only inches from her, his hands at his side.
"Then run along."

"Aren't you coming?"

"I have something I need to do first."

Impatient to be away, she headed for the door. As she
opened the panel, she heard him call her name. She turned
slowly to look back at him.

"When the years have passed, do you think you'll remember me?" he asked.

How could she not? Especially when his child would
always be there to remind her.

Again she felt her tears welling. "Aye. I'll remember."

Before she made an utter fool of herself, she was through
the opening, the door closing behind her.

Rolfe leaned his shoulder against a merlon, watching
Catherine as she took in the scenery at the adjoining crenel.
After joining her in the hall and partaking of his morning
meal, he'd suggested they go outside, where he led her up to
the battlements for a moment's privacy.

How could she think he'd ever forget her? he wondered, gazing at her profile. In his eyes, her beauty was unsurpassed. Not just outwardly but inwardly as well.

The thought that some day they would part pulled heavily at his heart, which at first surprised him. But then there was no woman quite like Catherine. Under different circumstances, he might consider asking for her hand in marriage. But, as a knight, his duty called. Always would.

Besides, she was accustomed to a life invested with riches. On the other hand, practically all he owned lay inside one coffer. Because of that, Rolfe knew she deserved far better than he could ever offer.

"Enjoying the view?" he asked, determined not to ruminate over things that could never be.

Smiling, Catherine turned to him. "Aye. 'Tis breathtaking."

Realizing he'd uttered those very words only an hour before, Rolfe chuckled. "Do you refer to the scenery or to me, milady?"

Her hazel eyes twinkled as she gazed up at him. "If you must know, the answer is both."

When she'd risen that morn, her mood was wistful. Now new life sparked inside her. She was suddenly playful. This was the Catherine who Rolfe most enjoyed. "Though I had hoped to score a point or two better, I am yet honored to find I'm at least equal to the surrounding hills. However, had you chosen the scenery as your preference, I fear my vanity would have been crushed."

Her eyes dancing with mirth, she tilted her chin most haughtily. "Your vanity, sir, could bear the weight of a thousand men and not suffer from the load."

Not so, he thought. Not if, after what they'd shared, she again sought her betrothed. She'd been given the truth about Miles, and if she went back to the man, Rolfe knew his pride would be dealt a severe blow. It would tell him she chose not to believe anything he told her.

He offered no comment on her statement, but instead instructed, "Close your eyes and hold out your hand."

"Whatever for?"

"For once, just do as I say without question." Her hand

rose from her side as her eyelids fluttered shut. Rolfe slipped the treasure from his belt, placing it on her palm. Her hand sank slightly from its weight. "You may look," he said.

Rolfe was at once amused by her reaction. Her jaw slackened in wonder as she stared at the solid gold bracelet. Her shaky fingers traced the circlet, which resembled twisted rope, then she touched the ruby eye of the serpentine dragon's head gracing the ornament.

"How beautiful," she whispered, reverence sounding in her voice. Her gaze met his. "Wherever did you get this?"

"I received it during my travels. It comes from a place which lies far beyond Persia, or so I've been told."

Her gaze again dropped to the bracelet. "Its worth must be immeasurable."

"Aye. Very much like you." She looked up at him inquisitively. "I give this to you, Catherine, as a keepsake to remember me by."

Her eyes glistened with tears. "Your gift is quite generous, but I need nothing more than what I already have to remind me of our time together. Truly, my memories of you will never fade. How could they?"

Her tone sounded lamenting while her expression appeared woeful, and Rolfe wondered if she deplored the thought of their parting just as much as he.

Without her, he knew his life would be lackluster, all joy abruptly abated. In spite of that, there remained the lure of his profession.

From the time he'd been taken into Robert de Bayeux's care, his goal had been to become a knight. The notion of traveling to far-off lands, of procuring untold riches, of righting injustices wherever they occurred had excited him. The enticement was yet there, but ever since he'd met Catherine, his need to follow those long-held dreams had somehow lessened.

As he gazed into her lovely eyes, he questioned which of the two was the most precious to him. The answer was upon him immediately. With the knowledge, he felt his heart swell with an emotion he'd never felt before. He understood what the sentiment was, could even give it a name. Joyfully he accepted the truth. Yet uncertainties abounded inside him, for he wondered if she might possibly feel the same. He had to know.

Stepping closer to her, he lightly brushed his knuckles along her cheek. "Catherine, I——"

A shout sounded, cutting into Rolfe's words. The guard who stood on the wallwalk just above the main gate announced the approach of riders.

"Stay here," he told her, then proceeded along the wall toward the south. Reaching the point where the guard stood, he noticed the three horsemen riding across the open fields. A quarter mile out, they were headed straight for Cart-bridge.

At first Rolfe thought they'd been sent by Henry, but as he watched the trio, he soon decided that wasn't the case. There was something about the middle rider that looked oddly familiar. The closer the man came, the more certain Rolfe was.

"Miles d'Avranches," he declared, just under his breath.

Stepping back from the wall, Rolfe signaled for the archers to come on high, then he turned to the guard. "They are not to come inside. Should they question you, nothing is to be said that would indicate the Lady Catherine is here. Do you understand?"

"Aye, sir. But what reason should I give them as to why we'll not allow them entry?"

"Tell them the place is filled with lepers. That should chase them off."

The guard quickly crossed himself. "Aye, sir. Lepers it is."

By now the archers had gained the top of the battle-ments, Garrick along with them. "What is it?" he asked Rolfe. "Her father?"

"Surprisingly, 'tis Miles. He comes with only two men, but you can wager the rest are out there, possibly hidden in the wood. For now, keep the archers back. If we show immediate signs of force, he'll know Catherine is here." He looked in her direction. Amazingly, she stood where he'd left her. "Take command, will you? I need to get her below."

The two men parted, Rolfe striding toward Catherine. "What's happening?" she asked the instant he reached her side.

"Nothing of import," he told her, catching hold of her arm. "Come, let's go below."

"Something of consequence has occurred or you'd not have called the archers to their posts." A look of dawning sparked in her eyes. "'Tis my father, isn't it?"

"Nay," he answered, attempting to direct her to the stairs. Her heels dug into the stones. "'Tis not your father, Catherine. I swear."

"Who then?"

"Some of Stephen's supporters," he said. He hadn't lied, for Miles, like his father, also gave his allegiance to England's king.

Rolfe again urged her toward the stairs, for he was impatient to get her below and into the keep. On this rise where the castle sat—especially here on its battlements— all sound from the valley below became amplified. Should Miles call out before she was safely down in the yard, Rolfe feared she might recognize his voice.

They were at the head of the steps when the shout came. Her betrothed's voice lifted on the wind and swirled over the wall, straight into Catherine's ears.

"'Tis Miles!" she said, looking Rolfe full in the face. Before he could stop her, she screamed her betrothed's name.

Rolfe cursed soundly, then motioned for a nearby guard. "Take her below," he ordered once the man was beside them. Handing Catherine over, Rolfe strode to a point just above the gate. "Did he hear her?" he asked Garrick.

"Aye," the older knight replied. "He's insisting that he be allowed in. Wants to negotiate for the Lady Catherine's release. He also says he and his attendants are alone and unarmed."

"The man's a fool if he thinks I'll believe that. Have you sighted any movement in the wood?"

"None, but that doesn't mean his men aren't out there."

Rolfe heard Miles's incessant demands to speak with the man responsible for Catherine's abduction.

"Are you going to show yourself?" Garrick asked.

"Why not? He knows she's here; therefore it stands

to reason the man who took her is also at Cartbridge. 'Tis time I faced the bastard and let him know who I really am." Motioning for the archers to take their positions, Rolfe stepped to the wall. "What do you want, Miles d'Avranches?"

Just beyond the moat, Miles's horse pranced beneath him as he stared up at Rolfe. "You know my name?"

"Aye. I know it well. What is it you want?"

"I wish to see my betrothed," Miles called.

"That's not possible."

"I demand to see her, so I will know she is well."

"She's well," Rolfe returned.

"Do you expect me to take your word, sir, as proof?"

"I've stated the truth. You may take it or leave it as you will."

There was silence between them, then Miles said, "I know you. But I cannot recall the circumstance in which we met."

"Considering the event, I can understand why you'd prefer to forget," Rolfe answered.

Miles frowned. "Who are you?"

"I am Rolfe de Mont St. Michel," he said, noting how the man had grown very still. "Remember, Miles? The road to Antalya? The hordes of Turks pouring down on us from the hills above? Coward that you are, you ran from the battle to hide in the rocks. Now do you recall the circumstance?"

"I recall no such incident, for I was never on the road to Antalya," he shouted. "You're mistaking me for someone else."

So, Rolfe thought. Even now the bastard refused to admit his cowardice. No doubt he held his tongue because he feared Catherine might overhear their conversation. "You were there. Sir Garrick, for one, can testify to such."

Garrick stepped to the wall to peer down on Miles. "Aye. I will bear witness you were there," he called. "And I know several other knights who will do the same." Then Garrick mumbled, "That's if any of them still live."

Pressing his lips together, Miles glared at the two men. "Where is Catherine?" he questioned with force. "I demand to see her."

"Methinks the weakling is trying to show he possesses some mettle, just in case his betrothed is listening," Garrick said to Rolfe.

"Once he sees the bows are set with arrows, he'll flee soon enough over yon hill," Rolfe commented, nodding at the distant knoll to the south. Then to Miles, he shouted, "You cannot see her. She's safe. That's all you need to know. Now be gone with you while you can yet ride from here."

At Rolfe's signal, the archers took their stance, nocked their arrows, and drew their bowstrings, Miles held closely in their sights.

"If you allow him to go," Garrick said, "he and his men will lay siege."

"Aye, that they will. We have enough stores to last six months. By then Henry should have his victory. I'd say we're prepared."

"Then so be it," Garrick returned.

Rolfe again looked down from the wall. Miles hadn't moved. He raised his arm, making certain his nemesis could see that he was about to issue the archers their command. "Be warned," Rolfe shouted, "their aim is true."

This time Miles didn't hesitate. He instantly reined his horse around. Smiling, Rolfe was about to gesture for the archers to stand at rest when Catherine suddenly bolted forward.

In her attempt to get at the wall, she bumped into one of the bowmen. His arrow released. Its cast was sure. Miles toppled from his horse.

"No!" she cried in utter horror, for Miles lay motionless on the ground. "Please!" she said, turning to Rolfe. "You must help him."

Rolfe paid no heed to her words. "God's wounds, woman," he bit out, grasping her shoulders. "I sent you below. How did you ever get back up here?"

"She got away from me, sir."

Rolfe looked in the direction of the voice. The guard whom he'd put in charge of Catherine hobbled toward him.

"I'm sorry, sir, but she took me by surprise," the man said.

Rolfe noted the guard's pronounced limp. "Obviously."

"Please," Catherine said again, her fingers curling against his chest. "You must help him."

Rolfe saw the tears welling in her eyes. "His men can assist him."

"He'll die if he doesn't get the proper care. Please. For my sake, don't let him just lie there."

"He may already be dead."

Her tears were now streaking her cheeks. "You can't be certain of that. Oh, please. If he is alive, I know we can help him. I beg you to let Eloise and me see to his wound."

Rolfe gazed at her for an endless moment. The joy that once filled him had slowly drained away. Her tearful pleas on behalf of her betrothed told him all he needed to know.

Releasing a long breath, he glanced at Garrick. "Bring the bastard inside."

CHAPTER
17

CATHERINE STOOD A DOZEN YARDS BACK FROM THE MAIN GATE, watching anxiously as Miles was carried across the drawbridge. Beside her, Rolfe firmly held her arm. His stance was rigid, his jaw set, and when she'd last looked at him, she noted the coldness in his eyes. His hatred of Miles was apparent, but, strangely, the emotion now seemed to extend toward her. Though troubled by his mood, she paid him no heed. Her concern currently lay with Miles.

The two attendants were led into the courtyard. Three horses followed. Next came Miles. As he was carried into the yard by Garrick and three other men, Catherine attempted to pull from Rolfe's grip. He held her fast.

"Let me go," she demanded, tugging against his hand.

"When the gates are closed and locked you may see to him. Not before."

An eternity passed as Catherine waited for the large wooden panels to swing shut. The huge crossbar dropped into place, and Rolfe's fingers uncurled from her arm. She ran toward the unconscious Miles.

"Is he alive?" she asked Garrick, her gaze on Miles. He was being carted face-down. The arrow protruded from his upper back near his left shoulder.

"He's breathing," Garrick responded as he and the others headed for the keep.

Catherine skipped alongside them. "Take him to the lord's chamber."

"The bastard won't be given any comfort in my bed," Rolfe said, coming upon the group.

At his motioning for the procession to stop, he caught hold of Miles's hair and lifted his head to look into his face. As though afraid of being infected with vermin, he let go of the brown locks; Miles's head dropped.

"Take him to the common quarters instead," Rolfe ordered. "I want guards posted around him as well."

Catherine stared after Rolfe as he strode on ahead across the yard. Handling Miles as he had, she believed he'd been deliberately cruel. If he wanted to blame someone for this current situation, he should look to her.

She'd been the one to disobey, the one to whack the guard's shins with an ax handle, which she'd grabbed on passing the barrel where it rested. Likewise, she'd been the one to run back up to the battlements and to rush the wall, wanting to see if her father were also with Miles. That the arrow flew, felling her betrothed, was also her fault.

She wasn't certain why she'd screamed Miles's name in the first place. She supposed in the excitement of learning that he stood just outside the castle she thought to alert him, hoping somehow he could magically transcend the walls and deliver her from Cartbridge before Rolfe discovered she carried his child. A foolish notion indeed.

Considering everything, she deemed that Rolfe's anger and hostility should be vented on her, not some helpless man who might in fact be mortally wounded.

When Rolfe disappeared inside the keep, Catherine immediately picked up her pace. "Hurry," she said to Garrick and the others. "His wound needs immediate attention."

By the time they entered the common quarters, Brother Bernard and Eloise were already inside the room. On his own entry to the keep, Rolfe had undoubtedly informed the pair that their services were needed, for a collection of articles meant for Miles's treatment were gathered close beside them.

Staying close to Miles, Catherine marked that Rolfe was also in attendance. He held to one side, his expression stoic. He refused to look at her.

"Lay him here," the monk instructed.

Garrick and the other men carried Miles to the place where Brother Bernard had pointed. Settling their load face-down on the pallet, the men stepped away. The monk gathered his robes and knelt beside Miles to inspect the wound.

"His injury doesn't look to be life-threatening," Brother Bernard announced, then grabbed the arrow's shaft. With a quick jerk, he pulled the thing from Miles's back. "As I thought," the monk said, holding the arrow's bloody tip on high for all to see. "The point penetrated his flesh by no more than two, maybe three inches. The angle indicates that the only thing harmed is muscle. If I'm correct, he'll recover. Unless, of course, he takes the poisoning in his blood."

At the first of Brother Bernard's statements, Catherine released the trapped breath from her lungs. Now she had something else to worry about. Moving to Miles's side, she knelt opposite the monk. "Do you think you can prevent such?" she asked.

"I believe it's possible," Brother Bernard answered. "But I will know better once I actually see the wound."

Fumbling at Miles's right shoulder, the monk released the brooch and then, with Catherine's help, drew the blood-stained mantle from his patient. Next he took hold of his dagger and sliced through Miles's tunic from neck to hem. Spreading the cloth apart, exposing the skin, he inspected the wound more closely.

"Hand me the wine, Eloise," he said, not looking at the woman, "so I might clean the area."

Catherine's nurse quickly shoved the metal flagon into the monk's hands, whereupon he poured wine into the wound.

"The herbs, please," he said. "And the grease."

The things passed to him, he set to making an ointment. Afterward he spread the paste over the wound. Requesting a square of linen, he covered the area, then bandaged the whole with a longer strip of the cloth, again with Catherine's help.

"There," Brother Bernard said, rising to his feet. "I believe the wound will heal quite nicely."

"Why hasn't he awakened?" Catherine asked, her fingers shakily stroking the right side of Miles's brow.

From behind her, Garrick chuckled. "Considering the injury wasn't of any consequence, you can wager the weakling fainted. Place something foul smelling under his nose and his eyes will open fast enough."

No sooner had Garrick finished his statement than Miles groaned. His eyelids fluttered. "Catherine?" he questioned, his blue gaze focusing on her.

"Aye. I'm here."

"I thought I'd never see you again."

He attempted to lift his head, but Catherine gently pressed it back to the pallet. "Keep still," she told him.

His left cheek settled again. "What happened? I feel so weak."

She nibbled momentarily at her lower lip. "You were wounded by an arrow, Miles."

He frowned. "The bastard shot me in the back."

Before Catherine could tell Miles the mishap was her doing, Rolfe announced, "You were warned. Next time take heed and move faster. Otherwise you might not fare as well as you have."

Gazing up and over her shoulder, Catherine noticed that Rolfe stood just behind her. When his voice had sounded she'd jumped, for she hadn't heard him approach. "If I may," she said, "I'd very much like to stay with him until I know he's feeling stronger, and that he hasn't taken a fever."

Emotionless gray eyes stared down at her. "'Tis your choice." He turned to Garrick. "Search him for a weapon."

As the older knight began patting Miles's body, eliciting several protests while he did so, Catherine surveyed Rolfe through her lashes. He'd saved her the embarrassment of telling Miles that she'd been the cause of his injury. Still, she couldn't fathom why he was acting so coldly toward her.

There had to be more to his sudden transformation than

just Miles's untimely appearance. At first Catherine couldn't fathom what it might be. Unless . . .

Her urgent pleas that she be allowed to attend to her betrothed's wound: Were they somehow connected to his shift in mood?

A strong possibility, she thought. Things had certainly changed between them since that morning when she'd awakened, had altered even more dramatically since they'd stood side by side on the battlements sharing a private moment together.

She wondered briefly what words would have passed through his lips had the guard not at that very moment sounded the alert. Considering Rolfe's present behavior, she doubted he would ever reveal them to her. If anything, Catherine understood one thing: Their relationship would never be quite the same.

Sighing, she let her gaze fall from his face. At his waist, she caught sight of the ruby-eyed dragon's head peeking from his belt.

The bracelet.

She now remembered how she'd held onto the keepsake from the moment he'd given it to her, only to drop it as she'd hastened against the wall. He'd obviously retrieved the ornament. She wondered whether he planned to return it to her. Or did he now intend to retract the gift altogether?

"Aha!"

Garrick's exclamation drew Catherine from her thoughts. She turned in time to see him stand away from Miles.

"Wicked-looking little thing," he said, his thumb lightly testing the tip of a knife. "I found it tucked in his boot."

"A person needs some sort of instrument to assist him while eating," Miles announced.

Garrick grunted. "Minding the length of the blade— a good eight inches, I'd say—you must be somewhat of a glutton." He handed the knife to Rolfe. "'Tis all I found."

"'Twas enough," Rolfe said, turning the knife in his hands. "A blade this size could gut a man." He looked at Garrick. "Come. We have things to discuss."

Catherine's heart sank when he offered not a word in

parting. He hadn't even accorded her so much as a cursory glance. His last words were to the guards.

"Watch them carefully," he ordered, his tone clipped. Then he and Garrick made their exit.

"Well," Brother Bernard declared, "I doubt I can be of further aid, at least for the time being. I've mixed some herbs in a cup of wine." He pointed at the vessel sitting on a stool beside Eloise. "Give it to him. 'Twill ease the pain. Now, if you'll excuse me, I shall also take my leave."

"I appreciate your help," Catherine told him.

"Think nothing of it, my child." With a wave, he left the room.

"I'll be staying," Eloise stated when Catherine looked her way. "You'll not have to attend to him alone."

"Then hand me that cup," Catherine said. At her prompting, Miles rolled to his right side, whereupon she aided him as he sipped the herb-laced wine. "'Twill give you relief." Miles nodded, and after handing the cup back to Eloise, she gently pulled his ruined tunic from his arms, then tossed it aside.

"Is it safe to talk?" he asked as Catherine covered him with a sheet of linen.

She glanced at the guards. Though vigilant, they stood far enough away so as not to intrude. "Aye. They cannot hear us."

"I had hoped to make a more dignified entry than what I had, but at least I got inside. That the bastard would order me cut down when I complied with his wishes is unconscionable. He'll pay for this infraction. Dearly at that."

Feeling guilty, Catherine was unable to hold his gaze. "'Twas my fault you were wounded, Miles, not Rolfe's," she said, deciding it was time to own up to her blunder.

His brow furrowed. "Your fault?"

"Aye," she replied, self-consciously plucking at her skirt. "I had broken away from my guard and rushed against the wall. As I did so, I bumped into one of the archers. He let loose his arrow. The next I saw you were lying on the ground. I didn't mean for it to happen. It just did." She remembered why she had done so. "My father—where is he? Is he all right?"

"As far as I know, he is fine. He and my father are seeking you out far to the east of here."

Catherine listened as Miles related the account of their search. She learned they'd started in the south, sweeping ever northward. He became annoyed as he spoke about their travels, but she imagined the irritation in his voice was simply a reflection of the exasperation he'd felt at not finding her.

Twice in telling his story he yawned, and Catherine realized that Brother Bernard's potion was taking effect. By the time he finished his tale, his eyelids were drooping.

"You should rest," she said when he yawned again.

"First I must know something."

By the way her betrothed stared at her, she knew what he was about to say. "What is it, Miles?"

"Has the bastard harmed you? Defiled you? I want to know, Catherine. Has he?"

Catherine knew this was her chance to absolve herself of any wrongdoing. She could readily cry rape and be believed. But Rolfe had never forced her into giving him her virginity, and she'd not claim that he had.

"No, he has always been most kind."

"Seems unlikely the bastard would know the meaning of the word."

"Miles," she stated firmly, "he has never harmed me. Now rest."

"Aye," he said, yawning again. "I grow sleepy." His hand covered hers where it lay in her lap. "But when I awaken, I want to know all that has happened to you."

His words were garbled, but Catherine understood him. "Rest, Miles. We'll speak of it later," she said, then saw he was already asleep.

She was relieved. He'd already suffered one blow to his system; she hated to deliver another this quickly. Whether it was today, tomorrow, or next week, soon enough he'd have the truth.

Standing on the wallwalk, Rolfe scanned the horizon to the south. "'Tis the same as with the other three directions," he said to Garrick, the pair having just circled the battlements. "I see no movement of any kind."

"Aye. But you can be sure his men are out there. Do you want to send an armed force into the field to see if they can be found?"

Rolfe shook his head. "I'll not risk losing even one of our men simply to seek their numbers. We're well fortified. Even if they come by the hundreds, I doubt they'll breach these walls. No, 'tis best we stay put."

"Then the waiting begins," Garrick said.

"Aye. 'Tis the way of it. At least we hold the prize," Rolfe commented.

"The Lady Catherine."

Rolfe nodded. "Since their objective is to see to her safe return, I doubt they'll willingly place her in jeopardy by attempting an attack. Wherever they are, they'll hold to their spot. As you say, the waiting begins."

"I wonder at Miles's stupidity for approaching as he did," Garrick said. "The fool was never much of a strategist."

"He probably thought he'd not be recognized. Posing as a weary traveler with two lone attendants—the first a lad who looks as though he just met his teens, the second showing every sign of being just a few years shy of the grave—he no doubt hoped to gain entry to Cartbridge without altercation. Did you check the others for weapons?"

"Aye. 'Twas the same as with Miles. Two knives, nothing more."

"I want them watched," Rolfe stated. "Before making his approach, Miles may have devised a signal by which to alert his men. Since he is presently unable to follow through, the others might attempt to send the message for him."

"What of the Lady Catherine? Do you think she will try to aid her betrothed?"

"Freedom beckoning to her, she very well might," Rolfe replied.

"Do you want her guarded as well?"

"No. When she's not busy nursing her betrothed," Rolfe said, his enmity for Miles again rising inside him, "I'll watch her movements myself."

"Anything else?" Garrick asked.

"Alert the men to look for smoke on the horizon. By the number of campfires set, we might be able to estimate their force. If there's no smoke by day, then have them watch for firelight at night. I have a feeling, though, they are far enough away that we'll not be afforded that particular advantage."

With a nod, his companion announced, "Then I'll see to passing your orders on to the others."

As Garrick made his way to the first sentinel, Rolfe turned and walked in the opposite direction. Coming upon the spot where he and Catherine had stood when the alert was sounded, he paused and wondered about his own sanity.

A moment of weakness, he thought, glad now the words he'd nearly uttered had never had the chance to roll from his tongue.

In some deluded state of euphoria, he'd assumed there might be a chance for them, conceived she was of greater importance than his duty, believed, of all things, that he'd fallen in love with her. He'd been ready to tell her so, to ask if perchance she felt the same, when Miles appeared. If he'd hoped her answer was to the affirmative, he was quickly dealt a blow, for within minutes the truth was handed to him.

By the horrified look in her eyes after her betrothed went down, by her forlorn expression as she was apprised the man could be dead, by the plaintive quality in her voice as she begged for Miles to be brought inside, Rolfe knew she was as enamored of the man as on the day she'd been abducted. With the revelation a heaviness had settled in his chest.

True, her reaction may have resulted from her own guilt at having caused Miles's injury. Even so, her incessant pleas triggered a rising resentment within him. He wondered briefly if he'd been stricken by that age-old demon called jealousy.

No, he decided, needing to deny that such a thing might be true. Anger was his response. After all they'd shared, after everything she'd been told about her betrothed, she yet chose to protect the man. To Rolfe that meant she still loved the bastard.

The coldness that encased him became brittle. If that were so, why had she given her virginity to him? Had she hoped to use her body in order to gain her freedom, so she could rush back to her betrothed?

Rolfe doubted that was the case. She'd known from the start that her release was in Henry's hands, not his. Considering that, it was quite possible she held feeling for both Miles and himself. Perhaps she suffered from the same sort of indecision as he. Where once he was trapped between his desire for her and his need for freedom, she now found herself caught between two men, one her lover, the other the man she was to marry. A hopeless situation, he knew.

As for himself, Rolfe was no longer torn. He'd made his choice. He now was grateful he hadn't said the words that had momentarily filled his heart. The break would be so much easier now. Though he cared for Catherine, and deeply, he could offer her little. There were yet battles to be fought. He could feel them beckoning. Wanderlust called again, and Rolfe understood fully that he was a knight, first and always.

And what of Catherine?

He desired her, and as long as she was willing, he'd seek his enjoyment with her. He'd do everything in his power to persuade her that Miles was not the man she wanted. She deserved far better in a mate. Somehow he'd make her understand that to be true.

And what was in the offing for them?

Knowing the connection would soon be severed, he slipped the bracelet from his belt. He'd return it to her when next he saw her. If not to be held as a keepsake, then to be applied as payment for all the misery he'd caused her.

Rolfe needed no such reminder. For in the future, wherever he traveled, for however long he lived, there was one thing he would always carry with him.

His sweet memories of Catherine.

The signs of fever began at sunset. Several hours later, Miles was suffering from the onset of chills. His brow burned as though it had been touched by a hot iron.

"I hadn't expected it to happen this quickly," Brother

Bernard said, Catherine having sent for him. "But the wound has begun to putrefy. We'll have to wait and see what comes forth before I can determine if he's taken the poisoning. In the meantime, I'll try another approach to his treatment."

The monk took hold of a small chest containing the castle's medicinals. He searched through its contents until he found what he sought. After removing the old dressing, he unfolded the scrap of linen resting in his palm and withdrew a generous portion of the remedy he now wanted to try. Earlier, the call went out to the servants to collect as many freshly made spiderwebs as they could find. Apparently Brother Bernard had anticipated the need of their use.

Once the wound was tended and a fresh bandage applied, Brother Bernard stirred another concoction of herbs into some wine. Together, he and Catherine forced the liquid between Miles's lips. He coughed and sputtered, cursing its foul taste, groaning his discontent when he was ordered to ingest more.

"It will take the fever away," Catherine said when he tried to push the cup from his mouth. "Now drink it."

The ordeal over, Miles fell into a restless sleep, whereupon Brother Bernard took his leave. Catherine settled back to wait and to worry.

Time passed slowly. Yet too soon, Miles stirred. He kicked the covers from him, and Catherine replaced them. He requested water, and she dribbled the cool liquid over his tongue. As the pattern repeated itself again and again, her guilt mounted. The monk came and went, checking on his patient. All the while, Catherine prayed that Miles would recover.

Screens were gathered around Miles as the castle's inhabitants began to retire for the night. Though Miles was in no condition to cause anyone harm, his guards kept to their posts. Eloise had twice insisted she take herself to bed; twice Catherine refused. With the soft sounds of slumber humming around them, she stayed at his side, a single candle burning lower and lower on its wick.

"I wish you would go off to bed," Eloise said anew. "You haven't eaten and you look worn."

"I'll not leave him," Catherine told her, "not until I know the fever has broken."

"I thirst," Miles croaked.

Catherine grabbed the pitcher, only to realize it was empty. "I need to get some more water," she said, touching his cheek, then his brow. He didn't feel as feverish as he once had, but he was far too hot. "I'll be back in a moment."

He nodded. "Hurry," he breathed.

Coming quickly to her feet, Catherine felt her head swim. Off balance, she stumbled slightly. Eloise was instantly beside her.

"What's wrong?" her nurse asked, her hand on Catherine's arm.

The dizziness had subsided. She knew its source, but she couldn't very well tell Eloise the cause. "Nothing," she lied.

"'Tis something," the woman announced. "Your eyes were spinning 'round like a top."

Knowing her nurse would not let her go until she had an answer, she said, "I felt a bit lightheaded, that's all."

Her jaw set, Eloise held fast to Catherine's arm. Her gaze ran Catherine from head to foot. "He's bedded you, hasn't he? You carry his child, don't you?"

The blood drained from Catherine's face. If anyone had heard those words . . .

"'Tis true, isn't it?" Eloise asked.

"No."

"Don't lie to me, Catherine. I've cared for you since the day you were born. I know you as well as you know yourself. As sure as I'm standing here, you're carrying his child. 'Tis true, isn't it?" she repeated.

Catherine wanted to deny Eloise's words, but she knew she couldn't. She could never hide the truth from her nurse. Why did she think she could do so now? "Aye," she admitted. "'Tis true."

"Does he know?"

Catherine glanced toward the guards. They gave no indication they were listening. "No. He's unaware of the fact. And that is the way it shall remain."

"'Tis his child. He should be made to marry you."

"That's the point, Eloise. I'll not force him to wed me. Not because of the babe."

"I take it you gave yourself willingly."

"Aye."

"You're in love with him, aren't you?"

Her throat tightening, Catherine nodded.

"Then why don't you tell him about the child?" her nurse asked.

"Because," she moaned, "he doesn't feel the same way about me. I cannot press him into marriage, knowing one day he'll resent me for it. He has to want to wed me for himself. Otherwise we'll both be miserable."

Eloise harrumphed. "I wonder what your father will have to say about this once he learns what has happened."

"When that time comes, I'm hoping Rolfe will be far away. In the meantime, you are never to speak of this to anyone. Do you understand? Not one word. If you divulge my secret, I won't ever forgive you. That I swear."

"Catherine?"

Her name sounded forlornly, and she glanced at Miles to see him rolling on his pallet. "I need to get some water," she said, trying to break free of Eloise.

"I shall get it," Eloise replied, taking the pitcher from Catherine's hand. "As for your secret, 'tis safe with me—with one provision."

"And what is that?"

"When I return, you'll take yourself to bed. I'll care for him." She jerked her head at Miles. "He'll not die. Not before sunrise, anyway."

That Eloise held no sympathy for Miles was apparent. "If he worsens, promise you'll come for me," said Catherine.

"Aye. But he'll not get any worse than he is."

Eloise was a capable healer. Even so, Catherine felt obligated to stay. After all, Miles's suffering was the product of her own foolishness. Yet if she wanted her nurse to remain quiet about what she'd learned, Catherine knew she had to agree to Eloise's terms.

"Then the bargain is made," she said, just as Miles again groaned her name.

* * *

A short while later, Catherine entered the chamber. Slumbering, Rolfe lay on the mattress, a sheet of linen draped low on his hips. As from the night they first shared the bed, he was nude.

Too weary to even snuff out the candle on the table beside him, she stripped from her clothes and sank down next to him. No more had she settled than he rolled toward her.

"I want you, Catherine," he whispered as he pulled her to him. Then his lips covered hers in a passionate kiss.

Even as tired as she was, she didn't object. She wanted to be held, soothed, shown affection in the only way he knew how.

His lovemaking was tender yet urgent, as though this joining might be their last. And when it was over, their mutual pleasure complete, he gathered her to him, holding her close.

As they lay quietly in the darkness, the flame now extinguished, the heavy gold bracelet gracing her wrist, Catherine wondered at his current mood. The coldness had vanished. A wistful quality had taken its place. Her heart aching, Catherine knew why, for the same sort of sadness had encompassed her as well.

Shared moments such as these were not destined to last. And though neither dared speak of it, the fact remained.

Soon—very soon—all this would be just a memory.

CHAPTER
18

"*OUCH!* THAT HURTS."

Catherine frowned at Miles. He sat on a stool near the open window in the common quarters. "I'm being as gentle as I possibly can," she replied, thinking he was acting like a child.

It was now the third week in July, a full month since he'd made his appearance at Cartbridge. From the time his fever had broken, he'd been throwing one tantrum after another, and Catherine was annoyed with his behavior.

Taking care, she again pulled against the bandage. He'd been slow to heal; the wound was still draining. As she lifted the linen swatch, the seepage causing it to adhere to the scab, he winced and hissed a curse. Gritting her teeth, Catherine had had enough. She ripped the bandage free.

The yell that went up drew several gazes their way, including those of the guards. Catherine noted how the two men chewed at their lips, trying to keep from laughing aloud.

"God's wounds, Catherine!" Miles exploded. "I believe you're trying to kill me."

Had that been her intent, she would have held her tongue

and allowed him to be left on the ground beyond the moat where Rolfe had wanted him to stay. Recently, because of Miles's surly mood, she wondered why she'd spoken up at all.

"It could not be helped," she returned, checking the wound. Puckered and drawn, the area around it was an angry red. "The thing was stuck." She spread a dab of Brother Bernard's ointment over the wound, working it into his skin. "We'll leave the bandage off. Maybe then you won't put up such a fuss."

Miles turned on the stool. "Have I been behaving that badly?"

"Aye," she said, wiping her hands on a scrap of cloth. She thought briefly of Rolfe and how, with his arm dangling uselessly, unspeakable pain tearing through him, he'd stood before her, protecting her from the wolves. Not once had he complained. "You have no patience, Miles. You are perpetually belligerent and haven't the decency to show the appreciation that is due those who have attempted to help you. Everyone here will be glad when you're gone."

"So will I," he muttered, not offering an apology. "That is the problem. We are held here against our will. The days grow tedious. I cannot wait until we are released. When that happens, in the first church we come upon, we can be married—finally."

The cloth in Catherine's hands stilled. She glanced through the window. Until this day, whenever he questioned her about her captivity, her only response had been to say she'd been treated kindly. The time for the truth had come. Drawing a breath, she released it slowly, then said, "We cannot marry, Miles."

His brow furrowed while his eyes searched her face. "What are you saying?"

"I'm saying that things have changed, and I cannot, in good conscience, marry you."

"Changed? In what way?"

"My feelings, for one."

He stared at her. "Your feelings? Are you saying you no longer love me?"

Catherine wished there were some way of telling him without hurting him. But she knew that, no matter what was said, he'd suffer, and so would his pride. "Aye. That is what I'm saying."

His jaw dropped. Disbelief marked his face. "You cannot mean that."

"I'm sorry, Miles, but I do."

He examined her at length, then his eyes narrowed. "At night, I've yet to see you come into this room to seek your own pallet. Where do you sleep?"

"In the lord's chambers."

"That's where *he* sleeps also, correct?"

Catherine understood whom Miles meant. "Aye, he sleeps there."

"Do you share the same bed?"

His questions were becoming too personal. Besides, they were not alone. "Miles—"

"Tell me!" he demanded, his anger apparent.

Catherine noticed how several heads had again turned their way. "I know this is difficult for you, but unless you can contain your temper and keep your voice down, I'll not go on with this conversation. Understand?"

"*Difficult?* Christ, Catherine, if you're about to say what I think, how can you expect me to remain calm?" He gave her no chance to respond. "He's bedded you, hasn't he? Forced you to become his whore! I'll kill the bastard for taking what was to be mine!"

"Miles, listen to me. He didn't—"

Before Catherine could finish, Miles sprang from the stool and gathered her into his arms. "Oh, my dearest, you shouldn't have tried to protect me by telling me you no longer love me. That you are not virginal matters little. You were defiled. I can only imagine the horrors you've endured, all because of his lasciviousness." He pulled back to gaze into her face. "I do know one thing: I forgive you. And even though you are no longer pure, I want to marry you."

Catherine gaped at him. Forgive her? If he believed she'd been defiled, why should she need to be pardoned? She shrugged from his hold and stepped back. "He didn't force me. Whatever has occurred between us was done by mutual consent."

"You gave yourself willingly?"

"I did."

He viewed her as though she were some odious creature that slivered through the mud. Catherine braced herself for what was to come.

"How could you have done such a thing!" Miles grated. "He's naught but a rogue and brigand. He doesn't even know his own sire. When I call him a bastard, I mean it literally. 'Tis beyond me how you could possibly switch your affection to some ignoble piece of rabble such as him."

Miles's words were telling, for as she was being escorted down the steps from the battlements she'd heard his claim that he had never met Rolfe. If that were so, she thought it rather strange that he knew so much about Rolfe's personal history.

"He said he knew you, Miles. Is that true?"

His expression grew guarded. "Until the day I was wounded I never set eyes on the man."

"Then how is it you are aware that he really is a bastard?"

His gaze was now shuttered, and though she waited, he didn't respond. Even when Garrick had confirmed Rolfe's story, Brother Bernard relating what he'd been told for good measure, she'd been willing to give Miles the benefit of the doubt. But now Catherine knew fully that all along Rolfe had been telling her the truth.

"Then you were once a knight, just as he said," she accused. "And you were on the road to Antalya, along with Robert de Bayeux and his son, Francis. You ran from the fight, didn't you? And because you did, both Robert and Francis were killed. Further, you were named a coward, your sword and spurs stripped from you and broken. That's so, isn't it, Miles?"

Enmity shone in his eyes as he glared at her. He gave no response, but Catherine was determined to have one.

"Don't be so bold as to deny it, Miles. Garrick has confirmed Rolfe's account. I imagine there are others who will do the same. All of it—it's true, isn't it?"

"Aye," he admitted, the utterance bursting through his lips. "But you don't understand. It was futile to stand against so many. They came by the dozens, wave upon wave. Had I stayed where I was, I also would have died. It was horrible." Moaning the word, he shook his head. "Horrible, I say."

Pity welled inside her for the man whom she once thought she loved. The terror he must have suffered at seeing the hordes of savages descending upon him was beyond her imagining. Still, others had stood and fought. Most had died, but some had lived, including Rolfe.

Even if Miles had stayed and faced the enemy, she questioned whether his doing so would in any way have changed the final outcome for both Robert and Francis. As Miles said, they might all have died. No one would ever know. Fate had decreed itself that day. And no amount of conjecturing could ever alter what had happened.

But one thing was apparent: Catherine now possessed the truth—or at least part of it. As she looked upon Miles, she wondered what else Rolfe had told her that might also be fact. Had Miles and Geoffrey sought another betrothal before seeking one with her? Was it actually their greed that had brought them to Mortain?

"Do you fault me for not telling you about my past?" Miles asked.

"No."

"Then why are you so determined to reject me? Despite what has happened, I want you for my wife."

Desperation sounded in his voice. Was it because he truly loved her? Or did it have to do, as Rolfe suggested, with his greed?

Catherine could have used this opportunity to question him about the young beauty he'd allegedly sought as his wife prior to making a betrothal with her. Six months before the answer may have mattered to her, but not now. Everything had changed.

"I cannot accept you as my husband, Miles, for I don't love you."

"And I suppose you think that because you've shared his

bed he has lost his heart to you? That he'll ask you to be his wife?" Miles laughed sharply. "You're a fool if you believe that. From what I remember of him, whether it was a woman or a battle, he was always eager for the next conquest. I doubt he'll abandon his wandering ways simply for you. His profession is his first and only love. Take my word for it, he hasn't changed."

The words cut deep, for Miles was probably right. By all indications Rolfe's devotion would last only until the day they parted.

She thought miserably of the bracelet that she'd tucked away, fearing it would generate way too much speculation about them. As far as Rolfe knew, the ornament was the sole remembrance that she'd carry with her once she left Cartbridge. Even given its worth, she believed the keepsake was scant compensation for the heartache she would bear. The one thing that could possibly counteract the abiding sorrow was their child. In that new life was where she'd ultimately find her joy.

"By your silence," Miles said, "I gather you know what I say is true. But if you doubt me, go to him and ask. I'll wager anything he'll choose his freedom well above you." He again took her by the shoulders. "Don't you see, Catherine? In his twisted need for revenge, he's attempting to turn you against me. He's used you, tricked you into believing he'll offer more. He's done this simply to get at me."

Could Miles's words have any merit? Did Rolfe seek his revenge through her? No. She'd not accept that as being true.

Breaking from his hold again, she said, "No promises were ever made, Miles. He's never been anything except honest. But that is not what's at issue here. I cannot and will not marry you. You may therefore consider our betrothal ended." She packed the medicinals in the chest and shut its lid. "I'll check on you later."

"Still hoping, aren't you?" he called as she headed for the door. "Remember, we have a contract. I'll not let you go that easily. Ask him—just ask him. You'll see what I said is true."

As Catherine walked along the corridor, her guard traips-
ing behind her, she decided she would indeed pose the
question to Rolfe. After all, there was a slim chance that
Miles was wrong.

Rolfe was striding across the courtyard when he glanced
at the window to the common quarters. His gut lurched, and
he stopped dead in his tracks. There, framed by the opening
in the stones, stood Catherine and Miles, locked in an
embrace.

Through narrowed eyes, Rolfe watched the pair. Soon
Miles pulled back and gazed at her upturned face. She
seemed entranced by his every word.

He'd seen enough. His jaw set, he aimed himself at the
keep.

Thinking about her discussion with Miles, Catherine
entered the lord's chamber. On closing the door in her
guard's face, she turned and gasped. "I didn't expect you to
be here," she said, her heart yet fluttering from the sudden
surprise.

"Where have you been?" Rolfe asked.

He lazed back in the chair by the table. Relaxed as a lion,
she thought. Just as dangerous, too. There was something
about his demeanor that warned her to be careful.

"I was tending Miles's wound," she said, crossing to the
table. She set the medicine chest down. "I thought you were
in the stables."

"I was, but now I'm here." He came to his feet and pulled
her to him. "Take your clothes off."

Catherine blinked. "'Tis the middle of the day."

"So? Don't you think it can be done in daylight?"

"The guard is standing outside the door."

Rolfe shouted the man's name. On the guard's acknowl-
edgment, Rolfe told him to take his leave. "Now he's gone,"
he told her. "Disrobe."

Something nettled him. Eyeing him cautiously, she wondered what it could be. "Why are you acting this way?"

"How am I acting?"

"Odd," she said. "Very odd."

"Do you consider my wanting to make love to you odd? Except for the few days you said you were unable to do so, we've enjoyed each other every night. 'Tis time we did so during the day."

Those "few days" were supposed to be her monthly flow. She'd lied—again. Not wanting to draw his suspicion, she'd told him her cycle had come.

His attitude was making her nervous, so she blurted, "The Church says we should not come together during the day."

He arched an eyebrow. "Nor should we come together if we're not married. But that hasn't been the case, has it? Actually, Catherine, if the Church had its way, we'd all remain celibate, married or not. Were we all to adhere to that doctrine, Christianity would soon die out. I'll wager anything the Church hasn't considered that." He pulled her closer, his hands settling on her hips. "I want you—now."

What did it matter if it was daylight or dark, they were married or not? She loved him, and their time together grew short. Whatever moments they could steal, adding new memories to the old, suited her quite well.

"Now," he repeated, his voice husky, and Catherine nodded her consent.

He led her to the bed and helped her from her clothes. His own garments fell beside hers on the floor. Then he pressed her down to the mattress.

"Open to me," he said.

Catherine complied, and they were instantly joined.

He was commanding, masterful, his lovemaking fast and hard, and when it was over she had the strangest feeling that she'd just been branded his possession.

Contented, she lay in his arms, wishing they never had to part. It was time to ask the question. But not forthright. A roundabout manner would be far better. That way, should Rolfe respond as Miles had said he would, she wouldn't look the complete fool, her hopes crumbling before his eyes.

She moved her head so as to see his face. "What do you plan to do when this is all over?"

"Are you referring to our lying here in utter repletion?" he countered. "If so, I thought we might start anew. Only this time, you may take the lead."

Catherine blushed. "That's not what I was talking about. I meant when I gain my freedom. What will you do then?"

Propping one hand against his head, he smoothed the other over her belly. It was beginning to round slightly. If he noticed, he'd never mentioned such, something for which Catherine was exceedingly grateful.

"I suppose I'll rejoin Henry."

She was silent, allowing his hand to play freely wherever it decided to roam. All along she gathered her courage. "Do you think you'll ever marry?"

His palm grazed lightly over one nipple, sending a delightful chill through her. "No. 'Tis not something I desire. Besides, I have no home, no means by which to support a wife. All I own sits in yon chest. And even if I were to find the right woman to love, I'd think twice about asking her to wed me. My profession always calls. When it does, I'd have to leave. I could be gone days, months, years on end. It wouldn't be fair to her or to me."

The right woman to love . . .

The phrase tumbled through her head. Apparently he hadn't found what he required in her. The hollowness inside her was unbearable. She fought to contain her emotions. "Why do you say it wouldn't be fair?"

"For one, I doubt either of us would remain faithful to the other, especially if I were to be gone months at a time."

"Are you saying that even though you loved her you couldn't be true to her?"

"I don't know," he replied with a half shrug. "The situation has never arisen."

Catherine stared at him. Even if he were to profess his undying love to her, she would never be certain he could be trusted. She imagined herself sitting alone at night while he rode from town to town, hopping from bed to bed, a new wench every night. That was not her idea of marriage.

Oh God, why had she ever fallen in love with him? And why had she posed all these questions? She thought her heart had just been shattered. Dazed, she saw his hand lying on her breast. She wondered if he'd somehow reached inside her and squeezed with all his might until something cracked, for that's precisely how she felt. She'd stupidly wanted an answer, and now she had it.

The urge to run welled within. Somehow she had to get away from Cartbridge, away from him, before she went thoroughly mad. She could see herself clinging to his leg as he dragged her across the courtyard while heading for his horse. All along she'd be begging him to stay. That would never do. If nothing else, she had to retain her pride.

"And what of you?" she heard him ask. "What do you intend to do once you're set free? Marry Miles, perhaps?"

So caught up in her grief, she missed the sarcasm in his voice. "I—I don't know. Even after what has happened, he says he wants me as his wife."

"Then he's aware I took your virginity?"

She viewed him closely to see if he gloated over the fact. If he did, he kept it hidden. "Aye. He's aware."

"Did you tell him?" he asked.

"No. He guessed. Despite what you may think, he's not a complete dolt. He knows we share the same room. It wasn't hard to surmise the rest."

"And he still wants to marry you?"

"Aye. He has mentioned the betrothal contract. If I refuse to consent to the wedding, he'll probably try to enforce it through the Church."

"Which brings us back to you: Do you still want to marry him?"

"I told you I don't know." What was one more lie added to the rest? She sighed. "If you want the truth, I am of a mind to place myself in a convent."

He gazed at her as though she'd just grown horns. "A convent?"

"Aye," she said, breaking from his hold. She rose from the bed. "That is what I'm thinking."

"You're jesting. Tell me you are."

"I'm not," she returned, her head popping through her chemise. "I'll become a cloistered nun."

"In a convent," he repeated.

"That's what I said," she announced, knowing that there,

in the security of a nunnery, she could wail away her misery in solitude.

His Catherine in a convent, Rolfe thought. It was several hours later, and he sat alone in the lord's chamber, questioning her sanity. Madness, he decided. Pure madness. Why in God's name would she do such a thing?

That she'd cloister herself made no sense. Were she here, he'd tell her so.

After their interlude, she'd dressed and asked permission to go below to the hall, saying she wanted to speak to Eloise. He'd called for a guard to escort her. Even though she'd been most compliant, following his rules meticulously since Miles had been carried through the gates, he didn't fully trust her. Especially after what he'd seen today.

The scene of the pair embracing revived itself in his mind. He felt his gut twist anew. If he didn't know better, he would swear he was jealous.

At first scoffing at the idea, he quickly sobered. If he weren't affected by that particular demon, why the hell had he been stricken with the swift urge to possess her?

Coming into the keep, he'd made his way to their chamber. On his way, he'd nearly knocked Aubrey down as he brushed by him, the lad asking if he could be of service to him. Once here, he'd thrown himself into the same chair where he was now sitting. Fingers drumming the table, he'd stared at the door, his anger mounting. The latch had clicked, and when he saw Catherine, he was more determined than ever to have her.

His lovemaking had been forceful, urgent. It was as though he had some perverse need to mark her with his ownership.

She'd given herself willingly, just as she always did, and when their joining reached its pinnacle, their cries of shared rapture filling the room, he'd felt at once satisfied that he'd mastered her. At the same time, he'd been racked by guilt.

Jealous?

Damn right he was.

Why hadn't he recognized the fact sooner?

Because he'd never suffered from the affliction until Catherine.

A convent, he thought anew.

She was far too vibrant to simply shut herself away like that. And far too beautiful to be perpetually frocked in black. No man would ever again hear her sweet laughter, see the mirth dancing in her ever-changing eyes. Her fiery passion for life, and for her lover, would be forever abolished in the required solemnity of a cloister. Only the shell of the woman he once knew would remain.

In exasperation, he released his breath. He didn't understand her abrupt need to lock herself away and disagreed with her choice entirely. The only thing that held some promise about her decision was that she'd not be marrying Miles.

Or would she?

She'd indicated that the bastard might try to enforce the betrothal. She was no longer virginal, but if he expressed his willingness to accept her anyway, the Church and her father might agree.

Rolfe sat forward with a jerk. *God's wounds!* He couldn't allow that. Catherine was his. No man should have her but him.

He recalled their conversation, this talk about his possibly marrying. As usual, that old barrier he erected whenever his freedom was threatened had leaped into place. He'd issued some sort of nonsensical yarn that if he ever found the right woman to love he doubted even then he'd wed. He knew it to be nonsensical because he'd already found the *right* woman.

Catherine.

That she could be forced to marry Miles or that she might sequester herself in a convent was ludicrous, especially when there was a simple solution.

Admit it, he told himself.

The words sprang forth in his mind with such ease that he knew them to be true. He loved her. Loved her with every fiber of his being. Without her, life would have no meaning. Without her, he'd wither and die.

Once more he believed Catherine felt the same.

Why else would she give herself to him so freely, even with her betrothed so close? The look in her eyes when she gazed upon him, the soft smiles she bestowed exclusively on him, the tenderness of her touch, the responsiveness of her lovemaking—all told him her affection was genuine.

There was only one thing to do: Given her betrothed's greediness, which nearly equaled Geoffrey's, Rolfe was certain it would work.

Bounding from his chair, he strode to the door, where he threw the panel wide. "You," he said, spying one of the sentinels.

"Sir?" the guard questioned.

"Bring Miles d'Avranches here at once."

CHAPTER
19

"LET ME MAKE CERTAIN I HAVE THIS STRAIGHT," MILES SAID. "You're offering me this pouch of gold for Catherine, correct?"

Rolfe eyed the man. Though he could barely abide being in the same room with him, he tempered his hatred and attempted to remain calm. "I'm not buying her, Miles. So stop trying to make it sound as though I am. The bargain is this: For that sack of gold, you'll relinquish all claim to Catherine by rescinding your betrothal to her. I want that set in writing. Likewise, you are never to mention our exchange to her. That also will be put in writing."

From across the table, Miles viewed Rolfe. "'Tis not enough," he said.

Rolfe's gaze narrowed. The bastard was twice as greedy as his father. Rolfe possessed more gold, but he needed the remainder for himself. For one, it might also be necessary to settle with William de Mortain. For the other, he required an acceptable sum so that he could support Catherine.

She'd not be able to live in the style to which she was accustomed, but they'd get by. At least for a year or so. Maybe longer. And once Henry's campaign was finished, the duke might be willing to reward those who were most faithful to him, Rolfe among them.

As far as his little infraction, when Henry discovered that the houses of de Mortain and d'Avranches would never be joined, the duke would undoubtedly forgive Rolfe, especially if he asked for Catherine's hand himself. Or so he hoped.

Rolfe smiled coldly. "You know, Miles, I could facilitate matters and save myself a small fortune just by seizing yon sword and running you through. I suggest you take what is offered before I retract the sum altogether."

"The amount you've tendered is not in question here. I seek something else."

"What?"

"My release," Miles announced. "On the morrow, my two attendants and I will be allowed to leave Cartbridge. Give me that, plus the gold, and our agreement is set."

"Done," Rolfe stated, knowing Miles posed no threat. Even if he went straight to Catherine's father, leading the man here, Cartbridge could withstand the siege. In fact, Rolfe believed William's arrival would be to his advantage. Inviting the man inside, he could begin negotiations for his and Catherine's marriage. Taking hold of a quill pen, he tossed it across the table. "Start writing."

As Rolfe dictated, Miles wrote. Afterward he affixed his signature, whereupon Rolfe dribbled some candle wax below it, Miles setting his ring into the seal. Taking the paper, Rolfe read Miles's scrawl, making certain everything was there.

"Is it acceptable?" Miles asked when Rolfe lowered the document.

"Aye. The bargain is made." He tossed the bag of gold at Miles. "I propose you start packing. By shortly after sunrise tomorrow, you'll be gone from here." He called for the guard. Opening the door, the man stepped inside. "Take him back to the common quarters."

Alone in the chamber, Rolfe smiled. How very easy it was, he decided, as he folded the signed agreement. Both Miles and Geoffrey were pair and kind, a perfect match. Tomorrow, once Miles was gone, he'd profess his love to Catherine. Considering how much his coffer had been lightened, he prayed he hadn't misjudged her feelings. What a coup for Miles it would be if in actuality Catherine didn't love him.

Rolfe frowned, wondering if he'd just erred.

"He has freed me," Miles said. "I leave here after sunrise tomorrow."

Catherine's hands stilled above his wound. "I don't understand. Why would he allow you to go?"

Miles chuckled. "Perhaps my belligerence has paid off. Maybe he wants me away from here before I drive everyone mad."

A sadness settled over her. Not because Miles was leaving, but because she was made to stay. After what Rolfe had told her that morning, she knew the situation between them was hopeless. Her heart ached, even more than before. She imagined the pain would always be with her.

"I am happy for you," she said, her fingers smoothing the ointment into his skin. "When you see my father, please tell him I'm well."

"Did you ask him?"

Catherine knew whom Miles meant. She had hoped he wouldn't quiz her about Rolfe, about whether she'd gotten an answer. But she supposed it was inescapable that Miles would toss the words at her. After all, he'd been so positive about Rolfe's choice he no doubt wanted to gloat at hearing he was right.

She'd not allow him the opportunity to throw the fact in her face. She was miserable enough already. To protect herself, she decided to play dumb.

"Him who?" she asked.

"Come, Catherine: You know what I'm talking about. Did you ask your lover if he ever intends to marry you?"

"No, I didn't."

She hadn't lied to Miles. Not exactly. The question she'd posed to Rolfe was if he thought he'd ever marry, not if he'd ever marry her. She noticed how Miles had turned his head and was now staring at her.

"Then he has never offered for your hand or professed his love?"

"No. He hasn't. I told you before, there were no promises

made." It was Catherine's turn to study Miles. "You act surprised. Why?"

He blinked, and his brow cleared of its furrows. "I'm not the least surprised by what you've said," he announced curtly. "'Tis as I told you. His profession is his first and last love. No woman will ever change that."

Though she wished otherwise, she knew Miles was right. Forgetting herself, she whispered, "Aye, 'tis true."

There was silence, then Miles asked, "Catherine, if there were a way for me to get you from here, would you want to escape him?"

Did she? No, but she had little choice. Her pregnancy would soon be noticeable. She could only imagine Rolfe's reaction when he discovered she'd lied to him. Besides, he didn't love her, so why prolong the inevitable?

To preserve her pride and to avoid any more hurt, she decided it was better for her to leave now. If Miles had a viable plan to gain her freedom from Cartbridge—and, sadly, from Rolfe—she'd latch onto it, the same as a drowning kitten would snag a passing log.

"Could Eloise come too?"

"I'm sorry, but that won't be possible. She'll have to stay. I doubt she'll be harmed. In fact, once you've escaped, she'll probably be set free. He has no use for her, does he?"

"No. Because your father's sympathies lie with Stephen, Henry ordered that I be taken."

"Why?"

She decided to relate what Rolfe had told her. "As I understand it, the duke feared that once we were married, your father might persuade my father to join against him and his campaign here in England. I was to be a diversion. If you were searching for me, you certainly couldn't fight Henry."

Miles emitted a short laugh. "From what I've heard, it hasn't been much of a fight. Other than at Malmesbury, there's been more posturing than anything. Henry has not yet won, so there's still a good chance Stephen will prevail. But 'tis as your father suspected. Henry is the real culprit. William will be interested to know he was right."

"I'll be glad to see him again," she said of her father.

"Then you wish to go?"

"Aye," she replied, knowing this would be her one and only chance. "Tell me your scheme."

As Catherine listened, Miles explained what he believed was a workable strategy. By the time he finished, Catherine also thought it was feasible.

"'Tis risky, Catherine," Miles said. "Should we be caught, there's no telling what will happen."

"'Tis a risk I'm willing to take."

"Good. Somehow I must get word to my men. That's if they haven't by now deserted me."

"Then you do have a force hidden somewhere outside the castle!"

"Aye," Miles replied. "Before I showed myself openly, my men and I watched Cartbridge for a full day under the cover of the trees. We set a place to drop a message had I been fortunate enough to get inside. With my being guarded, I've been unable to attempt any communication whatsoever. It has been the same with my attendants." Miles gave her the exact locale and explained further that a man was to come each night to look for any messages. "With this much time having elapsed and naught a word from me, they've probably given up their nightly run. Or, worse, they think me dead."

"Was someone watching when you approached the castle?"

"Aye. Undoubtedly he saw me fall."

Again Catherine regretted having rushed against the wall. Not only had Miles been wounded, but the force that had been with him may no longer be anywhere near. "We cannot give up hope. Tell me the message you wish to send, and I'll see that it is done."

"I want a rider sent ahead to your father's estate. We were all to meet there at the end of July if you weren't found. Even if the messenger has less than a day's start ahead of us, he'll be upon Oxford well before we will. 'Twould benefit us greatly if the others could join us somewhere between here and there, just in case your lover gives chase."

Miles's constantly referring to Rolfe as her lover set Catherine on edge. "His name is Rolfe," she announced. "Henceforth address him as such."

"*Bastard* would suit him better, but forgive me. Just in case *Rolfe* gives chase. Is that more to your taste?"

"Much," she answered, not liking Miles's sarcasm. For now, she let it pass. "Are you certain your man will agree to this plan?"

"A few gold coins should be enough of an incentive to earn his cooperation."

"I will enlist Eloise to help us. Your man can get the necessary things to me through her. In the meantime, I'll write the note and see it's delivered to the proper spot."

Miles smiled. "Your education is a benefit to us, Catherine."

She began packing the chest containing the medicinals. "There was a time, Miles, when you thought my knowing how to read and write was a waste of effort, maybe even a threat to your male vanity. You believed I was too independent and far too outspoken. As I recall, you wished I were more demure. Had I in actuality been the modest, timid creature you would rather I be, I'd not have survived the journey from Normandy to Cartbridge." She slammed the lid of the chest. "Excuse me, please. I need to seek out Eloise and set your plan into motion."

As she started to turn, Miles caught her arm. "Catherine, when we are free of this place and again in Normandy, I want to marry you."

"There will be no marriage between us. As I told you, I don't love you."

Catherine left the common quarters, her guard following behind her. If all went well, shortly after sunrise, she'd be riding away from Cartbridge, alongside Miles, in the guise of one of his attendants.

The bound stone sailed over the wall and across the moat, landing with a thud. Several guards on the battlements circled toward the sound. Searching the darkness, they apparently saw nothing out of sorts and turned back to their posts.

The stone's hurler kept stealthily to the shadows while moving around the perimeter of the yard, then at the right spot bolted toward the keep.

"What are you doing out here?" Garrick snapped, scowling.

"Getting some fresh air," came the surly reply.

"Well, take yourself inside," he commanded.

Tossing her head and lifting her skirts, Eloise mounted the stairs. She slammed the keep's door behind her.

A warm breeze lifted from the fields, sending the scent of wildflowers through the chamber's open window, but Catherine was unaware of the fragrance in the air.

Standing in the darkness, she stared at the courtyard below. The hard thud of the keep's door echoed upward, and she slowly released her breath.

She'd been watching Eloise as best she could, the dim light masking most of her nurse's movements. When Garrick's harsh voice rose, Catherine felt her heart stop, for she was certain they'd been found out. The rush of relief that flowed through her when the knight ordered Eloise inside left her weakened, her knees wobbly. She clung to the sill for support.

"Are you more interested in the stars than me?" Rolfe asked from behind her.

Her fingers uncurling from the stones, she turned toward him. "No, but 'tis a glorious night."

"Aye," he said. "We could find some of the same splendor here, if you'd just simply come to bed."

The realization that this would be their last night together brought tears to her eyes. She'd take the bit of heaven he offered, placing it alongside her other memories, to hold for all time.

"Are you coming?" he asked.

She heard the sheets rustle as he slid more to his side of the bed. "Aye."

As she moved toward him, she pulled her chemise over her head. The garment drifted from her fingers to the floor. All was in readiness for tomorrow's escape. The extra set of clothes, passed to Eloise by Miles's attendant, then carried

to Catherine beneath her nurse's tunic, were tucked away—
of all places, under the mattress. Catherine prayed they
could make the switch without being caught. If their plan
came unraveled, Miles would undoubtedly suffer. Sinking
onto the bed, she wondered what Rolfe might do to her.

His hand claimed her waist, pulling her to him. As he
pressed her back against the sheets, he inhaled deeply. "I
don't know which scent is more appealing: yours or the
blossoms in the field. 'Tis a night for lovers," he whispered.
"If you'll allow me, I'll make it one you won't soon forget."

Her fingers threaded through his golden mane. She urged
his face closer. "Forget?" she questioned. "Never."

Tonight's memories, Catherine knew, would have to last
her for a lifetime.

Rolfe stirred from his sleep just as the sky began to lighten
on the eastern horizon. Catherine clung to him, and he to
her.

Recalling the night past, he marveled at how very tender
their joining had been. There'd been no haste to seek a
climax, just long, deep kisses and easy, gentle caresses. But
when their rapture had come, it had been beyond anything
ever experienced or even imagined.

She'd whispered his name with such longing that his heart
had opened to her completely. He'd wanted to tell her then
how much he loved her. But he'd held back. Once Miles was
gone, he would speak the words he'd kept inside. He only
hoped she felt the same.

Easing away from Catherine, he rose and set to dressing.
When next he turned, his task finished, he saw she was
watching him. "'Tis early," he said. "Go back to sleep."

"Why are you up at this hour?"

"I've something to attend to."

"What?"

Not knowing how she'd react, he hadn't yet mentioned
Miles's departure to her. Apparently, neither had her betrothed.

Former betrothed, he corrected himself.

He'd thought briefly to keep the information from her but

decided that to do so wouldn't be fair. "A little after sunrise, Miles will be leaving Cartbridge."

She sat up. "Leaving?"

"Aye."

"But I thought he was your prisoner."

"No, Catherine. You were the one who asked he be brought inside. While here, he's been watched. He's healed enough that he and his attendants can now be on their way."

"Oh."

He cocked his head to one side. "Does the thought upset you?"

"No."

"Will you miss him?"

"Some," she said, shrugging.

Rolfe was relieved. Had she still been in love with Miles he would think she'd be prostrate with grief over the man's departure. She impressed him as being a bit saddened, but the emotion certainly didn't overwhelm her.

After last night, and with what had just transpired, Rolfe was almost certain her affections now lay with him.

He grabbed up his sword and strode to the bed. "I'll be back shortly."

Leaning over, he touched his lips to hers. One hand circling his neck, the other pressing at his waist, she deepened the kiss. Rolfe came away feeling pleasantly dazed.

"May I come down and say goodbye to him?" she asked just as he reached the door.

Rolfe turned to look at her. "If you hurry."

Striding the corridor, Rolfe was now twice as eager to see Miles on his way. A day spent with Catherine behind a locked door would certainly lessen the tension that flourished inside him.

Though the betrothal was rescinded, he had to face a far greater obstacle than Miles: Catherine's father. The man's hatred of him was probably insurmountable. Of course, if Catherine accepted his proposal of marriage, Brother Bernard could immediately perform the nuptials. Surely William de Mortain wouldn't kill his own son-in-law.

The idea was tempting, but Rolfe had no intention of employing more subterfuge. To honor Catherine, he'd ask for her hand as was the custom—through her father. And if William de Mortain refused, he'd go to Henry. In lieu of land or gold for his services, he'd request the right to marry her.

All this was conjecture, for one thing had yet to be determined. In Rolfe's mind, the same question arose.

Did Catherine love him or not?

The moment the door closed, Catherine looked at the key she'd filched from under Rolfe's belt. So far, so good, she thought, as she bounded from the bed and locked the door.

Heading again to the bed, she lifted the mattress and pulled the clothes from their hiding place. After snatching her chemise from the floor, she aimed herself at the table, where she placed the lot, then went to work.

With a wide strip of linen rent from the chemise, Catherine bound her breasts. Next she donned the attendant's clothes. Over those she threw on her chainse and yellow bliaud. Once she drew on her stockings, she shoved her feet into her slippers, only to stare at them.

Boots, she thought, kicking off her slippers. Her eyes darted from corner to corner. Spying what she needed, she dashed to the spot, praying Aubrey would forgive her for stealing his one other pair.

The boots now on, she found the fit a bit too roomy, but they'd have to do.

Catherine quickly brushed her hair, then plaited it. Grabbing the hooded shoulder cape, she tucked the article inside the boot's top.

Was that everything?

As she looked around the room, searching for anything she might have forgotten, tears stung her eyes. Several brimmed and fell, especially when she spied the bed. She wiped her cheeks, knowing she couldn't afford to start blubbering now. But then Rolfe might think her tears were for Miles. The effect should work well for when she was gone.

After one last glance at the room, she started for the door.

The bracelet. Dashing to where she had stored it, she found the remembrance and slipped it onto her wrist, then up her arm, covering it with her sleeve.

Finally at the door, she unlocked it and palmed the key, intending to pass it to Eloise for phase two of their plan. So much depended on her nurse's secondhand instructions to the attendant that Catherine hoped there had been no miscommunication.

Her gaze traveled to the stones framing the room, jumped to the spider web high in one corner, then dropped to the bed. Committing it all to memory one last time, she chewed at her lip, trying to keep the tears at bay.

Then Catherine stepped into the hall and shut the door.

Rolfe stood at the foot of the stairs outside the keep, watching as Miles and his two attendants checked their saddles. Their steeds were laden with their travel packs. From where Rolfe stood, all seemed in order. So what was the delay?

Just as he started to make his way to the area where the three were gathered, Garrick and two other knights with them, Rolfe heard the door open above him.

Catherine.

As eager as he was to see Miles gone, so he could return to her, Rolfe had forgotten he'd given her permission to say farewell to the bastard.

Once she was at his side, he walked with her to the center of the yard. He noted she was exceptionally quiet. The tip of her nose appeared a bit red. And her eyes . . . Had she been crying?

His heart sank a little. Miles d'Avranches didn't deserve her tears. Rolfe wondered what she'd say if she knew her beloved betrothed had given her up for a pouch of gold and his freedom.

Coming up beside Miles's horse, which the man had by now mounted, Rolfe looked up at him through narrowed eyes. "Is all in order?" he asked, his tone clipped.

"I believe so. Alaric," Miles called.

The boy looked around, his dark locks striking his shoulders.

"Do you have everything?"

"I think so, sir." His gaze fell on the attendant beside him. "My hood," he cried. "I left it next to my pallet in the common quarters."

Before anyone could react, the lad went scurrying for the keep. Garrick started after him.

"Leave him," Rolfe said. "He'll be in and out of there before you can make the top of the steps."

When he turned back, he saw that Catherine was holding Miles's hand. He'd obviously missed part of their conversation.

"Tell my father I am well," she said.

"Aye. I will. Take care, Catherine," Miles returned, his hand tenderly brushing her cheek.

That demon within began to claw at Rolfe's insides. He'd never known jealousy until Catherine. Then when Miles's thumb touched her lips, he'd had enough.

"See they find their way out," he said to Garrick. He took hold of Catherine's arm. "Come."

As he led her back across the yard, he looked at the stairs. Eloise now stood at their foot. He stopped several yards away from the woman and turned Catherine toward him.

Tears shimmered in her eyes. One broke free and trickled down her cheek. He caught it with his finger. "Do you cry for him?"

She said not a word, but spun on her heel; Rolfe was immediately after her. When he met the steps, Eloise blocked his path, Catherine already rushing up to the door.

"You know and I know he's not worth her tears," the woman said. "Let her have her cry. Once done, she'll know it too."

As Catherine disappeared inside the keep, Rolfe murmured, "I hope you're right."

Catherine shut the door and ran to the sheltered area beneath the stairs in the entry. Wiping her tears, she tore her bliaud over her head, then her chainse, tossing them into the corner. After wrapping her braids around her head, she plucked the hooded shoulder cape from Aubrey's boot and donned it. The cloth pulled low over her forehead and shielding the sides of her face, she ducked her head and was back out the door.

As she loped down the steps, she prayed Rolfe would indeed think she was Alaric. The boy had been chosen because his size and stature most closely resembled hers. Besides, she knew Rolfe wouldn't harm a lad who was not much more than a child.

Five steps from the bottom, Catherine bent her head further. "Excuse me," she grumbled, her voice purposely low.

Eloise moved sideways, her girth pressing Rolfe to the wall. Catherine caught her nurse's hand and squeezed, then bolted past the pair. In a few more strides, she was beside her horse. The beast wasn't very tall, so she had no trouble climbing astride it.

"Open the gates," Garrick shouted.

The wooden panels took forever to swing on their hinges, or so Catherine thought. She nearly fainted when she heard Rolfe's voice behind her.

"Remember our bargain, Miles," he said. "I expect never to see you again."

Wondering what he meant, she felt the horse lurch forward. Apparently someone had struck its rump. Then Miles was beside her, as was his attendant, their horses trotting toward the yawning gates.

Don't look back.

The refrain repeated itself over and over again in her mind. But oh, how she wanted to see his face one more time.

Hooves sounded against the drawbridge, then they were soon in the open field, where they set their horses into a canter. Only when she thought it safe did she glance over her shoulder.

He stood on the battlements, watching their departure, and she knew she'd always remember him thus: her golden warrior bathed in the rays of a rising sun somewhere in the green English countryside.

Two miles out, they were joined by a troop of nearly twenty-five men. "Milord," a knight greeted once they'd all reined in. "I received your message." He drew the scrap of linen on which Catherine had written the directive from his belt. "Three riders were sent toward Oxford. They should probably reach Lord William's estate a day or so ahead of us."

"Good," Miles said. "I had feared after all this time you may have left the area. If not that, then stopped the nightly run for my message."

The knight's face turned stony. "Our duty prohibited such. Lord William employed us to do a job, and it shall be done. Did you find the Lady Catherine?"

"She is there beside you, sir."

Catherine pulled the hood from her head. "I am Catherine de Mortain."

"Milady," the knight greeted with a nod. "Your father will be glad to know you are well. We sent two riders to find him when your betrothed did not return. I can only assume their search for him to the east went unrewarded, since he has not appeared."

"Thank you for your loyalty, sir, and your show of intelligence as well," she said. "But I fear we are not out of danger yet. I suggest we ride from here as fast as possible before we are pursued."

"You are right, milady. Let us be on our way."

The knight ordered his men to encircle Miles and Catherine; then at his command, the troop set their horses into a gallop, heading south.

Topping the next rise, Catherine again glanced over her shoulder. The crown of the towering keep peeked above the horizon. Tears glazed her eyes as she again thought of Rolfe.

From the start, she'd wanted to be liberated from her captor. Her wish had now come true. And with its fulfillment, Catherine understood all too well: She'd gained her precious freedom only to become, forevermore, a prisoner of her own heartache.

"Catherine, open the door."

It was Rolfe's fifth such command in an equal number of hours. Four times he'd been told to leave her alone. Four times he'd acceded to her wishes.

On those occasions, with her words coming through the door, her voice had sounded different. But he assumed she'd been weeping, so he'd paid the unaccustomed tones little heed. This time she responded not at all.

He stared at the lock. Just how she'd gotten hold of the key confounded him. He thought he'd tucked the thing in his belt. But, then, in his hurry to get to the yard that morning, he could have left it on the table. Hence he was stuck now talking to her through the wood.

"Catherine, my patience is wearing thin. Open the door. Please?"

The same as a moment before, she didn't answer; Rolfe jiggled the latch.

"God's wounds, woman. He's not worth your tears. Now let me in."

No reply came forth, and Rolfe's eyes narrowed on the wood. One hard kick and he'd be inside. Debating whether or not he should wreak havoc on the door, he heard footsteps coming along the corridor. Garrick strode toward him, a mixture of yellow and white cloth bundled in his hands.

"I think you've been wasting your breath," Garrick said once he reached Rolfe's side. "While sweeping, one of the servants found these under the stairs just inside the entry." He dangled the chainse and bliaud in the air. "Look familiar?"

Rolfe stared at the garments. If Catherine was *supposed* to be in their room, why were her clothes beneath the steps? Unless . . .

A curse hissing through his lips, he gave the door a mighty kick. Once. Twice. The third one brought results. The wood splintered, the panel flew wide, and Rolfe was instantly in the room. As he thought: *Alaric.*

"Where is she?" he demanded of the lad while striding toward him. Beside the boy, Rolfe caught his ear and plucked him from the chair. "Answer me."

"I d–don't know, s-sir," Alaric replied as he danced on his toes. "Honest."

Rolfe released the lad's ear and pressed him down into the chair. "Tell me what you do know."

"Only that I was ordered to give my other set of clothes to some woman," he answered, rubbing the side of his head.

"My master said that once we were ready to ride this morning, I was to claim I'd left my hood in the common quarters and to go back into the keep for it. I hadn't forgotten it, though. My hood was with my other clothes. Again inside the keep, I was then given that key." He pointed to the item resting on the table. "The same woman told me to lock myself in here with the instructions that if anyone asked entry, I was to tell them to go away. No matter what happened, I wasn't to unlock the door."

"What woman, Alaric, gave you the key?"

"The plump one with the graying hair."

Rolfe looked at Garrick. "Bring him," he ordered his companion. Heading for the door, he was bent on finding Eloise.

"If she continues to be uncooperative, we can always string her up by her toes and dangle her over the outer wall," Garrick stated. He spoke to Rolfe but was eyeing Eloise. "That should loosen her tongue fast enough."

"Come near me, and your shins will suffer anew," she threatened.

"Just try it, woman, and we'll see who will be suffering the most."

"Enough," Rolfe said, straightening from the edge of the table where he leaned. "This bickering is getting us no-where."

Not all that long before, Rolfe had found Catherine's nurse in the great hall. She sat on a bench, hands clasped in her lap. It was as though she'd been waiting for him to show, Alaric with him.

"'Tis obvious she'll offer us nothing," he continued. "We're losing time. Pick twenty of our best men. I want them fully equipped and ready to ride as soon as possible."

Rolfe turned, looking for his squire. He spotted him at the far end of the room with Brother Bernard. At his call, the pair hustled his way.

"Do you need my services?" Aubrey asked.

"Aye. Go to the kitchens and order a week's worth of provisions for twenty-three riders."

Brother Bernard frowned. "What's happened?"

"The Lady Catherine has escaped us," Rolfe returned.

"How?"

"She rode out under our very noses this morn with Miles," Garrick told the monk. Holding the back of Alaric's tunic, he shoved him forward. "Was wearing this lad's clothes."

"I take it you're going after her?" Brother Bernard questioned.

Rolfe nodded.

"I'll go with you," the monk stated.

"I'm going too."

All eyes turned toward Eloise.

"I'll not stay behind," she said, rising to her feet. "She may need me."

"Sit down, woman," Garrick ordered. "You'll be staying."

"Make that enough food for twenty-five," Rolfe told his squire.

As Aubrey dashed off to the kitchens, Garrick stared at Rolfe. "Surely you're not taking her with us?"

"Aye, I am," he responded, his gaze on Catherine's nurse. "As before, Garrick, something tells me 'tis best she comes along." He pulled Alaric forward, then motioned another man to his side. "Take this lad into your care and make certain he's fed. Treat him kindly. When I return, I'll decide what to do with him then." Handing the boy over, he looked back to the others. "Any questions?"

"Aye. Where are we headed?" Garrick asked.

"We have two choices," Rolfe announced, watching Eloise. "William's estate or Geoffrey's." The slight stiffening of the woman's face gave him his answer. "I say 'tis the former. We head toward Oxford."

CHAPTER

20

CATHERINE WAS WORN AND ON EDGE, MAINLY BECAUSE OF Miles. Since they'd escaped Cartbridge, he complained continuously. Either they were moving too fast, the constant shock of the pounding hooves eliciting pain in his shoulder; or if they slowed their pace to accommodate him, he became annoyed with their lack of progress. Hence everyone's mood had deteriorated. To say the least, it had been an arduous four days, especially for her. The only good thing was that so far her baby didn't seem to be suffering any ill effects. She prayed it remained so.

If she'd thought things couldn't possibly get worse, she was gravely mistaken. That morning her horse had gone lame, and she was now forced to ride with the ill-humored man whom she was once impatient to marry.

How she'd ever believed Miles to be the perfect mate was beyond her. Fortunately, fate had intervened, sparing her from a marriage that would have brought her nothing but unhappiness.

Yet Catherine wondered what she'd actually attained, for in actuality she'd simply traded one form of misery for another. Rejected by the man she truly loved, she was now destined to live out her days alone, bittersweet memories of her golden warrior her only companion.

Lost in her thoughts, Catherine started when Miles emitted a vivid curse. "Hold up," he shouted to those ahead of them.

Sir Balder, the knight who'd met them just outside Cartbridge, reined in his steed. A scowl marked his discontent. "What's wrong this time?" he asked when Miles came up beside him.

"My horse cannot keep up with two of us astride," Miles announced. "'Twould be better if we slowed our pace."

"We're not that far from Oxford," Sir Balder replied. "I'd feel far better about the Lady Catherine's safety if we tried to press ourselves a bit harder."

"How close do you think we are?" Miles questioned.

"Ten miles, maybe nearer," the knight replied.

"If the bastard hasn't caught up to us by now, 'tis unlikely he'll do so—that's if he gave chase in the first place. Even if he did, I doubt he'll follow us into Oxford." Miles shook his head. "There's no need to rush. We'll still make our destination before nightfall."

"If you insist," Sir Balder said. "But if anything happens, 'twill be on your head."

Turning his steed, the knight rode on ahead and ordered his men to slow their pace.

"Why do you think Rolfe won't follow us into Oxford?" Catherine asked.

"'Tis too close to Stephen's castle at Crowmarsh. From across the river, the royal troops have been besieging Henry's fortress at Wallingford for nearly a year now. I'm sure your lover is aware of that. Even if the aforementioned places do lie ten miles beyond Oxford, I doubt he'll risk his capture by coming so near to enemy territory."

From what Miles had said, Catherine grew worried about Rolfe. If he had followed them, his innate sense of duty having impelled him to do so, she feared he would indeed ride straight to Oxford, danger or no. The man was dauntless and, yes, reckless. Just knowing that she and Miles had duped him was more than enough to drive him onward.

Wanting satisfaction, he'd not rest until he'd settled with them both.

Catherine sincerely hoped he'd not be so foolish as to put his life in jeopardy. Certainly not for some mandatory sense of commitment to Henry, certainly not for his gnawing need for revenge, and, most of all, certainly not for her.

Looking to the blue heavens, she prayed: *Dear Lord, if he is in pursuit, please make him turn back before he comes to harm.*

Rolfe had no such compunction.

Riding ever closer to Oxford, he was determined to find both Miles and Catherine.

From the former, he wanted his gold, along with the opportunity to bring the bastard to his knees. His intention was to spare Miles, but oh what enjoyment he'd receive from watching the fool grovel at his feet while pleading for Rolfe not to take his life.

And from Catherine?

He wanted the chance to face her so he could profess his love and discover at last if she felt the same about him. Should she reject him, which he prayed she didn't, he'd already decided he would set her free. And if by some miracle she reciprocated his affection, he planned to allow her the choice of either returning to Cartbridge or seeking out her father.

Nearly certain she'd opt for the latter, he'd willingly comply with her wishes. Despite what he once felt, despite what he'd told her, his duty and allegiance to Henry no longer mattered. It was Catherine whom he wanted to please.

But above all of this, what concerned Rolfe most was the danger Catherine faced. Just before his riding out from Cartbridge, a messenger had arrived from Henry. The duke, he learned, was marching to the relief of his stronghold at Wallingford and planning to besiege Crowmarsh. Since it had taken a week for the messenger to arrive from Bedford, Rolfe imagined Henry was presently in position. Considering such, Stephen's troops had to be gathering in defense of Crowmarsh. What better place than at Oxford?

It was quite likely that skirmishes would break out all around the region, Stephen's troops meeting Henry's as they tried to station themselves. Therefore Rolfe knew he had to find Catherine before she found herself trapped in one such fray. There would be no mercy for her, especially when she was dressed as a man.

A shout rose from behind him. Rolfe looked around to see one of his men pointing at the opposite hillside. Focusing on the area, he saw a band of riders topping the knoll. Immediately he barked a command, then urged his stallion into a full gallop. His armed knights followed.

As sure hooves thundered beneath him, Rolfe smiled inwardly. His relentless pursuit had paid off. Catherine, he felt certain, was just over the next rise.

Cresting the hill, the group of riders descended the slope and started across the open field. Catherine was the first to notice that something was out of sorts. It was far too quiet.

The birds—not a twitter or a call rang from the treetops. She looked first to one side, then to the other, and studied the woods that lined the clearing. Way too quiet for such a balmy summer day, she thought.

Apparently Sir Balder was the next to notice. He raised himself up in the saddle to nearly stand in the stirrups. Turning, he viewed the field's perimeter.

Movement caught Catherine's eye. She was about to alert the knight when a clamorous cry sounded to their right. The yell was reciprocated from the left. Then from both sides armed horsemen bolted out of the woods.

Everything happened at once.

Miles issued a curse. The knights who surrounded them reached for their weapons. Before anyone could do much else, their attackers were upon them.

While swords clashed and clanged furiously in her ears, Catherine thought it might be Rolfe who'd been lying in wait for them. But as Miles constantly turned his horse, obviously trying to find an outlet, she swayed in the saddle and searched the faces of the men who were engaged in battle. Rolfe wasn't among them.

The fighting became more frenzied. Men were falling

around them. Miles was still unable to escape from the entangled mass. Unexpectedly he began shoving at her. Confused, Catherine turned her head. There was a wildness in his eyes that frightened her.

He shoved her again. "Bitch, get off."

Catherine gaped at him. Had he gone mad?

"Do as I say!" he grated through his teeth.

The force of his next push unseated her from the horse; Catherine sailed downward and hit the ground with a thud.

Her palms stung, her knees ached. Shaking her head, she dragged herself to her feet to see Miles, his sword drawn, breaking a trail through the pack. When she noted he didn't stand and fight, the realization struck that he intended to flee the battle. Rolfe was right: The bastard *was* a coward.

Knowing she had to get from the midst of this chaos, Catherine tried to pick a path through the crush of horses and men. She wended around one steed, only to find another blocking her.

Bumped and battered by the spinning destriers, she became frantic. She shoved and pushed her way from the center. Then, spying a break in the warring bodies, she dashed forward. When she next looked up, a rider came toward her, his sword swinging. Her mind whirling with thoughts of Rolfe, their unborn child, and her father, she froze in her tracks.

"Merciful St. Michael," she whispered, remembering the Archangel was Rolfe's protector, "spare me and his child. Please."

Catherine's entreaty was instantly answered, for a horse abruptly bolted in front of her.

Sir Balder.

Quickly tripping away, she was hit from behind. At the same time, Sir Balder's steed sprang backward. Catherine found herself pressed between the rumps of two horses. When they jolted apart she stumbled, then dropped to her knees, gasping for breath.

Steel struck steel above her. Glancing up, she saw the blade plunge. *No!* her mind screamed. The knight who'd tried to save her toppled from his horse. Protectively hugging her stomach, she rolled to the ground. The air rushed from her lungs as Sir Balder landed lifelessly atop her. For Catherine, all went black.

Rolfe topped the rise to mark the confusion below. The blood drained from his face, for in his mind he was reliving the road to Antalya. This time, though, it was Catherine's life that lay in jeopardy.

Dear God, don't allow it to happen again. Protect her, please.

The prayer streaked through his mind as he pushed the young stallion to its limits, his sword drawn and ready. While his men galloped behind him down the hill, Rolfe scanned the field. Relief washed through him the instant his gaze latched onto her. She was in the center, astride a horse with Miles. His sword swinging, Rolfe was at once in the fray.

Whether he fought Stephen's men, William's, or Henry's, Rolfe couldn't say. He cared less who fell by the wayside. His one goal was to get to Catherine.

By the time he next looked up, searching for her, four men had fallen under his sword. Across the way, he spotted Miles's back. The man's horse bolted from the crush.

From his position, Rolfe couldn't tell if Catherine were seated before the fleeing Miles. He had no choice but to chance that she was.

Backing the stallion out of the squeeze of bodies and steeds, he sheathed his sword, cut around the perimeter of the group, and gave chase. The yards between them dwindled. Two hundred. One hundred. Fifty. Rolfe was yet uncertain if Catherine were on the horse.

When he was nearly beside Miles, Rolfe's heart sank. Just as quickly, fury rioted through him. "Pull up!" he shouted.

Miles ignored the command and whipped his horse with the reins.

Rolfe gritted his teeth. Now even with Miles, he sprang from his steed. His body crashing into Miles's, both men sailed through the air and tumbled to the ground.

Rolfe was immediately on his feet, jerking Miles to his. With the action, the pouch that Rolfe had given Miles came loose from the man's belt. Gold scattered around their feet to glisten in the sunlight. Rolfe ignored his once precious treasure.

"You left her back there, didn't you, you bastard?"

Rolfe didn't wait for a reply. His fist slammed into Miles's jaw. Picking Miles up from the ground, he issued the punishment again. Then with a hard kick into Miles's side, Rolfe grabbed up his helm, which had flown from his head, and whistled for his horse. The stallion came running. In a few seconds, Rolfe was again headed toward the fray. Behind him, Miles was quickly gathering the coins.

A mile away, over the next rise to the south, William de Mortain rode alongside Geoffrey d'Avranches. Some fifty men followed behind them, including the three who had traveled from Cartbridge. They had arrived several hours before dawn. Now all were headed north to join with the group that was aimed toward Oxford.

As he topped the hill, William stared down on a lone rider and horse galloping pell-mell toward them. He noted how the man swayed disjointedly in the saddle. His tunic doubled against his belly, the rider looked to be more interested in what lay in its folds than the route ahead.

"The fool is going to kill himself," William commented to Geoffrey.

As though William had just foretold the rider's fate, the horse's forelegs plunged into a depression in the field that was hidden by the long grass. The beast toppled, its rider flying over its twisting neck. William cringed when he saw the man strike the ground headfirst. The rider tumbled along the earth for a short distance, then lay eerily still.

Beside William, Geoffrey was oddly silent. When William glanced at the man, he noted how his companion had gone pale. Then Geoffrey spurred his horse. As he rode toward the fallen rider, the lone word that broke from his lips told William all, for Geoffrey had shouted his son's name.

Directing his men down the slope, William came upon Geoffrey. He was on his knees, cradling Miles's limp form. Dismounting, William walked to the man's side and placed his hand on Geoffrey's shoulder.

"He's broken his neck," Geoffrey said, smoothing his son's brow.

With a compassionate squeeze of his hand, William left Geoffrey's side. If Miles was near, so was Catherine. He had to find her. As he approached his horse, he noted Miles's steed struggling to rise. Its forelegs were broken. "Slay the poor beast," he ordered one of his men.

Now atop his own steed, William spied a glittering trail. Gold coins spread along the ground from the fallen horse to where Miles lay. He wondered if that was what had held Miles's attention. Had the young fool been less interested in the treasure, William was certain he'd now be alive. Then with a stern command issued to his men, William set out in the direction whence Miles just came.

Rolfe's blade was red with the blood of another half-dozen men. On his return to the group, he was immediately drawn into the clash. He fought his way valiantly to where he'd last seen Catherine.

He swung his sword and another man fell, his arm severed. All the while, memories of that not-so-long-ago time kept flashing inside his head. Faces flitted. Robert's, Francis's, and yes, most of all, Catherine's. Determined that history didn't repeat itself, Rolfe struggled onward. She had to be alive!

Please, God. Let it be so.

Then as if by some miracle, the clash ended. The attackers, their numbers far less than they were, retreated across the field and into the woods. Rolfe quickly guided his horse to the spot where he thought Catherine might be. Dismounting, he began searching through the bodies strewn across the ground.

He heard his name shouted. Looking up, he saw Brother Bernard and Aubrey coming toward him. Between the pair was Garrick, his arms draped over their shoulders. Blood seeped from a wound on the knight's thigh. A second injury showed at his side. Behind them ambled Eloise.

Ten feet from Rolfe, the monk looked up. "Riders come," he said, pointing to the south.

Rolfe turned. This new force appeared to be just over a quarter mile away. "Get him into the wood, quick," he said of Garrick. Then spinning around, he frantically scoured the area for Catherine.

He heard Eloise cry out. Loping to her side, he gazed down on the fallen knight and the small form curled beneath him. A long braid snaked along the ground, sable brown in color. Rolfe felt his gut lurch.

Tearing the helm from his head, he tossed his sword to the ground, then rolled the lifeless form aside. He dropped to his knees. His hand shaking, he smoothed the other braid from her pale face.

"Catherine?" he whispered, as tears filled his eyes.

His heart twisting, he stared at her. Oh God, she was so still.

Her chest rose. Seeing the motion, Rolfe silently uttered his gratitude to every saint he could name, the Archangel in particular.

"Catherine . . . love. Wake up." He lightly patted her cheeks. "Open your beautiful eyes for me." She didn't respond. "Please, love. Awaken."

The sound of hooves thundered in Rolfe's ears. Not knowing who these new intruders were, he grabbed his sword and came to his feet. Poised to do battle, he stood protectively over Catherine.

The man at the group's fore bounded from his horse prior to the beast's stopping. He came at Rolfe, his blade swinging, a cry of fury vibrating in his throat. Rolfe deflected the blow; then as the blades sliced apart, he swung quickly, skillfully. The man's sword flew from his hand.

The tip of his blade pressed at the man's neck, Rolfe stared into his opponent's eyes, ready to skewer him. Then recognition took hold.

William de Mortain.

Aware his own life would now lay in jeopardy, Rolfe relaxed his stance and lowered his sword. Never could he harm Catherine's father. At once, Rolfe was surrounded by twenty of William's men. His hands were quickly bound behind him.

Brushing past Rolfe, William knelt at his daughter's side. Eloise was already on the ground, attending to her charge.

"How is she?" William asked.

"I'm not certain," Eloise responded. "She won't awaken."

William clenched his jaw and jerked his head. "Is that the bastard who took her?"

Eloise looked up at Rolfe. "He is the one."

"I am Rolfe de Mont St. Michel," he announced, his gaze on Catherine, "vassal to Henry, duke of Normandy, count of Anjou. Your daughter was ordered taken by my liege lord, but her injuries lay on my shoulders. I ask that you do not blame Henry for what has happened here."

William came to his feet. "If your duke were in this very spot, I'd tear his bloody heart out for all the misery he has caused," he snarled in Rolfe's face. "But since he isn't, you are the one who will pay."

"I accept your edict, sir," Rolfe said. "You should know I never meant for Catherine to be harmed. Readily, I'd give my own life if it would change what has occurred."

"And so you will," William stated.

At that moment, another rider and horse came galloping toward the group. Reining in, Geoffrey d'Avranches leaped down from the animal's back and strode to where William and Rolfe stood.

"'Tis he, isn't it? He's the bastard who caused my son's death." With that, Geoffrey spat in Rolfe's face.

Rolfe stared at the man, sputum dripping from his cheek. The last he'd seen of Miles, the man was groveling on the ground. Surely two punches and a kick hadn't done the coward mortal injury. But apparently, from what his father said, Miles was dead. Rolfe could muster no remorse.

"I want him, William," Geoffrey announced. "'Tis my right to take retribution for what he has done."

"And mine," William returned.

"Then we shall take the pleasure together." Geoffrey looked at Rolfe's guards. "Put him on his horse. We head for Farnham."

"Nay," William stated. "We head to my estate. 'Tis closer."

As Catherine's father ordered a litter made for her, Rolfe was spun around. There at the edge of the woods stood Brother Bernard and Aubrey, a struggling Garrick trying to break loose from their hold. All their gazes were upon Rolfe.

He shook his head, signaling them not to come nigh. There was no sense in their suffering a like punishment to his. Noting that Garrick gave up his fight, Rolfe was relieved when the knight's two companions pulled him into the woods. Then Rolfe was shoved toward his horse. Once he was mounted, one of the guards guided the stallion by its reins.

Rolfe watched as Catherine was settled onto the litter. Blessed St. Michael, he thought. Would she ever awaken? As the troop was ready to ride out toward William's estate, Geoffrey came up beside him.

"You contemptible bastard," he grated through his teeth. "By what I have planned for you in way of recompense, I suggest you say your prayers. 'Twould be far better if you were to die sooner than later."

Rolfe kept his gaze on Catherine, who was only a short distance behind him. He imagined Geoffrey's punishment would be severe. It didn't matter. As long as she lived, he'd gladly suffer whatever tortures were necessary in exchange.

And if she died?

Death, Rolfe decided, was far and away more preferable than a life without his beloved Catherine.

CHAPTER

21

"IT HAS BEEN TWO DAYS, AND SHE HASN'T AWAKENED."

"She will. But I caution you when she does come to, you had better keep your tongue between your teeth. If she has any questions, I will answer them."

From a distance, Catherine heard the voices. The first was Eloise's; the second, her father's. She didn't understand what they'd said. The familiar tones were what had drawn her from the depths of her oblivion. Her eyelids fluttered, and she focused on the two people who stood beside her.

"Father?"

"Oh, merciful Lord!" Eloise declared. "She's with us again."

As William turned to his daughter, Eloise crossed herself and voiced a prayer of thanksgiving.

"Catherine," he said, edging a hip onto the bed. "'Tis good to behold your lovely eyes."

Open your beautiful eyes for me.

Rolfe's voice sounded in her head. When had he uttered those words? Or was she just imagining that he had? Her brow furrowed as she stared at her father.

"What's wrong, Daughter? Are you in pain?"

"No. I simply thought . . . 'Tis nothing," she said. She looked around her. "Where am I?"

"At my estate," William replied.

Though nothing was familiar, she asked, "At Mortain?"

"No, Catherine. We're in England."

The grogginess instantly left her. Everything came flooding back. Under the covers, her hand immediately sought her belly. Feeling the slight roundness, she was relieved.

"How did you ever find me?" she questioned. "And Miles—where is he?"

"'Tis not important," William said. "All in good time, you'll be told everything. Right now you should rest." He took the cup that Eloise placed before him. "Here. 'Tis something to help you sleep."

She pushed lightly at the cup. "I don't want to sleep."

"Don't argue, Daughter. Now drink."

Lifting her head, her father set the cup to her lips; Catherine swallowed. As she lay back on the pillow, she spied the ruby-eyed dragon's head peeking from her father's belt.

"My bracelet." She slipped it from the leather band at William's waist and placed it on her arm.

"Where did you get that treasure, Catherine?" her father asked. "'Tis worth a small fortune."

She yawned. The herbs were making her sleepy. "From Rolfe. 'Tis a remembrance of the time we shared together."

"Was he kind to you?"

"Aye."

"You're certain he didn't harm you in any way?"

"Nay. He saved me from the wolves and the rats. Eloise will tell you."

William looked at Catherine's nurse; she nodded. "He always treated her well," Eloise confirmed.

"He was right," Catherine mumbled, the herbs taking her closer to sleep.

"Who?" William asked.

"Rolfe. He said Miles was a coward. And that he is. I don't want to marry him. Not anymore."

William frowned. "Why do you say Miles is a coward?"

"He pushed me from the horse and rode away. 'Twas

terrible. Everyone was fighting around me, and I couldn't get out of the fray. Sir Balder saved me, but then he was killed . . . fell on me."

As Catherine spoke, her words became more slurred. "Hush, Daughter. We'll talk of it later."

"I should never have doubted him," she whispered. "I'm glad he didn't follow, else my golden warrior may have come to harm."

Catherine didn't see the look that passed between her father and her nurse. Allowing Eloise's potion to claim her, she drifted off to sleep, believing Rolfe was safe.

Deep in the dungeon of William de Mortain's fortified keep, Rolfe drew a jagged breath. Needles of fire pricked along his arms as he dangled above a yawning black pit that no doubt led straight to the bowels of hell. His wrists were raw and bleeding from the rope that bound them. His lips were cracked, his throat parched; one eye was swollen shut from the hard blow Geoffrey d'Avranches had delivered.

From his good eye, Rolfe watched the iron that lay in the glowing coals. Geoffrey plucked the instrument of torture from its bed. He spat on the tip, then laughed when it sizzled.

The man was demented, Rolfe thought, then stiffened as Geoffrey swung the iron toward him. He jerked as the fiery tip seared his belly. Too weak to cry out, he endured the pain. Sweat poured from his brow as the putrid smell of burning flesh filled his nostrils. Would this agony ever end?

Rolfe went limp when the iron left him. As always, he thought of Catherine. Memories of her were his only comfort.

When times were their darkest or most painful, such as now, he envisioned their days and nights together. He heard her soft laughter, saw the look of passion in her ever-changing eyes, felt her lips as they traveled his body when they made love. It was those memories that gave him the impetus to survive.

But why?

He didn't even know if Catherine were alive.

More often than not, he thought it would be best if he

simply surrendered to the ever-lasting sleep; then the suffering would surely end. But the one hope that she still lived always prompted him to withstand the torture and the agony he was made to bear. Just to see her one more time, to know she was well—that's all he asked. Then he'd allow death its due.

The white-hot iron struck again, this time against his shoulder. His head pulling back, Rolfe gritted his teeth. He heard the hiss of searing flesh, smelled the rank odor, then felt the pain. His nude body was immediately slammed by a bucket's worth of frigid water. Chills ran the length of Rolfe's spine.

Geoffrey laughed uproariously. "'Tis only the beginning, Rolfe de Mont St. Michel. Just wait until tomorrow." He turned to the guards. "Bring him down and tie him to his cot. We don't want him to die too quick."

The wooden arm that suspended Rolfe over the pit was cranked to one side. The chain was unhooked, and he fell into the dirt. His hands yet bound, he was lifted by each arm and dragged to his bed, then tied hand and foot to the rails.

"Sleep well," Geoffrey said, grabbing the torch. "Tomorrow I think we'll try the rack."

All went black when Geoffrey stepped through the door. Rolfe heard the lock click. As he lay in the dark, shivering, the dampness of the dungeon piercing to his bones, he let his mind drift into the past and to the one thing that eased him . . .

Catherine.

He was dead.

Catherine couldn't believe it was possible.

Rolfe, her golden warrior, was dead.

"I cannot accept what you say is true," she said, springing from her chair.

Gripping her hands together, Catherine began to pace. It had been two days since she'd first awakened, almost the same number in which she'd lived with the certainty Rolfe was safe at Cartbridge. The confidence held until only a few hours before, when she'd snapped from her daze to stare at Eloise.

Whether it had been the herbs, which had kept her in a constant fog, or if it was simply that she was always so accustomed to having her nurse around, Catherine couldn't say. But when the realization struck, it nearly knocked her from her feet. If Eloise were here, then Rolfe had to have followed. Catherine's questions tumbled forth. What she was told, she couldn't countenance.

"And neither will I accept that he killed Miles," she announced, "though God knows, if anyone had the right to slay him it was Rolfe."

"Catherine—"

"'Tis not so." Her words cut over William's. "But if he did kill him, the coward deserved no less. I would have slain him myself had I the chance."

"You don't know what you're saying," William barked.

"Don't I? The last I saw of my *beloved* betrothed, he was running from the battle as fast as his horse could carry him, leaving me to fend for myself. That he died is a favor granted me from the saints. I won't have to marry the bastard. I'd not do so even if he were still alive." She turned on her father. "I want to see Rolfe's body."

"'Tis buried," William responded. "They are both buried."

She gaped at him. "I don't believe you. I'd know if Rolfe were dead."

"Daughter, 'tis as I told you. We found him on the battlefield, not far from Sir Balder. Eloise identified him. Why are you working yourself into such a frenzy over this man? Tell me."

Catherine ignored William's command. She began to pace anew. "Why is Geoffrey here?" she countered.

"He is too distraught to travel. I have invited him to stay until he feels up to removing himself to Farnham."

Not trusting the man one whit, Catherine said, "I'd prefer he left now."

"Daughter, you're being unreasonable. Crass as well. Your betrothed lies in a freshly made grave, and you're going on and on about this scoundrel who abducted you as though you hold feeling for him. Is that it? Do you fancy yourself in love with him?"

Aye, I love him.

Catherine wanted to shout those words, but she held them inside. She had no intention of explaining what she felt for Rolfe to anyone. Not at present. "He was good to me."

"Then you are drawn to him," William said, nodding. "'Tis not uncommon, Catherine, for a young woman in your situation, who has depended solely on one man for all her needs, to think she owes him her undying gratitude. He's wiled you. Have you forgotten he stole you from your betrothed, from me? Took you on a treacherous journey across sea and land? Placed you in danger at every turn? Pursued you from Cartbridge, whereupon you were thrust into a battle which nearly claimed your life? The man is a mercenary. The only reason he followed you is to make certain he collects his fee from Henry."

She again gaped at her father. "You keep speaking about him as though he were alive. Is he here? Is he your prisoner? Tell me."

"He's in his grave," William stated, then rose from his chair. "Now I'll have no more of this talk about Rolfe de Mont St. Michel. The hour is late, and 'tis time you took yourself to bed." He walked to the door, then turned. "Forget about him, Catherine, for you'll never see him again. Good night to you."

Long after the door had closed, Catherine continued to gaze at the panel. Something was decidedly amiss. She didn't want to believe her father had lied to her, especially when he'd never done so before, but she was beginning to think that was the case.

Then again, maybe she was mistaken. Perhaps she wanted so much for Rolfe to be alive, she refused to grasp the truth when handed to her.

Tears brimming in her eyes, Catherine glanced at her bed. Bruised, battered, and aching, she was still weak from her ordeal. Now this new blow, which pummeled her emotions and tore at her heart, had drained her completely.

Disrobing down to her chemise, which, along with her tunic and chainse, Eloise had sewn for her, Catherine climbed into bed. Having left the candle burning, she stared at its flame. He couldn't be dead. He just couldn't be.

Every memory she had of him filled her head. Virile, strong, handsome, he was far too vital to be gone.

Her tears streamed her cheeks, for the blame was hers to bear. Had she never fled Cartbridge, he'd yet be safe. And he'd be holding her in his arms once more.

Her sobs broke forth, and Catherine buried her face in her pillow, the same entreaty playing again and again in her mind.

Please, please, don't let it be true.

Far below where Catherine lay crying, Rolfe sat huddled on the dirt floor in the dark. He was filthy and smelled of sweat. Raw, open wounds festered all over his body. He was cold and hungry. Atop that, having pulled through the agonies of the rack, the instrument caked with years of dust from little or no use, he ached unmercifully. He was amazed his joints hadn't separated, especially at his shoulder.

But Geoffrey's torture was calculated.

The same as the man gave Rolfe just enough water to make certain he survived, Geoffrey inflicted the needed amount of pain to ensure that his victim lived to suffer for another day. Rolfe's death was meant to be slow, arduous. Geoffrey took great pleasure in seeing that it would be.

Rolfe heard the lock turn. Light poured into the dank room as the door opened. He squinted against this new sort of pain. Then he heard Geoffrey's voice.

"Hang him over the pit."

The guards came toward Rolfe and, catching him by the arms, dragged him to the center of the dungeon. The winch sounded, the chain was hooked to the rope binding his wrists, then his arms were pulled above his head. He was cranked slowly upward, then swung over the pit. He swayed when the wooden beam stopped.

Rolfe wondered why the rope securing his hands didn't just simply unwind, sending him to his death. With his luck, the hole had no bottom, and he'd fall through space for eternity. He'd only exchange one form of torture for another.

Torch in hand, Geoffrey stepped forward and drew his sword. Its tip skimmed lightly across Rolfe's groin. "You'll hang here the night through. If you live, tomorrow I think I'll geld you."

Nausea filled Rolfe as the cold steel grazed against his testicles. *Mother of God. End it now.* His prayer went unanswered.

Laughter trailing him from the room, Geoffrey slammed the door, leaving Rolfe to hang in the darkness.

Time passed endlessly, and he drifted in and out of consciousness. How much longer could he go on?

The words formed in his mind. He shouted them in silence.

Catherine, come to me, my love, so I may at last die.

She awakened with a start.

Rolfe?

She'd heard his voice.

Come to me, my love . . .

Was it a dream?

No. She actually heard him.

Tossing back the covers, Catherine scrambled from her bed and drew on her chainse. The candle yet burned on the table. Taking up its holder, she headed for the door.

Down the stairs she went, to the hall, then to the first floor. It was as though she were attached to a string and being drawn along a prescribed course. But where did it lead? And was Rolfe truly at the end of this route?

Catherine found herself facing a door. Her hand shook as she unlatched it. She prayed it didn't lead where she thought.

Pushing the panel inward, she stared at the winding stairs that descended even lower inside the keep. Perspiration dotted her upper lip; she began to tremble. Then the words floated through her mind once more: *Come to me, my love.*

She drew a deep breath and steadied herself, then passed through the opening. Eyes keenly watching every step, she circled down to the cellars. Once on level ground, she held the candle high, searching each corner for the ugly little creatures she so despised. It was then she spied another door.

Compelled to see what was beyond the panel, she rushed

toward it. The hinges moaned as she pushed against the wood. On the other side lay another set of stairs.

Thrusting the candle into the black well, she gazed at the steps. Footprints showed in the dust that had settled on the stone treads. The patterns were recent. Someone had traveled this way, no doubt just hours before.

Catherine harkened to the sounds below. Water dripped, its hollow echo ascending the stairs. Other than that, she heard not a thing. But that didn't mean they weren't down there.

Leaning back against the jamb, she closed her eyes and listened to the hammering of her heart. What if it had been a dream? Were she to descend to the bowels of the keep and she was met by a horde of rats, she'd surely go insane.

She couldn't do this. Rolfe was dead. She had to think of their child. Pushing from the jamb, she reached for the door's handle, intending to pull the panel shut.

Come to me.

The words tore at her heart. She couldn't ignore them.

Blessed St. Michael, give me your protection.

The prayer whispered through her mind as she stepped back into the stairwell and lifted the candle high. There on the wall, she caught sight of a torch. Taking it from its holder, she set the candle flame to its head. Light burst forth, illuminating the darkened hole. The intensified glow gave her comfort.

Before she again lost her courage, Catherine set the candle on the top step and wound down the rest. Coming to the bottom, she waved the torch back and forth, again searching each corner.

Empty.

Quickly she followed the footprints that marked the dirt floor. She came to another door. Trying the latch, she found the panel locked.

She stepped back, her gaze scouring each wall. A key dangled from a ring that hung on a peg.

As she tripped the lock, she wondered what might lie beyond. Her imagination took hold. She saw herself opening the door, a horde of rats sweeping from the room to envelop her. Catherine shuddered.

Stop it! she demanded of her own mind. Drawing a cleansing breath, she released the latch and pushed the door wide.

The torch held before her, light flowed over the area as she crossed the threshold. Her heart nearly stopped; her eyes widened.

"Oh, my God," she whispered in disbelief. "Rolfe?"

Naked, filthy, oozing wounds striping his body, he hung from his wrists over a yawning pit.

If there were rats crawling over every inch of the room, Catherine cared not. She rushed to the place where he hung. "Rolfe?"

He didn't respond, nor did he move, and Catherine's fears redoubled inside her breast. Reaching across the stones framing the pit, she lightly touched his leg. He was warm.

"Rolfe?"

She shook him; he jerked. Turning his head, he opened his one eye. He stared down at her as though he were seeing a vision.

"Rolfe, 'tis me, Catherine," she said, tears welling in her eyes. His once lustrous golden hair was matted with dried sweat, one eye was blackened and swollen shut, his lips were cracked and bleeding. "My God. What have they done to you?"

Noting the rawness at his wrists, she cringed. The pain. It had to be unbearable. She needed to get him down from there.

She planted the torch in a holder on the wall, then rushed back to the pit. Rising on the stones, she pushed against the wooden beam until he was free of the hole. Then unwinding the winch, she eased him to the ground.

Catherine was immediately beside him. She unhooked the chain from the rope at his wrists; then, cradling his head in her lap, she set to untying the knot. Her fingers ached by the time she'd loosened the rope. She stared at the raw wounds and moaned.

"Oh, what you must have suffered. Who did this to you? My father? Geoffrey?"

He gazed up at her as though she didn't exist.

She smoothed her hand over his cheek. "Rolfe, 'tis me. Truly, love. 'Tis Catherine."

Slowly recognition came to him. "Cath . . ."

The croak told her his throat was parched. How long had it been since he'd had water? "You thirst?"

He nodded, and she eased his head to the ground. She went in search of that vitalizing liquid. Finding a bucket, a dipper inside, she allowed the water to run over her fingers to the floor. Seeing it was clear, she took the bucket to where Rolfe lay.

He shivered uncontrollably, and Catherine set the bucket aside, then pulled her chainse over her head. When she settled next to him, she covered him with the garment, then placed his head in her lap again. The dipper in hand, she dribbled the water between his lips.

"Go slowly," she said when he began to cough. "That's it. A little at a time."

When she thought he'd had enough, she took the remainder of the water and washed his face with her fingers, patting his skin dry with the hem of the chainse.

He continued to stare at her. "Cath—" He cleared his throat. "Catherine, is it really you?"

His words were no more than a harsh whisper. Though her heart ached at the lack of strength in his voice, she was gladdened he was able to speak. He lived, and with care, he'd soon be well.

"I have told you several times I am here. Why don't you believe me?"

His hand inched across hers, and he squeezed lightly. Again Catherine was aware of his weakness.

"I believe you," he rasped. "All I wanted is to know you are well. Now death can claim me."

The statement pierced through her like a spear. His head rolled on her lap. He went limp in her arms. Hysteria bubbled inside her. She shook him. "You'll not die, do you hear me? Look at me," she demanded. "You'll not leave me. You'll not leave our child. How dare you . . ."

His eye opened, and he turned his head. "Child?"

"Aye." Her hand on the side of his face, she made certain

he attended her. "All those months ago, I lied to you. Our first time together, I conceived. I didn't want you to find out." Catherine still didn't know if he would spurn her. "Oh, damn you for making me tell you this."

He caught her wrist. "Why . . . why . . ." He licked his lips.

"Didn't I tell you?" she finished, and saw his nod. "Because I was afraid you'd reject me, reject our child. Worse yet, if Henry or my father discovered the truth, and you were forced to marry me, I feared you'd soon hate me for robbing you of your freedom. You always said your profession meant all to you. I couldn't abide seeing revulsion in your eyes each time you looked at me."

"Didn't you think I'd eventually learn the truth?"

His words were slurred, but Catherine understood him. "Aye. As time went on, I knew you'd discover I had lied. I kept praying Henry would gain his victory so I could be set free, but the days kept passing, and I was still at Cartbridge. That's why when Miles offered me the chance to flee, I took it. 'Tis my fault that you're like this. Oh, why did you have to follow me?"

He attempted to smile. "I had to tell you something."

She frowned. "What on earth could possibly be so important to say that you'd put yourself in such danger? Look at you. Look what you've suffered. I . . ." She felt his hand squeezing her wrist. "What did you want to tell me?"

His tongue ran across his cracked lips, and he swallowed. "Catherine, I love you."

CHAPTER

22

CATHERINE FELT HER HEART SOAR.

"I love you also," she said, as worry took hold.

How could she possibly protect him, keep him safe from Geoffrey and her father? Especially the former?

She couldn't imagine William de Mortain participating in such heinous acts. Even so, he had to know what Geoffrey was doing. Just by allowing Rolfe's torture, he was as guilty as the man who enacted it. She'd never forgive her father. Never.

Gazing down at Rolfe, she saw his eyelid droop. "Rest, my love," she whispered while smoothing his brow. "I'll be here when you awaken." And she would be, for Catherine planned to guard him with her very life. "Sleep. You must get better for me and for our child."

"How very touching."

Catherine started. Her gaze hit the doorway. Her arms tightened around Rolfe. "Geoffrey."

Eyes narrowed, he strode toward her. Catherine leaned over Rolfe, protecting him. Geoffrey stopped beside her.

"My son gave his life to save you," he said, glaring down at her. "And all the while you were the bastard's whore. Bitch."

Catherine took the full force of Geoffrey's hand as it slammed into her cheek. Her head snapped around, but she hugged Rolfe to her. Then Geoffrey's hand was in her hair. He pulled her head back. She stared up at him.

"Say farewell to your lover, Catherine de Mortain. His life is finished."

"No!" she cried, twisting her head. As Geoffrey's hand tightened, she held onto Rolfe. "You'll not kill him."

"See if I don't," he snarled, pulling at her hair.

Her scalp was afire, the pain growing unbearable, but she kept her arms fast around Rolfe. "Let loose of me, you bastard. You'll not have him."

Geoffrey gave a hard jerk; Catherine cried out. At the same moment, a voice shot their way.

"Unhand my daughter!" William demanded.

Geoffrey's fingers relaxed. Catherine drew a steadying breath and hugged Rolfe to her.

"'Tis not her I want but the bastard she's trying to protect. You know she's his whore, don't you?"

Catherine watched as her father stopped in his tracks. His face hardened while his gaze narrowed.

"Move away from him, Catherine, and let Geoffrey finish the deed."

"No. I'll not let him come to harm. You've done enough already. I shall never forgive you for this, Father. Never."

"Catherine, move—"

"No!" she shouted, cutting across her father's words. "I love him. Your grandchild grows in my body. You'll not kill my baby's father. Nor will you allow it done. Do you hear me?"

William was apparently having difficulty grasping all she'd said. Even more so, he seemed unwilling to accept her words as true.

"Father—"

"'Tis as I said. He holds you spellbound, Daughter. The man ravished you, and he must be punished."

Tears of anger blurred her vision. "He didn't ravish me!" she fairly yelled. "I gave myself to him willingly. Aren't you listening to me? I love him."

Their eyes held for the longest while, then William relaxed his stance. "'Tis over, Geoffrey. Let them be."

"You may be willing to excuse your daughter for her lack of morals, but I'll not forgive her lover for his having caused my son's death. He will pay for his transgression, and it will be with his life."

"You're mad, Geoffrey," William stated. "Your son died by his own negligence. You saw how he rode recklessly across that field the same as I. Had he not been so intent on keeping those gold coins gathered in his tunic, he'd probably be alive. 'Twas his own greed that killed him, not Rolfe de Mont St. Michel." He advanced three steps. "Now give it up and let them be."

Geoffrey was of no mind to listen. When William took another step, the man drew his sword and pointed its blade at his chest. "The bastard may not have been there when Miles fell, but he is the one who set everything into motion by abducting your daughter. I care not about the whore's sensibilities. For his part in this, her lover must die. Tell her to move, William, or I'll slay her too."

"If you dare harm her I'll kill you!" William thundered.

The sword swung; its tip was now only inches from Catherine's back. "Tell her to move," Geoffrey repeated.

"Daughter, do as he says," William ordered.

"No," she said anew. Then she felt Rolfe squeezing her wrists. She looked down at him.

"Go," he rasped. "Let him have his due, before he harms you and your father as well."

"I won't leave you," she said, tears falling to his face. "I couldn't bear to live without you."

"Think of our child, Catherine. Through him, I'll always be with you. Go, my love, and save yourself."

Oh, blessed St. Michael, she thought, rocking Rolfe in her arms. Wasn't there some way to stop this?

"Move, bitch!" Geoffrey commanded, again snagging her hair.

"No!" she cried, shaking her head.

"Then you'll die with him."

"I love you," she whispered to Rolfe. He again squeezed her wrist.

"Say your prayers," Geoffrey grated.

In her mind, Catherine saw the sword coming at her back. "Hold, I say!"

The voice boomed through the room; all eyes, save Catherine's, turned toward the direction whence it came. Geoffrey's hand relaxed from her hair. As she momentarily gazed at Rolfe, she saw his lips twitch as though he were attempting to smile. A look of relief spread over his features.

Wondering who this stranger was, she turned to view the man who moved forward from the shadows. A reddish mane of hair crowning his head, he possessed lionlike features. Though of average stature with slightly bowed legs, his presence bespoke royalty. His demeanor, she thought, in many ways reminded her of Rolfe.

The man spoke again. "Whoever dares to raise his hand against Beauclerc's son shall answer to me, Henry, duke of Normandy, duke of Aquitaine, count of Anjou. Now stand away from my uncle."

Uncle? The term surprised Catherine. She always believed Rolfe was of noble birth, but never did she suspect his sire was a king.

Despite the command, Geoffrey stood firm. Henry waved his hand. Several bowmen stepped from the shadows, their arrows aimed at Geoffrey's heart.

"Nothing would give me greater pleasure, Geoffrey," Henry said, "than to see your miserable life end. But I shall, in my benevolence, offer you one more chance. Stand away."

"Not likely," Geoffrey snarled, raising his sword. "The bastard will pay."

Catherine cringed as she hunched over Rolfe. She waited for the blade to plunge. Above her she heard a whizzing noise, then a thud. As she peered from the corner of her eye, she saw Geoffrey stumble, an arrow protruding from his chest. His knees hit the stones framing the pit, then he toppled over the side.

"He was warned," Henry announced as he strode toward Catherine and Rolfe. He hunkered beside them. "I always wondered why I was so fond of you, arrogant rogue that you are. Now I know 'tis in the blood. We are a match in many ways."

Catherine spied Rolfe's dubious frown. "I don't think he believes you," she said to Henry.

The duke inspected her. "You are the Lady Catherine, I suppose?"

"Aye."

"You protected him well," Henry said. "'Twould appear my maneuvering has spawned love between the two of you. 'Tis good. I shall be eager to attend the wedding." He looked at Rolfe. "I assume you plan to marry her."

"Aye," Rolfe croaked.

"Good." After patting Rolfe's arm, he rose. "Duty calls me, so I cannot linger. The monk will explain all that has transpired to you both. Fare thee well, my friend," he said with a wave, then turned. Two strides away, he swung around. "For your loyalty, Rolfe de Mont St. Michel, you shall be rewarded most handsomely." He winked. "'Tis always wiser to extend control of a castle and the lands around it to someone I can trust. Especially when that someone is a part of my own family." With that, the duke and his contingent of twenty men exited the dungeon.

As Catherine watched Henry depart, she saw Eloise step forth. "'Twas good I ordered the sentries to let him in," she stated.

"'Tis good for her," Garrick said as he limped from the shadows. "Had she not acted as she had when Henry gave the command, I'd have shown her no mercy."

Brother Bernard and Aubrey came forward. "I believe my prayers helped as well, Sir Garrick," the monk declared.

"Aye," the knight responded. "Those, along with my threats."

William was now at Catherine's side. He knelt in the dirt. "Forgive me, Daughter. I had no idea what Geoffrey was doing here. Had I been aware of the events I would have stopped them."

Her anger and disappointment with her father had not subsided. "Would you have?"

William could not hold her gaze. "He'd stolen my beloved daughter from me. 'Twas my anger at him that allowed me to look aside. No man should be made to suffer the way he did. Come. We'll discuss this later. Let's get him from this place and see to his needs."

"Aye. We'll discuss it later," she said.

While William motioned for Brother Bernard and Aubrey to help with Rolfe, Catherine gazed down at him. "You're safe, my love. Soon you will be restored to good health." As she inspected his bruises and wounds, she lamented openly, "Oh, how I wish you had never followed me."

"Besides needing to tell you that I love you," he whispered, "there was something I wanted to ask. But I think Henry has affirmed it."

She already knew the question, but she wanted to hear the words herself. "What did you want to ask?"

"Will you marry me, Catherine?"

Tears of joy stinging her eyes, she smiled. "Aye, I will. Most gladly."

Freshly bathed and robed, Rolfe lay in the bed where he was carried, Catherine sitting beside him. It had been two weeks since he'd been brought up from the dungeon, his suffering ended. Though he couldn't recall everything that had transpired from the time he'd been settled in his room, he did remember how she attended him day and night. Whenever he searched her out, she was always there.

His bruises were gone, his wounds healed, and but for several scars from the hot iron, which would always serve as reminders of Geoffrey's torture, he was well on the mend.

That he was made to stay abed was Catherine's doing. To humor her, he obeyed her wishes. Tomorrow, though, he'd be up and about. The inactivity was driving him mad.

Presently, they were sequestered in his chamber, listening to Brother Bernard's account of how, as a baby, Rolfe had come to be on the marshes just below the abbey at Mont St. Michel. Garrick and William were with them.

"Your mother's name was Lenore. The brothers and I didn't know this, not until Robert de Bayeux came to the mount. 'Twas no simple pilgrimage that brought him to Mont St. Michel. She was his sister, Rolfe. Robert was your uncle."

Rolfe felt the press of Catherine's hand on his own. "Continue," he said, grateful for her unspoken reassurance.

"From the accounting that your mother gave Robert just before she died, you were the result of a brief affair with the old king when Lenore was at court. Even to this day his reputation is well known. Truly, Henry Beauclerc had a way with the fairer sex, even in his later years."

Rolfe accepted he was Beauclerc's son, yet the knowledge evoked no emotion in him whatsoever. "I know he claimed at least twenty bastards as his own," he said.

"And he may have claimed you, had he known about you," Brother Bernard returned. "Though he had again married after his queen died that didn't curb his lusty ways. He took Lenore as his mistress for a short time. The affair had already ended when she was suddenly called home to Bayeux. Not knowing she had conceived, she learned from her father that a marriage had been arranged.

"The plans were in the making for a wedding that lay over six months away when she discovered she was pregnant. Fearing her father's temper, she asked to be allowed to go on a pilgrimage to ready her heart and mind so she could become a good wife to her new betrothed. Being a very religious man, he gave his consent.

"Lenore started on her pilgrimage, with twenty or more attendants, but to everyone's surprise, she soon disappeared. Just why she kept you so long after your birth, no one knows. Nor is it understood why she left you on the marshes. Over the years, her family kept searching for her. 'Twas Robert who found her in a convent not far from Bayeux.

"She was dying, riddled by disease, and some thought insanity, for she kept rattling on about her immortal soul, praying God would forgive her for having left her son— Beauclerc's son—on the marshes below Mont St. Michel.

Once Lenore had left this life, Robert couldn't erase her ramblings from his mind. He came to the mount in search of the truth. That is where he found you."

Rolfe stared at the monk. "If Robert knew all this, why didn't he tell me?"

"By that time, Beauclerc had died. The unrest that followed between Stephen and Matilda, and eventually Henry, caused him worry. Though you were never in line to the throne, Robert feared you would come to harm just by way of your blood. He resolved it was better you never know about your parentage. The decision was meant to keep you safe. My brethren and I kept his secret just as he asked us to do."

Rolfe held no anger toward the man whom he now knew was his uncle. He understood Robert's reasoning for not telling him of his parentage, understood it was meant to protect him. The times after Beauclerc's death were perilous, lasting even unto this day. Besides, if Rolfe had called anyone "father," it would have been Robert. He was the one whom Rolfe loved and revered.

As for Lenore, he pitied her. What she must have suffered over the years during her self-imposed exile from her family, disease and madness consuming her in the end. Still, the woman was a stranger to him. He felt no grief or remorse at not having known her.

He thought of Duke Henry.

Earlier Rolfe had learned that when Brother Bernard, Garrick, and Aubrey had seen him being taken prisoner, they'd followed. On discovering in which direction the group went, the three immediately set off to find Henry at Wallingford.

Learning of Rolfe's predicament, the duke was ready to send a small troop to William's estate. It was only after Henry had learned from Brother Bernard that Rolfe was Beauclerc's son that he decided to lead the force himself.

"Tell me: Why was Henry so willing to believe we were related? 'Twould be far easier to dismiss the story, especially when there was no confirmation."

"Henry is aware of his grandfather's liaisons. Names of many of his mistresses have surfaced over the years. Lenore de Bayeux was not lost on him. Besides, the family resemblance is strong. You may be taller and fairer in coloring, but one cannot miss the fact that you are Beauclerc's son." Brother Bernard rose from his chair. "'Tis lucky for you I decided to come along on your journey to England. Of the handful who knew of your heritage, only I survive. I doubt that without Henry his troops would have commanded the attention needed to enter this place. Things might have gone far differently had the duke not been along."

"Aye," Garrick said, swinging his gaze toward William. "I would have hated to be you if my friend had not survived. As the duke has said, he was always fond of Rolfe. Whether he knew about Rolfe's relationship to him or not, when he learned what had happened here, the duke would have made certain you joined Geoffrey in the pit."

William cleared his throat. "Believe me, Sir Garrick, I'm grateful things have turned out as they have. And I'm doubly grateful that Rolfe has forgiven me for my part in this matter. As for my daughter, I hope someday she too will forgive me."

Viewing Catherine, Rolfe said, "Were she my daughter, sir, I believe I would have reacted the same way. I hold no malice toward you. As far as Geoffrey goes, he deserved what he got. 'Tis over. And since you've granted me permission to take your daughter as my wife, I cannot be happier. What say you, my fair Catherine? Can't you find it in your heart to forgive him as well?"

Her chin rose. "I'll think about it."

Rolfe chuckled. "Have no fear, William. From experience, I can tell you she'll eventually come around."

"I hope so. I'd not like being made to stay from my grandchild." He looked at Garrick and the monk. "I believe we should allow the young couple some privacy. How about a game of dice?"

Garrick and Brother Bernard nodded their assent. Once the three had left the room, Rolfe pulled Catherine down beside him. "You certainly are a stubborn wench," he said, leaning over her.

"'Tis in the blood," she responded, her fingers feathering through his hair. "I'm my father's daughter. He is as stubborn as I. Knowing that, do you still want to marry me?"

"Aye. I do."

She grew serious. "Are you certain? You've always valued your freedom. Marriage was not something you wanted. You made that very plain. I'd hate to awaken one day to find you had upped and gone. I don't know if I could survive such a—"

"Hush, Catherine," he ordered, placing his finger over her lips. "All that is in the past. My days of wandering have ended. The restlessness inside me was because I was always looking for something. Now I know who I am, and I certainly know what I want." As he lowered his face to hers, his finger slipped to her chin. "'Tis you, sweet, and your love. If I have just those two things, never will I need anything more."

"You have them," she whispered.

As she sealed her words with a kiss, Rolfe knew his search for new vistas, for new adventures, was a thing of the past. The long journey was over.

It had ended here in Catherine's arms.

EPILOGUE

Cartbridge Castle
March 1154

CANDLELIGHT BATHED THE LORD'S CHAMBER.

As Catherine read the letter from her father, the man having been forgiven on the day of their marriage, Rolfe leaned against the headboard, his son cradled in his arms.

"Father says that Clotilde is betrothed. We are to tell Eloise that her niece is to be married this summer."

"And who is the lucky man?"

"'Tis one of Geoffrey's soldiers. Apparently the day she was questioned about my disappearance, she fled the hall in tears and ran straight into the man. He was at once taken by her. Began to court her immediately afterward. Father was unaware of this until his return to Avranches to deliver the news about Miles's and Geoffrey's deaths. They are now all at Mortain. Brother Bernard is again at Mont St. Michel."

"See?" Rolfe said, smiling. "Had I not caused all these problems for everyone—especially Clotilde—she'd not have met the man of her dreams."

"Nor would we now be married," Catherine countered, placing the letter aside.

"Nor would we have a fine son."

A light knock sounded on the door.

"Come," Rolfe called.

When the panel opened, Eloise stepped into the room. "I'll take the sweet darling from you," she said, ambling toward the bed. "'Tis time little Henry found his cradle. After Garrick and Aubrey see him, that is. And 'tis time you two got some sleep."

Rolfe handed his son over to Eloise. "I had something else in mind entirely, but 'tis both done in the same place."

Eloise blushed as she harrumphed. "I hope to teach Henry better manners than you have, sir."

"You have my permission to try," Rolfe returned.

Catherine sprang from the bed and kissed her son good night.

"I'll be back when he's hungry again," Eloise stated, then was out the door.

"Come here, woman," Rolfe said, reaching for Catherine's hand. "I have plans for us." She joined him on the bed. "Remove your chemise. I want to look at you."

"Then remove your braies, sir. My eyes are just as eager as yours."

In seconds they were both naked. They sank onto the mattress.

"Are you sorry that you paid all that gold for me or that you've given up your wandering ways?" she asked as Rolfe's hand roamed where it wanted.

He'd told her about Miles's duplicity, about his greed. She'd accepted Rolfe's words without question. "The only place I want to wander is all over this bed with you."

Catherine smiled. "You're a devil, Rolfe de Mont St. Michel. I should have taken note of such when I first looked into your eyes that morn in the chapel over a year ago."

"What? Didn't I look priestly enough for you?"

"Nay, you were far too handsome."

"Was that what you were thinking when your mind drifted away?"

"Drifted away?"

"Aye. I had asked you a question, and you just kept staring at me."

Catherine looped her arms around his neck and opened her thighs; Rolfe eased into her.

"Aye. 'Twas what I was thinking. I'm certainly glad you decided to hear my confession that morning."

He lay still above her, gazing into her wondrous eyes. "So am I."

"Do you want to hear my confession now?"

He nodded.

"I love you, Rolfe de Mont St. Michel. With all my heart."

"And I love you, Catherine de Mortain. I shall do so until the day I die. Till death takes me, my fealty belongs only to you."

"'Tis good," she said as the rhythm of his lovemaking began.

"'Tis more than good," he whispered. "'Tis splendor."

AUTHOR'S NOTE

At Wallingford, in late July or early August of 1153, Henry, Duke of Normandy, gained a victory of sorts. The win did not come from battle, but from a forced truce called by both Henry's and Stephen's countless barons and many earls. Although Henry and Stephen were ready to fight to the death, no one else wanted to stand against his fellow countryman. With the demand for peace coming from their most trusted supporters, the two men had no choice but to comply. Then on August 17, 1153, when Stephen's son Eustace died quite suddenly—supposedly struck down by St. Edmund himself for having devastated the lands and burned the crops at the monastery at Bury St. Edmunds—the future was set. Stephen's younger son, William, never sought to be king. Henry, by choice, was now the undisputed heir to the English throne.

Both men moved on to different campaigns—Henry to Stamford and Nottingham; Stephen into Suffolk—to at last meet again at Winchester on November 6, 1153. There it was decided that Stephen would remain king until his death, Henry his designated heir. On October 25, 1154, Stephen died, and on December 19, Henry was anointed and crowned king of England in Westminster Abbey.

NORTHERN WALES

April 1157

It was inevitable.

Even so, Alana had hoped Gilbert's death would draw no more than an expression of sympathy from his king. Instead, some four dozen mounted men waited beyond the palisade, their leader requesting entry.

She turned from the window in her chamber to look upon her trusted servant Madoc, the man having brought word of the group's arrival. "Is Henry among them?" she asked.

He shook his graying head. "I don't think so, milady," he replied. "The one who is at the fore calls himself Paxton de Beaumont. He bears a pennon of a black dragon on a crimson field. Claims he knew Sir Gilbert, says they were old friends. By his trappings, there's no denying he's a knight. He is Norman as well. You can wager he's one of Henry's vassals."

"And where is Sir Goddard?" she asked of the knight who was now in charge of the stronghold.

"As usual, he had far too much wine last night. He's still asleep, as are most of his companions."

Alana nodded and again faced the window. Through the breaks in the trees, she glimpsed the rippling river beyond the outer walls. Today its waters were almost placid, far from the raging torrent of six months past.

Time swept backward to that fateful day. From afar, she saw herself falling endlessly through space, experienced the breath-robbing plunge when she sank beneath the frigid waters, felt herself tumbling helplessly through the rain-swollen eddy, her body crashing against the rocks projecting from the river's bed. Deprived of precious air, her lungs threatened to burst. Somehow she clawed her way to the surface, where she gasped and sputtered, only to be dragged to the bottom once more. The cycle continued for what seemed an eternity. That she hadn't drowned was truly a miracle.

"Milady?"

Alana blinked, her trance broken. "What is it, Madoc?"

"Should I tell those at the gate to turn this Paxton de Beaumont away?"

She circled slowly toward her servant. "Nay. We have no choice but to allow him entry."

"But—"

"We must. Otherwise he'll grow suspicious. We can ill afford his mistrust. Besides, I'm certain he has come to secure what is rightfully Henry's."

"Rightfully Henry's?" Madoc snarled. "These Norman dogs are excessively brash. They invade our homeland, claiming it as their own. But just as with your dead husband, they too will know the wrath of our countrymen's blades."

"That may be so, Madoc. Still, until we are able to drive these *dogs,* as you call them, from our soil, we must temper our pride and act as though we accept them as our masters." Alana knew that was especially so if she hoped to keep the truth about Gilbert's death hidden from his king. "Since Sir Goddard is indisposed, order the gates opened and allow this Paxton de Beaumont and his men entry. Give them food and drink. I will be down shortly to offer them welcome."

Once Madoc exited the chamber, Alana pulled a comb through her hair, then hid the mass under a headrail. Hugging her mantle close, she followed after Madoc, wondering why Paxton de Beaumont had so boldly crossed the marches and Offa's Dyke into Cymru, what the Saxons had long ago termed Wales.

His name sounded familiar, but she couldn't remember Gilbert's connection to the knight or even in what context her late husband may have mentioned the man. But then Gilbert had shared little with her about his life before they'd wed. Alana wasn't surprised by the fact, for after the first six months of marriage he'd hardly spoken to her. The ensuing three years had become a study in silence.

Though their relationship was strained, Gilbert still expected his husbandly due. Save for the last four months of his life, he came to her bed regularly, expecting her to submit, which she did.

Alana shuddered as she remembered how without preliminaries Gilbert mounted her. After several thrusts and grunts, the latter culminating in a lengthy groan, he rolled away from her and quickly left her side. That she'd been freed of the odious burden of seeing to his needs was a blessing. As she saw it, lovemaking was a loathsome act, something she hoped never to suffer again from any man.

At the top of the stairs, Alana affected an expression of bereavement. Over the interim, she'd perfected her widow's mask and could execute it at will. She could even summon tears at the mention of her late husband's name. A ruse, yes. For when she first learned of Gilbert's death, she nearly jumped for joy.

Alana worried little whether her feigned grief was taken as genuine or not. It was Paxton de Beaumont who concerned her.

The knight's presence, she suspected, was at Henry's bidding. Certainly he'd traveled across the marches and into what most considered hostile territory in order to secure the castle for his king. But Alana doubted that was his sole reason for showing himself outside the gates. She had a strong feeling Henry mistrusted her account of Gilbert's drowning. Suspicion of foul play was the underlying motive that had sent his vassal this long way to the secluded fortress overlooking the small tributary that eventually flowed into what the English called the River Dee. She'd swear on her dead sire's grave this was so.

As Alana descended the stairs, she began to fret. She'd taken great pains to hide the truth about Gilbert's death from all who resided inside the castle. Only she and Madoc were allowed in the chamber as they both prepared her husband's body for burial once it was pulled from the river. The telltale wounds marring his flesh would have alerted whoever saw them that the frigid waters hadn't been the cause of Gilbert Fitz William's demise. No. It was the plunge of an angry blade, many times over, that had ended his life.

For her sake, and the sake of those whom she protected, Alana prayed Paxton de Beaumont never learned the truth.

As the blood-red pennon with its prancing dragon snapped in the wind above his head, Paxton waited patiently for the gates to be opened to him and his men. A strange land this Wales, he thought, glancing around him. Its rugged, slate-sided mountains, its forests of pine and oak, its open hillsides sheeted with purple blossoms of heather, the vaporous mists rising from its frigid streams, the country displayed an eerie sort of beauty, one he'd never beheld in all his travels. Wales, this land of strangers, it puzzled him, especially its people.

An unruly lot, he decided. If not bent on destroying their enemies, they were bent on destroying each other. Not a single Welshman could be trusted. He wondered about the women.

Alana of Llangollen, Gilbert's widow—what was she like? Treacherous? More to the point, had she been the cause of Gilbert's death?

The last Paxton had heard from Gilbert Fitz William was on the eve of his friend's union to the "lovely Alana." That was how Gilbert had described his bride in his letter. Paxton would reserve his opinion of Gilbert's widow until he met her himself.

For now, all he knew about Alana of Llangollen was that she'd been offered in marriage by her kinsmen to the new lord who had been sent to fortify the motte-and-bailey castle that had long since been abandoned beyond the fringes of the Welsh marches. It seemed she was a token of peace.

Over the years, his travels having taken him far and wide, Paxton never learned if Gilbert was happy with his marriage. The next he'd heard of his friend was not from the man himself but from Henry, who reported that Gilbert had drowned while attempting to save his wife from the raging torrents of the nearby river. Though he'd been sent to the fortress to make certain it remained in Henry's possession, Paxton was asked to look into the events surrounding Gilbert's untimely death. Henry didn't trust the Welsh. From all he'd heard, Paxton was of a like mind with his king.

The gates swung open and the group was granted entry by one of the guards. Leading the way, Paxton guided his destrier, along the darkened passage beneath the gate tower and into the courtyard, whereupon he examined the wooden structures that framed the area. Next he scanned the inhabitants who'd halted their tasks to view the newcomers.

"There seems to be an inordinate amount of Welshmen manning the place," Graham de Montclair commented as he rode up beside Paxton.

Paxton looked at his companion and fellow knight. "Aye," he replied, "and one of them comes our way."

"Good morn to you, sirs," the man hailed, halting before the pair. "My name is Madoc. My mistress has sent me to bid you welcome. Once you've seen to your horses, she asks that you come into the hall, where refreshment has been made ready for you and your men."

"Thank you for your courtesy, Madoc," Paxton said while dismounting. He stepped in front of his steed. "Where is your mistress? I'd like to greet her personally, if I may."

"She's inside," the man replied, jerking his head in the direction of the large building that stood opposite them. "She awaits you there." He hesitated, then cleared his throat. "I presume Henry has sent you, milord?"

Paxton surveyed the man. He appeared most eager for a response. "Do you pose the question for yourself or for your mistress, Madoc?"

"Since we rarely have visitors, my mistress assumed you were sent by Henry. I merely hoped to confirm such so I could inform her as to what capacity you have come."

"I will address her myself on that matter," Paxton replied. "For now, tell me: Who is in charge here?"

"That would be Sir Goddard. He's not risen as yet, nor have his men."

Paxton wondered at the laxness of those who were to defend the castle. Glancing around him, he noted it was the Welsh who protected the gates. "Then wake him," he stated, "and tell him I am here. I'll meet him in the hall."

Handing the reins to his squire, the lad having dashed up beside him, Paxton motioned to Sir Graham. Together the pair crossed the yard toward the building where Alana of Llangollen said she'd greet them.

Tall and self-assured, he came through the door with a confident bearing, his companion behind him. Removing his helm, he ran his long fingers through his thick raven hair, its lustrous length brushing his broad shoulders. From where she stood at the foot of the stairs, Alana had no trouble distinguishing which of the two men was Paxton de Beaumont. Prideful, he was. Commanding as well.

His gaze scanned the vast room. When he spied her, he strode toward her, his movement fluid and decidedly masculine.

Praying he wasn't as discerning as he appeared, Alana steeled herself for their first meeting. Shoulders squared, her mask in place, she waited.

"Alana of Llangollen?" he inquired once he was before her.

"Aye."

He bowed his head, then looked her in the eye. Alana was at once fascinated by his deep blue irises and the long black lashes framing them. Oddly, her heart skipped a little as she met him stare for stare. She was stunned by her reaction.

"I am Paxton de Beaumont, knight and vassal to Henry, king of England, duke of Normandy and Aquitaine. I am also an acquaintance and friend of your late husband. Please accept my condolences. I was grieved to hear of his death."

Deceptive tears were beckoned forth, and Alana gazed through their shimmering screen. "Thank you for your kind expression of sympathy. Although it has been six months, I feel Gilbert's loss as though it were just yesterday. That I was spared and he . . ." She allowed the rest to fade, her voice becoming purposely choked. She breathed deeply, jaggedly, another ruse she'd perfected. "Unfortunately, naught can change what has happened. Come." She waved her hand toward the table. "Food and drink await you after your long journey. I ask that you partake of our meager fare and accept it in way of welcome. But first, I offer you water so you may wash your feet."

He frowned down at her. "Wash my feet?"

"Aye. It is our custom. That is how we show favor to all our guests."

"An acceptable custom, it is, but I wouldn't call myself a guest. The term is reserved for those who intend to stay only a short—"

A commotion sounded at the entry, and Paxton swallowed his words. Turning toward the disturbance, he surveyed the man who had found his way into the hall. Unkempt, his reddish hair knotted and dirty, several days' worth of stubble shading his haggard face, he stood just inside the door, wearing naught but his braies and a mail shirt.

"Where is this Paxton de Beaumont?" he questioned loudly.

Paxton noted how the man weaved on his feet. Surely this wasn't Sir Goddard? If so, the knight was a sad testament to his profession. "Here," Paxton called across the way.

Staggering toward Sir Graham, the man spun none too steadily in Paxton's direction. His bare feet crushing the fragrant grasses covering the floor, he crossed the span separating them. "Are you Paxton de Beaumont?" he asked on reaching his target.

The man's stale, wine-laden breath struck Paxton square in the face. He stepped back and studied the disgusting sot. "I am," Paxton replied, noting that the man's eyes were red and watery. "And I suppose you are Sir Goddard?"

"Aye," the knight replied. "Did Henry send you?"

"He did."

The man jerked a nod. "More stomachs to feed," he grumbled. "Come with me, and I'll show you where the garrison is lodged."

"You have separate quarters?" Paxton asked.

Sir Goddard snorted. "Aye." His eyes narrowed on Alana. "'Tis the only way to assure we'll not be murdered in our sleep."

Paxton spied the man's belligerent look. He gazed down at the woman who stood at his elbow. Her long-lashed, dark eyes, which he thought were most alluring, remained fixed straight ahead. "Do you have reason to fear for your lives?" he asked the knight.

"'Tis well known that not a Welshman can be trusted."

"Even so, the entire yard is filled with their ilk. Why is that, especially if you feel they are untrustworthy?"

"'Twas Sir Gilbert's doing. And hers. They're her kin. Had the fool sent them all back into the wood, where they belong, he might still be alive."

Paxton noticed Alana hadn't moved, nor had her expression changed. She was indeed lovely. An incomparable beauty, in fact. But that didn't mean she was incapable of treachery. "Are you saying they had something to do with Gilbert's death?"

"Not them. 'Twas her," Sir Goddard proclaimed, swaying on his feet. "Had he not gone into the river after her, we wouldn't have pulled his body from the waters a day later. 'Tis her fault that he's dead."

Paxton marked how Alana stiffened. Then her eyes narrowed on the man.

"As always, Sir Goddard, you are feeling the effects of your night of drink," she accused. "Likewise, your hatred of my people has once again made itself obvious. Tell Sir Paxton why you have not sent us into the woods. Go on. Tell him."

Sir Goddard glared at Alana. When no response came forth, Paxton said, "Tell me why the Welsh are still here."

The man shifted his gaze. As he did so, he lurched sideways. "I don't have to explain myself to you."

"Oh, but you're mistaken, sir. I want an answer, now."

"By whose authority do you order my reply?"

"By Henry's authority. And by my own."

Sir Goddard's eyes widened. "Your own? Don't tell me you're the new overlord of this forsaken piece of land?"

"This piece of land and everything upon it," Paxton replied, "including you. Now answer my question, before I have you bound and hung, headfirst, over the palisade."

The man curled his lip. "There's no mystery to it. They remain as laborers, so as to keep the place in order. 'Tis not befitting for a knight to toil at such menial tasks."

"I presume they are paid for their work."

"They are fed and have a place to sleep."

"And are they allowed to come and go at will?" Paxton inquired.

"If you're asking if they are held prisoner behind these walls, the answer is no."

"I beg to differ with you," Alana stated. "Nary a man has left this place without some mishap befalling him once he's passed through the gates."

"If you're speaking about young Owain, he was punished for his thievery."

"He took no more than two days' supply of food to hold him until he reached his dying mother's side," she returned. "You sought not justice in your punishment. Instead, because of your twisted logic, you enacted naught but a grievous cruelty."

"'Twas justice," Sir Goddard insisted.

"By whipping him, then severing his right hand? In my judgment, such punishment goes beyond what is morally befitting the supposed crime."

"He deserved what he got," the knight snarled.

"Why? Because he is Welsh?"

Paxton had heard enough. "Sir Goddard, as of this moment, you are relieved of your duties at this fortress. Find your way back to your quarters and begin packing your belongings. I'll expect you gone from here in an hour."

"With pleasure," the man stated. "You're welcome to this wretched place and its ill-born inhabitants. 'Tis a cursed land. Why Henry seeks to lay claim to it is above me. I offer you a word of caution, Paxton de Beaumont: Keep the slut far from you, lest you also end up dead."

Paxton watched as Sir Goddard rolled on his heels and wobbled toward the door. Feeling a light pressure against his arm, he dropped his gaze to the small hand touching him. He looked into Alana's eyes.

"Thank you for sending him away," she said. "Ever since Gilbert's death, he's been exceedingly barbarous and spiteful. Truly, I'm grateful Henry has appointed you as the new overlord."

Eager to inspect the rest of the garrison and decide which men should depart with Sir Goddard and which should stay, he eased her hand from his arm. "In a few weeks, Alana of Llangollen, you may feel differently about that."

"I must warn my uncle," Alana said to Madoc hours later. The pair stood just inside the doorway to the hall.

"Let one of us go in your stead," her servant insisted. "'Tis far too risky. Unlike his foregoer, he hardly touched his wine. He may still be awake. If you're caught trying to slip through the side gate, he'll become suspicious."

She glanced through the opening at the building where the garrison was housed, Paxton de Beaumont and his men having retired there for the night. No light shone from its windows. "I'll not get caught. And I must speak to Rhys about other matters as well."

"Then let me come with you," Madoc countered. "The night wood is no place for a young woman alone."

"Have you forgotten my heritage?" she whispered, still inspecting the yard. "I can run these hills and forests as good as any man." She shook her head. "Nay, Madoc. I must go by myself."

"Once you reach your uncle's, stay there and do not return. This one is far more astute than was Sir Goddard. If he learns the truth—"

Alana's fingers fell across Madoc's lips. "I have to return," she said. "Whether Henry says otherwise or not, this land is my inheritance. It belongs to me and you and everyone else who resides here. I'll not desert what is mine. Nor will I leave my friends to fend for themselves against these dogs." She again glanced at the yard to see that no one was about. "I'll be back before the dawn."

Fearing Madoc would issue another protest, Alana was out the door, heading for the side gate. The sky was cloudy, masking the moon's glow. The better for her, she thought, knowing her trained eye could see twice as far in the dark as any Norman. The air smelled of rain. She prayed the skies didn't open until she'd crossed the river and back.

Rhys—she had to get to him so she could warn him and her cousins that Sir Goddard was no longer at the fortress. The knight had been lax, mainly because he kept his face constantly in his cups. But his replacement was every bit the warrior that Sir Goddard had failed to be. Paxton de Beaumont and his men, along with the twenty others he'd chosen to stay, could fend off her countrymen with ease, no matter how numerous they were.

Not that Rhys planned to attack, but she must apprise him to stay on the opposite side of the river, far from the stronghold, which overlooked the valley and the heavy wood. They could no longer meet as they once had, as they'd planned to do tonight. The risk was far too great.

On silent feet, Alana traveled from the sheltering shadows of one building to the next. Halfway along the side of the last structure, she spied the gate. Seeing that no one guarded the outlet, she broke into a run. Just as she cleared the building, a hand snagged her arm, pulling her up short. Though she nearly screamed at full voice from the sudden scare, no more than a soft cry escaped her lips. She stared at the man who had grabbed her.

Paxton de Beaumont.

"What are you doing?" she asked, attempting to shake from his hold.

"It would seem that is my question to you." He glanced at the gate, then back at her. "Where were you planning to be off to at such a late hour? Does your lover await you in the wood?"

Glaring up at the tall knight, Alana momentarily clenched her jaw. *Hardly.* She'd die before she lay with a man again. "I was going to Gilbert's grave."

"His what?"

"His grave," she lashed back. "It lies just beyond this gate, in a clearing in the wood. Sir Goddard would not allow me to leave the fortress. So at night, when he'd fallen drunk on his pallet, I would make my way to Gilbert's resting place to offer a prayer for his soul."

Paxton remained silent for such a long time Alana feared he didn't believe her. The tension drained from her when he said, "I'm not Sir Goddard. I suggest you remember that. When the sun has risen, we shall both go to Gilbert's grave, so I may offer a prayer for him as well. For now, you will return to the hall. To make certain you do, I will go with you."

As she was escorted back the same way she'd come, Alana thought of her uncle. Somehow she had to get word to him. *Madoc,* she decided, certain that from now on she'd be watched constantly. Not Madoc, she concluded, realizing Paxton de Beaumont was too clever by far. Someone else would have to take the message. Someone he'd not suspect. Maybe Owain.

They halted outside the doors to the hall. Alana waited for the new lord to release her arm. He held her fast and gazed down at her. "Is there something else you wanted?" she inquired after what seemed an eternity.

"A truthful answer from you."

Alana lifted her chin. "What is the question?"

"Did Gilbert drown? Or did you murder him?"

Look for
Everlasting
Wherever Paperback Books Are Sold
Summer 1995

Judith McNaught
Jude Deveraux

Jill Barnett
Arnette Lamb

❧❧❧❧❧❧

A Holiday
Of Love

❧❧❧❧❧❧

*A collection of romances
available from*

POCKET
BOOKS   1007-02

Experience the sweeping passions
of Linda Lael Miller's latest
historical romance

PRINCESS
ANNIE

Pocket Books proudly presents the sequel to
TAMING CHARLOTTE
and YANKEE WIFE

Available from

POCKET
STAR
BOOKS

979-01